"How the hell did you get up here?" Madison demanded.

Gabriel brushed past her as if he'd been coming to her apartment for years. "Some digs. I don't know why Cullen was so red-hot to have you on the team, but judging by this apartment, I'd say you two must have a cozy little relationship."

"The apartment belongs to me. A gift from my father."

"Daddy's little girl?"

Any restraint she'd had melted away at the taunt. Without thinking, she closed the gap between them and swung, wanting only to wipe the smirk from his face.

He caught her wrist, his expression amused. Fury combined with adrenaline to give her added strength, and she slammed her left leg into the side of his knee, using his hold on her arm to flip him to the floor. Still holding her wrist, he pulled her with him, rolling quickly to pin her to the ground, his body hard against hers.

"Nice moves." His voice was deep and smoky, his eyes darkening with an emotion she wasn't about to put a name to.

Madison's anger had somehow slipped away, the chemistry between them shifting. If she lifted her head even slightly, their lips would touch. Just centimeters and… "Get off me," she said, breaking the spell.

His smile was slow, and a little wicked. "I don't know. Seems pretty comfortable to me."

DARK OF THE NIGHT

"A highly entertaining read, both as a mystery and love story, [that embraces] all the components a reader could want."
—*Rendezvous*

"Full of suspense and intrigue…blackmail, murder, and a storyline that takes great unexpected twists will keep you at the edge of your seat!"
—*Old Book Barn Gazette*

"Intrigue, deception and murder make *Dark of the Night* a great way to spend your entertainment hours."
—*Romantic Times* (4 stars)

"A compelling, thoroughly entertaining tale of romantic suspense. Fans of the genre should add Dee Davis to their list of 'don't miss' authors."
—*AOL Romance Fiction Forum*

JUST BREATHE

"A wonderful, not-to-miss, stay-up-late read."
—*Philadelphia Inquirer*

"*Ally McBeal* meets *Mission: Impossible*…"
—*Publishers Weekly*

"A book that successfully merges the elements of a spy novel and romance comes around once in a blue moon.… I look forward to the next Dee Davis novel with excitement."
—*Bookaholics*

"Ms. Davis uses a deft hand in molding her characters…"
—*Under the Covers*

DEE DAVIS
ENDGAME

HQN™

ISBN 0-373-77036-7

ENDGAME

Copyright © 2005 by Dee Davis Oberwetter

In loving memory of my father

ENDGAME

Victory goes to the player who makes
the next-to-last mistake.
   —Savielly Grigorievitch Tartakower (1887–1956)

PROLOGUE

New York City

BINGHAM SMITH WAS LATE. Which wasn't all that unusual, but given the fact that his driver hadn't shown up, and that he was due to close a deal in less than an hour, it held the potential for disaster.

Cursing softly under his breath, he closed his umbrella, eyed the surging crowd and stepped onto the staircase leading into the bowels of the city. Subways disgusted him. Humanity pressed together, pushing and shoving, all decorum lost.

But he was pragmatic if nothing else, and given the downpour, there was no chance of catching a taxi, so the subway it was. An older, balding man stumbled against him, the spoke of an umbrella jabbing forcefully into Bing's side, the pain oddly localized, sharper than he would have expected.

With a curt nod, the man disappeared, swallowed by the crowd, and Bing turned the corner, stepping out onto the train's platform. An empty platform. It seemed he couldn't catch a break.

Turning his wrist, he consulted the face of his Piaget, and immediately wished he hadn't. A quarter of an hour wasted and no train. He debated making his way back to the stairs, and the relative sanctity of the street, but dismissed the idea almost immediately. Best to wait.

Nothing ever came from overreacting, and besides, his head was beginning to ache and the prospect of climbing stairs did not appeal. The people on the platform surged forward as a unit, a sure sign the train was coming.

Bing tightened his hand on his briefcase, and blinked as the lights seemed to brighten and then dim, a wave of dizziness making him stumble. Sucking in a breath, he let the crowd move him forward, fighting for composure, a dull ache radiating through his chest cavity and along his arm.

He ruthlessly pushed the thought of pain aside, twisting past a tweed-clad grandmother so that he stood poised on the yellow line just as the rumble of the oncoming train became audible. There was no time for illness. There was simply too much at stake. He'd worked long and hard to reach this point, and nothing—not his driver, not a rainstorm, and certainly not a stitch in his side—was going to interfere with his success.

The number six train roared into the station, sparks flying on the steel below. The pain in his chest had intensified, making it hard to breathe, and the single light at the head of the train mesmerized him, the rhythmic sound of the wheels seeming to mimic the frantic beat of his heart.

He closed his eyes, fighting for breath, and started to take a step backward, but before he could accomplish the movement, the crowd moved again, each person intent on claiming a spot in front of the doors of the incoming train.

One minute there was concrete beneath his feet and the next—nothing. He knew he was falling, even tried to throw out his hands to break the fall, but the pain was too strong, his heart pumping with an almost syncopated rhythm, the effort robbing him of all strength—robbing him of life. Which was probably just as well, because two seconds later the number six train smashed through Bingham Smith's body as if it were made of straw.

Six down, three to go.

CHAPTER ONE

New York City

INTERROGATION ROOMS RANKED only slightly above gas station restrooms in the stench and filth department. Which was too bad, considering the amount of time Madison Harper spent in them. Sucking in a final breath of semiclean air, she opened the door and walked into the room, immediately commanding the attention of the detective in the corner and the perp at the table.

The latter looked to be at odds with his surroundings, although he was showing some signs of wear and tear. His white button-down was starting to wilt, and the creases in his khakis weren't as pristine as they'd once been. With a little luck, she'd soon be responsible for adding some sweat to the ensemble.

With a subtle nod at the detective, she lifted the bag she held onto the table, making a show of pulling out a bloodspattered pipe. Still without breaking the silence, she carefully laid the pipe on a battered bookshelf, and then, just as carefully, turned her back on it.

"Mr. Jackson." She held her hand out to the man at the table, ignoring the flash of surprise in the detective's eyes. It was always the same. Derision, surprise, skepticism, and then ultimately resentful admiration. Profiler's lot in life.

"Who the hell are you?" Paul Jackson glared up at her through bloodshot eyes. She waited a beat, and then another, delighted to see him shooting a sideways glance at the pipe. So far so good.

"My name is Madison Harper." They shook hands as if they were at a business meeting, and then she sat across from him at the table. Detective Barton shifted, leaning back against the windowsill, eyes narrowed, arms crossed.

Skepticism.

Madison bit back a smile.

"You another detective?" Jackson was studying her now, trying to figure out who the hell she was, and more importantly if he could use her to his advantage. It was there in the tilt of his head, and the twist of his brows.

"No." She shook her head, pulling a stack of files out of the case and dropping them onto the table. "FBI. We've been working with the police. Trying to solve Connie Weston's murder."

Murder was a kind word for the act. A vivacious fifth grader, Connie had disappeared on a walk to the corner grocery, only to be discovered dead in an abandoned warehouse five days later. The child had been raped, sodomized, and then beaten in the head with the pipe on the bookshelf. There were no fingerprints, and no trace elements to tie Jackson to the murder, but Madison was nevertheless certain of his guilt.

The trick was to get him to admit as much.

"I already told Barney Fife there," Jackson inclined his head toward Barton, but his gaze was back on the pipe, "I didn't do it."

Barton shifted again, looking a lot like he wanted to tear into Jackson, but he had his orders, and to his credit, despite his obvious disapproval he didn't attempt to interfere. They'd been round and round their approach, and only when his lieutenant had insisted had Barton agreed to play it her way. But apparently he lived by his word.

"Maybe not on purpose," she said, noting that Jackson

had indeed started to sweat, his hands clenched in an attempt to hold on to control.

Jackson worked for the local cable company and had been in the area the day Connie disappeared. He was newly divorced, and recently discharged from the army. His sheet included a suspected rape and a couple of arson charges from his youth. And he'd been the primary suspect in a New Jersey rape a couple of years back, a hooker named Belinda Markham.

Until today he'd been the picture of helpful, cocky and confident. Even volunteered to take a lie detector test. He was definitely the kind of man who could have approached Connie without scaring her. The eleven-year-old would never have seen it coming. Not when she was so close to home. Even in New York there was a comfort zone.

"We know you did it, you sick bastard. Just tell us how." Barton evidently had lost whatever willpower he'd summoned, and he stepped menacingly toward Jackson, his face twisted in anger.

Jackson immediately regained some of his former bravado, glaring up at the detective through narrowed eyes. "I didn't do nothing."

Madison swallowed a rebuke, settling instead for a visual one, and then smiled at Jackson, reaching out to touch his hand, her skin crawling with the action, her body held in tight control so that her revulsion was not apparent. "We're not blaming you, Paul. I've seen the pictures." She made a play of pulling them out of an envelope.

She let her gaze sweep over the tiny form clad only in the plaid skirt of her school uniform, focusing instead on Jackson, who stared at the photograph as though in a hypnotic trance. It was as if he simply couldn't pull his eyes away.

"The man who killed her obviously felt remorse, Paul. See how he laid her jacket over her face? It's a protective move, meant to shield her from harm. Whoever did this obviously had a heart."

She swallowed the bile rising in her throat, and looked up to meet Detective Barton's eyes. His skepticism was fading.

"She was a pretty little girl." Jackson's voice was soft now, all traces of contentiousness gone. "Really sweet."

Madison grabbed onto the adjective. To call someone sweet you had to know them. Or at least have met them. She felt a flash of triumph, she was getting close. "Not so sweet, surely?" She looked up to meet Jackson's eyes, only to find he was again staring at the pipe, his breathing uneven.

"I mean girls that age—they don't know what they've got, do they?" She waited a moment, making sure she had his full attention. "Wearing their skirts so short. Their legs all tanned and bare. They hardly leave anything to the imagination. And girls like that hardly ever wear bras. It's enough to drive a man crazy, isn't it?"

Jackson nodded slightly, his gaze now alternating between the pipe and the photograph. There were circles of sweat under his arms now, and beads of it on his forehead. With a slight nod, Madison indicated that it was time for the final act.

Barton pushed off of the windowsill and walked over to pull out the chair beside Jackson. "Did you know that when a person is bludgeoned to death, like Connie here—" he poked a finger at the photograph "—blood flies everywhere?"

Unconsciously, Jackson looked down at his hands.

"All we have to do, Paul, is test you for trace." It was far too late for that, but the man had no way of knowing. Besides, he'd turned the corner, found his out. He'd never meant to kill Connie. He'd only wanted to seduce her. In his mind, her friendlessness had meant she wanted him. It was only afterward, when he realized the reality was nothing like the fantasy—that Connie was frightened and hurt—that he knew he had to kill her. To cover up what he'd done.

Madison knew it all. She could see it. See it with his mind. Feel his impotence. His building rage. She could smell Connie's fear as it filled the room, surrounding him, robbing him of his fantasy—of his triumph. She could feel his hand as it closed around the steel of the pipe. All he wanted was to erase his mistake. Stop the crying. Make it go away. He'd been wrong. She wasn't the one. And for that she had to pay. Remorse and anger twisted in his gut, until there was nothing left to do but hit her, and hit her, and hit her....

"I didn't mean to hurt her."

Madison jerked back to the present, her breath coming in gasps. Jackson was looking at her, his eyes begging her to understand.

"Of course not," she whispered, her hand still on his, not daring to break eye contact.

"It's just that she kept coming on to me." The words came out on a sigh.

Again Madison swallowed bile. "It's not your fault, Paul. How could you have known she'd fight you?"

"She did." He was earnest now, intent on explaining. "She screamed and she screamed, and she kicked me. I didn't know what to do. Then she tried to run away."

"And so you killed her." Madison kept her voice soft, noncondemning, almost as if she were consoling a friend.

He shot a look at the pipe again, and then buried his head in his hands. "I only meant to make her stop screaming." He looked up, nothing left of the confident man. "I just wanted to touch her. To show her what it was like to be with a man. I just wanted to make her feel good."

Madison refrained from voicing her real thoughts.

There was one more hurdle to jump first. "And Belinda Markham? Did you want to make her feel good, too?"

Jackson looked startled for a moment, and then suddenly dead calm. "No. *She* was a whore. I just wanted to fuck her."

With a sigh, she stood up and, without looking at Jackson or Barton, walked out of the interrogation room.

"Good work in there." Walter Blythe turned from the two-way mirror. Blythe was the director of the FBI's Behavioral Science Unit, and for all practical purposes he'd written the book on profiling. Furthermore, he had no business here, and her skin crawled with the premonition that something bad was about to happen. "You managed to solve a case that's been dangling over the NYPD for more than a year now."

"I did my job." It was a nonanswer, but it was the best she could do. Graciously receiving compliments had never been her strong suit. "Why are you here?"

Blythe smiled. "You don't beat around the bush, do you?"

"Not much purpose in it." She leaned back against the desk, watching through the mirror as Barton placed handcuffs on Jackson.

"I got a call today from the director. And his call came from the White House. It seems your godfather's got a problem, and he needs you."

"Something's wrong with Cullen?" Madison frowned. Cullen Pulaski wasn't the type of man to need anyone's help.

"He's fine. But he believes several colleagues of his have been murdered."

"And the FBI is getting involved?" Curiosity tinged with worry surged through her, cresting on a note of resentment. Whatever her godfather wanted, she wasn't going to like it.

"No, Madison." Blythe's expression was forbidding. "*You're* going to be involved. He wants you to head up a task force he's forming. And he's got the backing to do it. As of now you're relieved of your normal duties."

"But my cases…"

Blythe waved a hand through the air, cutting her off. "Will be handed over to another profiler. As of now, you're off the job."

She opened her mouth to protest, but Barton chose that moment to bring Jackson out of the interrogation room. It was as if he were a different man. Instead of jovial and cocksure, his demeanor was hangdog and defeated.

She'd won and Jackson knew it.

They walked past, Detective Barton's gaze colliding with hers.

Resentful admiration.

She'd danced with the devil and made him pay his due, but still she was being punished. She shot a look at Blythe, who shrugged in answer.

Hell of a world.

THE FLORIDA KEYS DINER was seedy at best, decrepit at worst, and nothing new in the long line of places he'd frequented of late. Decorated with gator heads, Formica and table jukeboxes in various states of disrepair, it was an odd fusion of swamp rat and Buddy Holly.

It suited his purpose. Hell, he blended right in. Which was more than he could say for the suits in the corner. Stoking his anger, Gabriel Roarke strode across the room, his movements calculated to go unnoticed. Odds were, his cover was blown, but old habits died hard.

A vague sense of unease mixed with his irritation as he recognized the men at the table. Something big was coming down if the director was here—something Gabe had the distinct feeling he wouldn't like.

Especially if it involved Cullen Pulaski.

The second man was recognizable if for no other reason than his face was plastered across the country's newspapers on an almost daily basis. It had been said on more than one occasion that the U.S. was run by the nouveau riche, and Cullen Pulaski was a card-carrying member. A renowned mathematician with a nose for business, Cullen had scored big during the tech revolution, placing him at the top of the industrial elite. His company, Dreamscape, was a permanent fixture on the Fortune 500, and that was just icing on the cake. Gabriel had worked with him years ago, and despite their differences, the two men had gotten along.

Grudgingly.

Gabe was a loner, and Cullen was as outgoing as they come, a politicians' politician. Only he preferred pulling the strings from a distance. And for the most part, what he wanted, he got. Which somehow only made Gabe angrier. To hell with the business of the CIA, when Cullen Pulaski called, everyone had damn well better come running.

"So, what the hell's this all about?" Gabe barked, sliding into the booth, his jaw locked in anger. "You're compromising my operation."

"It couldn't be helped." Cullen shrugged, dismissing Gabe's anger as if it were of no accord. "I needed you."

"And that was worth blowing a two-year investigation?" Incredulity and outrage washed through Gabe as he glared at the older man.

Evan Jensen lifted a hand, demanding silence. Not more than forty-five, Jensen was the CIA's youngest deputy director. But what he didn't have in seniority, he more than made up for with sheer presence. "I wouldn't have called you in if it wasn't important."

Gabe looked first to Pulaski and then to Evan, an eyebrow raised in question. It was a calculated look he'd practiced as a child, and once learned had never abandoned. "When I got the word, I assumed I'd been made."

"The operation hasn't been jeopardized." Jensen's voice was soft, but it was tempered with steel. "It's just been handed over to another operative."

Gabe opened his mouth to protest, and then shut it again. There was no point in antagonizing Jensen. Whatever was happening was obviously beyond his control. To hell with the fact that he'd sweated blood over this one. His was not to question why or some such shit.

"All right then, beyond Cullen's *needing* me, why don't you tell me what this is about?" There was cynicism in his voice, the overlay part and parcel of his personality. In the fourteen years he'd been with the company, he'd seen just about everything.

A waitress stopped at the table, set a cup of coffee in front of Gabe, and pulled out a pad, but Evan waved her away. So much for breakfast. Gabe reached for the coffee, sipping the acidic brew, the action soothing in its familiarity.

"What do you know about the American Business Consortium?"

"Not much." Gabe frowned. "It was formed in the wake of 9/11. An attempt at communication and cooperation among leading industrial bigwigs. If I remember right, the FTC had a field day, until the president stepped in and gave the consortium a get-out-of-jail-free card. All's fair in the fight against terrorism, I guess. Even collusion."

"There is such a thing as the greater good, Gabriel. You of all people should recognize that fact." Cullen leaned forward, his eyes sharp with intelligence. "The idea behind the consortium is really twofold. First, on a reactive front, it provides a communication base and a set of standard operating procedures, should something or someone try to bring down American commerce. And, on the proactive front, it allows for increased leverage in the international market. An opportunity to forge alliances that strengthens the United States' position worldwide, both economically and politically."

"A noble cause." Gabe said the words, but didn't for a moment believe them. As far as he was concerned, patriotism couched in economic gain was suspect from the get-go.

Evan frowned in warning, but Cullen only shrugged. "There are two sides to every coin. But in this case I honestly believe the primary beneficiary is the country."

"Gentlemen," Evan cut in, "we can discuss economic philosophy until we're blue in the face and never come to agreement. The fact of the matter is that the consortium exists, and if you're correct, Cullen, under possible attack."

It was Gabe's turn to frown. "From whom?"

"I don't know." Cullen shook his head, and took a sip of coffee. "I'm not even certain there's really a threat. I don't have anything definitive. Just a pattern. But in my business patterns are everything, and I can't ignore this one." He studied them both for a moment, leaving Gabe feeling as if he'd been found wanting. "A close friend of mine passed away recently. He met with an accident in a subway tunnel."

"Inelegant way to go," Gabe mumbled. "Was there an investigation?"

Cullen nodded. "He fell onto the tracks in front of a train, so there was of course suspicion of foul play, but the autopsy indicated a massive heart attack."

"Which would explain the tumble onto the tracks."

"Yes, but, the more relevant fact is that he was in perfect health."

"People have heart attacks all the time, Cullen. So what makes you think this one is questionable?"

"Cullen's friend is Bingham Smith, and he was on his

way to a meeting with the Chinese delegation," Evan said, his tone solemn, ominous. Bingham Smith made Cullen Pulaski look like chump change. The man was notorious for leveraging takeovers of even the most unavailable companies.

"The consortium has been working on a trade deal with China for almost three years now. And we were close to success. But Bing was our lead man. He'd built a relationship with his Chinese counterpart that can't easily be replaced."

"And you think someone purposefully took him out to quash the deal?"

"I think it's a possibility."

"But surely this is something the police should be handling." Gabe looked from Cullen to Evan in confusion.

"There's more," Evan said, shooting a sideways look at Cullen.

"I mentioned a pattern. The fact is that two other consortium members have died recently."

"More subway problems?"

"No." Cullen's smile was terse at best. "Totally unrelated as far as cause. Jacob Dashal was electrocuted, and Robert Barnes was killed when one of his warehouses burned to the ground. Both deaths were ruled accidental."

"So what's the pattern, other than the fact that they were also members of the consortium?"

"Nothing concrete. It's more of a feeling I have. But each man was significant in the effort to reach economic accord with China. And their deaths caused setbacks that have been difficult to overcome."

"How many people are in this consortium?" Gabe asked, setting his now cold coffee on the table.

"There are about fifty member companies, headed by an eleven-member board, of which I'm now the acting chairman."

"Bingham served as chairman until his death. And both Barnes and Dashal were key players in the negotiations," Evan added for clarity.

Gabe nodded, trying to assimilate the information. "So you believe that someone out there wants the trade agreement to fail. And that your friends' deaths have been an attempt to stop things from moving forward."

"Yes. But I've had trouble convincing local authorities of the same. All three men died in different states, which means different jurisdictions and varying degrees of interest in pursuing anything more."

"What about the Feds?"

"Same reaction. They gave it cursory attention. I demanded that much, but the conclusion was that although it was an unfortunate coincidence, there was no evidence to support a conspiracy of any kind."

"So he's brought it to the CIA?" Gabe frowned at Evan.

"No, Gabriel," Cullen said, forcing Gabe's attention back to him. "I went to the president. And once I'd explained my concerns, he authorized a task force, a group of experts to investigate the situation and report directly back to me. I've got carte blanche to pull the members from wherever I see fit."

"Our tax dollars at work." Gabe tried but couldn't keep the cynicism from his voice.

"Cullen wants you to head up the task force, Gabe. That's why I called you in."

"You risked my operation to send me on a wild-goose chase trying to find some illusive conspiracy dreamed up by an overmoneyed, highly imaginative computer magnate?" Gabe glared at Evan, purposely ignoring Cullen.

"Your job, Roarke," Evan growled, "is to go where I tell you to go. And while your operative skills are unimpeachable, your attitude is not. The president gave the order, and wild-goose chase or no, you will head up the task force, or find a job in the private sector. Am I making myself clear?"

"Yes." Gabe allowed his tone to border on subservient. If he hadn't been so tired he'd never have let his anger show, but he'd been undercover for months now, and the strain was obviously taking its toll. "I didn't mean offense, Cullen."

"None taken." Cullen waved off the apology. "I realize this is out of the ordinary. And the only thing I can say to reassure you is that this accord, if successful, has the power to change the face of international commerce. Which means it's as important as whatever you're doing now."

"*If* there's a conspiracy."

Cullen's eyes narrowed to slits, all geniality vanishing. "There is. I'm certain of it. A good deal of successful business is based on intuition, Gabriel. And I can feel this in my gut. Something's afoot. And I need you to figure out what it is." He leaned forward, his hand gripping the edge of the table, adding a feeling of urgency to his words. "You'll of course have all the funding you need. And any personnel you desire."

"I can pull together my own team?" The idea had a certain appeal, and since the assignment was inevitable, he might as well enjoy it.

"More or less. I am asking someone from the FBI to work with you. And I suspect she'll have some ideas as to the makeup of the task force."

"She?" His eyebrow shot up again, this time of its own accord.

"Madison Harper. She's with the Investigative Support Unit."

"A *profiler?*" The other eyebrow rose to meet its partner, his voice breaking on his surprise.

"An excellent one." Cullen nodded, ignoring Gabe's reaction. "She's also a friend. I trust her implicitly. And more importantly, I think she'll be the perfect complement to your more tumultuous style."

Gabe decided to let it pass. There was enough to deal with without further antagonizing the man who was apparently his new boss. "How soon do you want to get started?"

"As soon as possible. Evan has agreed to let you have anyone you need, and I have similar permission from other agencies. I want the best. And I trust that you can get them for me. Of course you'll probably want to meet Madison first."

Actually, she was the last person he wanted to meet. He wasn't a share-command kind of guy, and quite frankly the prospect of sharing it with some quasi-cerebral FBI guru made the idea that much more loathsome.

Especially when said guru was a woman.

CHAPTER TWO

NIGEL FERRIS LISTENED to the hum of the 747's engine, his ear catching the subtle whine as the pilot adjusted the flaps. Everything was fine. The fact that he was suspended in a tin can thirty thousand feet above the earth was non-negotiable.

Gabe called, and Nigel answered.

Even if it meant flying commercial.

It was ridiculous, really. He'd spent the better part of his career taking risks that no sane human would even contemplate, and here he was afraid of a bloody aeroplane.

Damn it all to hell.

"Can I get you something to drink, sir?" The flight attendant was a middle-aged woman, from La Paz by the sound of it. Not exactly the nubile nymphet one associated with the word *stewardess*.

Nigel contained a sigh. "I'll have a whiskey, neat, please." Might as well numb the discomfort churning in his gut. It wasn't just the plane. It was the whole damn thing. He smiled blankly as the woman handed him his drink, then took a sip, the accompanying burn doing little to assuage his worry.

Less than twenty-four hours ago, he'd been deep in the jungle, immersed in a world far removed from the quasi-luxury of whiskey in a plastic glass. Not that he was enjoying the fact. Truth was, he'd rather be back in camp.

He'd been close to accomplishing his goal, and now all that was blown to bloody hell.

Because of Gabriel Roarke.

Nigel leaned back against the seat, closing his eyes, the past tumbling through his mind, cushioned by the Maker's Mark. He'd first met Gabe in Saudi Arabia, part of a mission into Iraq so classified he still wasn't allowed to talk about it.

But he remembered. Dear God, he remembered. It was the stuff of his nightmares.

Taking another sip of his drink, he opened his eyes again to stare down at the open dossier on his lap. It might have been Gabe's message that pulled him out of the jungle, but it was another man that had clinched the deal, at least as far as Nigel's superiors were concerned.

Cullen Pulaski.

A man would have to be dead not to know who he was. His name was plastered across the headlines enough. Every news rag in the free world covered Cullen Pulaski. But Nigel wasn't interested in magazine articles. His connection with Pulaski was much more personal. And the idea of working with the bastard again wasn't exactly the thrill of a lifetime.

Still, it was bound to be interesting. Nothing about the man was ever boring. And if Gabriel and Payton were involved, he wasn't one to be left on the outside. Not that it had been an option.

His orders had come from the very top. The prime minister's directive. The objective abundantly clear.

And he supposed that, as much as anything, was causing his queasiness. Gabriel Roarke wasn't a man one wanted to cross, and certainly not betray.

And yet, if Nigel was to be true to his directive—that's exactly what he was about to do.

"I REALLY SHOULDN'T BE doing this, you know." Harrison Blake looked up from the FBI computer terminal, his hair sticking up every which way. He was the epitome of the boy next door, and one of the best computer forensic men in the country.

He was also Madison Harper's friend. They'd trained together at Quantico, and even when Harrison had left the Bureau for the private sector, they'd remained close. He was the first person she'd called after she'd received the news about the task force.

In the past twenty-four hours she'd managed to finalize the paperwork on Paul Jackson, update her replacement concerning ongoing cases, and meet with Cullen for a rundown on what he expected. All that was left was to assemble the team. But before that, she needed an ally, and Harrison fit the bill to a tee.

"It was either you come to New York, or me fly to Texas, and since you've got an expense account…"

"Which beats the hell out of what they offer around here." Harrison laughed as he shot a look around the cubicle Madison called an office. The FBI wasn't noted for its lavish perks, and the New York branch was no exception. "But I still could have accessed my own system."

"I know, but this is faster. And it's not like you're here to steal state secrets. I just want to know what, if anything, we've got on Cullen's theory, and you know your way around a computer far better than I do."

"You could have asked one of the computer techs here."

"And given up the chance to see you?" She smiled, but knew the gesture didn't quite reach her eyes. The whole task force idea left her with a bad taste in her mouth. She'd worked incredibly hard to rise within the ranks of the Bureau, and the idea of mavericking for Cullen, no matter how close they were, left her uneasy.

Harrison, as usual, read her mind. "The director approved this, right?"

She nodded, chewing on her lower lip, the habit ingrained since childhood. "He didn't have a choice. Cullen went through the White House."

"And you're worried that his strong-arm tactics won't sit well with the brass."

"Exactly," she sighed. "The last thing I need is to be accused of throwing around my pedigree." Her godfather and her father between them controlled a large chunk of the American economy. Which meant they also had political connections to rival the president. Her career, however, had been built on her own terms. She used her mother's maiden name, and was well into her work as a profiler before her connection to Philip Merrick had become public knowledge.

Until now, she'd never done anything that could even remotely smell of collusion with her godfather or her father, her need to stand on her own two feet almost second nature. But Cullen had blurred the line. And even if she'd wanted to say no, she doubted that she could have.

"I just don't want to lose all that I've worked for, and dropping three cases in order to unofficially chase after Cullen's shadows isn't exactly the way to make agent of the month."

"This one's totally off the record?"

"Yup. He's tried getting various agencies to investigate, but none of them bought into his theory. So, in typical Pulaski fashion he's cut through the bullshit and gone straight to the top."

"And tapped you to head up the task force." As usual Harrison was multitasking, talking and typing at the same time, the computer humming with activity.

"Not alone. I'm supposed to share that responsibility with some guy from CIA. We're meeting him at Cullen's offices tomorrow."

"You don't sound very excited by the prospect." Harrison swiveled his chair so that he could see her, hazel eyes concerned.

"I'm not. CIA types tend to be a bit over the top when it comes to macho, and I really don't want to have to prove myself yet again." There was a hint of bitterness that surprised her. She usually took sexual inequality in stride, the fact that she had to work harder than most men a given.

"I've no doubt you'll wow him." Harrison's grin widened. "You always do."

She bit back a laugh. "I'm glad you're here."

He turned back to the computer. "I just hope your macho man is equally pleased."

"I'm as much in charge as he is. I have every right to recruit who I want to help. Besides, how could he not want you?"

Harrison saw a computer as an endless puzzle, one that fascinated him to the point of obsession. That obsession had served law enforcement well. He could access almost any system, and in doing so, secure information that was otherwise unobtainable. He saw patterns in data that even seasoned detectives missed.

"It's not what he thinks that matters, anyway." She looked up to meet Harrison's questioning gaze. "Cullen is ultimately in charge, and he's delighted to have you on board."

Harrison grinned. "I thought you abhorred using connections to get what you wanted."

"It's not the same thing and you know it." She shrugged off a twinge of guilt, determinedly changing the subject. "What are you finding there? Anything of interest?"

"Well, the best way to test a pattern is to try and find an anomaly. So, using Cullen's database, I've been looking at records for all the members of the consortium. Each company has a designated representative. And in almost every case it's the president or chairman of the board. So I culled out the ones that have had a change in leadership within the last two years. Which ultimately gave me a list of fifteen."

"But there are only six here." She stared at the screen, reading through the names.

"That's because the others were legitimate changes of the guard. Retirement, takeover, that kind of thing."

"And these?" She recognized the names of the recently deceased board members and suddenly it clicked. "They're all dead, aren't they?"

"Yup." Harrison nodded. "And more interesting than that. Only two of the six died of natural causes. The other four met with rather untimely deaths. Seems they were a bit accident-prone."

Their gazes met and held.

"Or Cullen Pulaski is right."

THE CLINK OF glassware, low murmur of voices and static from the TV blended together to provide the perfect white noise. Panama City was perpetually full of tourists, people fleeing the cold northeast for sanctuary in the sun, but the Blue Room catered to locals. No umbrellas in pineapple glasses here. This was a whiskey-straight-and-beer-from-a-bottle kind of place.

Exactly what Gabe wanted. He sat in a corner, back to the wall, waiting. He'd put the word out a little over twenty-four hours ago, but he knew his friends would respond as quickly as circumstances allowed. There was a code between them, a bond forged in the fires of hell. There were things they could never talk about, even amongst themselves, but push come to shove, they could be counted upon.

And with Cullen Pulaski's long arm behind him, there would be no problem with approval. The powers that be would jump to make certain Pulaski's demands were met. Not that it really made a difference. If Gabe had called without any clearance at all, they'd still have come.

"I see you're still a creature of habit." Nigel Ferris materialized from the shadows and slid into the empty chair next to Gabe's. Ever-vigilant, his gaze swept the room. Apparently satisfied with what he saw, he smiled, the gesture not quite reaching his eyes.

Gabe shrugged and sipped his whiskey. "Old habits die hard. I didn't expect you until tomorrow."

"You shouldn't have expected me at all." The Englishman's eyes crinkled in genuine amusement. "Your message to London was routed through the Bolivian consulate. And those assholes are mired so deep in political bullshit it's amazing they manage to find the office each morning, let alone get a message to a supposed subversive working with left-wing anti-American guerillas."

"Undercover again, I take it?" Gabe raised an eyebrow, unimpressed with his friend's diatribe. Nigel hadn't changed a bit. British to the core, he had the breeding of an earl and the morals of a street urchin, the combination making him one of MI6's best operatives.

He'd been with Special Forces when they'd met, assigned as an adjunct to their Delta Force team. Not only had he proved himself a valuable team member, he'd won Gabe's trust, and the two of them had worked together on subsequent operations as their respective countries' needs had coincided.

"Let's just say I was working." Nigel shrugged. "That is, until I got your summons."

Gabe frowned. "I wouldn't call it a summons, exactly. More of a friendly request."

"Listen, mate, that *request* had to clear three countries' security levels, pass through at least five armed checkpoints, and then wend its way upriver to a place most Bolivians don't even know exists." He signaled a passing waitress, ordered a beer, then sat back. "So what gives?"

"Cullen Pulaski." Gabe spit the words out like a curse. "It's his game. He pulled the strings to call me in."

"And you used those same strings to get me."

Gabe nodded. "Misery loves company."

"He pulled you off a mission." It was a statement, not a question.

"Two-year op."

"You call Payton?" Nigel took his beer from the waitress and sat back, waiting.

"Yeah. His voice mail was routed through so many connections there's no way of knowing where the hell he really is, or if he'll get the message, but I tried."

"Last time I ran into the bugger he was in Singapore posing as a import-export man. Wouldn't have known him except for the scar. He had it camouflaged behind a beard, but if you know it's there you can still see it. Surprised he can still work undercover with a mark like that."

"He gets the job done. That's all that matters when you get right down to it. Hopefully he'll meet us in New York."

"New York?"

"Yeah, Cullen's corporate headquarters are there. Guess he thought it would be easier to have us operate off his home turf. He's supposed to be setting up some sort of command control. No idea what the hell that means exactly, but you can bet your ass it'll be top of the line. All that's left is to assemble the team."

"So, assuming Payton gets word, we'll be together again." Nigel frowned. "Not sure I like the sound of that. The last time we were together people died."

"That's a given in our line of work." Gabe tried to keep his tone even, to hide his own concern, but Nigel read the truth in his expression.

"You know what I mean." The Englishman released a sigh. "When Cullen Pulaski wants something, he doesn't give a damn what the price is. Payton's got the scars to prove it."

There were other scars, too. Less physical ones, and

Gabe knew only too well that they festered as easily. "You're not going to get an argument from me. But that doesn't change the fact that the man wants us. And basically—" he fought against a wave of bitterness "—what Cullen wants, Cullen gets."

"So what is it this time?"

"Three somewhat untimely deaths, and the foundation of a trade agreement with China. If Cullen's hunch plays out it could mean significant terrorist activity. That's where we come in." Gabe went on to fill in the details, sketchy as they were, including Cullen's grandstand efforts to gain their involvement.

"Well, you've got to admire the old bastard's spunk." Nigel frowned, his mind already at work on the puzzle. "How long ago was the first death?"

"About six months."

"I don't suppose he was kept on ice."

"Nothing so fortunate. There was an autopsy, though."

"And victim number two?"

"Four months ago. No autopsy."

"We're going to need someone with forensic experience. First to examine the autopsy and then if necessary to exhume the bodies. Even with decomposition there should be something left to point us on our way."

"We'll use the locals as much as possible, and if we need more help, I'm sure Cullen will find us an expert."

"He certainly seems to have a knack for it. Anyone else been drafted? Besides the three of us, I mean?"

Gabe stared down at the amber liquid in his glass. "I'm actually supposed to be sharing command with an FBI profiler. Woman named Madison Harper."

"Never heard of her," Nigel offered helpfully.

"She's a *friend* of Cullen's. Got the feeling that was his motivation for the decision."

"Wonderful. That'll either make her a tart or an

egghead. Just what we need. Either way, shouldn't you have cleared my coming through her?"

"Probably." Gabe suppressed a grin. "But I didn't. And quite honestly, I don't see Cullen being too concerned with the fact."

"And the girl?" Nigel asked.

"Will have to deal with it if she wants to stay on board. I've no interest in playing baby-sitter to Cullen's latest project."

"Have you considered the possibility that we're judging too quickly here? A profiler might prove very useful if there is indeed a connection between the board members' deaths."

"Sure, if the guy is Hannibal Lecter." Gabe tried but couldn't keep the derision from his voice.

Nigel shook his head. "You Yanks and your cinema. *Silence of the Lambs* certainly gave the profession notoriety, but anyone can be profiled. Number 10 Downing's had great success in using the same skill set to apply to suspected terrorists. If your Ms. Harper is any good, she could be a valuable member of the team."

Gabe shrugged. "I don't have anything against the woman personally. Hell, I don't even know her. I just don't like the idea of having her forced on me."

"So look on it as a challenge." His friend shrugged. "Something to sweeten the pot. You know you aren't happy unless someone's throwing the gauntlet down. Besides, like I said, maybe she'll be an asset."

"Yeah, and the Pope lives in Jersey." Gabe swallowed the last of his whiskey.

"Hardly." Nigel managed to look indignant and amused all at once. "So when do we leave?"

"We're catching the red-eye in a couple of hours. In the meantime," Gabe signaled the waitress for another round, "I suggest we drink up."

CHAPTER THREE

MADISON STARED down at the report, willing it to speak to her. Not so much the words on the paper, but the implications behind them. Six men dead. Their lives extinguished in an instant. The repercussions potentially global.

But there was nothing here to tell her why or even *if* they were connected.

"Hey, I think I've got something." Harrison looked up from his computer. They were ensconced in a conference room on the executive floor of Dreamscape's Manhattan offices. It had been converted for their purposes, state-of-the-art computers and equipment lining two walls. The third wall was partially covered by a white board, the remaining space designed to serve as a communications center complete with telephone bank and media consoles. The final wall was comprised completely of windows, their glass panes affording a magnificent view of Central Park.

From where she stood, Madison could see the wide expanse of green, leaves just beginning to turn, hints of gold and red making the trees seem like a kaleidoscope in the wind. "Something more on the dead men?" She turned from the window and walked over to the computer console, staring at the screen over his shoulder.

"Actually it's information on our Mr. Roarke." Harrison looked up at her with a grin.

"So what'd you find? His dossier was pretty slim."

"This isn't a lot better. Five years in the army, three of them with Delta Force. Operations too classified even for me. But whatever they were, they were significant. He's got a list of medals longer than my arm. After discharge, he pops up again at Langley. A couple of years training, and then what looks to be routine assignments in Europe for the next couple of years."

"So far that tracks with what we already know." Madison tucked a stray strand of hair behind her ear, her attention still on the screen. "What have you got after that?"

"That's where it gets interesting. According to the personnel file, Roarke had an altercation of some kind with a higher-up, was sanctioned and given a desk job, but—" Harrison tapped the monitor meaningfully "—with a little finagling I was able to access a more secure area and, interestingly enough, Roarke is listed here as an operative."

Madison read the screen. "Black ops."

Harrison nodded. "Which would explain the ruse of a desk job. If this adds up, I'd say he was underground for something like six years. But I can't say for sure because I couldn't get access any deeper."

"I thought you designed the system?" Harrison worked for Phoenix, a Texas company that specialized in computer forensics. In addition, they also developed secure systems for law enforcement agencies.

"We designed it. But that was before my time. I just know a few tricks. Anyway, just after 9/11 Roarke shows up again on regular listings assigned to counterterrorism. He's been working stateside ever since."

"With a heck of a lot of success, if that's to be believed." She nodded at the computer, chewing on the side of her lip. Roarke sounded like a testosterone junkie. Quick to put himself in harm's way, he'd command fierce loyalty among his friends, and probably be able to count them on one hand.

He'd be a loner, and have trouble with rules and superiors, but he'd be smart enough to have turned the detriment into an asset. A man who kept his own counsel, and would definitely not be interested in sharing command. Her guess was that he would be average-looking, the kind of man who faded into the background.

"Madison Harper?" The voice was deep, almost a bass, the sound sending a wave of something akin to pleasure coursing down her spine. She swung around, her eyes locking with pale blue eyes in the midst of a hard, chiseled face.

The eyes narrowed as the man with the voice let his gaze travel from her head to her feet and back again, the look measuring, weighing her worth. Black hair curled around his temples, a couple day's worth of beard decorating his chin. He should have looked unkempt, but instead the effect was rakish, the glint in his eyes letting her know he was more than aware of his effect on the fairer sex.

"Gabriel Roarke," he said, leaning against the door frame, crossing his arms over his chest, his mouth quirking upward ever so slightly.

She opened her mouth to say something pithy, but couldn't get the words past the cotton in her throat. Gabriel Roarke was anything but average. Seven years in the Bureau, five of them working with Investigative Support, meant that she could be pretty certain her reaction was well hidden. But the very fact that she was having it at all didn't sit well.

The last thing she needed was a pretty boy with attitude. "I wasn't expecting you until this afternoon." She carefully modulated her voice, keeping it neutral, almost bland. She'd used the exact tone on reticent offenders with great effect.

Gabriel's left eyebrow rose, the resulting expression

somewhere between amused and demonic. "I caught a ride on a cargo plane out of Tyndall."

"There was no need to rush over. You could have at least waited until you'd had a shower." It was her turn to measure him, and she had to admit there was nothing a good haircut and a shave wouldn't fix.

His lips parted in a smile, his teeth white against the beard, making her think of a pirate. "I've been here since yesterday evening, and if you'd care to check," he languidly lifted an arm, resting it on the door frame, "I think you'll find I've showered."

Their eyes locked, the air hanging between them, heavy as if it were laced with cyanide. One breath and—

Behind her, Harrison cleared his throat.

She exhaled and turned gratefully toward her friend. "I'd like you to meet a colleague, Harrison Blake. He's a genius with a computer, and I've asked him to join us. I hope you don't mind?" She smiled, knowing full well the gesture was empty. There was just something off-putting about Gabriel Roarke, as if he kept the world at arm's length, totally self-contained. A man of mystery.

Which simply meant he was a challenge. After all, cracking personalities was her specialty. The darker the better. And if she could successfully profile someone like the Sinatra killer, she could surely deal with a CIA operative—no matter his baggage.

Harrison, blissfully unaware of her turmoil, held out a hand to Roarke. "I'm not in the habit of horning in, but Madison can be pretty persuasive."

Gabriel shook Harrison's hand and smiled, the gesture lightening his face and making him seem infinitely more approachable. "I'm sure you'll be a wonderful addition to the team. I've added a couple of friends myself. People I can trust." The last was aimed directly at her. As if he were daring her to object.

Which, considering she'd just foisted Harrison upon him, wasn't a likely prospect. "Are they in town?"

"One is. Nigel Ferris. He came in with me last night. The other is still AWOL, I'm afraid."

"AWOL?" The question came unbidden.

Gabriel smiled, the gesture slow and amazingly sensual. "He's a bit of a wild card. Works for himself. Sort of a gun for hire. Last I heard he was in China. I've tried to reach him, but there's no telling how long it will take to track him down."

"When you say gun for hire, you mean mercenary?" Madison tried but couldn't contain her frown.

"Exactly." His smile widened.

"I see." She didn't see a thing, but it was all she could think to say. There was something about the man that put her out of kilter somehow, and she didn't like the feeling one little bit.

"Anyway," he continued, "Nigel insisted I come over and smooth the way before he arrives."

It was obvious he didn't believe anything of the sort was necessary, but it said a lot about his character that he'd defer to his friend. Loyal to a fault. She suspected the words more than described Gabriel Roarke. But that loyalty wouldn't come without price.

She shook her head, clearing her thoughts. She wasn't here to profile Roarke. "Cullen has the utmost faith in you. I'm certain whomever you've chosen will be a valuable asset to the team." God, she sounded just like her father. Just the right hint of superiority in her tone.

The eyebrow rose again, signaling the fact that Gabriel recognized the tone, as well, and just as easily dismissed it. "I was hoping you might bring me up to speed. Cullen said you'd already been looking into things."

"Why don't we sit down?" She gestured to the chairs, her mind turning to business. "Harrison did a little digging and found three more deaths. One seemingly from natural causes, and two accidental." They all sat down, Gabriel directly across from Madison, his icy gaze giving away nothing.

"Board members?"

Harrison shook his head. "But they were all members of the consortium, and key players in the move toward the trade agreement with China."

"Any sign of foul play?" He shifted his attention to Harrison, and Madison wasn't certain if she was relieved or disappointed.

"Nothing that triggered an investigation. One of them had an autopsy. Which means we're at three of six with forensic evidence."

"So what are your impressions?" Gabe frowned, his gaze returning to Madison.

She was fairly certain his use of *impression* was deliberate, a subtle dig at the inexact nature of her profession. "Profiling can't happen in a vacuum, Mr. Roarke. Without something more to go on, I can't even make an educated guess. Contrary to popular belief, we don't pull things from thin air."

"I didn't mean to imply that you did." He shrugged, the gesture robbing his words of sincerity. "I was just curious to know your thoughts."

"I think we've got to come up with a plan. Starting with procuring the necessary paperwork to gather forensic evidence from the victims. I've contacted a friend of mine in forensics. She can help cut through the red tape. Hopefully help us find any discrepancies."

"And if there aren't any?" He was goading her.

"Then we can all go home," she shot back.

"Don't think I wouldn't like just that." He crossed his arms, his icy stare sardonic. "But I'm not sure the word of a *friend* is going to sway Cullen."

"It will if she's the head of Braxton Labs." Madison drew out the last two words, waiting for him to acquiesce. Tracy Braxton was the best in the country.

"We'll see." He shrugged, his gaze dismissive.

Anger flashed, and she opened her mouth to retort, but Harrison cut her off, his expression carefully neutral. "I've also been studying the progress of the Chinese agreement, taking into consideration the effect on negotiations with each death." He pointed at his computer. "If someone is trying to damage the accord, there should be a correlation. In addition, I'm also in the process of gaining access to e-mail and computer records for all six men."

Gabriel nodded. "How about family members? Has any attempt been made to talk with them?"

"We've only been on the case for twenty-four hours." Madison tried but couldn't keep a note of exasperation from her voice. "We're not miracle workers. Besides, I was waiting for you. We are supposed to be collaborating on this."

"Well, I'm here now. So it seems the first order of business is for the team to meet." Gabriel stood up, his black brows drawn together, eyes narrowed in thought. "Since you've already done the preliminaries—" he nodded in Harrison's direction "—why don't you prepare an overview of what you've found? And Madison can bring us up to speed on the Chinese accord. If the two things are related we'll need to understand the ins and outs of what's gone into negotiations, as well as understanding who the remaining key players for the consortium are." He glanced down at his watch. "We'll reconvene here tomorrow morning."

"Is that all?" Madison fought to control her temper. She hated being dictated to more than anything, shades of a childhood spent with a business tycoon for a father.

"For now," Gabriel said, turning to leave the room, her sarcasm obviously sailing right over his head.

She turned back to Harrison, her mouth still open to retort. Harrison was grinning. And Madison suddenly felt the absurd desire to laugh. "Was it my imagination or did he have a bit of a God complex?"

"I think maybe you're overstating things just a bit." Harrison laughed, leaning back against the conference table.

"Not at all. The man practically dragged me back to the cave by my hair."

"Well, I'll have to agree with the cave part. But if your reaction is anything to judge by, I'd say he'd have gotten you there without damaging your do."

"What the hell are you talking about?" She was yelling, which was something she never did, the hot burn of her cheeks a telltale sign that she was losing it.

Harrison held up his hands in defense. "Nothing. I just call them the way I see them. And you've got to admit that Roarke has your number. He hit nine out of ten buttons and has reduced you to shrieking."

She shut her mouth with an audible click. Harrison was right. Gabriel Roarke had managed to completely unnerve her, probably intentionally. And she'd promised herself a long time ago that she'd never again let a man get to her like that.

No matter how much he intrigued her.

GABRIEL STRODE through the hotel lobby, trying to order his thoughts. Whatever he'd expected of Cullen Pulaski's protégé, Madison Harper wasn't it.

On the one hand she was a real beauty, complete with long legs, tight ass and silky blond hair he itched to bury his fingers in—California clean with a New York City edge. On the other hand, she saw a hell of a lot more than he was comfortable with, her piercing gray gaze stripping him naked with no more than a glance. It was enough to drive a man to drink.

He stopped at the door to the bar, the lively conversation inside enticing. Normally he didn't drink this early in the day, but at the moment the idea held real merit. Everything was happening too fast. He'd spent the last two days trying to pull out of his undercover persona, to recapture some sense of the real Gabriel Roarke.

But the truth was he'd lost himself years ago, his identity eroding away like a riverbank. Sometimes in tiny, almost unidentifiable bits and pieces—other times in huge chunks, the roaring water threatening the entire structure. What was left was an empty shell. A finely tuned machine.

And Gabe was comfortable with the fact, preferring it to the demons that haunted him. It was far easier to bury himself in work, to hide from the past and the mistakes he'd made. With a shake of his head, he turned his back on the bar and headed for the elevator. What he needed was a hot shower, and some time with the files Madison had given him.

Just the thought of her sent a riot of emotion rushing through him, a flood he wasn't certain he was equipped to handle. And that, added to his mixed emotions about the mission in general, made the present situation untenable. Cullen Pulaski wanted the Gabriel Roarke he'd been fourteen years ago. But quite frankly, that man didn't exist.

He stepped onto the elevator and stood silently, watching the light over the door move from floor to floor. With a subdued ding it stopped, the doors sliding open to expose a generically themed hallway. Hotels were all alike.

He inserted the key card and entered his room. After the artificial brightness of the hallway, it seemed abnormally dark, the heavy drapes closed against the city glare. The hairs on his neck rose as the instincts that had kept him breathing over the last decade kicked in.

He wasn't alone.

Automatically, he reached to his waist for his gun, dismayed to realize it was across the room in his suitcase. Moving with a stealth born of experience and adrenaline, he was across the room and reaching for his weapon when a voice broke the darkness.

"You're losing your edge, Roarke." Sunlight flooded the room as the curtains parted, and Payton Reynolds stepped out from behind them. "One more second and you'd have been a dead man."

"Or you." Gabriel swung around to face his friend, his gun barrel trained on the other man's chest. "What the hell are you playing at?"

"Just testing your wits." The younger man smiled, laughter quirking the corners of his mouth. "I thought you'd never get back."

Gabe returned the smile despite himself, and lowered his weapon. Payton hadn't changed a bit. He'd never had any patience—unless he was hunting someone. Then he was tenacious as hell, keeping at it until he had his quarry centered in the crosshairs.

He spoke seven languages, knew more guerilla warfare than possibly any man alive, and had an uncanny knack for thinking ahead of the game, seeing inside someone's head, guessing the direction of his thoughts before the poor bastard got there himself.

"And in the meantime you decided to break into my room?" Gabe walked over to his suitcase and dropped the gun inside, then turned back to face his friend.

Payton shrugged. "It wasn't difficult. And I needed a place to wait."

"You couldn't have just gotten a room of your own?"

His smile was slow. "And spoil the fun?" He moved forward and the sunlight caught his scar, the jagged line starting at his brow and cutting diagonally down to his chin.

"When did you get in?"

"A couple of hours ago. I'd have been here sooner, but

it was a little dicey getting out of Beijing. Some unfinished business." His face tightened for a moment, then almost as quickly relaxed. Payton kept his own counsel. Sharing only what he deemed absolutely necessary.

Always a loner, he'd beat around the army for several years before landing in Delta Force. But once there, he'd taken to operations like the proverbial duck to water, and Gabe couldn't have asked for a better man.

Until Iraq.

After that, he'd never really been the same. He'd spent almost a year in recovery, and then disappeared, going underground, supposedly selling his services to the highest bidder. Gabe had never asked for the truth. And Payton had never offered.

All that mattered was that he trusted the man. With his life, if necessary.

Payton moved farther into the room, his gaze assessing. "So where the hell have you been?"

"Meeting my counterpart." The word was innocuous enough, but somehow he'd managed to give it context, because Payton's smile widened.

"The profiler?"

"I see you read my files." Gabe shot a look at the open folder on the desk. Payton was nothing if not efficient.

"There wasn't much else to do." Payton shrugged. "Is Nigel here?"

"Yeah. I sent him over to get the medical examiner's final report on Bingham Smith."

"The one who fell in front of a train?"

Gabe nodded. "I figured we ought to check the details ourselves, rather than trusting someone else's sources."

"Ah," Payton said, "we're back to the profiler again. Surely she's not that bad?"

"She's fine." More than fine, actually. The woman was a looker, and the buttoned-up G-man persona had only enhanced the fact. "It's just this whole thing. I don't like being anyone's puppet."

"Then I'm afraid you're in the wrong profession, chum." Payton dropped onto a chair, suddenly looking tired, his scar white against his tan. "Dancing to someone else's tune is the name of the game. My guess is it's the puppeteer you're upset with more than anything. Cullen Pulaski has a way of rubbing folks the wrong way, you in particular."

"If I recall, you're not exactly a Pulaski cheerleader yourself."

"I pride myself on not cheerleading for anyone. Except maybe myself." The man's smile turned self-mocking. "You get anything new from the profiler?"

"Her name is Madison Harper." Just stating her name sent electricity coursing through him—the woman had definitely made an impression, but probably not the one she'd wanted.

"All right." Amusement colored Payton's voice. "Did *Madison* have any new information?"

"They found three more deaths that could fit the pattern."

Payton frowned. "They?"

"Seems I'm not the only one who brought in his own people. She's got a friend, Harrison something or other, a computer geek. He's the one who found the additional deaths."

"Sounds like the kind of man we can use. Know anything about him?"

"No. But I will." Gabe grimaced. "And in the meantime I gave them both assignments."

"And how did that go down?"

Again Gabe saw piercing gray eyes, silver laced with steel. There was more to the woman than looks. She had backbone, too. And he admired that in anyone. Even a female. "Not well. I think she took it as more of a challenge than an order. But the end result will be the same."

"And as far as you're concerned, that's all that matters?"

It was a question Gabe wasn't certain he could answer—at least on one level. But he quickly pushed the thought aside. "Of course. I want to find the answer to Cullen's puzzle, stop whoever is behind it, and get the hell out of here."

"And that starts with what the geek found."

"Yeah. All three dead guys were key members of the consortium. Which brings our total to six. All in the past thirty-six months."

"How long has the consortium been working on the Chinese accord?"

"Almost three years. But there would have been prep work so it could go back further than that."

"And our guys were involved?" Payton's brows drew together in concentration.

"Exactly. We'll know more tomorrow." Gabe let out a sigh. God, he hated working by committee, far preferring the ease of handling things on his own. But life rarely afforded that opportunity. Especially when Cullen Pulaski was around.

Besides, if he was honest, he'd have to admit that the only real fly in his ointment wore a blue suit and Chanel No. 5.

CHAPTER FOUR

MADISON WAS RUNNING LATE, a fact she loathed, but could do nothing about. All efforts to hail a taxi had been futile and she'd wound up taking the bus. Under normal circumstances she quite enjoyed the M31 and people-watching out the window, but today she was meeting with Gabriel Roarke and she didn't think that he was the type to tolerate anything less than punctuality.

She sighed, checked her watch, and hurried into the elevator, willing it to move faster. If everyone was already there, she'd have to make an entrance, and she abhorred that kind of attention.

Especially with *him* watching.

She got off on the 43rd floor and made a beeline for the conference room, her heart beating a staccato rhythm in her chest. The elevator door on her left dinged, and she glanced over as it opened.

"Madison, darling." Cullen Pulaski stepped into the hallway and pulled her into a bear hug. Not exactly a professional moment, but at least she didn't have to go into the lion's den on her own. "You remember Kingston and Jeremy?" He released her, gesturing to the men behind him.

Madison forced a social smile, and they all began to walk toward the closed door of the conference room. Kingston Sinclair was a longtime associate of her father's. Known for his unbending tenacity in business, his ex-marine attitude showed in both his work and his physique. Despite his age, he was in top physical form, his strength due more to years of routine than any vanity. She remembered him at family affairs, always in the corner with a colleague and a whiskey—straight.

Jeremy Bosner and her father were old friends. He had acted the role of kindly uncle most of her life, like Cullen, serving as a sort of stand-in for real family. She hadn't seen him much since she'd left home for college, but her memories were fond ones.

As the vice-chairman of the consortium, Jeremy should have taken charge after Bingham's death, but he'd been passed over when the board had selected Cullen instead. Today tension was evident in the line of his shoulders and his clenched hands. Maybe he wasn't as comfortable with Cullen in the chairman's seat as he'd have everyone believe. Or maybe he had other concerns. Madison forced herself not to jump to conclusions—an occupational hazard.

Cullen pulled the doors open and the four of them walked into the room. Sitting on the far side of the table, his grin rivaling the Cheshire cat's, Harrison was the first person she saw. But even so she could *feel* Gabriel Roarke, the current between them powerful and compelling. She pivoted slightly and their gazes met and held.

He was clean-shaven, dressed all in black and leaning casually against the windowsill. But there was nothing casual about this man. Even relaxed, he held himself under tight control, his expression giving away nothing. They stood for what seemed to be an eternity, eyes locked, until Madison grew uncomfortable, and despite her resolve, looked away—straight at the amused eyes of the man sitting next to him.

Curly brown hair framed a wonderfully craggy face highlighted by a pencil-thin moustache and neatly shaved half beard. He was dressed in a turtleneck sweater, tweed jacket, and corduroy pants. All that was missing was a pipe and a couple of dogs.

This had to be Nigel Ferris.

He coughed discreetly and she drew in a deep breath, surveying the rest of the room while she pulled her thoughts in order. Directly across from Gabriel and Nigel, a fourth man sat holding a cup of coffee, his dark hair spilling around a pale face bisected by a jagged scar. Knife wound, if she had to call it. An old one. He lifted his head, throwing his face into full light, as if daring her to comment, his green-eyed gaze assessing.

AWOL had evidently decided to return to the fold. She struggled to remember his name. Payton something. His expression was somewhat less forbidding than Gabriel's, but only slightly.

Wonderful.

"Morning, Cullen," Gabriel said, pulling Madison's thoughts firmly back to the matter at hand.

With a brief nod for Jeremy and Kingston, Gabriel's eyes fixed on her again, his lips curled upward in a mocking smile. "Glad you could join us, Miss Harper." His voice was dismissive as if she were a truant schoolchild.

Anger washed through her and almost unconsciously she straightened her stance. "It's Madison. And I wasn't aware there was a time card to punch." She purposely walked past him to take a seat by Harrison, turning her smile to the group at hand. "But now that everyone's here, shall we begin?"

Gabriel opened and then shut his mouth, as attention shifted to her. With an inward smile, she started the meeting, determined to maintain the upper hand. "I think first off we need to have introductions."

"You all know Cullen." She nodded in his direction. "And this is Kingston Sinclair. He heads up Radion Enterprises and serves on the consortium board." Kingston lifted a hand. "And Jeremy Bosner serves as VP for the consortium and owns Activitron Electronics." Both men, along with her father, Cullen, and a handful of others, were card-carrying members of America's industrial elite.

"We're delighted that all of you could come on such short notice." Cullen took over the meeting effortlessly. Madison sat back with a sigh, happy for the opportunity to simply observe. "You both know Madison." Cullen smiled benevolently in her direction. "And next to her is Harrison Blake. Harrison is an expert in computer forensics."

The man with the scar studied them both intently, as if memorizing their faces, then stared back down at his coffee cup.

"That's Gabriel Roarke." Cullen waved a well-manicured hand in Gabriel's direction. "He's heading up the team with Madison." He paused for a moment, studying the two remaining men. "The dapper fellow next to him is Nigel Ferris, and the quiet one with the coffee is Payton Reynolds."

Madison wondered how many times people introduced Payton by some nonessential identifier. Anything to avoid the scar. It was a natural reaction, a polite one in most cases, but she'd bet money that Payton Reynolds wasn't the kind of man who appreciated deception of any sort.

"Now that we all know each other, why don't we get down to business." Gabriel Roarke neatly assumed command, sidestepping her completely. Which was no doubt exactly what she deserved for letting her attention wander.

Still, she wasn't the type to just sit back and do nothing. "Good idea." She forced a smile. "I'll start, shall I? I spent the morning on the phone to Tracy Braxton."

"From Braxton Labs?" Jeremy asked, obviously impressed.

Madison nodded. "I asked her to examine all three autopsy reports."

Kingston frowned. "Jacob didn't have one. So there should only be two."

"Harrison has found three more deaths that fit into the pattern," Gabriel interjected, looking down at his notes. "Luther Macomb, Frederick Aston, and Alan Stewart all died within the last thirty-six months."

"People die all the time." Jeremy frowned.

"Yes, but these fit the pattern," Harrison said. "All three were members of the consortium, and they were all active in working on the accord. And—" he paused for effect, ever the showman "—all three were apparently quite healthy."

The room was silent for a moment as the three board members digested the information. Only Jeremy seemed genuinely surprised. But then, Cullen had already known, and Kingston Sinclair was notorious for holding his thoughts close to the vest.

"So did your friend find anything in the existing autopsies?" This came from Nigel, his lilting accent definitely not American. According to his dossier, he'd started life in rural England. A village in Gloucestershire. His accent, however, belied the fact, the product no doubt of intensive private schooling.

"Nothing that points to foul play," Madison told him. "She did ask for tox screens on Bingham Smith, though. Hopefully, we'll have those back tomorrow."

"Weren't they already run?" Payton asked, frowning.

"Not with the amount of detail Tracy wanted. She's looking for trace elements."

"Something to explain the heart attack," Gabriel said, getting it in one.

Madison nodded. "She's also checking to see if there were tissue samples for any of the others. If so, she'll probably request them and run some of her own tests."

"All of which will take time." Cullen's voice held a trace of frustration.

"It's a start, Cullen." Gabriel's voice had lost its edge. In fact, it almost sounded conciliatory. Madison bit back her surprise. "And we're making inroads in other places, as well. Nigel had a talk with the M.E. who handled Bingham's case."

"Nobody mentioned the fact to me." The words were out before she had time to think about them, and she immediately wished them back.

"There wasn't time." Gabriel's tone was mild, but his eyes spoke volumes, their icy depths reprimanding.

She opened her mouth to retort, then closed it, forcing a smile. "No problem. You just caught me by surprise."

Amusement flitted across his face. And Madison dug her fingernails into her palms, hanging on to her control by a thread. Harrison was right, the man knew how to push her buttons. But there was no sense rising to the bait. Instead, she turned her attention to Nigel. "Did the M.E. have anything to add to his report?"

"Not much." Nigel shrugged. "Only that he was surprised at how healthy Bingham's heart tissue was."

"He was in excellent shape," Jeremy interjected. "Worked out at least three times a week."

"Being healthy doesn't necessarily preclude a heart attack." Payton's voice was deep, almost inaudible, but there was an air about him that made a person want to listen anyway. As if when he deigned to talk, it was because there was truly something important to say.

"I just meant that…" Jeremy trailed off uncertainly.

"We know what you meant, Jeremy," Cullen reassured him. "It's what's been bothering us all. But Payton is right. Healthy men die every day from heart attacks."

"So why the bloody hell are we here?" Nigel summed up everyone's feelings in a sentence.

"Because I think there's something more," Cullen said simply, as if his word was enough. But then maybe it was. After all, they were all here, their respective agencies jumping when Cullen came calling. That kind of power could be heady. The sort of thing that led to God-complexes.

Fortunately, Cullen seemed to be immune to that. Not afraid to use his power, but holding off until all other avenues had been exhausted. It was one of the things she loved about him.

"If there's something there, we'll find it." Gabriel smiled, the gesture not quite reaching his eyes. "We'll just have to keep digging. Nigel also talked to Mrs. Smith."

"Tiffany?" Cullen snorted, and Kingston laughed. An inside joke, no doubt. "Sorry." He sobered. "It's just that she isn't known for her astute powers of observation."

"I'm guessing a second wife?" Nigel asked, amusement cresting in his eyes.

"Fourth," Jeremy offered.

"Ah." Nigel nodded as if that explained everything. "I did find her a bit incoherent, but I wrote it off as grief."

Another snort from Cullen, this time skeptical. "The only thing that would make Tiffany Smith cry is if someone took away her credit cards. Did she have anything at all helpful to say?"

Nigel shook his head. "Only reiterated what we already know. That Bingham was a healthy man."

"I know he played a crucial part in the negotiations, but why don't you spell out exactly what his role was?" Gabriel frowned, eyeing Cullen.

"Bingham had worked in China for years. Even when there were economic sanctions, he still dealt with Beijing."

Payton tipped his head slightly, his attention focused on Cullen, his gaze speculative. Madison wondered if he was familiar at all with the negotiations. According to Gabriel, he'd been in China when the call went out. An interesting coincidence.

"Bingham's contacts were crucial in establishing the foundation that led to our current negotiations. Without him we'd never have gotten a foot in the door."

"But surely now with things more established, his role was diminished?"

"On the contrary," Kingston said, "as chairman, he was taking a lead initiative in the talks. In fact, he was representing us at the upcoming summit in place of Robert Barnes."

"The man killed in the fire." Madison consulted her notes.

"Correct." Cullen leaned forward, his expression inscrutable. "He also had extensive dealings with the Chinese. They were our primary negotiators. But the others, Stewart, Macomb, Aston and Dashal were also involved. Stewart and Macomb were on the original steering committee. Aston was a close friend and confidant of Bingham's. And Dashal was coordinating our efforts with the Department of State. The president's been very interested in our work, and has given us his full support, and at least to a limited degree, governmental resources."

"Who is serving on the committee now?" Harrison asked, looking up from his laptop. As usual, he was multitasking.

"The steering committee disbanded when negotiations began in earnest. Kingston has replaced Dashal working with State. And of course, I, as chairman, have stepped into Bingham's role, with the aid of others on the negotiating team."

"We'll want a list of those participating in the negotiations. And anyone else you can think of that's connected to the summit." Gabriel jotted something down on a notepad, his brows drawn together in thought.

"Maybe I'm the only one here in the dark, but what exactly is the purpose of this accord, Cullen?" Payton's voice again commanded attention.

"I'm sorry. I should have stated that at the outset. I'm afraid we've all lived with it so long, we take it for granted that everyone knows what we're talking about." He paused to take a sip of his coffee. "Put simply, the accord is an attempt to trade U.S. technological expertise—specifically intellectual capital—for Chinese favored-nation status on certain U.S. technological exports."

"But with the Chinese propensity for communism, not to mention their record on human rights, why would the U.S. government be interested in an agreement like that?" Harrison stopped typing, his full attention on Cullen.

"Money, my dear boy. It's as simple as that. Despite the fact that the economy is beginning to recover, changes won't occur overnight, and for those of us in technology the battle is even harder. Even with increased spending power, large expenditures and capital equipment will be the last to recover. And with so many companies holding on by a thread…"

Harrison nodded. "You need an untapped market. And an agreement for favored-nation status would be just that. Not to mention a political coup for a first-term president."

"Exactly." Cullen smiled at Harrison as if he were a prize pupil. "Unfortunately, your original assessment was correct, too. There is a lot of opposition to the accord, both here in the U.S. and abroad."

"Foreign companies who stand to lose their own contracts if the accord goes through." Gabriel was still studying his notes. "As well as countries who don't want to see the Chinese grow in technological strength."

"But haven't we been dealing with the Chinese under the table all along?" Madison asked. "You mentioned Bingham. Surely he wasn't the only one?"

"There were loads of others," Jeremy said. "But nothing on this grand a scale. And certainly nothing as well organized."

"Don't you worry about how the Chinese will use this technology?" Nigel didn't say it, but his meaning was clear. Although the accord was delineated as nondefense, much of the technology being discussed could easily be used for military purposes.

"The truth is they're going to get it one way or the other. The black market is booming. The Israelis and Russians are making a killing. Seems foolish for us to bury our heads in the sand, both financially and militarily."

"That's a pretty hawkish position, surely?" Nigel's question was off the cuff, intended to sound almost flippant, but Madison could tell he was more interested in the answer than he was willing to let on.

"It's a financial position, Mr. Ferris," Kingston said. "Survival of the fittest."

"Gentlemen," Cullen interrupted, "we're not here to argue politics. The summit, and any resulting accord, has the full blessing of the current administration, and that, for the moment, is all that's necessary." There was a finality to his words that precluded further argument. "Our job," he gestured to his two colleagues, "is to make certain that the Chinese continue to work with us toward agreement. Your job is to find out if there is in fact a conspiracy to upset the accord. And if so, you are to eliminate that threat. Am I making myself clear?"

Despite the testosterone levels in the room everyone nodded. Cullen Pulaski commanded respect. Period.

"Good." His smile was genuine. "Why don't we turn this over to you now?" He shot a telling look at Madison and then at Gabriel. "I really just wanted Kingston and Jeremy to meet all of you, and to give you the opportunity to meet us. Obviously we'll want to be kept apprised of your progress and discoveries. And you can always come to us if you have questions." He stood up, and everyone else followed suit.

"I've tried to think of everything you might need." He gestured to the equipment-filled walls. "But I'm sure I've forgotten something. Don't hesitate to ask. I meant it when I said I'd spare no expense. I'm sure you can understand now how important this accord is to the well-being of our nation. It's the beginning of a new age, and I, for one, am not willing to see some disgruntled splinter group try to take it down."

It was a rousing political speech, but unfortunately Cullen had the wrong crowd. These men might be patriots, but they weren't the kind to worry overmuch about political correctness. What mattered to them was bringing down the bad guys—whatever the reasons.

And just for the moment, Madison was in total agreement.

"YOU REALLY THINK this team of yours is necessary?"

"I do." Cullen Pulaski steepled his hands on his desk, and met Kingston Sinclair's worried gaze. "If I'm right about this, everything we've spent the last three years working for could fall apart just as we come into the home stretch."

"But you're basing all of this on a hunch." Jeremy Bosner walked over to the mahogany credenza that served as a bar, and poured himself a glass of juice. Tall to the point of seeming gaunt, he looked more like a befuddled professor than a business tycoon, a fact which he used to his advantage more often than not. "It seems to me that this task force of yours only serves to reinforce the Chinese delegation's concerns on the matter."

Cullen sighed, his gaze encompassing both men. For industrial giants they could be incredibly shortsighted at times. "If anything, it will assure them that we're serious about protecting our interests and theirs."

"Maybe. *If* there's something to protect us from." Kingston fiddled with the earpiece on his glasses, a ploy he often used when playing for time. "It's within the realm of possibility, you know, that Bing actually died from a heart attack. The police certainly seem to believe that."

"Bing was in perfect health and you know it," Cullen snapped.

"Look, whether you're right or wrong, Cullen, the point is that we're dealing with a delicate situation here. Bingham's death, whatever the reason, is going to cause problems in negotiations. He had connections that we can't just reproduce at the snap of a finger." Jeremy ran a nervous hand across his graying hair, smoothing it into place. "And I, for one, can't help but worry that even the rumor of it being something other than a tragic accident has the power to squelch the negotiations altogether."

"That's why I called in Gabriel Roarke. The man's a spook. If anyone can stay under the radar, he can." Cullen waited as the other two men digested the information.

"What about Madison? She's FBI. That's certain to raise some eyebrows." Jeremy gulped the juice, almost choking, a sure sign he was worried.

"She's also Cullen's goddaughter, which means her presence here is already accepted." Kingston surprised Cullen with the defense, but he'd take his allies any way he could get them. "That's part of the reason I wanted her on the team."

"You were in on this?" Jeremy's anger made his face blotchy.

"I discussed it with Cullen, yes." Kingston shrugged.

"But you just asked him if it was necessary." Jeremy's expression grew skeptical.

"I'm still not convinced it is. But Cullen was going to

take action with or without us, and so I figured I might as well have some say in the matter."

"I see." Jeremy sat down across from the desk, still clutching his cup. "So it's two against one."

"I wouldn't put it like that." Kingston's tone turned defensive, and he fingered his eyeglasses again.

"Look, gentlemen, we're all in this together. We've invested time, money and a hell of a lot of sweat into making this agreement a reality. And I'm not about to let anyone or anything get in our way. This task force is insurance. A way to appease the Chinese and at the same time hopefully get to the bottom of what may very well turn out to be nothing." Cullen didn't believe the last bit, but that didn't stop him from trying to reassure them.

He needed their cooperation, and he needed their continued financial backing. But he also needed the task force. The truth was he had a hell of a lot more than they realized riding on the accord. And Bing's death had been a major setback.

Hopefully, with everyone's attention focused on the idea of terrorist intervention, other more pressing things would be overlooked. There was simply too much at stake to risk an ill-advised confidence.

Jeremy Bosner and Kingston Sinclair were barracudas. And if they smelled blood, he wanted to be absolutely certain it wasn't his.

CHAPTER FIVE

"I THINK THE FIRST THING to do is pull together what we know." Madison stood in front of a white board, her cool facade apparently running straight to the core. Gabe wondered what it would be like to pull her hair from its ponytail and loosen the buttons on her white blouse. Madison Harper could use a little rumpling.

He discarded the thought almost before it was finished. The last thing he needed was to involve himself in anything that even resembled a relationship. If he needed release, there were other ways. Right now he needed to concentrate on the task at hand.

"Of the six deaths, how many were from medical causes?" Nigel was studying the names written on the board—dead men who had to be coaxed into telling tales.

"Only two." Madison answered without checking her notes. "Aston and Smith. Both heart attacks."

"Which statistically isn't out of the norm." This from Harrison who was, as usual, typing on his computer. "What's more interesting is the positioning. Aston was the first to die, and Smith the last."

"With four accidents in between." Payton had retreated to a corner, protecting his space.

"An electrocution, smoke inhalation, a car wreck and an apparent drowning." Harrison stopped typing to look up at the board.

"Apparent?" Nigel asked.

"He fell. Hit his head and landed in the bathtub with the water running. Without an autopsy there's no way to know if he died from the fall or the water."

"So why wasn't there an autopsy?"

Harrison shrugged. "Happened in a remote part of Colorado. Way up in the mountains. Doubt they've got the manpower to deal with something like that. Easier to rule it an accident. And at least on the surface, it certainly looks like it was."

"You've got the police report?" Gabe asked.

"It's right here." Madison left the white board and reached for a file, handing it to Gabe. "The only one of the four we have an autopsy report for is Robert Barnes."

The insistent ringing of a cell phone broke the conversation, and everybody scrambled to find their phone. "Mine," Madison said, flipping it open, moving to the far side of the room so that she could hear.

Gabe turned back to the group. "Robert Barnes was the man who died in the fire." He scanned the file, trying to remember the details. "A warehouse, right?"

Harrison nodded. "His own. The autopsy said he died of smoke inhalation."

"Was there an arson investigation?" Payton had moved to stand by the window.

"Yeah." Harrison answered. "For insurance purposes. There was talk of arson, but nothing conclusive. The most likely person to have torched the place was Barnes, and since he died in the fire—"

"They were quick to close the case." Gabe finished for him. "Who was the beneficiary?"

"The bulk of his estate went to charity." Harrison searched his computer screen. "With the odd bequest to staff and friends."

"I take it there was no family?" Gabe asked.

"A couple of ex-wives. No children." Harrison

shrugged. "Certainly no one with motive to kill the guy, if that's what you're getting at."

"In order to have a conspiracy," Nigel's voice had turned cynical, "you have to have something to go on. And other than their business connections, I don't see a bloody thing."

"How about proof of murder?" Madison closed her cell phone with a decided snap, her eyes sparkling with excitement. "That was Tracy Braxton. She got the tox screen back, and guess what she found?"

"I assume you're going to tell us?" Gabe snapped, impatience making him speak more harshly than he'd intended.

Her mouth tightened into an angry line, and he wished his words back. Harrison reached over to touch her arm and she relaxed. "She found traces of potassium chloride."

"Son of a bitch," Payton swore. "Instant heart attack. Any idea where it came from?"

"That's the best part." Madison was smiling again. "Tracy examined the body and found an injection site. His right hip. The original M.E. missed it."

"I'd say it's a pretty sure bet that Smith didn't inject himself," Nigel said. "The question, of course, is who did?"

"And why." Payton had moved closer, taking a seat next to Harrison, his interest obviously piqued.

"Whatever the answer, it looks like Cullen was right," Harrison said, already working on the implications.

"Hang on a minute." Gabe held up a hand. "Not to ruin anyone's fun here. But one death doesn't make it a conspiracy. For all we know someone totally unrelated to the accord could have had it in for Smith. A guy like that is bound to have enemies."

"Except that there was another heart attack." Nigel's

eyes were narrowed in thought, his expression grim. "If it turns out that Aston had potassium chloride in his system, then we've got the makings of something bigger."

"That's a big *if*," Payton said. "And even if it were to prove true, there's still the other four. None of them had heart attacks."

"He wouldn't want to use the same method every time." Madison's brows were drawn together in a frown as she studied the board. "By using different methods, the odds are better that the crimes would go undetected."

"So if Aston's heart attack was deliberate, wouldn't that blow your theory?" Gabe asked, trying to contain his cynicism.

"Not necessarily. If he killed five people and got away with all of them, then repeating the methodology is less risky. If it suited his purposes, under these circumstances, I could see using it again." Her gaze met Gabe's, her eyes daring him to disagree.

"I repeat—all of this remains speculation until we know for certain what happened to Frederick Aston." Gabe hadn't wanted there to be any truth in Cullen's theory. But faced with the reality of Smith's murder, he felt a surge of curiosity. And an overriding need to find the truth.

"You said there was an autopsy, right?" Payton, as usual, provided the voice of reason.

Madison nodded. "And they kept tissue samples. The lab in D.C. shipped them to Tracy last night."

"There's obviously nothing in the initial report." Nigel leaned back in his chair, his arms crossed over his chest.

"No. But there wouldn't be unless someone specifically looked for it. And unlike Bingham Smith, Frederick Aston had a history of heart problems." Madison shrugged. "So there wouldn't have been any reason to suspect foul play."

"So we wait." Payton didn't sound at all thrilled by the prospect.

"Why don't you and Nigel start digging into Bingham's past? Let's see who his enemies were. Harrison, you look into the other deaths—maybe there are similarities we're missing."

"And what do you want me to do?" Madison asked, gray eyes shooting sparks.

"I'm thinking maybe we ought to pay a visit to Tracy Braxton. Nothing like getting the news firsthand."

BRAXTON LABS WAS LOCATED in what had originally been a meatpacking plant. The outside edifice of crumbling brick belied the remodeled chic of the laboratories inside. State-of-the-art equipment and cutting-edge personnel had made the company one of the top private forensics labs in the country.

Madison sat in the reception area watching Gabriel chat up Tracy's assistant. The woman was practically cooing, her smile just this side of simpering. Gabriel seemed to enjoy the game, his answering smile warm and sexy. Playing it for all it was worth.

Certainly a far cry from the cab ride they'd just shared. They'd barely managed to stay civil on the drive over, tension permeating the back seat. Not exactly chemistry conducive to working together. She sighed, wondering what Cullen had been thinking when he had chosen them to head up his team.

On a professional level it made sense, but Cullen knew them both, and it seemed to her that he should have realized they'd never be able to work comfortably together. Still, she wasn't one to back off of a challenge, and if Gabriel Roarke thought that she'd just fold up her tent and go home, he had another think coming.

"Couldn't wait, huh?" Tracy walked into the office, her white lab coat a contrast to her dark braided hair. With her high cheekbones and flawless ebony skin,

Tracy looked more like a *Victoria's Secret* model than a pathologist.

"Considering we now have an open murder case, it seemed prudent." Madison stood up. "This is Gabriel Roarke." She motioned toward the man. "He's part of the team Cullen set up."

Tracy frowned. "Sounds like the two of you will have your plates full."

"And then some," Gabriel said, shaking Tracy's hand. "Agent Harper speaks highly of your work."

"It's all about getting the dead to talk. Nine times out of ten, with a little prodding, they spill their guts."

"Morgue humor?" Gabriel's eyebrow rose, the corner of his mouth curving upward.

"Sorry," Tracy said, "occupational hazard. Why don't you guys come on in." She gestured toward her office door and they followed her inside. The room was beautifully appointed, blues and greens lending a calming touch—a far cry from the pictures spread out on her desk. "Serial killer." She shook her head. "Ten vics so far."

Madison was immediately interested. "Where?"

"Nebraska, of all places. Has a penchant for old ladies. Sick bastard."

Madison frowned. "I read about the case. Guy's got a real momma complex."

"Ladies, if we could get back to the business at hand." Gabriel's deep voice held a hint of rebuke and Madison resisted the urge to shoot him the finger. The man was a real pain in the ass.

"Sit." Tracy indicated the chairs in front of her desk, then sat down behind it, pushing the photographs out of the way. "I not only got the sections, I had a chance to look at them. I'll need to see the tox report of verification, but I'd say the odds are good that Mr. Aston ran into the same needle Bingham Smith did."

"You found potassium chloride." It was a statement, not a question, Gabriel's tone grim.

"Signs of it. As I said, we'll need to wait for the complete report to confirm it. In the meantime, I studied the photographs of the body, as well. Even had a couple of them blown up." She picked up an envelope and removed two photos. "Of course without seeing the body, I can't be certain, but I'd say these are puncture marks."

Gabriel took the pictures from her and examined each in turn, then handed them to Madison. "So we have the same cause of death and possibly the same M.O."

The photos each showed an exposed patch of skin punctuated with a small round red mark. "This won't stand as conclusive evidence." Madison's gaze encompassed them both.

"Doesn't have to. If the tox report confirms the presence of potassium chloride, that'll be enough. In the meantime, the possibility of needle marks suggests the beginning of a pattern."

"Except that Aston died in his home, not in a public place. Makes access a lot more difficult." Madison continued to study the photos, trying to assimilate the facts. "Could mean the killer knew Aston."

"Or that the man was injected on his way home." Gabriel, too, was puzzling it out.

"Potassium chloride works pretty fast if the dose is lethal," Tracy said. "He'd have had to be pretty close to have made it inside."

"Where exactly was he found? Does your report say?" Madison chewed on the side of her lip, waiting.

Tracy rifled through the file. "Says here he was found in the hallway at the bottom of the stairs."

"So someone could have been at the front door," Gabriel said.

"I suppose it's possible." Tracy shrugged. "If the

photos are right, the first injection site was his upper arm. The second his thigh."

"But according to this—" Madison was scanning the report "—there was no sign of a struggle. And if some guy tried to lunge at me with a needle, I guarantee you I'd be fighting back."

"Point taken." Gabriel shot her a look that was impossible to interpret. "What about the other autopsy?" His question was for Tracy. "Any chance there was potassium chloride involved there?"

"No." Tracy shook her head. "Because of the fire, Robert Barnes's autopsy was much more thorough. They did a complete tox screen and there was no potassium chloride present. Besides, he didn't die of a heart attack."

"So there's no relationship." Madison tried but couldn't keep the frustration out of her voice.

"Not with regard to injection, but I did find a couple of things that, as far as I'm concerned, makes his death look a bit more suspicious. In the original autopsy report the M.E. noted a contusion at the back of Barnes's head. The conclusion was that he hit it falling after he succumbed to the smoke. But I'm not convinced of that. According to the photographs in the file, it looks to me like the contusion was premortem rather than post."

"So he fell before he died," Gabriel repeated, his impatience evident.

"It's more than that. It's the placement of the body at the scene." She pulled out another picture. "The way he's lying doesn't track with the angle of the wound. If he struck his head when he fell, it would be on the opposite side." She traced the arc of his fall on the photograph underscoring her words.

"Could he have rolled over?" Madison asked.

"Anything's possible, but I don't think so. The positioning of the body is too unnatural." Again she pointed at the photograph. "See the way the leg is twisted. If he'd been conscious that would have hurt like hell."

"And he'd have moved again." Madison stared at the picture, wishing it could talk.

"Exactly." Tracy nodded. "But unfortunately all of this is nothing more than an educated guess. Another expert might disagree completely."

"But you're *our* expert." Gabriel said as he considered the photographs. "So what can you tell from the shape of the wound?"

"Blunt force trauma," Tracy said. "Something small and heavy. A hammer, maybe. If I could have seen the actual wound I could probably have told you definitively."

"That's still not enough to prove foul play." Madison hated to be the naysayer, but it was important that they be certain. At least as much as possible in light of the fact that the man was dead and in the ground.

"There's a little more." Tracy sat back in her chair, still holding the file. "The chemical residue in his lungs led investigators to determine cause of death as asphyxiation, but when you look at the sections under the microscope the magnitude isn't what you'd expect."

"Meaning what?" Gabriel asked.

"Well, considering the size of the fire and Mr. Barnes's proximity to it, I'd say he stopped breathing well before it got close enough to actually kill him. Again, without seeing the actual body I can't say for certain. But I'm betting Barnes died before the fire ever really got going."

"So the blow could have killed him?"

"I'd say so. He obviously lived long enough to breathe some smoke, but I don't think that's ultimately what killed him. My guess is he was out cold and probably dying well before the fire started."

"Maybe his fall started a chain of events that started the fire," Madison said, testing a theory.

"Nope." Tracy shook her head for emphasis. "Point of origin was at least one hundred feet away. And according to this—" she waved the file through the air "—the ATF wouldn't completely rule out the idea that the fire had been intentional. That's why the insurance company was so thorough."

"But they never proved anything," Madison said, remembering the report.

"It's hard to prove arson. And even if you do verify there was an accelerant, unless there's a footprint, it's nearly impossible to tie it to someone specific." Gabriel spoke as if he had firsthand experience, and Madison found herself wondering whether he had investigated a fire, or started one. "So how the hell did the M.E. miss all this?"

"Not ineptitude, if that's what you're thinking." Tracy's expression turned fierce. "It's not like *CSI* on television, or even a place like this." She gestured at her office. "Most forensics labs are underpaid, understaffed, and seriously overworked. It's easy to miss things like this without the proper equipment. And top-of-the-line machinery is expensive and way out of the budget of the average forensics lab. Add to that a caseload that numbers in the hundreds and there simply isn't motivation to spend more time than absolutely necessary."

Gabriel held up his hand. "Sorry. Didn't mean to tread on anyone's toes. It's just that we're looking at three apparent murders, none of which were identified from autopsy."

"Well, you know now." Tracy crossed her arms, unaffected by Gabriel's outburst. "What you do with the information is up to you. My job is just to report the facts as I see them." She stood up, the gesture signaling the end of the meeting.

"And we appreciate all you've done." Madison rose, too, smiling. "Thanks to you we've got a good start. The next step is to look into the other deaths."

"The ones without autopsy." Tracy nodded. "Let me know if you decide to exhume them. Even with decomposition I can still find an amazing amount of evidence."

"You'll send a report." It was a statement not a question, Gabriel's mind already moving on to the next step.

Whatever that might be.

NIGEL SLIPPED INTO the team control room, checking quickly to make certain that it was empty. Everything was dark, the only light coming from the wall of windows. He glanced over at them, thinking that if things went south, what seemed an obvious perk could easily make the room a death trap. Better that they were below ground level, but Cullen wouldn't know that. And in all honesty he had to admit that considering his directive, the windows could prove an asset. But only if things got out of hand.

He made his way over to the computer bank, relieved to see that the system was on. He hadn't been able to tell if it was encrypted, and although he would most likely still have been able to gain access, this would be much simpler.

He sat down in front of a monitor, pulled out the keyboard, and with a few simple keystrokes had full access to Cullen Pulaski's computer systems. The file he needed was easy enough to find.

He pulled a disk from his pocket, inserted it into the computer, hit a key and waited while it hummed into action. Nine minutes later, disk back in his possession, he made his way to the door, the computer screen behind him flashing green—

Strike F1 to retry boot, no data found.

CHAPTER SIX

MADISON STOOD at the window of her apartment looking out at the Manhattan skyline. Lights glittered from windows across the way, the towering buildings full of residents settling down for the evening. In the distance she could see the shimmer of the East River, its crazy currents flowing in whatever direction it chose. First upriver, then down, fluctuating with the tides.

Despite the fact that the apartment had come from her father, she loved it. It was as much a home as she'd ever had, filled with the bits and pieces she'd collected over her nomadic life.

Her mother had been the original free spirit, and not even Philip Merrick's power and wealth had been enough to hold her captive. Less than five years after the wedding, Alexis Harper had simply taken her baby and walked out the door.

For the next six years Madison had traveled around the country with her itinerant mother, never alighting anywhere long enough to call it home. When she'd reached school age, Philip had demanded his daughter, and in the usual way of things, gotten exactly what he'd wanted.

The challenge won, he'd immediately shunted her off to a myriad of nannies and private schools, the latter turning to boarding schools, with vacations wherever her father's latest venture had taken him.

She'd traveled the world, and been incredibly lonely. So

much so that when she'd graduated from Vassar, she'd married the first man who asked, certain that at last she'd found a home. But hasty decisions are seldom good ones, and her marriage was not the exception.

Rick, it turned out, was nothing but a prick in gentleman's clothing. Only interested in her money, he couldn't understand her need for autonomy, and once it had become clear that she wasn't content to sit back and enjoy her father's bank account, he'd started a one-man campaign to undermine her confidence. And it had almost worked.

Almost.

So, as predicted by both her mother and father, the marriage had ended in divorce less than a year after the nuptials. And Madison found herself once again adrift.

When her father had suggested the apartment in New York, her first instinct had been to refuse. After all, as a fledgling FBI agent, she spent most of her time at Quantico. In fact, she'd spent the better part of her adult years trying to establish a life separate from her father, to make her own way without benefit of his name—to prove to herself, in some misguided way, that she didn't need anybody.

The reverse, of course, was true, and Philip Merrick was not a man easily dissuaded. He wanted her nearby. So when her profiling work took her to the city for back-to-back cases, she was faced with the prospect of living with her father or living in a hotel, neither option alluring.

Never one to admit defeat, her father had seized the advantage and bought the apartment, offering it as a gift, presumably with no strings attached. A joke if ever there was one, as there were always strings where her father was involved, but he did love her in his own unique way, and so with some reservation, she'd moved in. And never looked back.

Her work kept her traveling, and the apartment had become a refuge, a place where the evil she lived with day in and day out could not penetrate. A safe house of her own making. And for that she'd be eternally grateful to her father.

There was peace here that she never found in other places. Not in her mother's sprawling home in New Mexico and certainly not in her father's penthouse on Central Park West. With a resolute smile at her reflection in the window, she reached for the cord and drew the drapes, shutting out the city, leaving only the soft warmth of lamplight.

She moved over to sit on the couch, reaching for her wineglass, relishing the peace and quiet of her apartment. Information about the case swirled inside her head, replacing all thoughts of the past.

None of it made much sense. They had two confirmed murders and a third that looked suspicious. What had been theory was clearly reality. Which meant that there was a killer out there. And worse, that he would most likely strike again.

Taking another sip of wine, she let the events of the day wash over her. Despite her aversion to Gabriel, she had to admit that his associates seemed more than up to the task at hand.

She looked down at the files Harrison had pulled together, everything he could find on Nigel Ferris and Payton Reynolds. Nigel's record was exemplary. A team player who'd made a career out of coming through in the most dire of circumstances. His loyalty to his friends came second only to his loyalty to country.

Payton Reynolds's record was sketchier. He'd served under Gabriel in Delta Force, his stint in the army ending abruptly with a myriad of awards and a lengthy hospital stay. Details were classified, but it had obviously been something traumatic, the scar on his face a permanent reminder of whatever had happened.

There was no way to know for certain, but Madison would stake a week's wages that the mark served as an outward sign of more significant internal damage. She'd seen men like Payton before. The walking wounded. He hid it well, but it was still there, reflected in his eyes, and she found herself wondering if Gabriel carried similar scars.

She looked down at the report, clearing her head of all emotion. She was trying to get a handle on the men she was working with, not dissect their leader.

After the hospital, Payton had simply disappeared. Harrison had been unable to ferret out more than rumors, none of them particularly favorable. The most prevalent was that he'd gone underground. Selling himself to the highest bidder—which fit with what Gabriel had told her, but not with her overall impression.

She'd watched Payton today, and despite what the facts told her, she trusted him. Or maybe she just trusted Gabriel's instincts—at least professionally. And considering they'd all be working together to track a killer, that was all that mattered.

The doorbell rang, pulling her from her thoughts. She stifled a flash of irritation. No one was supposed to get up here without being announced. Caution being second nature, she stopped at the breakfast bar to retrieve her gun before answering the door.

It was probably nothing, but taking chances was how an agent wound up dead.

She peered through the peephole, shock blending with relief as she lowered her weapon. Gabriel Roarke stood on the other side, a scowl coloring his expression as he rang the bell again.

With a second surge of irritation, she swung open the door. "How the hell did you get up here?"

"Nice to see you, too." He glanced pointedly down at the Glock in her hand.

"I asked how you got up here. This is a secure building."

"CIA credentials open a lot of doors." He shrugged, and brushed past her, acting as if he'd been coming to her apartment for years.

She followed him into the living room, trying to compose herself. The man had absolutely no sense of propriety. "I could have shot you."

"I doubt that." His smile was disarming. The first he'd ever graced her with. Of course, it was for all the wrong reasons—like the fact that he thought she wouldn't have the courage to use her gun.

It was tempting to prove him wrong right then and there, but it seemed a little shortsighted to shoot one of the good guys, no matter how many buttons he pushed. She dropped the Glock on the counter and turned to face him. "Well, don't do it again. I live in a secured building for a reason."

"Nothing is secure, Madison." It was the first time he'd used her name, and she found that she liked the way it rolled off his lips. "But I've got to say this beats the hell out of living at the Marriott."

Cullen had set them up at the hotel for the duration. Harrison had even moved over there. "I'm sure Cullen would be happy to put you up somewhere else."

"It still wouldn't be this." He waved his hand through the air to emphasize his point. "Some digs. I think maybe I missed the boat not working for the FBI."

It was not an unusual reaction to her apartment, but somehow coming from him it rankled more than usual. "Too bad you missed the memo."

"Right." His smile held a hint of laughter, but any amusement was more than offset by the cynicism reflected in his eyes. Gabriel Roarke obviously had issues. Big ones. But thankfully, it wasn't her job to deal with them.

"What's down there?" Gabriel had turned his attention to the view, and was pointing at something below him.

She moved to stand beside him, her gaze following his. "Health club."

The gym was located three floors below her, extending out from the building, its crowning feature a slanted roof of glass. From this vantage point, she could almost see the tenants below hard at work on treadmills and stair machines.

"*Wealth* club is more like it. Are those chandeliers?" His tone was incredulous, and she smothered a sigh of irritation.

"Just in the clubroom," she said, struggling to hang on to her temper. "The rest is pretty much your basic gym."

"I'm impressed." His tone made it clear he was anything but, and she watched him as he dropped down on the sofa, looking for all the world as if he belonged there.

Still frowning, she sat down in the chair across from him. "You still haven't told me why you're here."

"I thought maybe we ought to get to know each other a little better."

"And dropping by my home unannounced is the way to accomplish that?" She tried but couldn't keep the sarcasm from her voice.

"Would you have welcomed me with open arms if I'd let you know I was coming?"

She started to nod, but then thought better of it. This man would recognize the truth anyway. "No. Probably not."

"There you go." He smiled, his icy gaze warming for a moment. "Part of espionage is knowing how to approach the target."

"So what, now I'm a target?" Talking to him was like fencing—a sport she detested.

"No." He sobered. "But you're an unknown quantity and I don't like undefined variables."

"So you thought you'd just drop in and check me out."

"Something like that." He leaned back and crossed his legs. "Mind if I have some wine?" He nodded at the open bottle on the table.

"Help yourself." She'd be damned if she'd offer a glass, but that didn't seem to faze him a bit. He got up, walked over to the kitchen, found another glass, poured the wine, then returned to the sofa. After taking a sip, he reached for her glass, holding it out to her as if *he* were the host.

She toyed with the idea of tossing it in his face, but hated the thought of what it would do to her cream-colored sofa. "Thank you." The words came out of their own volition, good manners overriding even the worst of situations.

"Look, I don't know why Cullen was so red-hot to have you on the team, but judging by this apartment, I'd say the two of you must have a cozy little relationship."

Anger shot through her, white-hot and razor sharp. "Cullen is my godfather, and the reason he wanted me on the task force is because I'm very good at what I do."

"I'm sure you are." The spark in his eyes said more than his words, and she tightened her hold on the stem of her wineglass, fighting to maintain control.

"For what it's worth, Mr. Roarke," she ground out, slamming the glass on the table, "the apartment belongs to me. A gift from my father. Feel free to check with the front desk on your way out."

Instead of retreating, he stood up and took a step closer. "Daddy's little girl?"

Any restraint she'd had melted away at the taunt. Without thinking, she closed the gap between them and swung, wanting nothing more than to wipe the smug expression from his face.

He caught her wrist, her hand inches from his nose, his expression amused. "So, the cat has claws." His eyes raked across her, making her skin burn.

Fury combined with adrenaline to give her added strength, and she twisted forward, slamming her left leg into the side of his knee, using his hold on her arm as torque to flip him to the floor. Still holding her wrist, he pulled her with him, rolling quickly to pin her to the ground, his body hard against hers.

She turned slightly, pulling her knee upward at the same time in an attempt to dislodge him, but he was faster, grabbing her other wrist, holding her captive beneath him.

"Nice moves." His voice was deep and smoky, his eyes darkening with an emotion she wasn't about to put a name to. Her breathing was ragged, and she was pleased to note that his was not coming any easier.

Her anger had somehow slipped away, the chemistry between them shifting. His breath teased her face, and if she lifted her head even slightly their lips would touch. It was compelling, this need to move forward. Just centimeters and...

The little voice in her brain screamed for sanity and with an exhale of breath, she forced herself to break the spell. "Get off me."

His smile was slow, and a little wicked. "I don't know. It seems pretty comfortable to me."

Her anger returned, but this time she managed control. "I said, get off."

He searched her face, and then with a shrug rolled off, acting for all the world as if the moment had never existed. "You know your stuff, I'll give you that."

"Just because I work as a profiler doesn't mean I'm not a *real* FBI agent, Mr. Roarke." She stood up and adjusted her clothing, wishing him to hell and back.

"I thought we'd moved beyond the formality of last names, Madison." He reached out to tuck a strand of hair behind her ear, the gesture amazingly intimate.

She stepped back, struggling to keep her expression

neutral. "I don't know anything of the sort. To date, you've insulted me, my profession, my godfather, my apartment…" She trailed off, realizing her voice was rising with each pronouncement.

Gabriel held up his hands. "I call it like I see it. Sometimes being direct is the best way to cut through all the bullshit."

"By insulting me."

He narrowed his eyes, as if considering his response, then smiled at her, the gesture again disarming. "I think that had more to do with chemistry."

She didn't have an answer. Couldn't even think straight, truth be told. This man had a way of unnerving her like no one she'd ever met. One moment threatening, the next taunting, and the next, well—sexy as hell.

Shit.

She drew in a breath and pasted on a sweet, social smile. The kind she reserved for boring old leches. "All right then, *Gabriel,* what do you say we start over?" No way in hell was she letting him come out on top. If he could be disarming, so could she. "You said you wanted to know me better. What exactly would you like to know?"

He frowned, obviously not expecting Pollyanna Sunshine, and she mentally gave herself the point. Sitting on the arm of the sofa, she reached for her wineglass and took a sip, waiting. But she had underestimated her opponent.

With the hint of a smile, he, too, sat down, crossing one leg over the other, equally prepared to wait her out. Their gazes met and held, neither wanting to be the first to break the silence. It would have been funny, except for the tension stretching between them, an energy that hummed through her with surprising intensity.

"What say I save you the questions and just fill in the details?" she asked finally, certain if she didn't speak they'd be sitting there until they were old and gray. A prospect she didn't relish for any number of reasons.

"Fine." He nodded, his scowl firmly back in place.

"Okay, here it is." She leaned forward slightly, and sucked in a breath. "My father is Philip Merrick. And his best friend is Cullen Pulaski. And as is custom, when I was born, my father asked Cullen to be my godfather. In the real, bona fide, stand-up-in-church-and-say-so kind of way. There is no other relationship between the two of us. None at all. He asked me to be on the task force because I have expertise that he believes will be useful."

Gabriel opened his mouth to respond, but she held a hand up to stop him.

"As to my career. I graduated magna cum laude from Vassar, then attended Harvard Law to please my father. Upon graduating, *with honors,* I went to work for the FBI—for exactly the opposite reason. After finishing my training, I worked for three years as a special agent, received two awards of distinction, and then transferred to the Investigative Support Unit, where, to date, I have played a major role in bringing fifteen serial killers to justice. Without my profiles, these men would have continued to prey upon innocent victims. And while I don't mean to blow my own horn, *Gabriel,* I believe you'll find that I'm at the top of my game."

"Nice to know there's something beneath the window dressing." He dismissed her tirade as simply as that, and she bit her tongue to keep from lashing out at him again. There was simply no winning with Gabriel Roarke, and letting him goad her into revealing more of herself was certainly not a strategic move.

"More than you'll ever know." She bit the words out, knowing she sounded like a petulant child.

"We'll just have to see about that." His gaze caught hers, pinning her like a butterfly on linen, and her heart fluttered in protest. Slowly he leaned forward until his breath caressed her cheek. She knew she should move. Get up off the sofa. But she didn't. Instead she shivered in anticipation.

And then the phone rang, the shrill sound like ice water in the face.

She pulled back, almost falling off the sofa in the process. Fumbling for the phone, she listened to the other end, holding on to the connection like a lifeline. Then working to control her trembling hand, she put the receiver back in the cradle.

"That was Harrison," she said, still struggling for composure. "There's a problem with the computers."

"What kind of problem?" He was instantly alert, his voice disturbingly normal.

"The disk array has been wiped."

"Sabotage." It wasn't a question, but she answered anyway.

"He thinks so." She drew in a breath, feeling calmer, her thoughts on the problem at hand. "Cullen's with him. And they want us there as soon as possible."

"All right then, let's go." He stood up, closing the space between them, reaching out to trace the line of her lower lip. "But make no mistake, Madison, we're not finished here."

CHAPTER SEVEN

"HOW BAD IS IT?" Gabe asked, striding into the room, Madison at his side.

"Nothing's retrievable. It's been wiped clean." Harrison swiveled his chair to face them. "Everything was backed up, of course. But it'll take time to get it all running again."

"Is it just our system? Or Cullen's, as well?" Gabe asked, trying to assimilate the consequences of the crash.

"Cullen's was hit, as well, but not to the same extent." Harrison shot a glance at the man who was standing in the corner, talking on the phone. "With his people working on it, he should be back up by morning."

"Thank goodness we've got you here to work on ours," Madison said, moving to stand behind Harrison as he resumed working at the computer.

Gabe fought a surge of irritation. She'd hardly spoken to him since they'd left her apartment, and here she was practically fawning over Harrison. He shook his head, dismissing the thought. What the hell did he care who she shacked up with? "What caused the crash?"

"It wasn't a crash. At least not in the sense of mechanical failure." Harrison pulled up a diagnostics screen. "This was definitely sabotage. A virus, maybe. I don't know. After I restore the system, I can run more detailed diagnostics."

"You think it was a prank?" Madison asked, leaning over for a better look at the screen.

"No way." Harrison shook his head. "We've got a firewall, a secure Internet connection and about a dozen other security measures. If someone got into the system it's because they wanted to."

"But if it was intentional, why didn't it do more damage? You've already said everything was backed up. Surely a hacker would be aware of that fact." Gabe was far from an expert at computers, but this seemed a blinding glimpse of the obvious.

"That's exactly the question I've been asking." Cullen walked over to the computer bank. "If they were trying to destroy my system, why attack you? And if they were after your system, why didn't they do a better job?"

Madison shrugged. "Maybe they were just inept."

"No way." Harrison shook his head, underscoring his words. "This was deliberate. If they knew enough to get in, they knew enough to do more damage."

"So what was the point? To send a message?" Gabe couldn't contain his growl. It had been a hell of a day.

"No." Madison turned to face him, her brows drawn together in thought. "They wanted to cover something up."

"That doesn't—"

"Think about it," she said, cutting him off. "They wiped our system clean. And hit parts of Cullen's, as well. But didn't do any lasting damage. All that's lost is the record of activity after the backup."

"Which I did before I left for the night," Harrison said. "But I'm still not with you."

"Okay. Think about an intentional crime. I'm talking about something planned. Like a murder or a robbery."

Gabe watched as Harrison and Cullen considered her words. He wasn't sure exactly where she was going, but he was definitely interested in seeing how she presented her case.

"What's the last thing the perp would do? After completing his objective?" Her gaze encompassed them all, waiting, and Gabe fought against the urge to answer, to win her approval, knowing he was just caught up in the moment. He needed Madison Harper's approval like he needed another assignment in Iraq.

"I get it." Harrison said, his enthusiasm rising. "He wipes the room down. Gets rid of any evidence he's been there at all."

"Exactly." Madison beamed, her attention still on Harrison.

"And that's what our perpetrator did," Cullen said. "He hacked into the system, then covered his tracks."

"Seems a big leap to me," Gabe said, watching as Madison's smile turned to a scowl.

"I think it makes a lot of sense, actually." Harrison was quick to jump to Madison's defense. "When you access a computer—any computer—you leave a trail. Sometimes it's really obscure. But it's there. And if a programmer knows where to look, he can find it."

"But if the system has been erased, there's nothing to find." Cullen, too, was obviously on Madison's side.

"All right," Gabe said, his tone grudging. "I'll admit the idea has merit. But in order for it to have value, we need to find out what he was after."

"That's going to be a bit trickier." Harrison turned back to the computer. "Once I've restored the system, all traces of the failure will be eliminated. I've run almost all the diagnostics I can without rebooting. So it's sort of a rock and a hard place."

"What about tackling it from Cullen's end?" Madison had moved over to look at the computer screen. "You said they had damage, as well. But his system wasn't wiped clean, right? Maybe you can work backward from there."

Gabe had to admit it was sound thinking. "Is that possible?"

"It might work." Harrison frowned, obviously considering the idea. "A lot of it depends on if the perp actually accessed Cullen's computer or if the failure there was merely a proximity problem. Our servers are linked by necessity."

"You certainly have my authorization to have a look. Anything we can do to find out what's going on. If an unauthorized access was made to either computer I want to know about it." Cullen's expression was grim. "Could the problem have generated from my computer system?"

Harrison shook his head. "Based on what I'm seeing I'd say it definitely started with us."

"Which leaves us with some really big questions. Not that many people know we're here, right?" Gabe asked.

"I haven't broadcast it, if that's what you mean." Cullen shrugged. "But I haven't kept it a secret, either. I thought your presence might actually act as a deterrent. So I imagine most of the employees here are aware of your existence. And of course, the consortium members know."

"So we're talking at least a couple hundred people." Madison sighed. "Which means finding the culprit will be next to impossible."

"At the moment, I'm more interested in what they wanted." Gabe walked over to Harrison. "I want you to see if you can use Cullen's system to back in to the information. We need to get someone over here to check for physical evidence. Although I suspect it's been destroyed." He glanced down at the keyboard.

Harrison winced. "Sorry. I should have thought about that. I was just so shocked to find the system failure."

"It's totally understandable," Gabe said. "I'd have probably reacted the same way. Still it's worth checking out. I'll put a call in to Nigel."

"I already contacted him." Madison's gaze held just a hint of one-upmanship, and despite himself, he smiled. "He's on the way."

Yeah, he'd definitely underestimated her. But the jury was still out on whether that was a good or a bad thing.

"YOU'RE WIRED tighter than the Energizer Bunny. Something else going on?" Harrison asked, his keen eyes seeing far more than Madison wanted him to.

They were sitting in the Marriott's bar. Harrison had gone as far as he could with Cullen's computer system, the rest would have to wait until morning. She hadn't wanted to go back to her apartment and hadn't been up to staying at the scene. Besides, her expertise was putting together who from what, so she was better off letting the others work on the *what*.

"Only three murders, a hacked computer, and an apparent conspiracy with the potential to affect all international trade as we know it. Not to mention Cullen's involvement. I don't like the idea that he might be a target."

"How about your dad? He have any dealings with the consortium?"

Madison shook her head. "He's not interested in China. Not until they're more technologically advanced, anyway. I think the truth is that he doesn't want the political ramifications. His bread is buttered on the other side."

"Frankly, I don't see how you keep up without a scorecard."

She allowed herself a smile. "I've had lots of practice."

They sat for the moment, letting the sound of the bar wash over them, happy conventioneers whose only care was which seminar to attend in the morning.

"Have you formed any impressions about who might be behind all of this?"

"Isn't that the question of the hour." Madison sighed, and took a sip of wine. "The first two deaths point to someone with experience and contacts. Either someone in the medical field, or a pro. And based on the way things went down with Bingham Smith, I'd lean toward assassin. But the fire is another thing entirely. Really messy. Hit the man, then burn the evidence."

"Seems logical to me."

"In a situation where the murder was unplanned, or unintentional maybe. But if we're to believe it was planned, then it doesn't follow. The fire didn't destroy the evidence. Granted, the first M.E. missed the details, but Tracy didn't."

"She didn't miss the potassium chloride, either. So does that count as a mistake?"

"No. A pro. He doesn't care if the method is discovered as long as it doesn't point to him. Ultimately, he just wants the man dead—preferably with as little fanfare as possible. That's the problem with all three murders really. If it was terrorists, why not a more dramatic attack? Something to really hit the news and make waves. Surely that would be the best way to guarantee the accord failed."

"Maybe not." Gabriel's baritone filtered down from above her, and she looked up to meet his glacial stare. "Mind if I join you?"

Yes came to mind, but it probably wouldn't stop him, so she resisted the urge to voice it. Instead she waved at the empty chair next to Harrison, but he ignored it and sat beside her, his thigh grazing hers in the process. She waited for him to move it, but he didn't, instead leaning back, the movement pressing him closer. With a feigned sigh, she shifted her chair away from him.

Gabriel lifted an eyebrow in amusement, but stayed put, signaling a passing waitress and ordering a whiskey on the rocks. "You were saying that the obvious ploy for a terrorist is to make a splash."

"And you, as usual, were disagreeing." She hadn't meant to snap, but the man was trying, to say the least.

Harrison's lips quivered as he tried to contain a laugh.

"The problem with your logic is that there is more than one kind of terrorist." Gabriel went on as if they were having a normal conversation. "The first is the kind you referenced. They're in it for the impact. And publicity only helps that. They jump at the opportunity to claim responsibility."

He paused to pay for his drink, then continued. "But some terrorists are more like soldiers. Attacking an enemy using less-than-acceptable means to achieve their goals."

"How does that differ from Delta Force, or black ops?" Madison voiced the question before she thought about how it sounded. Or maybe some part of her had asked it on purpose, wanting to goad him the same way he did her.

"It doesn't, really." He shrugged, ignoring her barb. "It's all a matter of perspective. If someone is fighting for your interests you're much less likely to question their methods or label them. If it's the enemy, then…"

"Surely there's a difference between someone righteously striking an enemy even under clandestine circumstances, and someone who randomly blows away innocents." Harrison leaned forward, interested.

"Morally, there is definitely a difference. But righteousness is in the eye of the beholder. And in either case the attackers could be termed terrorists."

"While I appreciate the lesson, I don't see how it applies here." She still sounded snippy and hated herself for it. She'd always prided herself on her self-control. "We're not talking about either flagrant attacks, or anything remotely righteous. In fact, if I had to call it, I'd say that greed was the most likely motivation."

"Bigger crimes than this have been committed for less." Gabriel shrugged. "The point is that even with the lack of splash, this could still be considered terrorism. If some entity is determined to stop the accord, and killing the consortium's key members to do it, then the methodology doesn't matter. They're still considered acts of terror. Especially in today's political climate."

Madison nodded, not really listening to his argument, a new thought having occurred to her. "Has anyone thought to check the Chinese delegation? Maybe they're having the same kind of problem."

"One step ahead of you." His smile was smug, or maybe it was just a trick of the shadows. "Payton did some checking before he left China. He knows Beijing and he's familiar with most of the players on that end."

"I suppose there's no point in asking why he knows so much about them?" Harrison queried, idly turning his beer glass with his fingers.

"None at all." Gabriel grimaced. "And believe me, I tried. But according to his intel, none of the Chinese involved have died from natural causes or otherwise."

"So whatever is happening here, it's targeted at the American side of things." Madison took another sip of wine, her mind turning over all that they knew, trying to assemble pieces into a recognizable whole. "At least that limits the investigation."

"But it still leaves us with a lot to prove. Although it goes a long way, three of six doesn't establish conspiracy." Gabriel's icy gaze encompassed them both.

"Don't forget the computers." Harrison leaned back in his chair, still playing with his beer glass.

"I take it you've finished your analysis?" Gabriel asked.

"I still have a few more tests to run." Harrison shrugged. "But I've exhausted most of my options. I even checked Cullen's tracking system. Old bastard designed a hell of a program. But whoever did this wiped it clean, as well."

"So you think they were after something of Cullen's?" Madison frowned.

"It makes more sense than wanting something off of

ours. All of the accord records are stored on his system. But it's still only an educated guess. One that I certainly can't prove. Once everything is back online, I'll finish the diagnostics. But I wouldn't hold my breath." Harrison sat back with a sigh. "Did Nigel find anything?"

Gabriel shook his head. "Nothing conclusive. Some partial prints. Most of which are probably ours. Anything that we can't identify will be checked against Cullen's employee list. He's got prints on everyone in the building."

"Nice of him." Harrison smiled. "And I suppose if we still have any unidentified we can run them through the computers at Langley just to be certain."

"Exactly, but my guess is they won't turn up anything significant."

"Even if we don't identify the hacker," Madison said, "I'd still say the fact we had one, combined with the murders, is a pretty strong indication that we're on the right track."

"It would seem that way, certainly. But until we verify that the other three deaths were also intentional, I'd prefer we maintain our skepticism." Gabriel sat back, finishing the last of his whiskey.

"Well, without an autopsy, how do you suggest we proceed?" Harrison asked. "They're all in different jurisdictions."

"Divide and conquer." Gabriel smiled, and Madison was certain she wasn't going to like the rest of what he had to say. "Harrison, you can check out Macomb's death. The car wreck happened in Albany, so you should be able to request records from here and still finish your work on Cullen's computers. Payton and Nigel can head for Virginia. Dashal has family there. And we already have the police report."

Madison's stomach churned. Alan Stewart had died in Colorado. In a remote mountain town.

"And you and I—" Gabriel's gaze collided with hers, a smile playing at the corner of his mouth "—will head for the mountains."

Madison looked to Harrison for support, but he only shrugged.

Some best friend.

There had to be a way out. Something she could say. But her brain stubbornly refused to provide an excuse, choosing instead a completely reprehensible route, and before she could stop them, the words tumbled out of her mouth.

"What time do we leave?"

CULLEN PULASKI SAT at his desk, staring at the computer screen. The list of files stared back at him, the cursor blinking, waiting for him to take action. He entered a series of keystrokes and a password, and the machine buzzed, then presented him with a list of documents. Opening one, he skimmed the pages, wondering if the intruder had made it this far.

He'd set up safeguards. But nothing was impregnable. Whoever had broken into the computer system had obviously known what they were doing, and what they were after. Cullen entered more keystrokes and checked the hidden log. He hadn't shared its existence with Harrison. The man had found the decoy. And searched it. But of course there was nothing to find.

Cullen had almost told him about the second one, wanting to share his genius with someone who could appreciate it. He'd designed the program himself. A way to track activity within his systems. An extra set of eyes watching his back.

But in the end, caution had won out. He needed to look on his own. See what, if anything, was there. He scrolled down the screen, stopping when he reached the record of the day's activities.

It took a moment to isolate, but it was there. An unauthorized entry. Someone had gained access to his files. Unfortunately there was no identifier. Just as Harrison had predicted, the pathway had been wiped clean. There was nothing left to tell him who it was.

Nothing at all. Only the fact that someone had been there. Someone who desperately wanted to bring Cullen down. But Cullen couldn't let anything get in his way now. He was too close. Everything depended on these final moves, the death dance of opponents in a battle for survival.

And despite all he had accomplished, Cullen Pulaski was afraid.

CHAPTER EIGHT

TOWN WAS PROBABLY too optimistic a word for Creede, Colorado. Situated on a horseshoe bend in the highway, there wasn't much more than the main street, but the way that street settled into a majestic crag in the mountains went a long way toward explaining why summer homes had sprung up all along the valley. That and the fact that the Rio Grande was prime fishing water.

There was big money here. Discreet money. A far cry from the town's heyday as a rip-roaring boomtown, but no less important to its survival. Gabe drew in a cold, cleansing breath. Winter was in the air, but hadn't come yet, the aspens still decorated with gold.

The streets were fairly deserted—tourist season was on the wane. Some of the shops had already closed for the winter. It gave the street a desolate feeling, as if it didn't really exist. Gabe swallowed a laugh. He'd gone poetic.

"We're almost there." Madison pointed toward an open parking area between two buildings. "The one on the left should be the courthouse, and according to this map, the sheriff's office is just beyond that."

They'd flown into Alamosa a couple of hours ago, rented the Jeep, and had been on the road ever since. Between red-eye flying, jet lag and the tension emanating from the woman next to him, it had been a hell of a ride. A sort of pleasurable pain. He liked to keep his edges sharp, and Madison Harper, it turned out, was the perfect hone.

He pulled the Jeep into the parking lot, and without further conversation they got out and walked back to the main sidewalk. The sheriff's office looked more like a house than a public building, but the truck out front was clearly marked and the man getting out of it was unmistakably the law.

"Gabriel Roarke?" The big man closed the distance between them quickly, already extending his hand. "Patrick Weston."

"Thanks for agreeing to meet with us." Gabe shook the offered hand. "This is my associate, Madison Harper."

"Not sure what I can give you that you don't already know, but always glad to lend a helping hand." The sheriff's eyes crinkled at the corners. A lifetime spent laughing. Gabe wondered idly what that would feel like.

"We've read the report of course," Madison said, looking up at the sheriff as they walked. "But you know as well as I do that sometimes things are omitted."

Weston nodded, his expression turning serious. "I take it you all are considering something more than an accident?"

"It's possible," Gabe said, not willing to reveal too much too soon.

The sheriff shrugged, leading them up the path to his office. Gabe put him somewhere between forty and forty-five. A career lawman, if he had to call it, but with the rugged look of an outdoorsman.

"Did you know Mr. Stewart?" Madison asked, her brows drawn together as she studied the man.

"Everybody knows everybody up here. Or has heard about them." Weston held the door open, then followed them into the office.

The room was a hell of a lot like every sheriff's office

in the country, right down to the smell of burned coffee. They followed Weston into a cramped space that served as his office, taking seats in the perfunctory metal chairs that were meant, no doubt, for guests and suspects alike.

"Alan Stewart was a good man." Weston leaned back in his chair, tipping it to balance against the wall. "Gave a lot to this community, even though he was only a part-time resident."

"Part-time?" Madison pushed a strand of hair behind her ear. Gabe noted that Weston followed the motion with his eyes, his gaze appreciative. Not that he could blame the man.

"Yup." He nodded. "Creede isn't the most hospitable of places in the dead of winter. And without the draw of major ski runs, most of the population clears out at the end of October, leaving only a handful of full-timers until the spring thaw."

"Did you actually see the body, Mr. Weston?" Madison looked up, her gaze searching, and the sheriff's focus returned to matters at hand.

"Nope. I was over in Del Norte at a meeting. By the time I got back, everything had already been taken care of."

"How do you mean?" Madison's frown deepened.

"Alan's death had been ruled an accident, and arrangements had been made to take his body home."

"To Texas," Gabe said. When not in Creede, Alan Stewart had made his home in Austin.

"That's right. Body was transported directly from their cabin. So I never saw it."

"But you wrote a report." Madison paused, her gaze meeting the sheriff's. "Who gave you the information?"

"Got some of it from the widow, and the rest from Doc Martin. It was all pretty routine and my report was just for the record. We had no reason to believe there'd been any foul play." Suspicion colored Weston's formerly genial face. "Are you saying I did something wrong?"

"Not at all." Gabe held up a conciliatory hand. "We're just trying to understand what happened."

The sheriff nodded, but his expression remained watchful.

"So who is this Doc Martin? A local physician?" Gabe asked, on a breath of frustration. They were getting nowhere fast.

"Nah." Weston shook his head. "Another part-timer. From Oklahoma. Has a house out in Rio Grande estates."

"Is he even a real doctor?" Madison's frustration was apparent, mirroring his own.

"Hell, yeah." The flicker of anger was back, but to his credit Weston held it in check. "A heart surgeon. Retired. Lives just upriver from the Stewarts."

"I don't suppose he'd happen to be out here," Gabe threw out, even though he was already fairly certain of the answer. The crisp fall wind was enough to tell him that most residents had already closed their houses for the season.

Weston's grin widened. "Well, now, seems in that you've got a bit of luck. The Martins are still here. Not due out 'til the end of the week."

"You think he'd talk to us?"

"Don't see why not." Weston shrugged. "I can go with you if you'd like."

"I STILL WAKE UP at night and expect to find him next to me." Alicia Dashal's smile was melancholy and a bit apologetic, as if she wished she were made of stronger stuff.

Nigel exchanged glances with Payton, wishing he could get the hell out of there. Interviewing widows wasn't exactly his cup of tea. He'd much prefer the Bolivian jungle.

"Where exactly did the accident happen?" Payton had morphed into the role with the ease of a chameleon, his tone the perfect blend of solicitude and authority. The bloody git should have been an actor.

"In his workshop." The widow dabbed the corners of her eyes with a tissue, her carefully made-up face accentuated with a permanent smile, the effect of one too many plastic surgeries. "He liked to work with wood. It helped him clear his head." Her smile was bitter. "Sometimes I think it was more about escaping all of this." She waved her hand at the perfectly appointed living room, the Georgetown brownstone probably worth a small fortune.

"I think most men need a retreat," Payton said, his words erasing the bitter expression from her face.

"Yes. I suppose they do." She nodded, as if reassuring herself. "I was the one who found him, you know."

"It must have been awful," Payton said, his tone encouraging her to share with them.

Stupid woman. She'd opened her home without question to two strangers claiming to be insurance investigators without even asking for identification. Nigel shook his head and forced himself to focus on the conversation.

"I don't think I'll ever forget it. Jacob slumped over the workbench like that. He'd been using the saw."

"An electric one?" Payton asked.

She nodded. "Circular, I think you call it." She paused to blow her nose. "The paramedics said he died instantly. Some sort of power surge."

"And you didn't call the police?"

"There was no need." Her eyes widened. "Was there?" The last was said on a whisper, almost as if she was afraid to voice the actual words.

"Probably not." Nigel shook his head, trying to reassure the woman, knowing that he hadn't accomplished the goal. He was not a man to suffer fools lightly and this woman represented everything he'd been brought up to despise. Too much money, too much time, and not the sense God gave a goose.

"We just need to cover all the bases." Payton smiled. "You understand."

"Of course." The woman nodded, then frowned, something unpleasant occurring to her. "There won't be any problem with the money…" She trailed off, her expression somewhere between alarm and embarrassment. Perish the thought that Alicia Dashal wouldn't get even more money.

"I couldn't say for certain at this point." Nigel drew out the words, watching as she blanched, then feeling absurdly guilty, he put her out of her misery. "But let me hasten to add that we've no reason to believe there'll be a problem."

"There's no need to worry, Mrs. Dashal." Payton reached over to pat her hand. "Everything will be just fine. As I said, we're just here to dot the *i*'s and cross the *t*'s. In fact, all that's left is to see the workshop. Would you mind showing us?"

Her smile was genuine this time, if a bit water-logged. "Of course." She stood up, tottering on high heels meant for a much younger woman, and led the way through the house into the back garden.

The enclosure was immaculate. Nigel couldn't help wondering if there was staff waiting in the wings to dash out and catch a leaf should it dare fall from the tree. The shed in the corner had a derelict look, as if it had been dropped into the garden by mistake.

Mrs. Dashal opened the front door and motioned for them to enter. "I haven't been in here since he died, you understand. It's only been four months." The tears appeared again, and Nigel tried to determine if they were driven by real emotion or were just a show for the two of them. "I just can't face it. Do you mind?"

"Not at all," Nigel assured her, relieved that they would be able to examine the shed on their own. She nodded once and turned for the house, and Nigel stepped across the threshold into the musty shadows of the shed.

Payton was standing by the workbench, his gaze encompassing the room. "She said he was using the circular saw, right?"

"Yes. Is that it on the workbench?" Nigel wasn't big on tools. In truth he couldn't tell a circular saw from a jigsaw.

"Looks like it." Payton frowned reaching over to pick the saw up using a piece of scrap wood. "Based on the dust, I'd say no one has touched this thing since the accident."

"Judging from the amount of corrosion I'd say the thing has seen better days."

Payton turned the saw slightly, examining the casing. "It's vintage, actually. Which goes a long way toward explaining what happened."

"Come again?" Nigel asked, feigning interest. What he really wanted was a drink. He'd done his bit for country and queen, and there was really nothing to do but wait it out. Preferably in the hotel bar.

"These things aren't insulated like they should be. And judging from the rust, I'd say this shed isn't exactly the ideal place to be operating electrical tools." Payton shot a look at the rickety, rotting walls.

"So the poor sod was doomed from the start, eh?"

"Looks that way." Payton nodded. "No GDI, no insulation. Combined with an old machine and I'd say electrocution was pretty much a forgone conclusion." He bent over to look at something behind the workbench.

"So this has all been a bloody waste of time." Nigel tried but couldn't keep his temper in check.

"Maybe." Payton reappeared holding the end of an extension cord. "And then again maybe not." He held it out for Nigel's inspection. "The ground pin is missing."

Nigel frowned down at the plug end. "But doesn't that happen a lot? I mean especially when the wall plug is two prong."

"It's possible," Payton said, his tone preoccupied. He had picked up a screwdriver and removed the saw's casing. "But not when you consider this." He pointed to the end of the saw where the cord joined the base.

Nigel leaned over for a closer look. The wires emerging from the cord had clearly been cut and resoldered. A makeshift booby trap that, combined with the missing ground, had shocked Jacob Dashal quite literally to death.

THE MARTINS' *cabin* was more like a small resort. Complete with satellite TV, the two-story structure had a wrap-around porch and a two-car garage. Situated among a stand of spruce on a spit of land that dropped down to the Rio Grande, the property was worth a small fortune.

Peace and tranquility, it seemed, always came at a price.

Still, as retreats went, this one was first-rate. Christened *Lands End* by a signpost at the head of the driveway, it was a beautiful place, and despite Gabriel's presence and their reason for being here, Madison closed her eyes and let the rustle of the trees and the whisper of the river soothe her.

Gabriel must have noticed her withdrawal, because she felt his hand on her elbow, urging her forward. She opened her eyes, and with a sigh, moved on, patently ignoring the touch of his fingers against her skin.

A tall man Madison guessed was in his late sixties stepped down from the porch, outfitted in waders and fishing vest. He lifted his hand in welcome. Sheriff Patrick Weston had obviously reached him.

Although they had declined the sheriff's offer to accom-

pany them, he'd insisted on calling Ronald Martin to let
him know they were coming, much to Gabriel's chagrin.
The man obviously preferred popping in on everyone unannounced. She shot Gabriel a look, managing at the same
time to disengage her elbow.

"I'm guessing you're the folks from New York?" Dr.
Martin's voice still held the command of his profession,
his bushy eyebrows rising in tandem, the combined effect
off-putting. "My wife just got off the phone with Weston."
There was a hint of rebuke in his voice.

So much for the sheriff paving the way.

"We've got some questions about Alan Stewart's
death." Gabriel as usual took control of the situation, and
Madison stifled a surge of irritation. "Sheriff Weston
thought you might be able to help."

Martin studied Gabriel for a moment and then with a
nod motioned to some Adirondack chairs on the deck.
"Why don't you have a seat and we'll talk out here?" They
followed him up onto the porch. "Virginia doesn't allow
me in the house in my gear."

Madison took a seat facing the river, the sound louder
now that they were out of the Jeep. Gabriel leaned against
the railing, waiting for Dr. Martin to sit.

"So what's this all about? Alan died almost two years
ago. Seems a little odd that you people are finally getting
interested."

"Finally?" Gabriel's eyebrow rose, punctuating the
question.

"I tried to drum up interest in Alan's death at the time.
Something just seemed off to me. The angle of the body,
the timing. Did you know Alan?"

Madison shook her head as Gabriel replied in the negative.

"Well he wasn't a trip-and-fall kind of guy. I just
thought there ought to be an autopsy."

"You thought there'd been foul play." Gabriel's comment was terse, his expression thoughtful.

"Lord, no." Dr. Martin held up both hands, looking at Gabriel with horror. "I merely thought there could be some medical cause."

"Like a heart attack." Madison's comment was soft, almost an afterthought, but both men turned to look at her, the doctor with something akin to relief on his face.

"Exactly."

"Did Stewart have problems with his heart?" Gabriel shifted against the railing, his body tensing.

"That was what was so odd. He'd just had a complete workup and everything had checked out fine. But I was one of the first on the scene, and based on years of observation, I'd have been willing to bet the farm it was some sort of cardiac event."

"And so you advised Mrs. Stewart to consider an autopsy."

Martin nodded. "But she wasn't sure, and when she talked to Patrick he assured her it wasn't necessary."

"Without seeing the body?" Gabriel's tone was dry, his expression condemning.

Martin shook his head. "Patrick's a good man. Been the sheriff a long time. But he's a don't-rock-the-boat kind of guy. "

"And so he ignored your concerns?"

"Not exactly." Martin shrugged, obviously uncomfortable with the conversation. "It was more that I was overruled."

"By whom?" Gabe was leaning forward now, his attention focused solely on the doctor.

"A colleague of Alan's. Man named Cullen Pulaski. I'm sure you've heard of him."

CHAPTER NINE

"FINDING ANYTHING?" Cullen walked over to the computer console where Harrison Blake was examining a string of code.

"I'm not sure." Harrison didn't bother to look up, merely typed in a command and pulled up another string. "I think maybe I've got a signature from last night's sabotage, but I'm not certain. I need to run a few more tests." He swiveled around to look up at Cullen. "If I'm right, we just might be able to trace back to the computer the hacker used."

Cullen felt a surge of excitement. "When will you know for sure?"

"Hopefully in couple of hours. I'll let you know as soon as I have something definitive."

"Excellent. Any progress on Luther Macomb?"

Harrison shook his head. "Unfortunately that's been more of a dead end. The police records are sketchy at best. Apparently it was raining that night. Visibility was poor, and the road conditions sucked. Macomb's car evidently went into a skid, slid through a guard railing and off an embankment. Unfortunately, the car exploded on impact."

"Meaning there's no way to verify for certain. Maybe you could talk to the officer of record?"

"I already did. The guy couldn't remember much of anything. Claims it was too long ago. Basically he just recited the facts he'd noted on the report. I followed up by talking to the towing company, but the guy said they compact as soon as the case is officially cleared. And since this one was ruled an accident, that would have been immediately. He's double-checking to be certain, but if there was any evidence, I'm betting it's long gone. After all, it's been two years."

"Maybe it won't matter. I just heard from Payton. They found evidence that Jacob Dashal's electrocution may have been intentional. Which brings us to four murders—two proven and two likely. That ups our statistics substantially."

"You heard anything from Madison and Gabriel?"

Cullen shook his head. "Nothing. I tried both their cell phones. Evidently they're too high in the mountains for reception. I've got the local sheriff's land line if we really need them, but they're due back tomorrow, so I figure we'll just wait."

Harrison nodded. "Regardless of what they find, I'd say that we have more than enough evidence to prove that there's a killer out there. And since the dead men's primary connection is the accord, I'd say we're looking at conspiracy. Unfortunately, that still leaves us with two major questions—who's pulling the strings and why?"

"Actually you've omitted one, Harrison, and I'm afraid it supersedes the others. The most important question is 'who's next?'"

"SO DID YOU GET hold of Cullen?" Gabriel walked over to the bedroom door and dropped her carryall. He'd already left his duffel by the fold-out sofa.

"No." Madison shrugged. "I couldn't get my cell phone to work. And I'm afraid this place doesn't run to a land line."

"Not exactly the standards you're accustomed to," Gabriel said with a smile that held little warmth.

Madison had to admit the cabin did lack certain amenities. But it had a roof and two beds, and for the moment that was more than enough. With the season dying, most of the accommodations in the area were closed. The XO was a dude ranch that attracted fishermen by the droves during the summer months, and thanks to its location higher up the valley, a smattering of hunters in the fall.

"Beats sleeping in the Jeep." She stood in the corner that passed for a kitchen, cleaning up the meal she'd made from the meager supplies they'd bought in town. They were booked on a flight tomorrow morning, which meant an overnight somewhere, and she had to admit that despite the rustic accommodations the view was amazing.

Perched on a cliff overhanging the Rio Grande, the cabin had a huge picture window framing the splendor of the mountains surrounding the valley, although it was too dark to see it now. The sound of the river filtered through the open door, the entire scene one of domestic bliss.

She shook her head. There was nothing domestic going on here, except maybe the dishes. "You should try your phone."

"Already did." Gabriel had moved to the window, his profile forbidding. "It doesn't work either. So we'll just have to wait until tomorrow to talk to him."

Madison walked over to stand beside him. "There's got to be a logical explanation."

"Maybe." His tone was noncommittal.

"Cullen was the man's friend, after all. And Alan Stewart was the third to die. At that point Cullen had no reason to believe something nefarious was afoot. He probably just wanted to make it easier on Mrs. Stewart."

"Cullen doesn't strike me as a particularly compassionate kind of guy."

"Then you obviously don't know him very well." Actually, he'd hit the nail on the head. Although Cullen cared deeply for the people in his life, he wasn't particularly good at showing it. But still she couldn't stand to hear Gabriel maligning her godfather. Or maybe she just hated the fact that he was right. Either way, she wasn't about to let herself agree with him.

"I know him as well as I need to." He trailed off, still staring out the window.

"Dr. Martin seemed fairly certain that Stewart had had a heart attack." She tried a different approach, determined to get him to engage. "If that's true, we could have our third death by potassium chloride."

"Seems possible." He turned around, his icy gaze meeting hers. "But unfortunately, even with an exhumation I doubt we can prove it conclusively."

"Maybe not in court, but I think we have enough to prove the pattern." She sat down on the fold-out sofa, and blew out a breath, her mind turning over the details. 'Four murders out of six deaths is statistically sound."

"Yes, but one of the four died by significantly different means. And you said yourself that the probability of it being the same killer is unlikely."

"No, I said that serial killers usually don't vary their methods. Professional killers, on the other hand, tend to do what it takes to get the job done."

"But the fire seems particularly unprofessional to me."

Madison shrugged. "It's a puzzle certainly, but not completely inexplicable. It's possible that more than one killer is involved, which makes particular sense if the thing is politically motivated. It's also possible that something went wrong with Barnes's murder. I mean, if the fire had caught hold, there wouldn't have been any forensic evidence."

"Still seems to border on inept to me." Gabriel's eyebrows were drawn together into a frown, the effect making him appear even more formidable.

"I agree. But even so, it still doesn't rule out the fact that Cullen was right. People involved with the Chinese accord are being killed. We just don't know who is behind it."

"Isn't that where your profession is supposed to come in?" His tone for once held no condemnation.

"Yeah. But only with all the facts in evidence. It's hard to put together a picture without knowing why these particular people were chosen. I need to get a look at the data Harrison has put together. Maybe he found something on the computer that can identify the person behind the sabotage. And if so, then maybe we can start there, assuming that the events are related."

"And we need to talk to Cullen." On its face the sentence meant nothing, but taken together with the intensity of Gabriel's expression and the ticking muscle in his jaw, Madison knew they were back to talking about Dr. Martin's disclosure.

"You're still thinking there's something sinister in Cullen's quashing the autopsy."

"Yes."

"Well, I don't." She shook her head for emphasis.

"Why not?"

"I already told you. I think he was trying to protect the widow. Spare her from the needless agony of having her husband cut open and dissected."

"Maybe." Gabriel rubbed his jaw, the bristles of his day-old beard dark against his fingers. "But then again maybe there's something else going on. He obviously knew firsthand about Stewart's death, and most likely he was aware of Aston's and Macomb's, too, yet despite all his talk about patterns and conspiracies, he doesn't mention them at all. Only Smith, Dashal and Barnes."

"He could have started investigating the most current deaths and when he met with resistance, he stopped and called us in. Or maybe he didn't connect the first three to his supposed pattern. There's a fourteen-month gap between Barnes and Stewart, after all. And the negotiations were only in the infant stage when the first three men died."

"It took Harrison about fifteen minutes to come up with the connection, and he doesn't even know the players. There's no way I'm buying into the idea that Cullen didn't make the same leap."

"Maybe he wanted to be certain we were up to the task." Madison frowned, not certain she liked the train of thought he was following, but unable to dismiss it out of turn.

"And so he purposely left out information?" Gabriel shook his head, moving to lean against the arm of the couch. "I don't think so."

"Then what?"

"I don't know. But I don't like being played. And no matter what his reasons were, Cullen intentionally kept information from us."

"But for what purpose? He was bound to know we'd find out eventually."

"That's another thing that bothers me." Gabriel crossed his arms, his expression thunderous. "It seems to me that it's been too damn easy to establish the murders. It's almost as if someone wants us to find out."

"I'm not sure I know what you mean."

"I mean that with very little effort we've managed to prove that Smith was murdered, that Aston was murdered, and that most likely both Stewart and Barnes were murdered."

"We have Tracy to thank for that."

"Do we?" Gabriel interrupted. "It still smells like a

setup to me. I mean how logical is it that two men are murdered with the same drug and the same M.O. and yet two different medical examiners missed the whole thing?"

"You heard Tracy. They're understaffed—"

"And underpaid," he said, cutting her off. "Yeah, yeah, I know. But what if it's really just a matter of someone wanting the information to come out now?"

"Cullen?"

"I don't know who else it could be. I mean you saw yourself, he wasn't at all surprised when Harrison announced the additional deaths."

"He wouldn't have been." Madison shrugged. "I told him."

"When?"

"After I talked with you. I ran by his office to let him know we'd met." And to vent, but she wasn't about to share that fact. "And told him what Harrison had found."

"What did he say?" Gabriel closed the gap between them, his expression if possible more intense.

"Nothing, really. I admit he didn't seem all that surprised, but I certainly didn't get the feeling he was hiding something." She tried to replay the conversation in her mind, but instead found herself caught in Gabriel's steely-eyed gaze. "You honestly believe Cullen is manipulating the investigation to facilitate some hidden agenda?"

Gabriel shrugged.

"Well, I don't buy it." She stood up and walked over to the window, feeling suddenly restless. "He wouldn't do something like that."

"If it was to his advantage he would." He'd come up to stand beside her, his proximity unnerving. "And you know it as well as I do."

"Maybe." She nodded, determined to keep her emotions at bay. "But it still doesn't make sense. If he were manipulating things to aid the success of the negotiations, he'd keep the murders under wraps, not drag them out in the open. The more it seems like a conspiracy, the more it's going to scare the Chinese, and that would ruin any attempt for alliance."

"It would."

Anger flooded through her. "Cullen has spent the past three years living, eating and breathing the accord. There is nothing on this earth that would make him do anything to sabotage those efforts. Calling us in to investigate just underscores the fact."

"Maybe." His propensity for one-word answers made her want to scream.

She spun around to face him, mouth open to retort, but stopped when she saw the expression in his eyes.

"I don't want to believe Cullen has anything to do with this, Madison. But I don't like the way this feels. And I always trust my gut." His face was so close she could feel the heat of his breath.

"Then we're not as different as you'd like to believe. Gut feelings are a major part of profiling." She licked her lips, her body responding to his nearness, blatantly disregarding the fact that she didn't even like the man.

"My instincts are built on years of experience. Not a lot of psychological bullshit."

Anger beat out pheromones. "Profiling isn't about mumbo jumbo. It's about learning from past experiences. Taking known information and applying it to new situations. There are commonalities among serial killers, or among terrorists. You know this as well as I do. Profiling just takes the similarities and uses them to predict behavior. Or to narrow an investigation to probable offenders. It isn't a hundred percent accurate, but it's a damn sight better than shooting in the dark."

"Hey, I didn't mean to bring out the claws." His smile was crooked, and despite herself she felt her anger evaporate. "I just have a problem with things I can't quantify."

"I imagine it ranks right up there with your dislike of authority."

Something flashed in his eyes, but before she could identify it, he managed to mask it. "Practicing on me?" There was a hint of mockery now, the sparring begun in earnest.

"I don't need to practice. You're easy enough to read." She shot him what she hoped was a self-satisfied smile. "You get off on adrenaline rushes. Take what you want. And are quick to put yourself smack-dab in the middle of danger. How am I doing so far?"

His eyes narrowed slightly, but he didn't say anything, and ignoring the signs, she continued, "You're a natural leader, but you've never been comfortable with the role. You're a loner. Command loyalty, but don't allow yourself to get close to anyone."

He moved closer, his expression controlled, but the tic in his jaw gave him away. She fought against the urge to step back, instead holding her ground. "You probably come from a troubled background, self-reliance the only thing that got you through. You think you have the whole world fooled, Gabriel, but I can see who you really are."

She'd meant to hurt him. To get back at him for maligning her profession, but somewhere along the way, she'd lost her taste for blood. A shadow in his expression told her she'd hit home, and she wanted nothing more than to take back her words.

His lips curled upward. He'd recognized her moment of doubt. She sucked in a breath, ready to add insult to injury, anything to stop his smirk, but he beat her to the punch, closing the distance between them, his mouth taking possession of hers.

There was nothing tentative in the kiss. It was a declaration of war. Take all or perish. His fingers curled around the back of her neck, pulling her closer, their tongues dueling for position, for fit.

Some part of her not yet consumed knew she should stop this. That there was danger. But she pushed the thought ruthlessly aside, giving in, instead, to the sensory onslaught. He backed her against the wall, his body pinning hers, and she pressed back against him, determined to give as good as she got.

The air around them sizzled with electricity, as if their joining had completed a circuit. Positive to negative. Pole to pole. She twisted her fingers through his hair, the black strands wiry and strong. Like the man.

He cupped her breast, his thumb circling her nipple, and she swallowed a moan, the action only heightening her desire. His mouth moved to her cheek, then her ear. Waves of pure physical pleasure washed across her as his tongue found the soft whorl of her ear. This time she couldn't stop her cry, and he pulled back to look at her, his smile slow and sure.

Madison fought for breath, and met his eyes full on, their wills battling even as their bodies pressed closer. She licked her lips, the skin raw from his bruising touch, but all she wanted was more.

With an exhale that resembled a sigh, he closed the scant distance between them, his kiss different this time. Possessive. As if he was sealing a bargain she'd no idea they'd made. A shiver of worry rippled through her but was gone before she had time to think about it, replaced by the white heat of his touch.

His hands explored her body, and though they still wore their clothes, she might as well have been naked. His heat invaded every part of her, a raging fire that she had no desire to extinguish.

He pushed her blouse off her shoulder, his lips branding her, and she reached for the buttons on his shirt, determined to taste him as he had tasted her, needing him even now to know that she was a worthy opponent.

She slid her hands inside the cool cotton, splaying them across his chest. She could feel his heart beating wildly against her fingers, her own matching the rhythm, as if they could only operate in tandem.

His mouth found hers again, and they pressed close, her hands trapped between them, raw physical need overriding all other thought. She ground against him, rewarded by his muffled groan, and he cupped her buttocks, their bodies rubbing together in an age-old dance.

Madison let conscious thought go, intent instead upon riding the wave, finding release from the glorious pain building inside of her. Release that only he could give her.

The door shook with the force of a knock, the noise taking its own sweet time to register in Madison's beleaguered brain.

"Excuse me?" The soft western drawl on the other side of the glass was hesitant. Embarrassed.

The emotion hit Madison with the force of a tornado. *Embarrassed.*

Sweet mother of God, what was she doing? She pushed away from Gabriel, fumbling with the buttons on her shirt, trying to ignore the still smoldering embers in his eyes. Turning, with what she hoped was a half-coherent smile, she walked to the door.

The ranch manager was standing on the other side looking through the window, shifting from foot to foot, looking extremely uncomfortable. Madison wished herself on another planet, but of course nothing happened, so instead she opened the door and apologized in a breathy voice that no doubt confirmed anything the woman had already seen.

"I didn't mean to interrupt," the woman said, her gaze darting back and forth from Madison to Gabriel who was leaning languorously against the wall. "It's only that there was a phone call for you." She looked down, consulting a piece of paper in her hand. "From Cullen Pulaski."

"What did he want?" Gabriel pushed away from the wall, his expression fierce.

Despite the screen between them, the woman took a step back. "He wants you to call immediately." She paused, twisting the paper in her hands. "He said to tell you there's been another murder."

CHAPTER TEN

MORGUES SMELLED LIKE HOSPITALS. The fact had always seemed surreal to Gabe. People fighting to live shouldn't smell like people who had already lost the battle. He'd spent a hell of a lot of time watching people die. He supposed if he thought about it, he'd have to say he was an expert. But he'd always made it a point not to dwell on anything.

Ever.

Candace Patterson lay naked on the table, the three-inch gash in her abdomen a stark contrast to the pallid color of her skin. The victim of an apparent mugging, the body had originally been sent to the medical examiner's office, but once Candace's connection with the accord had been established, she'd been transferred to Braxton Labs.

Cullen Pulaski in action.

"I thought you were in Colorado?" Tracy Braxton's smile was warm, a pleasant contrast to the harsh reality of the lab.

"I came straight from the airport."

"Which explains why you look like hell." It was just a comment, her gaze neutral, but Gabe flinched anyway.

Sleep was the least of his problems, actually. He and Madison had driven to Denver to take a red-eye in absolute silence, the black mountains echoing their mood. He'd wanted to reach out to her. To tell her that he hadn't meant to kiss her. Hadn't meant to want her. But he couldn't find the words, and she so obviously regretted the kiss, he'd decided finally that the best way to handle the situation was to pretend it had never happened.

Coward's way out, the voice in his head taunted, but he pushed it aside. It had been a mistake. It was as simple as that. A heat-of-the-moment reaction that had nothing to do with reality. Still, he was glad Cullen had ordered her back to headquarters. A little distance would do them both a world of good.

"Hey, you still with me?" Tracy's voice penetrated his ruminations, and with a wry grin he pulled his attention back to the present.

"Jet lag. Sorry."

"No problem." She shrugged, expertly cutting open the chest cavity to reveal internal organs. "I'm just glad you're here. Seems the death toll is rising."

"Looks like she met with the wrong end of the knife." Gabe tilted his head toward the wound. "Cullen said she'd been robbed?"

Tracy nodded, her braids swaying with the motion. "I'm guessing post mortem. That's when she was stabbed."

"You certain?" Gabe frowned, digesting the new information.

"Absolutely. Body temperature combined with lack of blood loss makes it certain. If this had been a mortal wound it would have bled like the dickens. But there was hardly any blood on the body at all, and according to the forensics folks, very little at the scene. My guess is someone found the body, and after making certain she was dead, stripped off her valuables."

"So you got any idea what did kill her?"

"Single shot. Back of the head." Tracy put down her scalpel and reached for a plastic tray behind her. Using forceps she picked up a bullet from the tray, holding it up for

Gabe to see. "Hollow point. Whoever the killer was, the guy meant business."

Gabe took the forceps, examining the tiny lump of metal. "I'd say that changes the rules of the game a bit."

"Ups the ante, if I had to call it." Tracy's somber gaze met his.

"Whatever this is about, I'd say it's coming to a head."

Which meant he needed to get back to the operations room, to discuss this newest information with Madison and the team. It was time to put her profiling to the test. They needed to discover who was behind the attacks—before someone else wound up dead.

"SO YOU THINK Alan Stewart was murdered." Harrison sat across from Nigel at the conference room table eating an Egg McMuffin. The table was littered with the residue of the rest of his breakfast, including a hash brown wrapper and the styrofoam container for pancakes. The man ate like a horse and never showed an ounce of it.

Madison pushed the hair out of her face, wishing she'd stopped to take a shower before coming to the operations room, but Cullen had demanded they come posthaste, and so despite her exhaustion, here she was. If Gabriel Roarke could keep going, then by God, so could she.

"Madison, are you listening?" Harrison was frowning, his brows drawn together to form a line, all semblance of the boy next door vanishing with the motion.

"Sorry. I guess I'm more tired than I thought." To emphasize the point, she yawned, then smiled ruefully. "You were asking about Alan Stewart, right?"

Harrison nodded.

"One of the first on the scene was a cardiologist. He believes Stewart had some kind of cardiac event. Combined with Aston's and Smith's cause of death, I think it's a definite possibility that Alan Stewart was injected, as well."

"But you don't have any physical proof." This from Nigel who had moved to stand by the window.

"No. But we were planning to contact the widow to obtain permission for an exhumation. That way Tracy could prove the presence of potassium chloride. But in light of Candace Patterson's apparent murder, it may prove unnecessary."

"Same for Luther Macomb," Harrison said. "Which is probably just as well, as I suspect it's a dead end anyway. The scrap metal from the car is probably part of a hundred different machines by now."

"We can add Jacob Dashal to the confirmed list." Payton Reynolds spoke up from a corner where he'd pulled something off the fax machine. "This is forensic verification that the saw was tampered with." He waved the paper for emphasis. "The man's electrocution was definitely not an accident."

"Which means we're at three confirmed murders, two that seem likely, and one that fits the pattern but without evidence of foul play." Madison glanced over at the white board and the black-and-white photos of the deceased. Real people. All dead.

"Make that four confirmed."

Madison jumped at the sound of Gabriel's voice, wishing again that she'd grabbed a shower. Not that she cared what he thought, it's just that dueling with him took a lot of energy, and at the moment she felt as if she'd slept in a bus depot. Which wasn't far from the truth.

What she really needed was a way to erase the last twelve hours, or at least the part she'd spent in liplock with the man. What in the world had she been thinking? Fortunately, he seemed prepared to pretend the whole thing never happened, which suited her just fine.

"Candace Patterson was shot in the head." Gabriel's words jerked her out of her reverie.

"Do you have ballistics?" she asked.

"Just a slug. Hollow point. Tracy's folks are running it for ID. But I doubt she finds anything. The whole thing smells like a hit."

"Which is yet another change in M.O." Harrison pushed away the last of his food. "So where does that leave us?"

"Trying to establish a link between the victims." Madison leaned forward, reviewing the facts listed on the white board.

"I thought we'd all agreed that the accord was the common link." Nigel turned a chair around and straddled it, crossing his arms on the back.

"There are a lot of people working on the accord, Nigel," Madison said. "But not all of them are being targeted. It's important for us to establish why these particular people were chosen."

"Which brings us to their role in the accord," Gabriel added. "Harrison, what have you got?"

"Not as much as I'd like." He shrugged and picked up a piece of paper. "The first three men killed, Aston, Macomb and Stewart, were all members of the consortium, but not members of the board. Their key activity in the accord seems to be that they all served on the steering committee."

"Preaccord you mean," Payton clarified, his words as usual barely audible.

"Exactly." Harrison nodded. "Barnes also served on the steering committee, but unlike the other three he went on to serve on the consortium board, and in addition was the first chair of the active delegation meeting with the Chinese."

"So the initial murders might have been an attempt to retard the process, and when that failed, they attempted to take out a major player," Nigel said.

"Except that this has been a team effort from the beginning. With Barnes out of the picture, his second in command, Jacob Dashal took over."

"Until his untimely death and Bingham Smith stepped in." Gabriel, too, was turning Harrison's information over in his head.

"That's where the first deviation occurs," Harrison continued. "Interestingly enough, Smith had no involvement in the planning of the accord—his job was simply to negotiate. He'd had private dealings with the Chinese for years, and so this was par for the course for him, but his involvement appears to be mainly at the behest of Cullen Pulaski."

"Meaning what, he wasn't interested in the success of the accord?" Payton was pacing in front of the window as if the movement helped him think.

"From a political standpoint he stood to gain a great deal. Economically, however, it would have been a wash for him."

"And he was on the board," Madison said, beginning to see a new pattern.

"Yes." Harrison nodded. "The third board member to die. A double hit if you will, because as with Barnes's, Dashal's and Smith's deaths not only had an effect on the accord, but on the consortium itself."

"So the change in strategy might be related to more than just the accord." Gabriel met Harrison's gaze across the table.

"Hard to say definitively, but it's something to consider."

"What about Candace Patterson? How does she fit in?" Nigel was leaning so far over the chair it was in danger of tipping.

"Another deviation. She was neither on the original steering committee nor on the board. But Cullen had tapped her to fill in Smith's vacancy on the negotiation team."

"What's her expertise?" Madison asked, caught up in Harrison's speculation.

"She's fluent in eight Chinese dialects. Studied abroad and worked for two years as a missionary. Since returning to the U.S. she's worked for Lexco, first heading up their Asian division, and then moving to corporate. She was recently promoted to VP, and became active in the consortium only when Lexco decided to get on board with the talks for the accord."

"So what we're looking at is an escalation in pattern," Madison mused. "We start with practically untraceable murders in the very beginning stage of talks about a possible economic accord with China. When those fail to derail plans, the targets change, and people higher up the ladder begin to die. But again there is little impact on the accord itself."

"Everyone, it seems, is expendable and as people die, they're replaced without question," Harrison continued, expanding on her thoughts.

"Except Cullen," Gabriel added, glancing at Madison, his message clear.

"Which is interesting in and of itself, but we'll examine that later," Nigel said, cutting in on the conversation. "The point you're making here is that as the accord gains popularity and moves closer to reality, the importance of the targets grows."

"Not only that, the M.O. for murder becomes more haphazard." Madison blew out a breath, trying to quantify her thoughts. "What began as a carefully orchestrated campaign, something almost undetectable, gradually begins to unravel until our most recent victim is killed in cold blood."

"But surely it was made to look like a robbery," Nigel said.

"If Tracy is to be believed that's pure coincidence,"

Gabriel answered. "A case of the body being in the wrong place at the wrong time."

"Which leaves us with a desperate enemy," Payton said, cutting to the heart of the matter.

"Does anyone know what the Chinese reaction has been to the latest murders?" Harrison had risen to stand behind his chair, his hands gripping the back.

"I don't know that there's been time for them to understand the ramifications of Candace Patterson's death," Madison said. "But according to the media, Bingham Smith's death, accident or no, has caused something of a stir."

"The Chinese won't like the two murders happening so close together." Payton stood by the window, his face in silhouette, his scar highlighted in the light. "They'll view them as omens of bad fortune."

"Which might mean our killer has achieved his goal." Harrison's tone was thoughtful.

"No." Madison shook her head. "Whoever is behind this won't stop until he's certain the accord is dead—*if* killing the accord is in fact his objective."

"Of course it's the objective. Harrison just spent the last fifteen minutes proving it." Nigel had obviously had enough of their deliberations, clearly preferring action to talk.

"I'm not saying it isn't." Madison raised her hands in defense. "I'm just saying that it's a little early to declare anything absolutely."

"Seven murders is pretty damning, don't you think?" Nigel's voice was clipped, even for a Brit.

"Look, Nigel, she's only saying we need to tread cautiously here. Not jump to any conclusions. We need to wait until we have all the facts."

Madison tried not to show her surprise. Gabriel was defending her. Something was definitely out of kilter with the universe.

"Right." Nigel nodded once, agreeing. "But in the meantime I say we need to identify possible suspects. Groups that stand to gain should the accord fail."

"Easier said than done." Gabriel's expression was grim. "There are any number of organizations, on both sides of the law, that would be happy to see economic harmony between Chinese and American business go the way of the eight-track. Narrowing it down to one won't be easy."

"I might be able to help," Harrison offered, looking pleased with himself. "It's too early to say for certain, but I think I've got a lock on the originating IP used to hack into our system last night."

"You've identified who it was?" Payton actually looked excited. Or as excited as Madison assumed he ever got.

"Hold on," Harrison said, shaking his head. "I didn't say that. I said I have a fix on the Internet address. Unfortunately those things can be used in relay, and it'll take me a while to verify the source."

"And even then you won't be able to say with certainty who was operating the computer." Payton leaned back against the windowsill, his casual stance at odds with the intensity of his gaze.

"Maybe not an actual user, but a computer. And from there it's usually possible to narrow down the odds."

"Good," Gabriel said. "Keep hunting. Right now it's our best chance. And in the meantime, we need to find out what we can about any enemies of the accord. Payton, you've got contacts in Asia. See what they know. Nigel, you and I will work on Lexco. Maybe there's something about Candace Patterson we don't know."

"And me?" Madison wished the words back almost as soon as she'd said them, hating the way they made her sound.

Gabriel's smile indicated he'd followed her train of thought and was amused. "Besides working on a profile for our killer, why don't you talk to Cullen and his cronies? I want to know which players left in the game hold the power. And more importantly, I want to know exactly what Cullen's involvement in this process has been, starting with Frederick Aston and moving right through to Candace Patterson. We know he was involved immediately following Stewart's murder. I want to know if he was involved with the others. And you, Madison, are just the person to find out."

From anyone else it would have been a compliment. But Gabriel didn't do praise. From him it was a gauntlet, a goading challenge to find out what exactly her godfather was up to, how deeply he was involved. And if she'd truly believed in his innocence, Gabriel's challenge wouldn't have bothered her.

But it did.

CHAPTER ELEVEN

"ALICIA STEWART NEEDED peace. It was as simple as that." Cullen leaned against the windowsill in his office, watching Madison, trying to ascertain the impetus behind her questions. "She was walking a fine line and I didn't want to push her over the edge."

"But according to Dr. Martin, there was some question as to cause of death."

"At the time it seemed likely that the fall killed him. And even if I'd suspected a heart attack, I wouldn't have had reason to believe there'd been foul play. Not then. The sheriff was convinced that it was an accident. And even Dr. Martin didn't suspect anything nefarious. So I told Alicia to bury her husband." Cullen shrugged and picked up a pencil, twirling it between his fingers. "I wish to hell I'd done it differently, but it's not like I can go back and change it."

"So why didn't you tell me?" There was a note of doubt in her voice. A niggle of worry made him wish he'd left her out of this. Maybe she was *too* good—saw too much.

"I didn't think about it. I mean really, Madison, it's not exactly earth-shattering news."

"It depends on how you look at it, I suppose." She sat back, her eyes narrowed in thought. "You're the one who started this investigation, after all. So I guess it seems a bit surprising to find out that you actually did something to hinder our chances of finding the truth, and then, conveniently, forgot to share the fact."

"You're making more of it than necessary. I'm not the enemy. And my telling Alicia Stewart she didn't have to subject her husband's body to an autopsy is hardly cause for concern. In hindsight it turns out it would have been helpful, but there was no way I could have known it at the time." He watched her face, relieved to see her relax.

"I'm sorry to be such a pest about this." Her smile was apologetic. "But Gabriel was concerned, and—"

"And sent you in to handle the old man?" Cullen cut her off with an answering smile.

"Something like that." She shrugged.

"So what do you think of Gabriel Roarke?" Cullen sat down behind his desk. It was time for a change of subject, and Gabriel seemed just the ticket.

"He's a bit arrogant."

"An understatement surely, but he's good at what he does and his attitude only contributes to that success."

"How did you first get to know him?" Madison sat back in her chair, her fingers tightening on the arms. It seemed his goddaughter was not immune to Gabriel's charms. Or perhaps she simply couldn't abide working with the man. Either was a possibility and would most likely lead to the same conclusion. At least he hoped it would.

"When he was in Delta Force, he was assigned to a mission I commanded."

"Come again? You were never in the army."

"Maybe commanded is too strong a word. But it was my mission nevertheless. A man in my employ got stuck behind the wrong border during the first war with Iraq. He was captured and held hostage. The official U.S. stance on the matter was, of course, that we don't negotiate for hostages. But I needed him out, and with a little cajoling, the powers that be agreed to a rescue effort."

"And Gabriel headed the team."

"Exactly." Cullen nodded. "He was the leader of a black ops group referred to as Logistical Command, the kind of men who are called in when all else fails. In fact, they used to refer to themselves as Last Chance, Inc."

"And your man was last chance status?"

"Unfortunately, yes. I'd tried every other avenue, and nothing could be done. Gabriel and his men were my last option."

"And did they succeed?"

"Yes," he said. "But not without cost. My man got out alive, but the others weren't so lucky. Eight of them went in. Only three came out."

She stared down at her hands, digesting the information and then looked up to meet his gaze. "Payton and Nigel were part of the team, as well."

"Nigel was serving as an adjunct to Delta Force at the time, and Payton was part of Gabriel's team."

"And that's why he asked them here. To be a part of your latest last-ditch effort."

"I suppose so. All I know is that I'd trust Gabriel with my life."

"You might have to." She stood up and walked over to the credenza, picking up a photograph, one of her when she was about twelve. "Why me?"

He considered deliberately misunderstanding the question, then thought better of it. Madison would see right through it. "I thought you'd add something to the mix. Gabriel is sort of a wild card, shooting from the hip, so to speak. He's good, but I thought you'd provide much-needed balance."

"Except that the man can't stand me." There was a flash of something across her face, something personal. Cullen contained a smile.

"I think you're overreacting. He's aloof, I'll grant you

that. And he certainly doesn't like the idea of sharing command, but it isn't personal. Unless there's something you're not telling me."

"No." Madison shook her head, still staring at the picture in her hands. "There's nothing."

"Then I predict you'll manage just fine. You're a valuable asset to the team, Madison, whether Gabriel realizes it or not."

"Thanks." Her smile was warm, and he felt a flood of emotion. She'd been a part of his life practically from the day of her birth, and at times it was hard for him to realize she was no longer a little girl. "It's not like I haven't handled worse."

Rick Wagner. He'd taken Madison to the cleaners, both financially and emotionally. She'd fallen for his charm and good looks, not realizing it was only an illusion, that the man himself was nothing but a leech.

Cullen sighed, sorry that she'd had to find out for herself. That she still bore the scars. But there was nothing he or her father could have done. Some things children had to learn for themselves. No matter the consequences.

"Cullen, we've got to talk." Jeremy Bosner burst into the room, his face flushed, his anger apparent. He stopped, momentarily flustered to find Madison in the office. "Oh, God. I'm sorry. I've interrupted something."

Madison held up a hand, shaking her head. "I was just leaving."

"No, stay." Cullen kept his voice personable, but it wasn't a request.

Madison shot a look at Jeremy, who nodded his agreement. With an answering nod, she replaced the photograph, moved to sit again in her chair.

"I just got off the phone with Chiao Chien." Jeremy gave Cullen an appraising look. "We've got to get this thing under control or we're all going down with the ship."

"I wasn't aware you knew him," Cullen said. Chiao was the primary negotiator for the Chinese delegation, and as far as Cullen knew not a close confidant of Jeremy's.

"I know who I need to know, Cullen." Jeremy shrugged, walking over to the bar to pour himself a drink.

"Anything to protect your interests." Cullen sat back watching his friend, trying to read between the lines. Jeremy always had hidden agendas.

"As if you haven't been doing the same thing. The honest truth is that we both have a hell of a lot riding on the success of this agreement. And with consortium members dropping like flies we've got problems. According to Chiao the delegation is restless—afraid that whatever it is that's plaguing us will turn on them, as well."

"I don't think that's going to happen." Cullen steepled his fingers, still studying the man. "And I've said as much to Chiao."

"Well, I think you're wrong, especially if the media keeps us front and center." He tossed a copy of the *Daily News* on the table, Candace Patterson's face splashed across the front page. "I thought the task force was supposed to take care of this." He shot a look at Madison, his expression a mixture of anger and apology. He'd always had a weak spot for Madison.

"Jeremy, we've only been working a few days." Madison's tone was neutral. "These things take time."

"I know you're trying." Jeremy's voice rose, his flush deepening. "But time is running out."

"They're professionals, Jeremy. They'll get to the bottom of this." Cullen pushed the newspaper aside, and leaned forward to meet his friend's gaze.

"Well, they'd better do it quickly or it'll be a pointless exercise." Jeremy sighed. "The Chinese are ready to walk. All we need is one more murder and they'll be signing with the Russians. And I don't have to tell you how that will sit with the president."

"It's a bluff. You know as well as I do that Russian technology is far from cutting edge. The Chinese need us. Their threats are nothing more than posturing. At most it might cost us a bit in the deal, but they won't walk."

"You'd better be right." There was an implied threat there that Cullen couldn't afford to ignore. "Or we may just need to rethink your value as a member of the consortium."

Cullen's laughter was forced, a cover for the surge of dread that ran through him. "I don't see how you can lay any of this at my feet. I've been screaming about conspiracy for months now."

Jeremy shrugged. "Let's just say if we need a scapegoat, you're it. You knew the risks when you stepped in to take Bingham's place."

Madison shifted slightly. Cullen had almost forgotten she was in the room. He returned his attention to Jeremy, struggling to hang on to his composure. "I did what I thought was best for the consortium."

"Without asking anyone else's opinion."

"Are you saying that Cullen assumed the chairmanship unilaterally?" Madison asked, her voice deceptively soft.

"Not exactly," Jeremy allowed. "I only meant that there were others equally qualified. Possibly even more so."

"You're talking about yourself." Cullen threw the word out like a gauntlet.

"I was next in line." Jeremy shrugged, feigning nonchalance. "And there are people who think I might have been a better bet. Look, the whole idea was to keep this all on the back burner until we got to the bottom of what was happening. But thanks to all of this, we're getting more attention than ever. The murders are continuing. And your team has done nothing."

"I told you, we've been together for less than a week,"

Madison interrupted, anger flashing in her eyes. "In that amount of time you can't expect miracles."

"I know that, Madison. And I'm not trying to throw stones. Especially at you." His look was imploring. "But I need this accord to go through, and for my investment to pay off. It's as simple as that. And no matter how unpleasant the prospect, I'll do whatever is necessary to make sure that's exactly what happens." His attention shifted back to Cullen. "Am I making myself clear?"

Cullen swallowed a bitter retort. There was no sense antagonizing the man. "I hear what you're saying, but I think you're worrying about nothing. Madison and Gabriel have excellent credentials. Between them they'll put a stop to this. Mark my words."

"I hope so," Jeremy said, his gaze encompassing them both. "If not, there'll be hell to pay. If this accord fails, Cullen, I'll be the least of your problems."

"WELL, IF THIS IS HOW the other half lives, I, for one, wouldn't mind giving it a go." Gabe stepped into the heavily paneled entry hall, his eyes passing over the lavish fittings to settle on what could only be an original Picasso.

"Appearances can be deceiving," Nigel whispered, watching the butler disappear behind a pair of double mahogany doors. Candace Patterson's family was definitely part of the moneyed elite that made up much of Westchester County.

"You sound as if you know." Gabe pulled his attention from the Picasso to frown at Nigel.

"Only secondhand. But believe me, that's enough."

Gabe opened his mouth to retort, but before he could do so a woman stepped into the foyer. She looked to be about sixty, her white hair fashionably cut and arranged with the precision of a military assault. Her suit reeked of money, and Gabriel had no doubt that the diamonds at her throat and ears were real.

"I'm Bertrice Patterson." Her voice was low and husky, the telltale mark of a smoker. "Gibson tells me you're with the police?"

"Actually, we're a bit higher up the ladder." Gabe flashed his credentials. "Special Agent Roarke."

"The FBI? I'm afraid I don't understand."

Gabriel didn't bother to correct her. The less she knew about who they really were, the better. "We're investigating your daughter's murder."

"I thought it was a robbery?" She fidgeted with her bracelet, spoiling her studied impression of calm.

Gabe exchanged a glance with Nigel. "Forensics indicates she was already dead when she was robbed."

"Oh, dear God." The woman's hand rose to her throat. "I had no idea."

"Preliminary findings supported a mugging. You'd no way of knowing." Nigel's voice was calming, his smile gentle.

"I think I'd best sit down." She drew a deep fortifying breath, and motioned them through the mahogany doors.

Gabriel followed her into the room, taking in its understated opulence. "Did your daughter have any enemies, Mrs. Patterson?" It was a standard question, and he didn't expect her to have an answer, but it was a way to relieve some of the tension, to focus her grief toward a solution.

"Not that I know of." She'd linked her hands together, her knuckles white with the effort. "But then we hadn't talked recently."

"You were estranged?" Nigel had taken a seat on a chaise, his posture giving the illusion of breeding, as if he sat in millionaires' mansions on a daily basis. Mrs. Patterson's smile was weak, but genuine.

"Not at all. We were quite close. Normally, we talked daily. But she was so busy at work. She hardly ever even made it home."

Gabriel raised an eyebrow.

"She had an apartment in the city. When she had an early meeting or was planning on being out late, she stayed there instead of coming home."

Nigel frowned. "What about her husband?"

Bertrice shook her head, disapproval radiating from her very pores. "He rarely goes to the city anymore."

"Is he unwell?" Nigel asked.

"No." She shook her head, her diamonds swaying with the motion. "Just lazy. Fundamentally so, I'm afraid."

"Is the marriage sound?" Gabriel wondered suddenly if perhaps they'd missed the boat on this one. Maybe there was another suspect.

"In its own way, I suppose. They seem to tolerate each other. And for whatever reason Candace showed no interest in divorce."

"Is it possible he may have felt differently?"

Bertrice laughed, the sound hollow. "Believe me, he hasn't the gumption for something like that. And besides, there's a prenup. With Candace gone, he's left high and dry."

"What about work?"

"I wouldn't know anything at all about that." She shrugged. "You'd need to ask her father."

Nigel frowned. "I wasn't aware that Mr. Patterson had anything to do with Lexco."

Again she laughed, but this time the sound was more natural. "He doesn't. But then he isn't Candace's real father. I'm afraid I was a bit indiscreet in my younger days. Fortunately Harold overlooked the fact." She waved a be-jeweled hand through the air as though dismissing the memory. "Lex Rymon is Candace's father. Although it was years before Candace got him to own up to the fact. Rather a complicated mess, our family."

"Was Mr. Rymon close to your daughter?"

"They got along, but I'd say it was more a business understanding than a father-daughter relationship. My daughter was single-minded about making it on her own. Lex gave her the opportunity to do just that."

"Work for her father." Nigel was stating the obvious, but his tone conveyed much more.

"In a manner, yes. But not in the usual Daddy's-little-girl way. Believe me, she wouldn't have lasted at Lexco if she wasn't up to it. Lex simply wouldn't have allowed it."

"I take it he's not the sentimental type."

Her smile was brittle. "In our circles sentiment is dangerous."

Gabe sensed the interview was over. He stood up, not sure exactly what they'd gained, but accepting that it was time to move on. "Thank you for your time."

Nigel followed his lead, standing up, his expression conciliatory. "We're sorry to have intruded."

"It's all right," she said, her gaze encompassing them both. "I want to know what happened to my daughter, and anything you gentlemen can do toward that end is a welcome intrusion."

The butler materialized at her side, almost from thin air, and with a stiff nod, escorted them from the room. Gabe stepped out into the sunlight, squinting in the afternoon glare.

"Well, that was a colossal waste of time." Nigel reached into his coat pocket for his sunglasses, and put them on, the action masking his expression.

"Probably so. But at least we can be fairly certain that Candace's relatives didn't do her in. From lack of interest if nothing else."

Nigel shrugged, lighting a cigarette. "They don't call them the idle rich for nothing, mate."

Gabe laughed. "It was sort of Stepford-wifeish, wasn't it?"

"And then some. Still, all of it added together makes her involvement with the accord seem a likely motive. The question, of course, is how do we prove it?"

"Well, first off, I think we have to talk to Lex Rymon."

CHAPTER TWELVE

MADISON SAT BACK in her chair, massaging her temples. She'd reread the files, trying to find something that tied the victims together. But beyond their wealthy background and their ties to the consortium and the accord, there was nothing unique. Which meant that it was going to be hard to predict who would be the next target. Like looking for a needle in a haystack. A defined haystack, but nevertheless a difficult if not impossible task.

The most obvious targets were Cullen, Kingston and Jeremy. They each had principal roles in the upcoming summit and all three held positions of power within the consortium. Although she'd also been able to identify about six others who held similar roles, and another twenty who had primary roles in one area or another. Add to that the fifty member companies, and the list could potentially be inexhaustible.

The primary question, of course, was how much they should be told. Obviously some degree of concern for safety was necessary. But too much information would only cause panic, the result being that the Chinese would head for the hills and the accord would be dead. A rock and a hard place if ever there was one.

Madison sighed and pushed her hair behind her ears. She needed a break.

Payton was over in the corner, typing on a laptop that looked like more like it belonged on the starship *Enter-*

prise than in their operations room. He'd sequestered himself almost as soon as Gabriel had issued orders, and best as she could tell, hadn't moved since.

"Any luck?" She walked over to lean against the corner of a desk, looking down at him.

He closed the computer with a snap and swiveled to face her. "Nothing concrete. I've been talking to some of my Chinese contacts, and they're definitely aware of what's been happening. Not only the deaths, but the fact that we've been called in."

"And is that a good thing or a bad thing?" She wasn't sure what to make of Payton Reynolds. He was self-contained like Gabriel, but without his sense of confidence. Almost as if Payton forced himself to keep the world at bay.

Despite the scar, he was the kind of man who could easily disappear into the background. Which if his dossier was to be believed, he'd made into an art form. Stealth as a commodity. But it had taken its toll. Too many hours on his own, pretending to be something he wasn't. It was there in the lines of his face and the hollows under his eyes. Dancing with darkness had a price. And Madison had the feeling that Payton Reynolds had paid—more than once.

"A little of both, I suspect." His answer was clipped, as if he really wasn't prepared to offer anything more, but she was his commanding officer in a way, and if she wanted to actualize the role she had to be willing to stand her ground.

"Meaning what, exactly?" She straightened up, giving her an even better height advantage, prepared to go the distance if he continued to hold out on her.

Instead, he smiled, the gesture changing his face, casting the scar into shadow, his craggy face suddenly handsome. "There's nothing I'm keeping from you, if that's what you're implying. Unlike Gabriel, I've got no problem with chain of command."

He'd read her like a book, and Madison found herself smiling in return. "I just need to know where we stand with the Chinese. It'll make it easier to decide how much of what we suspect should be made public."

He nodded, considering the question, then tipped back his chair so that he could see her more easily. "As I said, I talked to some of my contacts, and most of them seem to agree that although the delegates are getting restless, they're not ready to pull out of the game just yet."

Madison frowned, leaning back against the desk. "You said most of them. Was there a dissenter?"

"One." Payton crossed his arms. "Lin Yao. Not his real name, of course." His eyes flickered with mischief. "I'd have to kill you if I told you that."

He was laughing, but there was unmistakable sincerity in his voice, and Madison wondered for a moment what exactly Payton had been doing in China.

"I just want to know what he said."

"First you have to understand that not all the Chinese want the government to make a deal with the United States."

"I realize we have enemies in China, Payton, but surely it's getting better."

"No." He shook his head. "You're missing the point. The United States isn't the problem. The Chinese government is. And there are forces at work within the country that would do anything to make sure that the current régime is unable to maintain its power."

"And getting technological aid from the U.S. would be counter to that mission."

"Exactly. Unfortunately Lin Yao has no solid evidence. Just innuendo and rumor. My guess is even if Chinese dissidents are involved, they've hired an outside source. Someone with nothing to lose except a paycheck."

"A mercenary."

The word hung between them for a moment, and then Payton's grin reappeared. "Something like that. Or maybe someone who has another gripe with the accord. Someone who couldn't be traced back to the Chinese."

"And of course he has no idea who this person might be."

He shook his head. "Nope. But he's going to do some digging."

"Why would he help us?"

"He wouldn't." Payton shrugged. "But he owes me. And I owe Gabriel. So there you go."

"The mission in Iraq?" The question was out before she could stop it.

Payton's expression hardened. "It was a long time ago." It was a clear dismissal, but she pressed on anyway, compelled by something she couldn't quite identify.

"Cullen told me a little bit about it."

"Cullen Pulaski is a fool." There was no mistaking the animosity in Payton's voice.

"Then why…"

"I told you—" he waved a hand through the air, cutting her off "—I owe Gabriel."

Full circle stop.

"I'm sorry. I didn't mean to pry. I'm just trying to understand the dynamics of the group. I mean, it's not like I really know any of you."

Payton visibly relaxed, as though whatever demons she'd called forth had settled back into the dark recesses of his mind. "There's not much to tell really. I served under Gabriel for two tours."

"Delta Force."

He nodded. "We were tasked with some of the more unsavory missions. Including the rescue of Pulaski's underling."

"He said it was a rough mission. That people died."

His dark gaze met hers. "It was a hell of a lot more than that—" He cut himself off, his face shuttering again, whatever he'd been about to say firmly locked away. "Look, the reality is that Cullen Pulaski snaps his fingers and people jump to do his bidding, no matter the cost. Just look how fast you came running."

There was an element of truth in what he said, but she felt compelled to defend her godfather. "Whatever he does, he has good reason. You can count on that."

"What seems reasonable from one point of view often seems less so when viewed from the opponent's side."

"And you think that's what's happening here? That Cullen is manipulating this whole thing to his advantage?" It was exactly what Gabriel had said, the thought at once repulsive and cogent.

"The thought has crossed my mind, but I don't have anything concrete to back it up."

"Just a hunch?" Madison shivered, certain that if Payton Reynolds had a hunch, there would be something behind it.

"Something like that." He shrugged, another shadow chasing across his face. "Or maybe it's just that I don't like the man. Anyway, we'll just have to wait until we gather more information. First up, I want to see what Lin Yao finds."

Hopefully, something that cleared Cullen of involvement. Madison shook her head, pushing thoughts of her godfather's innocence from her mind. Payton was right, time would tell.

"In the meantime," she said, forcing a smile, knowing that he could probably see right through her, "maybe Harrison can uncover the identity of the hacker. In my experience, once you attach an IP address to a physical one, it's only a short hop to a suspect."

"It might work that way with domestic crimes, but if

this is really the work of Chinese dissidents you can be certain that tracing them won't be as easy as finding the computer used to hack into our system."

This time her smile was genuine. "You've obviously never worked with Harrison."

LEXCO HAD corporate headquarters in three countries, but their chief financial operations remained in New York. Which meant the obligatory high-rise power building, in this case black glass and steel at the southernmost tip of Manhattan. Lex Rymon had run his company with an iron fist for almost fifty years, and his success was evident even in the steel and concrete of the building.

The executive dining room was no exception, the plush bar appointed with crystal and velvet. Gabe and Nigel had already cased the place and found two security cameras and an acoustic panel that no doubt concealed recording devices. Seems Mr. Rymon liked to check in on his execs.

It had been tempting to disable the devices, but until he'd talked to Rymon, Gabe figured there was no sense in raising suspicion. As far as the man was concerned they were here to ask questions about his daughter's murder—nothing more.

"I'm sorry to have kept you waiting." Lex Rymon walked into the room, his expression clearly contradicting the sentiment. He was a big man, rough around the edges despite the Canali suit. His handshake was firm, and Gabe could feel calluses beneath the hundred-dollar manicure. He might be a billionaire, but he had blue-collar in his pedigree somewhere.

"Thanks for agreeing to see us." Nigel was, as always, the consummate diplomat. Maybe it was something in all that tea. "We've just got a few questions."

"Bertrice called me. But I'm not sure what I can add that you don't already know." He motioned to a glass-topped table, and then walked over to the bar. "Can I get you a drink?"

Gabe waved away the suggestion, taking a seat at the table. Nigel followed suit, although he looked longingly at the bourbon Rymon was pouring.

"Bertrice said you suspect something other than robbery." He didn't sound surprised or particularly concerned, just curious.

"Your daughter was robbed postmortem." Nigel looked over at Gabe, the question in his eyes indicating he too had noticed Rymon's lack of emotional response. Either the old boy was good at hiding his feelings, or Bertrice had been right when she'd said there was little love lost between father and daughter.

"That means someone else is responsible for her death. Do you have any leads?" Rymon picked up his glass and brought it to the table, sitting down across from Gabe.

"That's why we wanted to talk to you. We thought maybe you could shed some light on Candace's last few hours. According to your statement, she was working late that night."

Rymon nodded. "She was here, but it wasn't Lexco business that had her here after hours. She was working on that damned accord. It was all she talked about."

"Isn't Lexco a member of the consortium?" Nigel asked, leaning back slightly as if he were only marginally interested in the question.

"Yes. But we're not all that interested in the accord. In fact, I voted against it initially."

"But your company has had dealings with China for years. I'd have thought the trade agreement was tailor-made for Lexco."

"I already have the alliances with China that I need." The man's smile was slow, and wasn't reflected in his eyes. "Why would I want to help other companies encroach on my business?"

"Then why belong to the consortium at all?" This from Nigel.

"Why not?" Rymon shrugged. "This way I can keep tabs on what they're doing."

"But obviously you changed your mind about participating. I mean, you let your daughter take Bingham Smith's place as a negotiator."

"Gentlemen, you've got the wrong impression of my relationship with my daughter if you think I controlled anything she did. Candace has always done exactly what she pleased. And even if she had felt the need to consult someone over a decision, it wouldn't have been me."

"So why have her work here?" Gabe leaned forward, trying to get a bead on the man sitting across from him.

"In a word, she was brilliant. If she didn't work for me, she'd have worked for someone else."

"And you didn't want her working for the competition."

Again the man shrugged. "Would you?"

"What else can you tell us about the night Candace was killed?" Gabe asked. "Were you working late, as well?"

"Yes. In fact, Candace and I had dinner together up here. But she was interrupted by a phone call. Something urgent."

"What time did the call come in?" Nigel asked.

"I can't say exactly. Somewhere around nine-thirty. I know I came up here around nine. And we had a drink before dinner. We were just starting the second course."

"That fits. M.E. puts time of death around ten-forty," Gabe mused, trying to fit the facts into a recognizable whole. "What can you tell us about the call?"

"Not all that much. I admit to listening, but it was still one-sided. From the tone of the conversation, I'd say it was something to do with the accord. She talked maybe two minutes, then rushed out of here like a house on fire. Said something about meeting someone." He stared down at his hands. "That was the last time I saw her."

For a moment Gabe thought he'd misjudged the man, that he had in fact cared for his daughter, but then he looked up, his gaze cold and assessing.

"Will that be all?" He glanced at his watch. "I'm due in a meeting in five minutes. I hate to rush you out, but I've told you everything I know."

They stood to go, walking together toward the door. "Mr. Rymon—" Gabe fought to keep his tone civil "—did Candace use the phone over there?"

"No." The older man shook his head. "It was her cell."

They reached the door, and Rymon headed off in the direction of an open conference room. Nigel and Gabe walked toward the elevator in silence, each lost in his own thoughts.

"Not exactly father of the year material," Nigel said as the doors closed. "You think he had anything to do with his daughter's death?"

"I wouldn't put it past him." Gabe stared up at descending floor lights. "But no, I don't think he was involved. There's no motive."

"Well, he's clearly not a fan of the accord. And Candace was obviously a supporter." Nigel trailed off with a shrug.

"Doesn't play out." Gabe shook his head. "If the accord goes south, any American involved with the Chinese is going to be hindered. Maybe even cut off. I don't see Rymon as the kind of man to take that kind of chance. There are other things he could do, which bear a hell of a lot less risk."

"Great," Nigel mumbled as the elevator dinged open. "We're right back where we started."

"Maybe not." The night air was cold as they stepped out into the parking garage. "There's Candace's cell phone. If we pull the LUDs, we'll know who the hell it was that called her. And I'm betting whoever it was will be a direct link to the killer."

CHAPTER THIRTEEN

"GOOD MORNING, SUNSHINE. Payton told me he thought you were down here." Harrison plopped down in the over-stuffed Starbucks chair. "Latte fix?"

"Something like that." Truth was, it had been a long sleepless night, and she'd spent most of it analyzing and re-analyzing her attraction to Gabriel Roarke. Not that it amounted to anything except a momentary lapse in judgment.

Squaring her shoulders, she met Harrison's questioning gaze with a smile. "I just needed some time to think without everyone watching over my shoulder."

"It's not as bad as you're imagining it is," Harrison said. "The only one who seems to have issues is Gabe, and that's really only about his preference for doing things on his own."

"You sound like you're on his side." It sounded childish and she immediately regretted the words.

Harrison smiled, sipping his chai tea. "I wasn't aware there were sides."

Madison fought the urge to throw something, settling instead for the acid heat of her coffee sliding down her throat. "There aren't. Not really. It's just that…" She stopped, not certain how much she wanted to admit to Harrison.

"He's a bit overbearing?"

Not exactly what she'd been thinking but there was definite truth there. "Among other things."

"Methinks the woman doth protest too much." Harrison's grin faded as he studied her face. "Did something happen between the two of you in Colorado?"

Madison swallowed, searching for words, knowing her hesitation was probably answer enough. "Nothing that mattered."

"It obviously mattered, Madison, or you wouldn't be down here brooding."

"I'm not brooding." She tightened her hand on her cup, letting the warmth soothe her.

"Hey," Harrison held up a hand, "I just call it like I see it. I've seen the sparks between the two of you. And you've definitely been avoiding each other since you got back, so I put two and two together."

"And got five. There's nothing going on between us except mutual dislike. Whatever else you think you saw was in your imagination."

"Or you're lying to yourself." Harrison saw far more than she wanted him to. "Either way, I get the picture. It's none of my business."

Madison opened her mouth to retort, but thought better of it and instead changed the subject. "Any luck with the IP address?"

"Actually that's why I was looking for you." His eyes brightened with excitement. "I think maybe I've got a name. It took a while to narrow it down to an Internet service provider. As I suspected, there were relays, but I finally worked my way back to point of origin—and an owner. Guy named W. Smith."

"No relation to Bingham, right?"

Harrison shook his head. "That'd be too easy. Fact is, I really don't know too much about him. He hasn't got a record and no prints on file. And with a name like Smith he's not exactly easy to isolate. There was a phone number and a P.O. I got it from the ISP. I tried the phone, a Virginia exchange, but it was disconnected. The box is in Charlottesville. Place called Mail Smart. But according to the manager the guy who rented it closed his account a couple of days ago."

"The name match?"

"Yup. But the application didn't provide much info. Same disconnected phone, and a physical address that would mean he's living in the middle of Downtown Mall. Bogus all the way."

"The manager remember what the box owner looked like?"

"Nope. Not a thing. Charlottesville is a college town, so it's not unusual for people to come and go."

Madison blew out a slow breath. "Looks like our Mr. Smith covered his tracks. If he exists at all. Any chance it was just another relay point?"

"No. The hacker was definitely working from that IP. But he could have used a computer from anywhere."

"How about a driver's license?"

"Found a couple thousand in the U.S." He grimaced, swallowing some of his tea. "There weren't any in Charlottesville, though. Although I found around fifty in Virginia. We're sorting through them now."

"So we're back to the needle in the haystack." And then some. Madison would bet her life savings that W. Smith didn't even exist. At least not under that name.

"It would seem so. But I'm not ready to throw the towel in yet. Payton's working on aliases. Maybe we'll get a hit there. And I've got a few more things I want to try. If he exists, we'll find him."

Of that Madison had no doubt. Harrison took this sort of thing as a personal challenge and he wouldn't quit until he'd found everything there was to find about Mr. Smith. Trouble was, that kind of searching took time. And quite honestly, she had the distinct feeling that time was running out.

GABRIEL STOOD in the doorway of the operations room, automatically searching for Madison. She was in the corner at the computer. Her ponytail spilled out across the blue of her shirt, and he crushed the urge to taste the soft satin of her neck, instead settling for the simple pleasure of goading her.

"You were gone when I came back last night. You have other plans?" He purposefully kept his voice brusque, waiting for the rise, knowing it was coming from the sudden tension in her shoulders.

She whirled around, anger flashing, and he felt a moment of triumph. If he couldn't arouse her passion the old-fashioned way, this would just have to do. "I waited until almost nine and then gave up. I gather you decided to sleep in?" She shot a pointed look at the clock. "I've been here since six."

It was only 7:30 a.m. but he still felt as if she'd scored a point, and the idea didn't sit well. "So what are you doing sitting here? I thought I told you to talk to Cullen."

"I did." She paused for a beat, her smile overly sweet, the exact opposite of the expression in her eyes. "*Last night.* And your suspicions were groundless. He was trying to help Alicia Stewart, just like I said. Under the circumstances, he had no reason to believe there'd been foul play. It was only later, after Jacob Dashal's death, that he began to have questions."

"Convenient answer, don't you think?"

"Or maybe, considering what happened in Iraq, you just want Cullen to be guilty of something."

Her words took him by surprise, hitting closer to the truth than he cared to admit. "Who told you about Iraq?"

"Payton." Her eyes darkened with regret. "He really only mentioned it in passing, and I shouldn't have said anything about it. Certainly not like that."

"Contrite" was an emotion she didn't wear well, and he

almost wished he hadn't snapped. Almost. "He shouldn't have talked about it at all."

"I was just trying to understand the bond between the three of you." Her hand fluttered aimlessly through the air. "I didn't know that it was off-limits." Her color rose, a bit of the spark back in her eyes. Madison wasn't the type to stay down for the count.

A part of him was glad.

"It's not off-limits *per se.* It's just ancient history. I don't talk about the past. Frankly, I'm surprised you got Payton to tell you anything."

Her smile was brittle. "It's what I do, remember?"

Maybe he'd underestimated her profession. Payton wasn't an easy mark. If she'd gotten him to open up… He considered the thought, and then dismissed it. The woman was causing enough trouble without him allowing that she might actually have value beyond decoration. "Regardless of what he told you, what happened all those years ago in no way affects my ability to lead this team."

"If your relationship with Cullen is colored by what happened, then I think it does." She was standing now, hands on her hips. "Maybe that's why he wanted me along for the ride."

"To keep me in line?" He took a step toward her, but she held her ground. "Honey, there's not a woman alive who can do that."

"A moot point, surely—" she moved forward, eyes narrowed, her gaze locked with his "—since no one is likely to volunteer for the job."

"Are you sure?" She was so close now he could count the freckles spattered across her nose, feel the warmth of her breath against his skin. "Seems to me you were more than ready the other night."

He felt rather than saw her intake of breath, and saw the

slight dilation of her pupils. He'd hit home, but she wasn't about to admit it.

"I think you've got it backward, Mr. Roarke." The whispered name might as well have been a blasphemy. "If I recall correctly, it was you who chose to engage. And you who lost control. And, if I had to call it, *you* who wouldn't have been able to stop."

"Are you implying I forced you?" The words came out on a rush of anger, the emotion cresting inside him, red-hot.

"Of course not," she snapped. "I never do anything I don't want to." She blanched as she realized what she'd said, taking a step backward in defense.

With a twisted smile, he moved in for the kill. "Checkmate, I believe."

"Hardly." Her lips twisted into the semblance of a smile. "I never said I wasn't involved, Gabriel." This time his name came out sounding like cream for a cat. "Merely that I wasn't the one who lost control."

Again he felt a surge of admiration. Madison Harper was a worthy opponent. Not that he wanted one.

"Hello, you two. Having a bit of a spat, are we?" Nigel's voice broke between them like ice water, and Gabe turned to face his friend, but not before he saw Madison's hand rise to her throat, the look of relief passing across her face just this side of insulting.

Damn the woman.

"We were just discussing Cullen, and his involvement in the murders." Madison stepped around him, all signs of their quarrel successfully banished from her voice. "Gabriel seems convinced that Cullen's been holding out on us. And I was just trying to prove that he was wrong." She shot him a simpering smile. "But as you're no doubt aware, he's not an easy man to convince."

"Yes. I'm afraid, he's far more the yours-is-not-to-question-why type. But then, I'm told some people seem to prefer that." He shot a knowing glance at the two of them, clearly not fooled for an instant. "Despite that, however, I do hope you'll allow me to interrupt your tête-à-tête. I come bearing gifts." He held up a manila envelope.

"The LUDs." Gabe reached for the envelope, but Nigel shifted, moving it just out of reach.

"Now, now, surely you're not going to rob me of my triumph." His eyes sparkled with mischief, and Gabe contained a sigh of frustration.

"Nigel, I have no idea what you're talking about." Madison was frowning at the two of them. "Care to enlighten me?"

"With pleasure." He waved magnanimously at the table behind them, and they all moved to have a seat. "Besides discovering that Candace Patterson had an amazingly dysfunctional family, we also learned that she'd been called away from work by a telephone call the night she died." He patted the envelope.

"And you've brought us the LUDs." Madison nodded with a smile, clearly up to speed. "So what do they have to say?"

"There are two incoming phone calls that fit the time frame, the first at nine forty-two and the second ten minutes later. Each lasted less than three minutes." Nigel opened the envelope and pulled out a sheet of paper. "The first was from a number in the East Village. I'm having it traced, and the second was from here."

"Our operations room?" Madison took the sheet of paper, scanning the contents.

"No. The call went through the main switchboard at Dreamscape."

"Cullen." Gabe said the name softly, almost as an afterthought, but Madison heard him, her gaze colliding with his.

"We don't know that." She chewed the side of her lip, returning her attention to the sheet of paper. "This isn't a very good copy."

"It's the best I could do." Nigel shrugged. "And I almost didn't get that. There was the little matter of authorization. They weren't all that impressed with my British credentials. I'm afraid I had to resort to flattery or we'd have had nothing at all."

"All that matters is that you got it." Gabe reached for the page, taking in the two highlighted lines. "And that we've got the numbers. Based on what Lex Rymon said, I think we can be fairly certain the first call is the one he referenced. She must have gotten the second after she left."

"So either one could be the killer," Nigel said.

"Well, Lex said the first call made her angry, right?" Madison looked to Gabe for confirmation. "And then she ran out of the dining room. So that makes caller number one look pretty darn suspicious."

"And since she was working with Cullen, a call from Dreamscape isn't all that unusual." Nigel said.

"But it's certainly not conclusive. The second caller could be the one."

"Is there a telephone log?" Madison asked, propping her elbow on the table, resting her chin against her palm.

"No. At least not at the switchboard. The phone company has one. But unfortunately it doesn't show extensions," Nigel said.

"So it could have been anyone." Gabe fought to control his frustration.

"Well, that late at night there has to at least be a record of who was in the building." Madison frowned.

"One step ahead of you," Nigel said, pulling more papers from the envelope. "There were around sixty people present that night. And over a third of them have had some contact with the accord or the consortium."

"It might be worth running the list by Cullen." This from Madison. Gabe frowned as their gazes met and held. "He might be able to shed light on who did or didn't know Candace."

"Maybe. Unless, of course, he's the one who made the call," Gabe said, knowing he was baiting her.

"I'm sure he'd have told us if he'd talked to her." Her voice conveyed an assurance that wasn't reflected in her eyes. It was a solid attempt at defense, but he could see she had doubts. He ought to count it as a victory, but somehow the taste of success had turned rancid in view of her distress.

Nigel cleared his throat. "Why don't I check on it? Under the circumstances, it might be better than one of you taking the old boy on."

Gabe started to argue, then lifted a hand in surrender. Maybe Nigel was right. Hell, maybe Madison was right. Maybe he was still holding on to his resentment. If Cullen hadn't gotten them all involved…

But that was stupid. What happened hadn't been Cullen's fault. No, that blame rested securely on Gabe's shoulders. Nothing would change that fact, and he'd do well to remember it.

"Fine," he said, pulling his thoughts from the past. "You handle it. But don't let Cullen snow you with rhetoric. It's his specialty."

"I think I can handle him." Nigel grinned. "After all I've been known to turn a pretty phrase when the moment called for it."

"Fine. And in the meantime we'll wait to ID the first number."

"No problem there." Harrison strode through the doors, carrying his laptop. "Ran into Nigel in Starbucks," he said by way of explanation. "And I've got an address."

CHAPTER FOURTEEN

THE BUILDING WAS a walk-up, the kind with boxes for rooms that sometimes rented by the hour. Gabriel was leading the way, Nigel manning the alley, with Payton watching the entrance.

Madison had Gabriel's back, much to his annoyance. And after the sixth flight of stairs, she had to admit the victory was losing its thrill. He'd hardly said a word on the way over, not an unusual state of affairs, but the tension between them had only increased with their most recent battle.

Something about the man just brought out the worst in her. When Nigel had interrupted earlier, she'd felt as if she'd been rescued from the maw of a tiger, yet at the same time she'd resented the Brit for intruding. Hell of a conundrum, and to further complicate matters, now she was climbing stairs with the man—guns drawn.

As they rounded the corner onto the sixth-floor landing, Gabriel motioned her against the wall. Apartment 6A was just ahead of them, the "A" hanging perpendicular to the six. According to Harrison's information the rooms were rented to a W. Smith, the same name used in Charlottesville.

Obviously not a coincidence. Which probably meant there wouldn't be anything to find. After all, the phone call had emanated from a cell phone, and even though this was the address of record, it could easily be a fake. Still, there was no sense in charging in unprepared.

She slid her back along the wall, trying not to think about the grime embedded there. They inched forward until Gabriel was beside the door. Quickly he knocked, and Madison held her breath, counting to ten as they waited for a response.

Nothing.

Gabriel knocked again, and Madison's heart pounded in rhythm against her ribs. This time there was a clatter, followed by the unmistakable scrape of a window opening. With a nod in her direction, Gabriel moved to face the door, Sig Sauer ready.

He kicked once, the door splintering open, and stepped into the apartment, Madison following on his heels. There were two rooms, and as Gabriel rushed the living room window, she released the safety on the Glock and swung into the bedroom. The bedclothes were scattered, as if someone had left them in a hurry. And the curtains in the window swung ominously in the breeze.

Hopping over the bed, she crossed to the window. The fire escape had been released, the ladder taunting her. With a groan of frustration, she threw a leg over the sill and was out on the grating in less than a minute. Still, that combined with valuable time lost in the hall meant whoever had been in the apartment had a heck of lead.

She was halfway down the first ladder when she heard Gabriel calling from above. At first she thought he was calling to her, but then she realized Nigel was standing below her.

"If he came this way he's a bloody ghost. He's not down here," Nigel responded, frustration evident in his tone.

The man must have gone up. Madison started moving in that direction, only to find that Gabriel had the same idea, his big body blocking her way as he vaulted the windowsill. Swallowing her irritation, she began climbing behind him, eventually emerging on the tar roof of the eight-story building.

The wind blew cold across her face as she scanned the flat open space, a soft cooing accompanied by a flutter of wings the only sign of life. Pigeons. If anyone had been here, they were long gone.

"There's nobody here." Gabriel spoke from near a chimney stack, his attention on the neighboring roofs. To the north the adjacent building rose straight up, a good ten stories higher than its neighbor. No escape that way.

Madison nodded, and made her way over to the door that led back into the building. It was locked, and from the looks of it rusted shut to boot, probably breaking all kinds of city codes in the process. "He didn't get out this way." She rattled the padlock for emphasis.

Gabriel nodded, crossing to the opposite corner. "He could have jumped here, but I don't like his odds."

She joined him at the edge of the roof, eyeing the twelve-foot gap separating the two apartment buildings. There were no other ladders, the fire escape and the door providing the only real exits. "Maybe he didn't come up."

Gabriel shook his head. "Nigel would have seen him."

"Maybe." She looked down into the alley. "But there's a door down there and a couple of windows. He could have slipped through one of those."

Gabriel holstered his gun and blew out a breath. "Whatever he did, he's gone now."

"Damn it, Gabriel, if you hadn't been in my way." She spit out the words, her anger not at him but the missed target.

"What? You'd have flown up the ladder? He was already gone. Nothing either of us did would have made a difference."

He was right, of course, and in light of his more than reasonable tone her anger deflated. "I suppose you're right. So what now? Search the room?"

"Yeah. And we'll check the alley." He started to turn back toward the fire escape, then stopped, his dark brows drawing together. "You were good in there."

Coming from anyone else she'd have taken it in stride. After all, she'd trained with the best, but coming from him it was different, and she couldn't find words, just stood there staring stupidly.

For a moment they were connecting on levels that had nothing to do with chasing suspects, or following procedure. And then it was gone as if it had never existed, the cold wind blowing it away in a whisper of fall leaves.

"We'd better get down." He started his descent, and she stood for a moment looking out over the rooftops, knowing that something had changed between them, something core-deep and unimpeachable. The thought elated her. And scared her to death.

And so, in the way that she'd handled most everything tricky in her life, she chose to ignore it, instead concentrating on matters at hand. With a sigh, she abandoned the roof to follow him down the ladder.

"YOU SAW NOTHING at all?" Gabe tried to contain his fury. This was quickly turning into a farce, someone leading them around by the nose with gleeful intent.

"Not a thing. The alley was deserted the whole time." Nigel sat on the arm of what passed for a sofa.

The apartment was furnished, although the word was more a euphemism than a reality. There was a table and a couple of chairs, along with the decrepit sofa and the mattress on the floor of the bedroom.

"No other means of egress? What about the windows and door opening off the alley?"

"All duly checked, I assure you. The door was locked, and two of the windows were barred. The third window only opened about six inches, which means unless the man was a contortionist he didn't get out that way."

"He didn't come my way, either." Payton leaned, arms crossed, against the battered table. "The only way out was the front door or the alley and the only person I saw there was Nigel."

"So that leaves the roof," Madison said with a sigh, the wind from the open window ruffling her hair. "Except that there wasn't any sign of him up there."

"Well, he had to have gone somewhere." Gabe ran a hand through his hair, knowing his frustration showed in every gesture. But it couldn't be helped. There were answers to be found. And, damn it, he was in charge of finding them.

"If he was here at all." Payton put voice to the thought they'd all been avoiding.

"Someone was here," Madison insisted, tilting her head toward the bedroom. "I definitely heard the window go up."

"I heard it, too," Gabe confirmed.

"But did you actually see anyone?" Payton asked.

They shook their heads almost in tandem. "Still, the window didn't open itself. Someone was here," Madison said, walking over to the bedroom door. Tracy's techs were still in there, scouring the room for tangible evidence of the room's occupant.

"Someone who's obviously having a bit of fun at our expense." Nigel frowned. "Anything from the bedroom?"

As if on command one of the techs walked into the living room. "Place is clean. No personal possessions. No hint of occupancy at all. And to top it off the room's been wiped down."

"So no fingerprints." Gabe's comment was meant to be rhetorical, but the tech answered anyway.

"No," he said, shaking his head. "Although they're still dusting the window ledge and the fire escape."

"I doubt you'll find anything there but my prints," Madison said, an edge of disgust in her voice. "I wasn't exactly careful when I hopped over the sill."

"You were just doing your job." Gabe wasn't sure why he felt the need to reassure her, but now that it was said there was no taking it back. "Besides, I was right behind you."

Madison's eyes widened in surprise, the look on her face almost worth the price of his conciliatory action.

"So where the hell do we go from here?" Nigel asked. "We've got a string of seven dead, all of them invested, to more or less degree, in the consortium and the accord. M.O. seems to change at random, repeating at will, and then veering off into something different, the latest out-and-out homicide. We've got a bloke hacking into our computer conceivably from Virginia, but then the man turns up on the phone records of our seventh victim—here in New York. And when we try to track him down he disappears like Casper the fucking ghost."

"What's interesting to me," Payton said, "is the fact that there's nothing here. Nothing personal. So if the guy really rented the place, where's his stuff?"

"He moved out." Gabe shrugged.

"And then what?" Payton asked. "Came back to wait for us to drop by? I find it difficult enough to accept that he just vanished into thin air. When you add luggage to the picture I'd say it's impossible."

"There's no reason to believe he'd have had personal effects here. In fact, we don't even know that *he* was here at all. Maybe we scared a vagrant," Gabe said. The option had a certain merit. "People like that survive by knowing how to fade into the woodwork."

"So you're saying our target, if he ever was here, was long gone by the time we arrived. And that all we've been doing is chasing our tails?" Payton flushed with anger, his scar white by contrast.

"It's possible." Gabe lifted his hands in defeat.

"It seems to me then that the pressing issue is to figure out who W. Smith is." Madison stood up. "So far he's done a pretty good job of covering his tracks. But everyone makes mistakes. We just need to find his weakness."

"Before someone else winds up dead," Nigel agreed.

"SO WHAT HAPPENED?" Harrison was following her around like an eager puppy dog, and although normally she was glad of his company, at the moment she needed time to think. To try and find logic where seemingly there was none.

"He got away," she said with a sigh, "or was never there to begin with."

"Was the apartment registered to W. Smith?"

"Yes. Three months, paid in cash." They were walking along the corridor to Cullen's office. Madison hadn't even known she was going there, but suddenly she liked the idea. Surely Cullen could help her make heads or tails of the whole thing.

"Did the manager give you a description?"

"What?" Madison pulled herself out of her thoughts, scrambling to remember what Harrison had asked. "I'm sorry, I'm a bit distracted."

"I asked if you got a description."

"From the manager? No. Everything was done by mail. It wasn't exactly a check-your-credentials kind of place."

"So we really have nothing." Harrison's frustration mirrored her own.

"That's not true." She laid a hand on his arm. "Thanks to you we have a connection between the hacker and Candace Patterson. She obviously knew him. And I think it's valid to assume that he may have killed her. That's a heck of a lot more than we knew this morning."

"Yes, but it still doesn't get us any closer to finding the

man. And if the pattern holds true, there will be more murders."

"Any luck with the alias angle?"

Harrison shook his head. "I'm still working on it. And Payton has feelers out with some of his colleagues. But nothing so far. Gabe's given me access to the antiterrorism database. I suspect it's got more concise information than anything I've been able to look at so far."

"I'm surprised he agreed. The man guards his territory with the ferocity of a pit bull."

"Maybe where you're concerned." Harrison's smile was sly. "But he's seemed happy enough to help me. Maybe it's all in the way one asks." His tone was teasing, but there was a message there, as well.

Something about drawing flies with honey…

She shook the thought away. "Have you started your search?" The question was brusque, but then Harrison had been baiting her.

"Not yet." His expression turned serious. "I was waiting to see if you all found anything. Guess I'd best get at it."

Madison smiled and reached for his hand. "Sorry I snapped. I'm afraid we're all running on a bit of a short fuse these days."

"And will be until we get to the bottom of this." He squeezed her hand. "No worries."

"I think that's a bit of an understatement." Gabriel walked out of Cullen's office, his expression thunderous. "Looks like the two of you have been busy." His tone was snide, his gaze locked on their clasped hands.

Madison flushed, dropping Harrison's hand like a hot potato, feeling all of about twelve.

"She was filling me in on what happened in the Village," Harrison said, apparently unaffected by Gabriel's implication. But then of course he would be. "Sorry you didn't catch the bastard," he continued. "But we'll get him next time. I was just heading for the operations room to start searching the Homeland Security computers. Hopefully that'll turn up something."

Gabriel nodded, seeming to find focus. Madison, still tongue-tied, was grateful for the reprieve. "I've just been talking to Cullen. It seems the Chinese are threatening to walk." Gabriel included them both in his somber gaze, his anger vanishing as quickly as it had come.

"That's what Jeremy said," Madison responded, delighted to hear that her voice sounded normal, "but Cullen assured him it was more talk than action."

"Not anymore. Kingston evidently got a call an hour ago. And unless we get things under wraps fast, all bets are off. As you can imagine, Cullen's fit to be tied."

"Did you talk to him about adding security? I'd say he's as likely a target as anyone." Harrison as usual cut right to the chase.

"He's already got quite a bit, but he's aware of the need. We need to talk to Kingston and Jeremy. They're also likely targets."

"Security might not matter much," Madison said, a new thought pushing its way front and center. "I'm sure we've all thought it. But no one has said it out loud. If Candace Patterson knew W. Smith, then it's possible that Cullen and crew do, too." She paused, her gaze encompassing them both. "And if it's truly an inside job, he's already got access."

"Yes." Nigel moved farther into the shadows of the alleyway, his cell phone held tightly in one gloved hand. "Everything's going as planned. They have no idea."

He listened to the voice on the other end of the line, wishing that someone else could have been chosen for the job. His loyalty was clear, but his conscience was not.

People were dying. And while he knew it was the price of the game, he didn't have to like it.

"Yes, yes, I will." He nodded to no one in particular. "It's all in place. There's nothing to worry about. It's not exactly my first mission, is it? I'm very good at what I do. Plus I have the added advantage of knowing how the man works." He clicked off the phone, swallowing a surge of disgust.

Oh, yes, he knew how he worked. For the last decade he'd even called the man friend. But then, in this business, there really was no such thing.

CHAPTER FIFTEEN

"I WOULD HAVE TAKEN YOU to Nino's, you know." Philip Merrick laid down the plastic fork and shot his daughter a frown.

"I know." Madison shrugged. Nino's, an Italian restaurant on First Avenue, was a favorite, but when her father offered to take her there, it invariably meant he wanted something, and tonight she wasn't up to the fight. "I just thought it would be better if we ate here."

"So you could keep on working." It wasn't a question, and his voice held a note of frustration. "You work too much."

"People's lives are at stake, Dad. It's not exactly a situation I can control." She pushed away her plate, suddenly losing her appetite. The ops room was empty, everyone gone for the night. If she'd had her way, she wouldn't have stopped for dinner, but her father had been insistent, and this was the compromise.

"Which is exactly why I think you're out of your league. You're supposed to be holed up in Virginia probing into the psychological whys and wherefores. Not on the front lines here in the city. Cullen told me what happened today. Hell, Madison, you could have been killed." Philip's expression darkened, his gray eyes the mirror image of Madison's, and she realized that she'd made a tactical error. Nino's was a public place and her father would never make a scene. Here, on the other hand...

She sighed. "There was no one there. I couldn't have been hurt."

"You didn't know that. Cullen said—"

"*Cullen* should mind his own business." She cut him off with the wave of an arm. It was an old argument, but she never seemed to quit rising to the bait. If her father had it his way, she'd be home baking cookies for his two-point-one grandchildren. "Besides, he's the one who got me into this."

"I know. And believe me, I've given him a piece of my mind on that subject. But unfortunately, neither of you has ever listened to a word I say. Sometimes I think you're more his daughter than mine." If Madison hadn't known better, she'd have said there was a touch of jealousy in his tone, but Philip Merrick wasn't the jealous type. He just liked maintaining control.

"Look, this case is no different from any of the others I've worked on. There's always some degree of danger, and you know it. But I'm careful."

"It's not you I worry about." Their gazes met and held. "I had the men you're working with investigated. A bunch of hotheaded daredevils. According to the information I got, they're not exactly play-by-the-rules kind of guys."

"They walk the line, I'll grant you that." She fought to keep her tone even. No sense starting a fight. "But they're trained professionals, and Cullen's worked with them before."

"Cullen wants what he wants." Her father waved a dismissive hand. "But that doesn't give him the right to put you in danger. There's a murderer out there, Madison, and now, thanks to Cullen, you're in the line of fire."

"I can take care of myself." She sighed, silently counting to ten. "If you'd pay any attention at all, you'd realize that I'm not a little girl anymore. This is what I do, and it doesn't matter if it's for the FBI or Cullen Pulaski. Either way, the job is the same. I'm out there to stop the bad guys. An honorable ambition, surely."

"Not if it gets you killed." Her father had crossed his arms, his expression mutinous.

"I'm not going to get killed. And I'm not going to quit the team, either. So you might as well give it up. Nothing you say will make a difference."

"What about your mother? Shouldn't you be thinking of her?"

Leave it to her father to try every angle. "Mother doesn't care what I do. She's far too busy fighting for the Ganges mountain beetle or whatever cause she's adopted of late. Besides, unlike you, she's accepted that I make my own decisions."

"Well, I don't know why that should surprise me. She never did have the sense God gave a goose." Despite their divorce, Madison's parents were actually quite comfortable with each other. Time, it seemed, did in fact heal all wounds. "And just because she doesn't see the risk doesn't mean it's not there."

"Dad," Madison ground out, her patience stretched to the limit, "I'll be fine."

"What about this Gabriel Roarke person? He sounds just like Rick."

There were similarities to her ex, but Madison wasn't about to discuss them with her father. Besides, she was beginning to think that maybe she'd underestimated the man, and quite honestly, she wasn't about to admit that, either. "It's not the same. For one thing, I'm not involved with Gabriel." *At least not yet.* The thought caught her by surprise, the accompanying rush of heat telling. "He's a colleague. Like Harrison."

Her father's expression said it all. In his world there could be only one relationship between a man and a woman—a horizontal one.

"I'm not interested in Gabriel Roarke. And even if I were, it has nothing to do with my ability to do my job." She loved her father, really she did, but sometimes she wanted to throttle him.

"I just want what's best for you, Madison." There was real concern in his eyes now, and Madison felt a rush of guilt.

"I know you do, Dad. But you've got to accept that I'm not going to change my mind about what I do."

"Maybe not. But it's my duty as your father to make sure you don't get in over your head. Even if it makes you angry."

"I'm not quitting the task force." They were at an impasse again. God save her from overbearing men.

"Fine." Her father stood up, his face flushed with anger. "Then I'll just have to talk to Cullen."

"Do what you have to do. But it's not going to change anything." She was wasting her breath—he'd already pushed past her, heading for the door. It swung open and her father barreled right into Gabriel. The two men stopped for a moment, assessing each other, and then her father shouldered by him, dismissing Gabriel with the gesture.

"Not a happy camper." Gabriel's dark brow arced upward, his expression amused.

"My father," Madison admitted, crossing her arms to hide the fact that they were shaking. "It seems the two of you have something in common." She fought against her anger, knowing it wouldn't solve anything, but she'd simply had enough. "He wants me off the task force, too."

Gabriel shook his head. "I never said that I wanted you off the team. I just don't like the idea of sharing command."

"It's more than that and you know it," Madison snapped, common sense taking a back seat to her indignation. "You think what I do is a waste of time. That I'm nothing more than a woman with a crystal ball."

"Don't put words in my mouth." He frowned, his anger rising to match hers. "I'll admit I'm a bit skeptical about profiling as a valid tool, especially with regard to terrorists. But that doesn't mean it doesn't have a place."

"In the back room of some flophouse."

"Madison," he reached out to take hold of her shoulders. "I don't know what's going on here, but you're mad at your father, not me."

Her anger deflated like an old balloon and she blew out a long breath. "You're right. I shouldn't have lashed out at you. It's just that I get so tired of having to prove myself over and over again." She was talking about more than just her father now.

"Then don't do it." Gabriel's hands burned into her skin, and she fought the urge to throw herself against him, to seek comfort in his arms.

Stupid notion.

"Look." He lifted her chin with a finger, their gazes locking. "The most important person you have to please in life is yourself. And if your father can't live with the choices you make, then so be it. You can't spend your life trying to gain his approval—" she opened her mouth to protest, but he cut her off "—or trying to shock him into paying attention. Either way you lose, because you're not living for yourself. You're living for him."

"You sound like you're talking from experience," she grumbled, not completely comfortable with the fact that he seemed to read her like a book. That was supposed to be her area of expertise.

"I'm not. At least with regard to parents." He shrugged, the gesture calculated to camouflage any emotion. "I didn't have any."

"Everybody has parents." The words were out before she could think better of them.

Gabriel's smile was hollow. "My father, whoever the hell he was, didn't stick around long enough for introductions, and my mother died when I was born. Too damn young to be having a baby."

"How awful." She stifled the urge to smooth the pain from his face, knowing he wouldn't appreciate it.

"It was what it was." He shrugged again with the same sense of overly orchestrated bravado. "I spent most of my life as part of the system. Foster care and juvenile homes. It wasn't until the army that I really found my niche."

"Regulation as a substitute for family." It was a predictable outcome for someone who grew up more or less on his own. And it certainly fit his profile.

"Don't analyze me, Madison, I don't fit into a box."

She believed that. Gabriel Roarke was definitely one of a kind. But it still explained a lot. "I'm not profiling you. It's just that a lot of kids from broken homes find comfort in the structure of the armed forces."

"My home wasn't broken. It didn't exist." His words were sharp, edged with long-ago pain. "And we weren't talking about me. We were talking about you—and your father."

"And how alike the two of you are." She couldn't resist the barb, but he ignored it.

"I've had experience with my share of overbearing commanders who thought they knew what was best for me."

"But they didn't?" She couldn't help the question.

"Not by a long shot." His steely gaze skewered her. "The only person I really trust, Madison, is myself."

"That's a lonely way to live."

"Maybe." He shrugged again. "But I find it's safer that way. And I think maybe you understand more about it than you're letting on. I don't think you trust people any more easily than I do."

Again he'd nailed her. And she didn't like the feeling. "I trust my father. I just choose to disagree with him. And there are others I know I can count on. Harrison, for one."

Gabriel's eyes narrowed. "Yeah, the two of you looked thick as thieves earlier." There was an undercurrent to his words, and she wrenched away, angry at the implication.

"Harrison is my friend. Nothing more. And if you'd get your head out of the gutter, you'd realize that."

"I just call it like I see it." He shifted so that they were standing toe-to-toe again.

"Well, then you're blind." She wanted to move away, but held her ground, not wanting to let him get the better of her. "I didn't mean that the way it sounded."

"Of course you didn't." His smile bordered on wicked, and he reached out to tuck a strand of hair behind her ear, the gesture sending rockets of fire racing through her.

Damn the man.

"I just meant that I'm not involved with Harrison. I'm not involved with anyone." She was babbling now, and the more she talked the deeper it got. He had a way of discombobulating her with only a word, or a look.

"Good." He'd moved even closer, his gaze dueling with hers, his breath teasing her cheek.

She stepped back, more because she needed to breathe than because she was running away. This was not how things were supposed to go with Gabriel Roarke. She was supposed to be able to manage him like she'd managed everything else in her life. Or at least compartmentalize him.

Not that Gabriel was the kind of man one could relegate to a back burner.

"We've got work to do." She reached for a file on a nearby desk and started flipping randomly through it, hoping he'd take the hint.

"It's late." His voice was gruff with an emotion she was

certain she didn't want to identify. "Maybe we should call it a day."

Her gut twisted as her mind presented a picture of the two of them naked, tangled in the sheets, body-to-body, as he stroked her, filled her. "You go on." She set down the file, trying frantically to pull her thoughts to safer ground. "I think I'll stay for a bit."

She kept her gaze on her hands, determined not to look at him, to face the challenge she knew was reflected in his eyes. It would be so easy to give in, to let her baser instincts take control…

She raised her head, drawing a breath to change her mind, but before she could utter the words, she realized the room was empty.

Gabriel Roarke was gone.

"YOU'RE BURNING the midnight oil." Kingston Sinclair walked into the operations room just as Madison was yawning over an autopsy report. Truth be told, she hadn't gotten as much done as she would have liked, her thoughts centering instead on the abstruse man she shared command with. But she wasn't about to tell Kingston.

"What are you doing here?" She put the report on the table, tipping her head back so that she could see him better.

He was older than her father by about ten years, but that hadn't hindered their friendship. Kingston had been a part of Madison's life as long as she could remember. Never as much of a family member as Cullen, but still someone she knew and trusted.

"I was meeting with Cullen, and saw the light on. Figured it was probably you." His smile was tolerant. "Do you ever sleep?"

"Not when there's a killer out there."

"I was shocked to hear about Candace." Kingston sobered. "And then Cullen told me about today's fiasco."

She winced at his choice of words, knowing that at least part of the fault lay with her. She'd ruined any chance they had for taking fingerprints off the window. "It could have gone better."

"You really shouldn't put yourself in danger like that." He had moved closer, his face reflecting his concern.

"It sounds like you've been talking to my dad." Madison grimaced.

Kingston shrugged. "I will say he's furious with Cullen. He thinks the two of you are in cahoots."

"Right." Madison shook her head, frustration cresting. "He and I got together to try and find a case that would put me front and center dangerwise just to piss off my dad."

"Hey," Kingston laughed, holding up his hands. "I didn't say it. Your father did."

"Well, he needs to lay off. I'm a grown woman. Not that he ever notices."

Kingston walked over to the window. "Honey, he notices. Believe me. That's why he worries. And it wouldn't hurt you to be careful, you know."

"I am careful. And besides, if anyone needs to be cautious, it's you. You know as well as I do, you're high profile when it comes to the consortium and the accord, and that makes you a target."

Kingston laughed, reaching over to pull the blinds. "How's that? Protecting my back."

"I'm not joking. You need to be careful. You and Cullen both."

"I know." His expression turned thoughtful. "It's getting down to the wire. The summit is just around the corner. If someone is really trying to stop things, he'll be full out now."

"We'll find him."

Kingston studied her for a moment, as if considering the

possibility, then sighed. "I'm sure you will. That's why—"

"Oh." Harrison drew to a stop as he walked through the door. "I didn't know anyone would be up here. Sorry to interrupt."

"You're not interrupting a thing," Kingston said. "I was just trying to get Madison to take care of herself. Her father and I rather like having her around."

"They're up in arms because I went up on the roof today," Madison explained.

"I just wish I'd been there." Harrison sounded like a petulant child. "The computer guy never gets to have any fun."

"Like you haven't handled your share of cases." Madison rolled her eyes. "He loves to play geek. But no one's buying."

"Well, you've both got more energy than I do." Kingston's smile encompassed them both. "And on that note, I think I should be heading home." He headed for the door. "Keep me posted. And watch your backs."

Harrison frowned. "Optimistic guy."

"He means well. But I'm afraid he's been listening to Dad more than he should." Madison sighed, rubbing her temples. "I'll be glad when this is over."

"Me, too." He walked over to one of the PCs. "Thought I'd take another crack at the Homeland Security computers."

"Still hoping to find an alias?"

"Yeah. Payton and I were talking and he thinks I should be trying translations of the name. Maybe it's got a correlation in another language." He ran a hand through his hair, the gesture making him look like a kid. "There's got to be something. Nobody exists in a vacuum."

"Maybe not. But sometimes it's damn close."

"You going home?" Harrison was already typing. In another minute he'd be lost in his own little world of bits and bytes.

"No." She was feeling restless, and an empty apartment was only going to magnify the problem. "I thought I'd swing by Jeremy Bosner's. I told Gabe I'd talk to him about beefing up his security. And now seems as good a time as any."

Harrison swiveled around to look at her. "It's almost ten o'clock."

She looked at her watch, surprised that it was so late, then shrugged. "Better safe than sorry. Besides, Jeremy's always been a night owl. He'll be up."

"You and Gabriel all right?" The question came from left field, and Madison worked to cover her surprise.

"Everything's fine, why?"

"Because he stormed through the hotel lobby, just as Payton and I were heading to the restaurant. And based on your earlier encounter, I figured maybe the two of you had gone on to round two."

"We talked," Madison said, knowing full well they'd done a hell of a lot more than that. "I might have hit a few sore spots."

"If his glower was anything to go by, I'd say more than a few."

"He'll survive." She shrugged. "Besides, he got no more than he deserved." That wasn't exactly true. He'd scared her. But not with words. In fact, it had been his gentle perception that angered her the most. She didn't want to be understood, and she certainly didn't need advice from Gabriel Roarke.

The man had nothing she needed.

Nothing at all.

CHAPTER SIXTEEN

THE BAR WAS CROWDED, the kind of place that only Nigel could have sniffed out. Molly Malone's was as close to a British pub as one was likely to find this side of the pond. At the moment, Nigel was bellied up to the bar having a spirited discussion with the bartender about a soccer match on television.

Payton sat in the corner, nursing the same beer he'd ordered an hour ago, while Gabe, sitting across from him, was well into his third whiskey. Probably not a strategic move, but at the moment, it suited his mood to dull his brain, twelve-year-old Bushmills being his weapon of choice.

The bottle sat open on the table and he stared at the amber liquid as it glowed in the lamplight. "Why the hell did you tell Madison about Iraq?"

If he'd had one less drink, he probably wouldn't have asked, but it irked him that Payton had shared secrets with Madison. Partly because he wanted that part of his life dead and buried, and partly because he didn't like the idea of Payton sharing anything with Madison.

Payton twirled his beer glass idly, considering the question. "I didn't tell her anything she didn't already know."

"Then how did…" He trailed off, realizing immediately where the information had come from. "Cullen."

"So she said. Look, in her defense, she's just trying to understand you." Payton's expression was inscrutable, the shadows of the pub hiding even his scar.

"Me?" Gabe choked out a laugh, remembering her earlier dismissal. "Believe me, that's definitely not what she's doing. More than likely she's trying to profile us. Identify all our little idiosyncrasies and then categorize us—tying everything up in neat little boxes."

Payton raised his eyebrows, not saying a word, the hint of a smile playing at the corners of his mouth.

"I hope you didn't tell her anything." Gabe could no more explain his anger than he could explain his attraction for the woman, but at the moment both were undeniable.

"Of course not." Payton's expression darkened. "I don't talk to anyone about what happened. You better than anyone should understand that." He finished the beer, slamming the glass back on the table. "I told you I just confirmed what she'd been told."

"I'm sorry. I overreacted."

"The woman gets to you." Payton's lips quirked upward again. "Anyone can see that. I kind of like knowing you aren't immune to the species."

"She pisses me off, if that's what you're talking about. But beyond that I don't give a flying fuck what happens to her as long as she stays the hell out of my business." At the sound of his rising voice, the couple at the next table turned to look at him, and Gabe felt heat rushing up the back of his neck.

"Obviously I think she's less of a menace than you do. Why don't we leave it at that." Payton was openly smiling now.

"Leave what at what?" Nigel walked up, slid into the chair next to Gabe and handed Payton a new beer.

"Nothing," Gabe barked, his anger receding but not vanished. "How'd the game come out?"

"We always lose in the clutch." Nigel shrugged cheerfully. "But I never give up hope. Any chance you solved the case while I went missing?"

"No." Payton met Gabe's gaze, ignoring the message there. "We've been talking about Madison Harper."

"Quite a girl, our Madison." Nigel's grin grew wolfish.

"She's off-limits." Gabe glared at his friend. "We're working with her. Period."

"Ah, so that's the way the wind blows, is it?" Nigel pursed his lips and swallowed a laugh. "I should have known."

"There's no wind." Gabe wished suddenly that he'd stayed in his room. His bottle of whiskey would have tasted just as good there, and he wouldn't have had to endure his so-called friends' abuse. "I just want everyone's mind on business. Madison is a part of the team. Deal with it. And keep your goddamn hands to yourself. Got it?"

"Sir, yes, sir." Nigel saluted smartly, still laughing.

"Have you heard anything else from Lin Yao?" Gabe asked, determined to change the subject.

Payton put his glass down, his expression turning serious. "Still nothing substantiated. But there's definitely something going on. Two antigovernment groups in particular have popped onto the radar. One is based in Northern China and keeps a notoriously high profile."

"Meaning they're not our boys," Nigel said, leaning in to keep his voice low. "If they were, the murders would have been splashed across the headlines."

"Exactly." Payton leaned back against the wall, his eyes traveling around the room, automatically checking for listeners. "But it doesn't completely rule them out. The second group is more likely. They're headquartered in the high Himalayas. Sort of the Chinese equivalent to the Hole in the Wall Gang.

"Stealth is their main mode of operation, and Yao's sources confirm they're not happy about the accord. He has one source who believes there's been activity in the U.S., but he wants to confirm it independently, so I'm waiting for word. In the meantime, Harrison is checking for movement and also for anyone who is associated with them that might use W. Smith as an alias."

"I've been over the potential target list," Gabe said, "and I think the clear winners are Cullen, Kingston Sinclair and Jeremy Bosner. Cullen is aware of what's going on of course, as is Sinclair, and I asked Madison to talk to Bosner." Gabe twirled the whiskey in his glass.

"You realize there could be others," Nigel said to no one in particular.

"Yes. Unfortunately there's no way to watch over everyone. In fact, I'm not sure it does us any good to watch anyone. It's far more important that we work toward finding the bastards behind this."

"Preferably before anyone else dies." Payton blew out a breath. "Anything come in from the lab?"

"Nothing substantial. They lifted three prints and a partial. Two of Madison's and one of mine." Gabe couldn't keep the chagrin from his voice.

"And the partial?" Nigel asked.

"No identity so far. But they're still working on it. I'm not expecting much. The rest of the apartment was clean. If our man was there at all, he's hardly likely to have wiped down everything but the windowsill. I expect it will turn out to be one of ours or someone in the apartment building."

"How about interviews—anyone in the building see Smith?" Payton's frown mirrored Gabe's. It seemed every step forward resulted in another two or three back.

"I can answer that one," Nigel said. "I talked to everyone on Smith's floor. There were three other apartments. And typical of New York, everyone claims not to have seen him."

"You think someone's lying?"

"Unfortunately, no." Nigel shook his head. "In places

like that people work to mind their own business. If you don't, you wind up dead. A couple of Tracy Braxton's techs did the lower floors. And again there was nothing. Someone on the second floor thought maybe they'd seen him, but when pressed couldn't come up with anything except that he was white."

"It's something, I guess." Payton didn't sound hopeful. "But I'd say the odds are against it. Unless he *wanted* to be seen."

"If this is meant as a wild-goose chase then it's possible, I suppose." Nigel leaned back in his chair, his brows drawn together in thought. "But I'm thinking that more likely he knows we're on to him and simply cleared out."

"So how do you explain the ghost act?" Gabe asked.

"The vagrant idea actually has merit," Payton said, draining the last of his beer. "That particular neighborhood is full of them. So it isn't too much of a stretch. Maybe the partial will confirm it."

"Even if it was a vagrant, that doesn't explain where the hell he went."

"He must have jumped the gap between the buildings. It's the only logical explanation," Nigel said.

"But it was at least twelve feet." Payton looked to Gabe for confirmation, and then back to Nigel. "That's one hell of an agile tramp."

"Takes all kinds." Nigel laughed.

Gabe realized suddenly that he was tired and it was late. He wondered where Madison was, then quashed the thought. Fatigue did strange things to a man. Lowered his defenses. Opened doors he'd thought firmly closed.

What he needed was a good night's sleep. Everything would look clearer in the morning. And in the meantime, he'd simply banish all thoughts of her from his mind.

IT WAS TOO COLD to be walking, but Madison didn't care. She needed to clear her head. She'd taken a taxi to Fifty-seventh and Second, and then on impulse made him stop and let her out. Jeremy Bosner lived at Sutton Place, so she really hadn't far to go, and the crisp October night was just the tonic she needed.

The wind blew sharply off the East River, cutting through the leather of her coat as if it were cotton or chintz. She pulled the collar closer and tipped her face to the breeze, letting it wash away the frustrations of the day.

They'd found nothing, just chased their tails around while the murderer yanked their chain. Of that she was certain. Whoever had hacked into the computer had wanted them to find him, or at least the trail he'd left. He was toying with them.

Just as Gabriel Roarke was toying with her.

Madison stuffed her hands into her pockets, picking up the pace. There were people on the street, but not as many as she'd have expected this time of night. Light spilled across the pavement as she passed storefronts and apartment buildings. Above her, wildly gyrating leaves were lit by the adjacent apartments. People safe and warm.

Home.

A rush of longing swept over her, the need to belong swamping all other emotion. It was a stupid thought, of course. The wistful dreams of a foolish girl. And she was no longer that girl. She had a home. Just blocks from here. And her father and her mother, and friends, and a job she loved.

She needed nothing else. It was only the past reaching out to pull at her. Like the wind. She pulled her arms into her sides, attempting to lock in the meager warmth her jacket provided. She should have stayed in the taxi.

She stopped, half thinking that she'd flag another one, when something, a movement or a noise dragged at her subconscious. Slowly she turned around, her gaze sweeping the street, looking for the source of the worry blossoming in her gut.

The last of the evening's stragglers seemed to have disappeared. She was nearing York and the river, Fifty-seventh Street shifting from retail to residential seemingly in an instant. Behind her, about a half a block away, a man walked his dog. Or more precisely, his dog walked him.

A couple across the street stood in the shadows, making out, their arms locked around each other, oblivious to everything else. Jealousy tickled her mind, but was dismissed easily in her need to find the source of her concern.

She waited in the lamplight, watching the street for signs of something amiss. Nothing moved except the man and the dog, the lust-filled couple, and an elderly man and woman who emerged from a building just up the way. Everything was as it should be. Her imagination was simply getting the best of her.

With a shiver she hurried forward. Jeremy lived just past York, his brownstone part of a cul-de-sac that had held court for a couple hundred years, the graceful buildings harking back to a more elegant time.

She passed the police booth at the corner, noted it was unmanned, and made a mental note to see that the NYPD were alerted to the situation. No sense in not taking advantage of what would seem normal observation.

The light changed and she pushed on across York, the wind stronger now that she was so close to the river. It stung her cheeks, dancing in her hair, whipping the strands into her eyes, only to die down to nothing once she reached the shelter of the row of brownstones.

She was relieved to see light coming from across the street—Jeremy's parlor window. She'd been to the brownstone many times over the years, usually at Christmas. It was beautiful in a Dickensian kind of way, complete with gabled windows, wrought-iron fencing and a Scroogelike lion head that served as a door knocker.

She was also delighted to note that the twenty-first century prevailed in the form of a security camera mounted above the door. After opening the gate, she climbed the steps to Jeremy's red-painted doorway, thinking that the only thing missing from the picture was a planter with a bay tree.

The wind whistled behind her, and again the hairs on her neck prickled. She spun around, eyes straining into the dark for something out of place. She could hear the quiet whoosh of the traffic on the FDR, and see the white caps of the waves in the river.

Everything in its place. She was just jumpy.

The brownstone immediately across the way was covered with scaffolding, home improvement New York–style. The flanking buildings were also dark but obviously occupied, their residents most likely already in bed for the night. Which was no doubt exactly where she should be. Shaking her head at her own folly, she started back down the steps, only to turn again when she heard the door behind her opening.

Jeremy stood in the warm light that spilled out across the stoop, his gaunt face creased with worry. "Has something happened?"

"No." Madison shook her head, embarrassment coloring her words. "I came by to talk to you about security, but I hadn't realized how late it was."

"Thank God." The older man's face relaxed into a smile. "I was afraid there'd been another murder."

"No, nothing like that."

"Good. I'm glad to hear it. I just poured myself a brandy. Why don't you come in and keep me company? It's a dreadful night to be out." He shot a look into the shadows almost as if he, too, feared something was out there. But then again, he would be worried, Madison thought.

"Come on. I've been meaning to talk with you anyway." He moved to the side, gesturing her to enter.

"All right." She walked past him into the lovely marble foyer. "If you're certain I'm not intruding." Just at the moment a brandy seemed the perfect way to abolish the uneasy jitters that had followed her down Fifty-seventh. And she did need to talk to him.

Jeremy closed the door and led her into the parlor, a beautiful walnut-paneled room with a fire blazing cozily at one end. There was an open bottle of brandy sitting on a drinks table beside a velvet sofa, and across from it, next to the fire, a half-empty glass balanced on the arm of a wing chair. An open book sat next to it. Madison could just make out the title—*Nine Coaches Waiting*. A great story, but an odd choice for Jeremy, surely?

It was only then that she noticed he was wearing a velvet smoking jacket, faded gray flannels adding to the sense of timelessness. An era long gone, yet still preserved here as if it had only been yesterday. Madison smiled and held her hands out to the fire. "It's wonderfully warm in here. I really do feel as if I've interrupted your evening."

"Nonsense, my dear. You're just the tonic this old man needed."

She turned to face him, accepting the glass he held out. "I'm afraid I haven't come with any answers. If you talked to Cullen, you'll know that today wasn't much of a success."

Jeremy nodded, and settled back into the wing chair, brandy in hand. "He mentioned that the killer managed to slip through your fingers. But that isn't what I wanted to talk about. The truth is, I owe you an apology."

"For what?" Madison sank down onto the sofa, trying to follow the turn of the conversation.

"I was out of line yelling at you. I know that the task

force is working as quickly as possible. It's just that my conversation with Chiao Chien was frustrating to say the least. We've worked so hard to lay the groundwork, and to think that some dissident could undo the whole thing by randomly killing the principal players…" He stared morosely into his brandy glass.

"It's certainly not random." Her response came out sharper than she'd intended, and Jeremy's head popped up, his gaze meeting hers.

"I didn't mean to sound so condemning. And I certainly didn't mean to make light of my colleagues' deaths. It's just so…so inconceivable. I mean, how does something like this disintegrate into something so squalid?"

"You know as well as I do that politics isn't a by-the-rules game. When the stakes are this high, sometimes it can seem like there's no other way."

"And so people die." Again he stared down into his glass, and Madison wondered if he'd had more than a little nip. She shot a glance at the decanter and saw that it was more than three-quarters empty.

He noticed her scrutiny and smiled. "It's not as bad as all that. It was already half-empty. And if I'm flushed, it's only because it was stuffy in here. See, I even opened a window." He waved a hand toward the large casement windows flanking the street, one of them cracked to let in the breeze.

"It's just that between the tensions of the accord, and everything you've uncovered, I've been a little tense. And this—" he held up his glass, the brandy flickering in the firelight "—helps take the edge off, if you know what I mean." He sat back, as if waiting for a verdict.

Madison sighed. "I wasn't being judgmental, honestly. Just feeling all over again as if I'm intruding." She leaned forward to put her brandy on the coffee table. "Why don't I just call you in the morning?"

"You'll do nothing of the sort. Drinking alone is a dangerous proposition. Besides, you look like you could use a break." His eyes darkened with concern, and Madison realized with a start that he really did care about her.

She smiled, and reclaimed her drink, settling back against the sofa again. "I'm fine, really. Just feeling the same frustration you are."

"Well two's company." There was a trace of melancholy in his voice and Madison realized with a start that he was lonely.

Despite his wealth and success, he was all alone.

A kindred spirit.

She fingered her glass, considering her next question. She hated to ruin the solidarity of the moment, but something he'd said yesterday had bothered her. "Are you really angry that Cullen assumed control of the consortium when Bingham died?"

Jeremy's eyes widened in surprise, then crinkled with his smile. "Good heavens, no. I was just posturing. Partially because I was angry and partially because it's good to shake Cullen up now and then. I have absolutely no desire to be chairman."

"But you're the vice-chair…." She trailed off, waiting for his answer, watching his body language for signs that he was lying.

"I like being second in command. All the glory, none of the headaches." He paused, studying her face. "But you don't want a flip answer do you? So I'll tell you. I was concerned that something exactly like what has transpired would occur." Madison frowned, opening her mouth to respond, but Jeremy waved her off. "Not the deaths. God knows I couldn't have dreamed up something like that, but the idea that something might happen to queer the deal wasn't that big of a leap. And quite frankly, I didn't want to be the one to take the fall."

"So you let Cullen assume the risk."

"No one *lets* Cullen do anything, Madison. I just didn't stand in his way. And the fact remains that regardless of who is at the helm, the stakes are the same. That's why your team has got to find answers as quickly as possible."

"We're trying." Madison sighed, and stood up to walk over to the window. The wind was still blowing, ginkgo trees bending in protest, the cool draft brushing against her hair. "The current idea is that the killer may be using an alias. If we can tie the name he's been using to something tangible, we might be able to work out his real identity."

"Sounds a bit like finding a diamond at the bottom of a waterfall."

"Unfortunately that's an apt analogy." Madison smiled into the dark, her gaze held by a sense of movement in the brownstone across the way.

"Can I freshen your drink?"

She held up a hand to silence him, something out there setting off alarms in her head. She stepped closer to the window, eyes scanning the darkened building across the way. There was a flash, and instinctively Madison pivoted and dived toward him, her eyes recognizing what her ears soon confirmed.

Someone was trying to kill Jeremy.

CHAPTER SEVENTEEN

GABE SIGNALED for the cabdriver to pull over and got out near the corner of York and Fifty-Seventh, wondering what in hell he was doing. He'd called the operations room looking for her, only to have Harrison tell him she'd already left. Heading for Jeremy Bosner's. She probably wasn't even there anymore—if she'd even come at all.

He glanced down at his watch realizing just how late it was. Still, he couldn't seem to stop himself, some insane compulsion to see her, to talk with her, driving him onward. Clutching the piece of paper containing Bosner's address, he crossed the street and headed for the little cluster of brownstones fronting the river.

The street was unusually dark, two of the three street lamps burned out or broken. Not something he'd have expected at this address. Usually when something happened around here, there were four or five city employees waiting in the wings to immediately right all wrongs.

Still, there was enough light to find his way, and he started up the street, then froze as a sharp hiss separated itself from the whining wind. His heart rate ratcheted up as his mind sought a logical explanation, but he'd heard the sound too many times to mistake it.

Someone had fired a gun, the silencer only partially muffling the sound.

He sprinted across the street toward the house belonging to Bosner, his imagination going into overdrive, his concern not for the man who lived there but for Madison. His heart twisted at the thought that she could be hurt, and suddenly he found himself empathizing with her father. Anything could happen in a profession like theirs.

Old memories fused themselves with the present to escalate his fear, his mind blanching at the thought of her dead, lying on Bosner's carpet, a bullet through her brain. He pushed the thought aside, not letting it find purchase. It couldn't happen again.

He simply wouldn't let it.

MADISON HIT JEREMY at waist level, her forward motion sending them both sprawling backward to the floor. She shifted to cover him as a second bullet slammed through the open window, this time shattering glass.

"Jeremy? Are you all right?" The whisper sounded louder than a cannon, and she waited, heart pounding for another shot. "Jeremy?"

There was no answer, and nothing more from the window except the shush of the wind as it slid through the broken glass, setting the curtains swaying. Carefully rolling to her side, she turned so that she could see the old man, her heart twisting at the sight.

Blood stained the front of his smoking jacket, the thick fluid darkening the velvet, matting it like old fur. Coming to her knees, she reached for his neck, her fingers confirming what she already knew.

Jeremy was dead.

Pulling her gun from its holster, she moved toward the window, careful to stay below sill height. Counting to ten, and satisfied that there had been no more shots, she inched up until she was level with the bottom of the window, staring out into the night, trying to locate the shooter.

The buildings across the way were still dark, and except for a swirl of dead leaves in the wind, nothing moved. No light. No flash. No gunshot.

She estimated no more than a few minutes had passed all told, which meant the shooter might still be there. Judging from the flash, her guess was that he'd been waiting in the abandoned building, his shot clear the minute Jeremy paused in front of the window.

In her mind's eye, she saw him standing there holding out the brandy glass. *Her* brandy glass. Ruthlessly she pushed all emotion away. There'd be time enough later.

Still holding the Glock ready, she moved quickly through the room and out into the foyer. The front door was closed, and on the other side she knew she'd become a target. She thought about calling for backup, but knew that it would take too long. If there was any hope of apprehending Jeremy's killer she had to move now.

She jerked open the door, staying behind it until she was certain there was no accompanying gunshot. Then, leading with the Glock, she swung out onto the stoop, keeping to the shadows, moving quickly down the steps, her gaze locked on the building across the way.

As she pulled open the gate, a shadow moved, and she swung her gun to the left, holding it carefully in her sights. For a moment nothing moved, and then suddenly the shadow stepped into the light.

"Gabriel." She released her breath, her lungs collapsing like an accordion. "What the hell are you doing here?"

"I heard a shot." His dark brows were drawn together, his eyes shining almost silver in the half-light. "I thought that—"

"Jeremy Bosner's dead." She cut through whatever he'd been about to say, recognizing the emotion in his eyes, and not ready to deal with it. "Two shots through the window. It came from over there." She gestured toward the scaffolded building with her gun. "I was just going to check it out."

"You're sure you're okay?" His gaze slid from her head to her toes, leaving a burning sensation following in its wake.

"I'm fine," she assured him, fighting to keep her voice level. "We're losing time."

He nodded, his attention shifting to the building across the way. "You stay here, I'll check it out."

A surge of anger hit her broadside, and she struggled to maintain control. It was a rerun of a common story. Most men she worked with ultimately tried to protect her, it's just that somehow coming from him it hurt all the more. "I'm coming with you. You need someone on your back."

He started to argue, then apparently thought better of it. With a nod, he started across the street, gun drawn. She followed, sequestering her resentment. The building's entrance was on ground level, and Gabriel motioned her to one side as they ducked under the scaffolding, the darkness intensifying.

She turned her back to him, the Glock trained on the street, her gaze vigilant. Nothing moved except the leaves rustling in the gutter and the trees bending in the wind, but she wasn't taking any chances.

The light from Jeremy's window spilled out across the sidewalk, giving the illusion that everything was all right.

"I'm in," Gabriel called, and she turned to follow him into the hallway. Unlike Jeremy Bosner's, this brownstone had been converted into apartments, one on each floor, with the staircase connecting the common space. There were drop cloths everywhere, paint cans and tools the only ornamentation. The building was obviously deserted.

Gabriel opened a door on the right and swung inside. "Clear," he said emerging again into the hallway. Madison opened the next door following the same procedure, and they alternated until they'd checked the entire floor.

"You said the shot came from up there?" Gabriel gestured toward the ceiling with his gun.

Madison nodded, already moving for the stairs. "Just above us, the room facing the street." She forced herself to climb slowly, pausing every couple of seconds to listen. Gabriel was right behind her, his eyes and gun on the hallway below.

Sirens wailed in the background, and Madison shot him an inquiring glance as they stepped out onto the landing.

"I called as soon as I heard the shot."

She nodded, grateful suddenly to have him here, despite his antiquated notions about women on the job. There was only one door on the second floor, and it stood open, light from the street filtering through, giving a sense of movement to the shadows.

"I'm going in," she whispered, steadying her hand on her gun.

Gabriel nodded once, his weapon trained on the landing, his eyes on the stairs, keeping watch. He had her back. There was an odd comfort there. And with a deep breath, she swung into the room.

The drapes rippled in the wind as it moaned through an open window. Shadows danced on the floor and wall, but other than their ghostly presence, the room was empty.

The killer was gone.

A TECH ZIPPED the body bag closed, and Madison shivered. Jeremy had deserved better. The little parlor had lost its cozy feel in wake of the forensics team, the fire gutted to embers, the overhead lights exposing fading upholstery and worn fittings.

She tipped back her head, rubbing her neck in an effort to relieve the tension radiating down her spine. It had been a long day. First the near miss at the apartment, and now again here in the brownstone.

Harrison hovered beside her, his concern written across his face. "You really ought to go home." His voice was a whisper, but it carried anyway, and Gabriel, standing beside the fireplace, frowned.

With a conscious effort, Madison straightened her back, and shook her head. "I'm fine, Harrison."

The twist of his mouth indicated that he didn't believe a word of it, but thankfully, he held his tongue.

"Would you mind walking through it with me one more time?" Nigel asked, and she turned to face him, forcing herself to focus, exhaustion warring with emotion to leave her more than a little woozy. "I just want to be sure I have it straight."

She'd already gone over it two or three times, but she understood the need to visualize, so she stood up, ignoring Harrison's hand. "We were talking. Jeremy was over there by the fire."

Gabriel continued to watch her, his eyes hooded, making it impossible to tell what he was thinking. They hadn't said anything much since the others had arrived. In fact, she got the distinct feeling he was trying to avoid her.

Not that it mattered what he was doing.

She returned her gaze to Nigel and continued her explanation. "I was over on the sofa. We talked about this morning's fiasco. I think quite honestly he was enjoying the excitement."

"And then you walked over to the window?" Nigel cut in.

"Yeah. Well, more to the left of it, I guess. It was open, and I was cold, so I didn't want to stand directly in front of it." She shivered at the memory, and then squared her shoulders shaking it off. "I was looking out the window, watching the wind in the trees, when I thought I saw something."

"And that's when Bosner got up?" Nigel was standing

by the wing chair now, moving in an approximation of Jeremy's path. Harrison was watching him as he too tried to visualize the events leading up to Bosner's death.

"Yes," Madison said. "He offered me another drink."

There was a cough from the direction of the fireplace, and Madison shot a look at Gabriel. His expression was impassive, but something glittered in his eyes, and Madison was pretty certain she knew what it was.

Blame.

Not that the sentiment wasn't deserved. If she'd been paying attention instead of chatting over brandy, Jeremy Bosner might still be alive. It *was* her fault. All of it.

"Madison?" Nigel interrupted her thoughts, his gaze going from her to Gabriel and back again.

"I'm sorry." She held up a hand. "It's been a long night." Gabriel moved again, this time turning his back on her, and she pushed all thoughts of him aside, focusing instead on Nigel. "I didn't actually see him move because I was still watching out the window. I shifted front and center, so that I could see better, and that's when I saw the flash."

"The shot."

She nodded. "From there I reacted on instinct, diving for Jeremy and pushing him to the floor. There was another shot. It's probably embedded in the wall somewhere. And then nothing."

"Forensics found it." Payton walked into the room, glancing down at the chalk lines marking the place where Jeremy had died. "Rifle cartridge. .223. Hopefully we'll get something from ballistics."

Madison nodded again, releasing another breath, trying to sort through all that had happened. Eight deaths. All of them murder. But definitely not by the same hand. Whatever was happening, the assassins were changing.

"This guy knew what he was doing." She glanced back

out the window, her gaze locking on the building across the way. "And he wasn't worried about hiding his actions. He had to have known I was in the house, and that I'd come after him. But it didn't matter, he killed Jeremy anyway."

"You could have been killed." Gabriel pushed away from the mantel, one fist clenched against his side.

"But I wasn't." She shrugged, avoiding his gaze.

"Only because he saw me coming." He took a step toward her and then checked the movement. "You shouldn't have come here on your own."

"I did what needed to be done. It's part of my job, in case you've forgotten." She clenched her jaw, hanging on to her control by a hair. "There was no way to know that the killer would strike tonight. My only mistake was reacting one second too slowly. If I had moved faster, maybe Jeremy would still be alive." Tears threatened, and she choked them back, cursing under her breath.

"Your reactions were fine." Harrison's hand on her arm was meant as comfort, but just at the moment that's the last thing she needed. She shook him off, still glaring at Gabriel.

Their gazes met and held, and she tried to read the expression in his eyes, but whatever he was thinking, it was well masked. With a sigh, she turned her thoughts back to the situation at hand. "Whoever the guy is, he's done this before. *Professionally.* There's nothing emotional going on here. No sacrifice for the cause, or anger at perceived wrongs. This guy calculated his every move."

"You're saying it's different from the earlier murders." Harrison sat on the arm of the sofa, the wheels in his head obviously turning as he, too, considered the situation.

"The first ones, certainly. There's a degree of intimacy involved with injecting someone with a drug, particularly with Aston and Stewart as they were killed on home ground. It would take a certain amount of nerve, but the risk is only worth it if the killer knew them and therefore had easy access, or if he wanted them to know who he was before they died. That's a far cry from a hit."

"And that's what you think Bosner's and Patterson's murders were." It was a statement not a question, but Madison answered anyway, her gaze meeting Gabriel's.

"Yes."

"What about the others?" Nigel asked, his brows furrowed as he weighed her words.

"Even more personal than the injections. Especially Robert Barnes. If our theory of the crime is correct, the killer knocked him out before the fire. Possibly an act of passion. Anger or something else. But either way, again he was there facing his victim. We see the beginnings of the change with Dashal and Smith. Although both murders were still rigged to appear as accidents, there was the start of a move toward the impersonal."

She stopped for a minute, gathering her thoughts, trying to see with the eye of the killer—or killers. "The killer wasn't present when Dashal was electrocuted. Or if he was, it was secondhand. It's doubtful Dashal saw him. And Bingham Smith was killed in a crowd."

"Same M.O. though as Aston and Stewart," Gabriel said, watching her with something akin to approval.

"Yes." She nodded, her confidence growing as she trod on familiar territory. "But with a major difference. There was calculation here. A plan. Busy platform, quick jab. And the killer is gone long before Bingham even realizes something is wrong."

"So our killer is learning?" Harrison offered the idea, but didn't sound as if he believed it.

"No." She shook her head for emphasis. "I think it means we've got more than one killer."

"Which begs the question why." Gabriel had shifted so that he could watch her, his expression inscrutable.

"It's hard to say. Shift of motive seems most obvious." She met his gaze full on, determined to hold her own. "Maybe whoever's pulling strings got tired of getting their hands dirty."

"Or maybe—" Payton picked up the thought "—in the beginning he actually believed one murder would be enough to throw off the accord, and when it didn't work, he tried again."

"And failed again," Gabriel added. "But if that's the case, then we're most likely talking about an individual rather than a group. Which would exclude our Chinese dissidents."

"Not necessarily," Payton said. "We've thought all along that they were using someone to do their dirty work."

"Yes, but that would mean they switched killers midstream." Gabriel frowned at his friend.

"It's not that unusual." Payton shrugged. "We're talking about a span of nearly three years, and our intervention has certainly changed the name of the game. If whoever is pulling the strings is worried that we'll get to the bottom of things, there'd be a need to escalate matters. That could easily explain the change of personnel and dropping any need to pretend the newest deaths were accidents."

"That makes sense, Payton," Madison said, her head starting to throb. "But it doesn't feel right. If someone overseas is pulling the strings, why not just use a professional from the beginning?"

"We don't know for certain that it wasn't a pro," Nigel said. "You said yourself that using potassium chloride isn't easy."

"No," she said, shaking her head. "I said it was personal. Shooting someone from a window across the street is impersonal. Looking them in the eye and stabbing them with a needle full of KCl is pretty much in your face. And the personality that is capable of one may very well not be capable of the other."

"So we're at an impasse. With one or possibly two killers and eight victims. And no sign at all of an answer." Harrison's voice seemed to be coming from far away.

Madison struggled to hear what he was saying, but the lights seemed to flicker, dark then light again, and she reached for the windowsill to steady herself. "I'm sorry, I…" A wave of dizziness washed through her, robbing her of speech, the reality of the evening's events suddenly hitting home with a vengeance.

Gabriel was at her side in less than a stride, his hard arms closing around her. She knew she should shake him off, assure him she was more than capable of standing on her own two feet, but just for the moment, she wanted nothing more than to let him hold her.

Damn it all to hell.

CHAPTER EIGHTEEN

"I DON'T WANT TO GO to the hospital, I want to go home." Madison sat back against the taxi seat and closed her eyes. "There's nothing wrong with me that a hot shower won't cure."

Gabe glanced over at her, not liking the pallor of her skin. "I think you should be checked out."

She crossed her arms, her expression mutinous even with her eyes closed. "I said no."

He'd never met a woman as stubborn. Or if he had, he'd obviously had the good sense to walk away without looking back. "So you're telling me your collapsing in the brownstone was just an act? That Jeremy Bosner's death didn't touch you at all?"

"You know it did." She acquiesced with an overly dramatic sigh. "But that doesn't mean I need to go to the hospital. There's nothing physically wrong."

"That's just the point, Madison. You watched a man die tonight."

Her eyes fluttered open, her brows drawing together in a frown. "That doesn't mean I need psychiatric help, either, if that's what you're getting at."

"Maybe not, but it wouldn't hurt to talk to someone."

"Not right now." The lights from the city illuminated her beautiful face, the pain etched there palpably visible. She might want to deny it, but Bosner's death had hit her hard. Still, he couldn't make her do something she obviously didn't want to.

"All right. You can go home. But only if you let me stay with you." He regretted the words as soon as they came out of his mouth. He had no interest in spending time with her. Especially not when she was so obviously vulnerable.

"I don't need a baby-sitter." She was so insulted she'd missed any sign of innuendo.

"No. You don't. But you also don't need to be alone. So here are the choices. Me or the hospital."

If he'd been a sensitive man, he'd have found fault with the length of her pause, but finally she sighed. "All right, then. I choose you."

He leaned forward to tell the driver, then sat back with a sigh. The undercurrent had returned, connecting them, the enclosed space of the cab adding to the intimacy. He shook his head, determined to ignore it, turning instead to her recent brush with death. "Have you ever seen someone die before tonight?"

"Not up close and personal." She released a breath, the sorrow in her voice ripping at him.

"Well, it takes a toll." His grip tightened on the armrest, dark memories giving credence to his words in ways she couldn't possibly understand.

"You've seen a lot of men die." There was a finality about the statement that resonated through the car.

"More than I'd have liked," Gabe admitted, uncomfortably aware that she was staring at him.

"Any of them your fault?" It was a fair question, but not one he particularly liked having to answer. Still, considering she was trying to deal with similar guilt, he felt compelled to do so.

"Most of them." *All of them,* his mind whispered. "I think you always believe there was something you could have done. Some precaution or other you should have taken. But hindsight is harsh. All your actions and their results clear to see. Carved in stone. In the heat of the moment, though, when things are happening too fast to process, all you can do is trust your instincts, rely on your training and then try and live with the results."

"And how do you do that?" Her voice was soft now, almost wistful.

"I don't know." He stared out the window, keeping his mind firmly on the present. "Day by day, I guess."

She nodded, the accompanying silence almost peaceful, the fragile thread of connection strengthening between them. He found himself wishing it could last, but knew from experience it would not.

"I'd gone to warn him about security, there's a laugh." It was a non sequitur, and there was nothing resembling humor in her voice.

"I'm the one who told you to talk to him."

"Not in the middle of the night." She was looking out the window now, staring without really seeing. "But I was restless."

"Madison, Jeremy would have died whether you were there or not." He pointed out the fallacy of her logic, knowing that she wasn't really listening, locked instead inside of her guilt.

"Oh, shit." She blew out a long breath, her hands clenching, knuckles white.

They had pulled up in front of her building, and he reached for her hands, surprised at how cold they were. "What is it?"

"That's my father's car." She tipped her head toward a black Beemer parked just across the street. "He must be up there waiting for me." She sighed again. "This is going to sound awful, but I don't think I'm up to seeing him right now."

"Madison…" He stopped, realizing his reassurances

weren't enough. She needed time to deal with it all on her own. He leaned forward and barked a new order at the driver, who quickly pulled out into traffic again.

"What are you doing?" Equal parts of hope and relief washed across her face.

"Getting you out of here." He shot her a grin, and received the ghost of a smile in return, the gesture making him feel reckless. Playing knight errant certainly had its benefits. "The great Philip Merrick will just have to wait."

MADISON STOOD in the doorway of the hotel suite, torn between gratitude and apprehension. On the one hand, Gabriel had saved her from an unpleasant confrontation with her father. On the other hand, they were now alone together in a hotel room, which, however innocent the reason, didn't negate the fact that the current running between the two of them was becoming impossible to ignore.

Gabriel was checking the room. Force of habit, no doubt, since no one knew where they were, or as far as she knew was threatening them. Still, it made her feel oddly protected to watch him checking the windows, light fixtures and telephone.

"It's clear. Why don't you take that shower? And I'll see about getting us something to eat."

She wasn't the slightest bit hungry, and the idea of being naked with him just on the other side of the door seemed at the very least a blatant come-on to temptation. But the idea of warm water won out, and she nodded, not certain she could actually find words, and headed for the bathroom.

There wasn't a lock, but she told herself it didn't matter. Just because her body was primed and ready didn't mean his was. He was watching out for his partner. Nothing more, nothing less. And she'd do well to get her mind out of the gutter.

She turned on the taps, and then turned to face the mirror, its candor not exactly welcome. Pale was an understatement; her eyes seemed three times their normal size. She'd been through far more horrific situations, and come out the other side without a scratch. But none of them had been personal.

Jeremy Bosner's life had been in her hands, and she'd failed him. She swallowed a sob, knowing that if she let the tears come, she'd never be able to stop them. And the one thing she was certain of in this life was the fact that you had to stay strong, no matter the obstacles. Only by focusing on facts and squeezing out emotion could she come out the winner.

She sighed, recognizing that she wasn't just thinking about her profession, she was thinking about her life. Stripping off her clothes, she stepped into the bathtub, and sank down into its soothing depth. Her problem was she thought too much. Overanalyzed everything. And just because the men in her life all seemed to think she needed protecting didn't mean she had to give in to the notion.

Her father meant well, she knew that. But it didn't excuse his cavalier behavior. In that he and Gabriel Roarke were cut from the same cloth. Or were they?

She settled back into the water, letting the warmth seep in. He'd been so different in the cab. More open than she'd ever seen him. Vulnerable, even. She laughed at the notion. Nothing about Gabriel Roarke was vulnerable.

He was one hundred percent man. The very definition of alpha male. And she'd had her fill of testosterone. The chest-thumping, hair-dragging, me-Tarzan-you-Jane scenario left her cold. Been there, done that.

So why, the little voice in her head nagged, did she still feel so attracted to him? She closed her eyes, willing the water to wash away her troubled thoughts, but instead it enhanced them, the soft lapping erotic, loverlike, against her skin.

In her mind's eye she pictured Gabriel's body hard against hers as he filled her, the exquisite sensation threatening to shatter her into pieces. Stifling a moan, she pulled herself out of the water, pulling the drain, and started the shower. Cold water was what she needed. Something— anything to banish her current train of thought.

Exhaustion played havoc with the mind, and she'd be wise not to give in. Even in fantasy, Gabriel Roarke was a dangerous man.

GABRIEL REPLACED THE TELEPHONE in its cradle, trying hard to ignore the sound of the water running and the torrid pictures it invoked. He'd called Cullen and assured him that they were all right, at the same time refusing to divulge their whereabouts. Madison needed some time, the night at least, to deal with things in her own way. And having seen her father in action, he understood her need to escape—at least for a few hours.

What he didn't understand was his need to help her. Something about her called to him in a way he couldn't explain. He'd fought against it, distancing himself from her in every way possible, but somehow despite the anger they always seemed to generate, he still was drawn to her. And if something had happened to her tonight...

But it hadn't. She'd performed like a pro. And he should be commending her, not wishing she'd change professions. A woman like Madison couldn't be coddled. That was the mistake her father was making. Sequestering her away from the world and all its dangers wasn't the answer, despite Gabriel's desire to join forces with the man and make it so.

Someone knocked on the door and he jumped, reaching automatically for his gun. A glance through the peephole assured him it was room service, and with a rueful shake of his head, he holstered the weapon and opened the door.

The kid behind the trolley looked all of sixteen, his uniform immaculate and about two sizes too big. Handing the kid a five, he closed the door, locked it, and pushed the cart to the center of the room, inhaling the wonderful aromas of the food.

He hadn't known what she'd want, so he'd ordered across the board. Appetizers, main courses, a salad, and even waffles for good measure. Surely something there would appeal to her. Again he marveled at the realization that he cared what she thought. When exactly had things changed?

Or more precisely, when had he accepted the fact that she was different from the others? An equal with whom he could share not only his body, but his thoughts? He frowned, pushing his rambling thoughts aside. He was acting like the kid with the trolley, all elbows, knees and hormones. And it didn't suit. Not at all. She was a colleague, and he was protecting her. He repeated the words again aloud, just to make sure they sank in.

Hormones were nothing more than a chemical reaction, and that was something he could control. There was nothing between him and Madison Harper. She wasn't his type, and he wasn't in the market anyway. Just because they'd been thrown together didn't mean he had to act on every foolish impulse he had.

For a moment he was tempted to call room service and have them remove the tray. Afraid suddenly of what she'd read into his apparent thoughtfulness. But he didn't have the chance.

A muffled sob caught his attention. At first he thought he'd imagined it, but then he heard it again, and as he stepped closer to the closed bathroom door, he was certain of what he was hearing.

Madison was crying.

He knocked, softly at first, and then when there was no answer, more firmly. He heard her moving, and what sounded like an answer, followed by more tears. A part of him wanted to move away, to ignore what he'd heard, but another part of him wanted to help, to make it better.

Without giving himself time to retreat, he pushed open the door, the misty steam pouring out around him. She was standing in front of the mirror, clad only in a white terry-cloth robe, her hair slicked back to outline the curves of her face, her feet and calves bare, the sight making his heart pound and his mouth run dry.

Both hands gripped the counter, as if by sheer force she could will away all emotion, the tense line of her shoulders an obvious contradiction to the effort. She turned to face him, still fighting for control, her pallor indicative of her torment.

But what touched him, what unmanned him, was the stark vulnerability in her eyes. He knew the look, had been there himself. She was doubting herself and her actions, uncertain suddenly of her ability to cope with a job that she loved.

Lust fled in a wash of empathy, the need to comfort overriding all other thoughts. He took a step, and without realizing it, opened his arms, and with a strangled cry, she threw herself against him, sobs ripping through her as if the world had gone mad. Maybe it had. He pressed his lips against her hair, the sweet smell of soap arousing in its simplicity.

"It's going to be all right." He knew that it was a senseless phrase, that it had no real meaning as he hadn't the power to make it okay. But he said it anyway, repeating it for good measure, holding her close, letting her cry, knowing that in doing so there was healing.

He'd been there. More than once. Second-guessing the past. Wishing for a second chance. And always with the same sense of hopelessness. Knowing that despite the best of intentions he hadn't made a difference. And someone had died.

He pulled her over to a wing chair and sat down, holding her in his lap, whispering nonsensical nothings, wishing he had the power to take the pain away, knowing that he didn't, that the only way she would heal was to face her fears herself.

CHAPTER NINETEEN

SHE SWALLOWED A SNIFFLE, and pushed away from him, mortified that she'd let herself go. "I don't—I mean, I—" She stopped, feeling every kind of fool. Gabriel Roarke didn't cry on his partners.

"I ordered food." He smiled at her, the gesture threatening to bring the tears all over again, but she held on to the last shreds of her dignity and took the offered escape.

"Wonderful." She slid off his lap, pulling the robe more tightly around her. "I'll just get changed and then we can eat." She refused to meet his eyes, staring instead at the red paint on her toenails, a foolish bit of vanity she clung to in the light of her often mannish apparel.

"Nonsense." He stood up, too, moving over to the cart. Madison could smell something wonderful, and to her consternation, her stomach rumbled happily in response. Out of the corner of her eye, she saw him smile. "The robe is fine. It covers more than an overcoat."

She wasn't completely convinced of the fact, but it was warm and comfortable, and she'd already spent a lot of time crying on his lap wearing the thing. Surely a little bit longer wouldn't hurt anything. And truth be told, she was famished.

She sat down on one of the chairs he'd pulled up, waiting expectantly as he pulled the lids off various dishes. It was as if she'd landed in the middle of a feast. French fries, hamburgers, pasta with some sort of vegetable sauce—and waffles. "You thought of everything." She grinned up at him, their gazes locking, and she immediately looked down again, not willing to accept the invitation she saw in his eyes.

Or thought she saw. As overwrought as she was, it wouldn't be impossible for her to be seeing something where nothing existed at all.

"Hopefully something here will appeal." He waved a hand at the table, a hint of uncertainty in his eyes.

"It's marvelous," she said, surprised at how very much she meant it. "I'll have the waffles. They're my favorite." She took a bite and sighed. "When I was really little I lived with my mother. And every Sunday she'd make waffles. It was sort of our special thing. No one else was ever invited. Just the two of us. And ever since, when things have been tough, I have a craving for them. Like they're some sort of panacea, I guess." She regretted sharing the minute she opened her mouth. Gabriel didn't care about her childhood desires.

"French fries always do that for me. Preferably McDonald's." He reached for the plate of French fries, his smile warm and encompassing. "Are you still in touch with your mother?"

Madison shook her head and swallowed a mouthful of waffles. "Only a couple times a year. She and my stepfather live in New Mexico on a ranch. It's just too far away from New York for regular visits." Put that way it sounded silly. Planes did fly both directions. "I was just a kid when I went to live with my father, and I'm not sure that Mother and I really ever reconnected."

"It happens." Gabriel shrugged. "But at least you still have her as a part of your life."

"I didn't even think about your parents. I'm sorry. You must think I'm awful. My mother is a free spirit. And it's always been hard to pin her down for visits and the like.

But she loves me. I know that. And I am grateful to have her around." It wasn't absolutely true. If she were honest, she'd have to admit she'd spent a lot of time wishing her mother was more accessible and her father was less demanding. Maybe if she'd spent more time accepting what she did have rather than trying to change what she couldn't…

"Everyone has to look at life from their own perspective, Madison. You of all people should know that. Just because I didn't have parents doesn't mean you can't be angry with yours." As usual he'd read her like an open book, the idea at once infuriating and intriguing.

"When you come right down to it though, for someone like you, my life must seem pretty damn easy."

Gabriel shrugged, reaching for a hamburger. "Everyone makes their own hell."

It was an innocuous statement, almost throwaway, yet she had the feeling it was also very telling. A defining statement that ought to give her insight into the man sitting in front of her. But for once her intuition came up empty.

She wrote it off to exhaustion, but a part of her recognized that maybe she was just too close to be objective.

"I agree with that, I think," she said, leaning back to look at him. "But there's more to it than that, isn't there? The key is what one does next that determines character."

"You mean whether they have the courage to claw their way out?" His crystalline gaze was assessing, and she shivered under the examination.

"Something like that. There are people who can't escape. Who only compound the problem, making it worse." She ate another forkful of waffle, turning her thoughts over in her mind. "And there are others who wallow in it. Taking pleasure from their own pain. So, yes, I guess I think the winners are the ones who find a way out."

"And what if there isn't a way out? What if the home-made hell is so deep and dark that there is no hope?" His gaze was intense now, as if the answer mattered very much.

"There's always hope." The words were out before she could stop them, and she watched his face darken. "No, wait." She held up a hand, stopping his retort. "I really do believe that. I think sometimes you have to search for it. And that it doesn't always present itself in the way you'd like. But I do believe that it's always there."

"Hope springs eternal." Cynicism colored his voice.

"Maybe not eternal, but often." She smiled, the gesture a peace offering. She hadn't meant to debate the fundamentals of life with him. "Maybe it's just a matter of knowing where to look."

He nodded, setting down the hamburger. "And maybe sometimes, it's just too much effort to find it."

They sat in silence then, and Madison wondered how she could feel so intimately connected with him, while at the same time he had withdrawn completely. It was maddening and compelling all at once.

Gabriel Roarke was a paradox. And though there were parts of him she frankly couldn't stand, there was a lot about the man that appealed to her on the most primitive of levels. Soul-to-soul.

Despite the differences in their backgrounds and personalities, there was a similarity she couldn't deny, and he recognized it just as clearly as she did, both of them simultaneously entertaining thoughts of running for the hills—even though neither of them was going to give an inch.

"WHERE THE BLOODY HELL is my daughter?" Philip Merrick spat at Cullen, pacing the Turkish carpet like an enraged sultan. His eyes were narrowed to slits, his mouth drawn into a tight line, his voice strung tighter than a Strad-ivarius.

"I've told you, Philip, I don't know." Cullen's voice wasn't exactly tranquil. The events of the night were quickly spiraling out of hand. First the near-miss with the purported hacker, then Jeremy's murder, and now Gabriel disappearing with Madison. "Gabriel just called to say that she needed a little time. He'll watch out for her."

"Like hell he will." Philip's voice had risen to a shriek. "You know as well as I do he's far more likely to use her and then leave her high and dry like that prick she married. You said the bastard called. Where did the call come from?"

"I don't know, he wouldn't tell me." Cullen did not like being put on the defensive, even when it was Philip. Especially when it was Philip. They'd been friends for a long time, but there had always been an air of superiority about the man that had irked Cullen. And there'd been times when Cullen quite cheerfully would have paid good money to see Philip being taken down a peg.

But now wasn't one of those times. Not when Madison was involved. On one thing they absolutely agreed, and that was their shared love of Philip's daughter. "He's not going to hurt her."

"You don't know that." Philip had calmed a little, if only so that he could think. "Did you star sixty-nine him?"

Cullen shook his head. "It didn't occur to me. I trust the man, Philip."

"Do it now." Philip was already looking around the room for the telephone.

"I can't. I've received other calls."

"Well, check the caller ID," he demanded.

"I'm not going to second-guess my command team just because you feel like you've lost control of your daughter." Cullen shook his head regretfully, knowing his friend was about to explode.

"God damn it." Philip didn't disappoint. "I want to know where my daughter is."

And so they'd come full circle.

"She'll be back in the morning. Gabriel said so. She just needed time to sort through what happened. She was there when Jeremy was murdered. And you know as well as I do that she'll be feeling guilty about it."

"It wasn't her fault," Philip snapped.

"Of course not, but that's not the way she'll see it. Gabriel's been through this kind of thing before." He reached out to pat his friend, an obviously ineffectual way to placate him based on the glare he got in return. "He'll know how to help."

"I don't want him to help her. I don't want him to do anything to her." This last was said through gritted teeth.

"I know that, Philip. But she's a grown woman, and she has to make her own choices."

Philip sank down on the sofa, burying his face in his hands. "I should never have let her get involved in all of this."

"You couldn't have stopped her." Cullen sat in the chair across the way, exhaustion gnawing at him.

"But you could have." Philip lifted his head, his eyes flashing with accusation. "It's your fault she's part of this. You used her."

An unaccustomed wave of guilt crept up the back of Cullen's neck. "Maybe so," he acknowledged on a sigh, "but she came willingly. And she's not the innocent you pretend she is, Philip. She's an FBI agent, along with all that entails. Furthermore, she's good at what she does. Quite possibly the best. And I need her expertise, it's as simple as that."

"It's not that simple and you know it. She's your goddaughter, for God's sake. You're supposed to care about her." His voice was rising again. "But instead, as usual, you've put your interests ahead of everyone else's. Has it occurred to you, Cullen, that she could have been killed tonight?"

"Of course it occurred to me." He clenched his fists, fighting the emotions rippling through him. "And scared the hell out of me, as well. But again, I remind you, it was her choice to put herself into the line of fire. Not mine."

"And how do you figure that?" Philip asked, his voice deceptively soft.

"She's a professional. How many times do I have to say it? If she wasn't here, she'd be off on some other case, and for all you know it could be even worse."

Philip stood up, crossing over to the chair, towering over Cullen. "If anything happens to my daughter, Cullen, I swear on everything I hold holy that I'll kill you myself. Am I making myself clear?"

"Perfectly," Cullen said, holding himself together by the most tenuous of tethers.

Philip strode from the room, anger radiating with every step. Cullen could almost smell the rage. Or perhaps it was fear.

His fear.

Nothing was going as planned. Everything seemed to be falling apart.

Dear God, what had he done?

"I'M SORRY, I didn't mean to sound so philosophical. Guess it's just the morbidity of the evening," Madison apologized, pulling the robe closer about her shoulders.

Gabe pushed away the last of his burger, and tried not to stare at the expanse of skin exposed by the vee of the robe. She'd hit a nerve. Several in fact, but he wasn't about to reveal more than he'd already let slip. If concentrating on her more salacious assets would keep his mind occupied and his mouth shut, then so be it.

"It was just talk." He shrugged, managing to keep his voice light, almost flip, but he could tell she wasn't buying. "You get enough to eat?"

She glanced down at her plate, looking almost surprised to see it empty. "I'm fine."

"There's still dessert." He lifted the lid on a piece of chocolate pie, his mind already picturing her savoring it.

"No thanks." She smiled, her expression suddenly guarded. "I think I've already had enough."

He wondered if there was really subtext to her words, or if he was merely projecting his emotions onto hers. Either way he needed to pull back. This wasn't what he wanted. If he couldn't still see the signs of her exhaustion, the barest hint of pain, he'd be heading for the nearest bar.

But he couldn't leave her on her own.

She needed someone with her. And if her father was out, so was Cullen. And he sure as hell wasn't going to leave her with Nigel or Payton. They were his friends, but he was also more than aware of the fact that they were full-blooded males, and Madison in a terry-cloth robe would try the sexual patience of a saint.

And his friends weren't exactly deity material.

Harrison Blake was even worse. Just a friend. *Yeah, right.* Not unless the man was a eunuch. Gabe frowned, emotions swirling inside him with the force of a whirlwind.

"Are you okay?" Her face was creased with concern, the expression sending his heart hammering. If she only knew….

"I'm fine. I was just thinking about the case. About Bosner's murder." As soon as the words left his mouth he willed them back.

Her face tightened and she wrapped her arms around her waist, the combined gesture making her seem all at once lost and frightened.

"I'm sorry, I shouldn't have said that."

She shook her head, visibly pulling her emotions into control, or at least keeping them well masked. "Don't be ridiculous. It's our case. We have to talk about it. I don't know why I'm letting it get to me this way. I know better."

She said it as though she could control the emotion, but Gabe knew better. Guilt was an insidious thing, whittling its way deep inside you, twisting around your gut until it was almost inextricable.

"You can't control what you feel, Madison."

"Of course I can." The words were uttered with enough gusto for four people, but it still didn't sound as if she believed them. "I don't have a choice really, do I? Not if we're going to figure out who's behind all of this. One thing's for certain, I don't want Jeremy's death to have been for nothing."

He had to admit she had spunk. Still, he worried that suppressing it would only make it all that much worse later on. Not that there was a thing he could do about it. She had to find her own way. He more than anyone recognized the truth in that.

"They'll go over the apartment and the building across the way with a fine-tooth comb. If there's anything to find, we'll find it."

"That's just the problem." She chewed on her lower lip, a sure sign she was wrestling with something. "Whoever our assailant is, he doesn't make mistakes."

"Everyone makes mistakes. We just have to find them."

"Maybe." She was frowning now. "But it's almost like two different things are happening here. First the murders. And then the hacker and our attempt to catch him."

"What are you getting at?" Gabe asked, intrigued.

"I'm not sure really." She leaned forward, the robe gaping open a bit, but Gabe forced his mind to stay focused on her words. "The murders, even in the beginning, have been performed with a certain degree of skill. At first in an obvious attempt to avoid being caught, and then with the proficiency of a hit man."

"Right. You said earlier that it almost seemed like two different killers."

She nodded, her brow still furrowed in thought. "I think that makes sense. But what I'm talking about here would be a third player."

Gabe's eyebrow shot up in question, his disbelief palpable.

"Not a third killer," she clarified. "But I'm not convinced the hacker is related to our killer. At least not directly. I mean, look at the merry chase he's been leading us on. It's almost like he wants us to catch him."

"Which is the exact opposite of the killer. But maybe he's playing two games with us. A blatant attempt to confuse."

"Maybe." She tilted her head and sighed. "But it doesn't feel right to me. Why would he make the effort?"

"To distract us? Or maybe it is a separate person. Someone who is part of the same group and therefore honestly playing the role of decoy."

She sat back, playing with a now cold French fry. "It's possible. Maybe even makes sense. Especially since the diversion—if that's what it is—didn't start until we were on the job. But I'm still thinking the explanation is something more than that." She shook her head. "But I'll be damned if I know what."

"Payton and Harrison are working on finding something to tie W. Smith to a flesh-and-blood person. And if he's one and the same as the killer, we're in business. If not—" Gabe shrugged "—then maybe he'll be attached to our terrorists and through that link we can find the killer."

"All of which takes time." Madison stifled a yawn. "And that's something we simply don't have."

"Not with consortium members dropping like flies." She shuddered, and he immediately regretted his choice of words. "When exactly is the summit scheduled?"

"In ten days. Which means that the Chinese are likely to go ballistic when they hear about Jeremy's murder. And unfortunately there's not a lot we can do to soothe their fears. The truth is, someone out there is murdering people faster than we can process them. All of which spells trouble for both the consortium and the accord." She paused, her eyes saying what her mouth could not.

Cullen and the others were in immediate danger. And for Madison at least, that was more frightening than anything else the killer might hope to accomplish.

"Cullen knows how to take care of himself. I've seen the man in action, remember?"

"But you had his back." She was chewing her lip again, the strains of the day clear against the pallor of her face.

"I've got it again." Her face hardened, and he immediately amended the statement. "*We've* got his back." Unless Cullen was the one pulling the strings. Gabe didn't want to believe that, but it wasn't something he could ignore, either.

"We don't know that he's involved." Madison sighed, the lines around her eyes deepening. It seemed they were now communicating without words. A heady thought.

"All we can do is examine the evidence. You know as well as I do that eventually it will tell us what we want to know."

She nodded, but looked so forlorn, he reached out to touch her hand, not certain whether he was doing it for her or for him. He just knew he needed the contact.

Fire danced along his skin. He almost jerked back, but she turned her palm, her fingers closing around his.

"We'll make this right." It was as much a question as a statement, her eyes begging for reassurance.

His hellcat had a softer side, and the idea warmed him all the way through, her humanity lending her an air of vulnerability that he found enticing.

Hell, downright sexy.

Unfortunately she was also nearly asleep on her feet, which meant that her needs superseded his. So for the moment, it seemed, he'd been given a reprieve. Although it sure as hell didn't feel like one.

CHAPTER TWENTY

MADISON WOKE with a start, the neon lights from Times Square flashing a pathway of pulsing light across the floor. She could almost feel a tangible beat. The city breathing. She rolled over and stared at the ceiling, her mind turning to the man on the other side of the closed door.

Gabriel Roarke.

Just the thought of his name made her shiver in anticipation. She rolled over onto her stomach and pulled the pillow over her head. What she needed was sleep. Or rather, rest—honest-to-God, peaceful rest.

She flopped onto her back again.

Fat chance of it happening here. She toyed with the idea of getting dressed and going home. Surely her father was gone by now. She even went so far as to swing her legs over the edge of the bed, her eyes lighting on the closed door.

Leaving would mean walking right by him, and just at the moment, she didn't trust herself to successfully make that journey. Which meant she was stuck here until morning.

With a sigh, she stood up and walked to the window, looking down at the street. Even at this hour there was activity below. People walking along, some sauntering in groups, others hurrying, on their way home or off to meet friends.

New York—the city that never sleeps.

She laughed at her own silly thoughts. She'd lived most of her life here, and still she found it oddly foreign, as if she could never predict what might come next. It was exciting, but also a little insular, as if she were marooned in the middle of nineteen million people.

A lonely thought. She shivered, wrapping her arms around herself.

"I thought I heard you moving around." His voice was as smoky as the night. "Are you all right?"

She sucked in a breath and turned to face him. "I was just feeling alone."

"Part of what you do, I guess." He walked toward her, stepping for a moment into the dancing neon light. He'd pulled on his jeans but hadn't bothered to fasten them, the hair on his chest narrowing to a thin line that disappeared into the open zipper.

"No, it's more than that." She had the fleeting thought that she shouldn't be sharing—that it was too intimate—but the words pushed out of their own accord. "I mean, you're right of course, I do spend a lot of time living in killers' minds. Part and parcel of their nightmares. But this is something more, something I've felt ever since I was a little girl. Silly, I guess, but I've never been able to shake it."

"It's not silly." He took a step toward her, the dark engulfing him again. "I know the feeling. Or at least something like it."

There was always the chance that he was taunting her. In the dark it was impossible to see his face. But some part of her urged her to take the chance. To believe.

"It's almost as if you're alone in a room full of people." He spoke softly, as if to himself. "I spent my entire childhood like that. Always on my own, never trusting anyone. And then somehow it just spilled over into my adult life." She heard him release a breath, a sigh. "You may live in the monster's nightmare, Madison, but I have to live with him. Pretend I *am* him. And sometimes I wonder if there's anything left of me at all."

"What a pathetic pair we are." Her laughter rang hollow, and she felt the momentary fear that in saying it she'd somehow made it true.

"Not pathetic. Just self-aware." He was slightly mocking now, but the words included them both, giving a sense of connection rather than rejection.

She liked the way it felt. Liked the way the darkness enclosed them, a cloak protecting them against the dangers of the night. As if he'd read her mind, he closed the gap between them. His breath brushed across her face, and then he was kissing her, his hunger only surpassed by her own.

She wound her hands through his hair, savoring its soft, springy texture. They pressed together, the heat of the moment combusting between them in a spiral of passion she hadn't believed existed in the real world.

Everything that was hard and unyielding about him came together in the moment, hot and demanding. And she matched him thrust for thrust as their tongues met and dueled. Each of them striving for power. Possession.

There was a current arcing between them, the connection incendiary. He was a take-no-prisoners kind of man and she reveled in the thought of what that might mean. His hands found the smooth plane of her back beneath the undershirt she slept in, massaging in circles, the friction from his callused palms erotic.

He moved slightly, his mouth trailing kisses along her brow line and down her cheek, finding the soft whorl of her ear, his tongue stroking the tender skin, a prelude of things to come. She pressed closer, feeling him hard against her abdomen, and knew he was aching for her as much as she longed to have him hot and ready inside her.

They danced around in a circle, Madison running her hands along the velvet muscles of his chest, while he felt for the hem of her camisole. She leaned back, lifting her arms, her eyes boring into his. In one fluid movement he stripped away the cotton chemise and, with a swallowed moan, pulled her back into his arms, his skin hot against hers, all velvet and steel.

He kissed her, then bit her bottom lip, the sensation somewhere between pleasure and pain, traveling first to her belly and then trailing fire to the wet place between her legs.

God, she wanted this man.

With a blatancy that surprised her, she slid her hand into the open waistband of his pants, gliding along the smooth skin of his abdomen until her fingers closed around him and moved rhythmically up and down.

With another groan, he swung her up into his arms and moved to the bed, setting her amidst rumpled sheets of cool cotton. She arched her back, her hands on her own breasts, their gazes colliding in a heat that was palpable. She let her hands trail slowly down her stomach to the apex of her thighs, teasingly running a finger across the crotch of her silk panties.

Silvery sparks flashed in his eyes. She shivered in anticipation, watching as he pulled down his jeans, his penis springing free, hard and solid, and one hundred percent male. With a smile that would no doubt melt icebergs, he straddled her, two fingers hooking into the elastic at her waist.

He slid the silk off, and she opened for him, her body humming with a life of its own. Dipping his head, he found the tender crest of one breast, drawing the nipple into his mouth, sucking it with a strength that sent heat rippling from breast to groin.

There was nothing soft about Gabriel Roarke, and she

realized that making love with him would be much like dancing with the devil, hot and fierce.

He let his mouth trail lower, his fingers massaging the soft flesh of her inner thighs, his tongue finding the hole in her belly, driving in, pressing skin against skin in a way that made her writhe against him, wanting more. Needing more.

His thumb found the soft skin of her labia, and quickly laid her defenses to waste, his fingers sliding deep inside her, his tongue still twisting into her belly button. She swallowed, the delicious tension inside her ratcheting up to levels beyond anything she'd ever experienced.

His thumb flicked against her like a mischievous feather, and she threw back her head and moaned, the sound guttural, coming from deep inside her. His mouth found her then, tongue replacing thumb in a flittering dance that made her buck against him, then struggle to escape the finely drawn pain he was creating.

But his hands found her hips, cupping her bottom and holding her in place, his tongue moving faster and faster, lightning streaking through her with each and every touch. She wanted more and yet she wasn't certain she could survive the passion he was unleashing inside her.

He sucked then as if she were nourishment, food for his soul, and she climaxed. Sensation, white-hot, breaking in icy shards around her, sending her beyond all reason, internal contractions so powerful that she thought she might die. She fought for breath, her mind swirling, and then cried out as the heat enshrouded her and there was nothing but sensation and the feel of his mouth upon her.

He moved, sliding his body along hers, until they lay pressed together, fitting like two pieces of a puzzle. She reached for him, and pulled his lips to hers, the kiss slower than before, but no less hungry. This time she explored the hot crevices of his mouth, the smooth surface of his teeth, feeling the heat rise in her again.

This was a game for two, and with a slow smile, she pushed him back, rolling over to straddle him. He reached for her breasts, the feel of his fingers against her skin exquisite. He rubbed both nipples until they were hard and throbbing, mimicking the shaft that pulsed between her legs.

She tightened her thighs, holding him locked against her vulva, the tiniest wriggle sending pleasure rippling through her.

"I need you, Madison." His words were low, almost a growl, and she marveled at his strength, his male sensuality. "Now."

Her lips curved into a knowing smile, and she enjoyed the moment of control, knowing full well that if he chose, he could change their positions in an instant.

Using her hands and legs she massaged his penis, loving the velvety feel of the head, envisioning it inside her, stroking her, filling her.

With a muffled groan, he lifted her with both hands, and together they worked to impale her. He was big and he filled her completely, her slick passageway stretched tight. Slowly, she slid upward, moving almost to the end, and then down again, pushing to take him deeper.

Amazingly the tension inside her was building again, stronger than before, demanding release, promising pleasure beyond imagination, the only reality the sensation between her thighs.

His hands circled her hips and he began to move with her. Up, down, in, out. Over and over again, deeper and deeper, their eyes locked together, a connection beyond the physical.

The heat between them built, flames of passion licking at them both, winding them tighter and tighter, pulling the thread taut, and then, with a shatter of sparks, sending them both flying toward the sun.

GABRIEL LAY BACK against the sheets, loving the feel of her body against his, her heat mixing with his, their breath twining together as they fought to slow the pounding of their hearts. He'd heard the term "little death" all his life, but he'd never really understood its meaning until now.

Madison had pulled things from him that he'd never even allowed himself to acknowledge. There had been more than a meeting of bodies here. Their climax had been intense, more than physical, his mind coming along with his body, the combination devastating and stimulating all at the same time.

Little death.

He smiled, stroking the damp hair from her face, even that simple gesture pleasurable. She shifted against him, turning her head so that he could see her face. Her eyelids were still half closed, her gaze still clouded with passion. He felt a surge of possessive pride. She was a wildcat. Giving as well as taking. The kind of woman a man dreamed of in the dark lonely hours of the night.

"That was wonderful." A lazy smile twitched at the corners of her mouth, then flickered away as if the movement simply took too much effort. She ran a finger along the plane of his chest, stopping to circle each nipple.

"More than wonderful, Madison." Her name sounded sweet in his ears. "Fucking amazing."

Her lilting laughter was better than any music he could think of. "That's certainly one way of putting it. But I can tell you it's not going to get you into the romantics' hall of fame." Her fingers had moved lower, grazing along his flaccid penis, each stroke awakening the fires inside. "Looks like with a little encouragement you might be up for a second round."

No talk of love and romance for this woman. Instead, she shifted so that she straddled his legs, leaning down to take his penis in her mouth, the wet heat getting an instant response. Her hand circled him just below her lips, and gently squeezed as she sucked, his mind turning to jelly as his hormones hit high gear.

She laved him with her tongue, the rasping almost painful to his oversensitized flesh, but wonderful nevertheless, and he twined his hands through her hair, urging her onward, loving the sight of her taking him deep into her mouth.

The spring inside him wound tighter and tighter, pleasure turning to need, need to desire. He wanted to be inside her. To watch her come even as he did. He moved slightly, pulling her head back, and she sat back on her heels, her eyes meeting his.

"Now?" Her smile was a little wicked, her fingers still kneading him.

He nodded, struggling for words, amazed at the emotions she aroused in him. "If you do that one moment longer it will be too late."

Her grin widened, and she moved to lie on top of him, her knees on either side of his hips, her breasts tickling his chest. Oh God, if there was a heaven, surely this was it. With a groan, he pulled her against him, rolling over so that he was on top, one knee between her legs.

It was his turn to torture, and sliding his fingers deep inside her, he began to move, his thumb flicking against her clit, watching as her laughter faded, replaced with passion. She pushed upward, taking him deeper, and then bit at his lips, forcing her tongue inside his mouth, finding the same rhythm as his fingers, her action reversing their roles yet again. The tortured becoming the temptress.

He moved his hand, and lifted his body, bringing it home with one smooth motion, driving deep, feeling her tighten against him in welcome. He stayed still for a moment, enjoying the simple pleasure of connection, the binding of his body to hers, and then unable to stand it any longer, he began to move, first withdrawing, and then driving deep and then deeper still.

She rose to meet him thrust for thrust, their bodies moving in mirror image, up and down, thrusting, parrying. A dance that drove him to the brink of exaltation. His body tightened in anticipation and then, with no further warning, exploded in a symphony of sound and light, the release beyond pleasure, beyond pain.

Madison arched against him one last time, thrusting upward, pulling him deep inside her. And then, crying his name, she came, her eyes wild, her hands linked with his, her body's shudders engulfing him, humbling him.

And just like that, Gabriel Roarke fell in love.

CHAPTER TWENTY-ONE

THE SUN STREAMED through the window, splashing across the comforter and into Madison's eyes. With a groan, she flopped over, trying to grab a minute more sleep, wanting frantically to hold on to her dreams.

Amazingly erotic dreams. She sighed and ran a hand over her breasts, then sat up, clutching the sheets, reality hitting her like a force ten hurricane. She'd slept with Gabriel Roarke. Well, sleep hadn't exactly been on the agenda. To underscore the fact, her muscles rebelled as she moved to sit on the edge of the bed, her eyes sweeping the room for some sign of the man.

His jeans were missing from the floor.

Surely a bad thing.

Or was it a good thing? Relief warred with alarm, leaving her giddy. On the one hand, she'd had the most adventurous night of her life. On the other, she'd strayed into dangerous territory. Caring about Gabriel Roarke would be a one-way ticket to heartache.

Despite the amazing connection between them, he'd admitted to being a loner, and more than that, she knew him to be something less than a liberated male. And her last experience in that department was enough to make her run for cover. She'd fought too hard to recover from the damage Rick had inflicted to jump right into that kind of relationship again.

But then, Gabriel wasn't Rick.

Her mind was quite emphatic on the point, and her body echoed the sentiment with a shiver of corporeal memory.

She pushed her hair from her eyes, confusion warring with desire inside her. She didn't regret last night, not one mind-shattering minute of it. She'd even be up for a repeat performance, but not if it cost her her heart.

Of course the point might be moot. Gabriel had apparently had similar qualms, the fact that he was currently MIA mute testament to the hard truth of the matter. The thought hurt a good deal more than she would have liked it to, and she realized that a part of her had already surrendered to the man—to the feelings she had for him.

Damn it all to hell.

She swung out of the bed, defiant in her nudity. Besides, there was no one here to see her. She'd just take a shower, find her clothes, and get back to business as if nothing had changed between them. It'd be a cold day in hell before she'd let him know the power he held over her. A romp in the hay. That's what it was. And that's the way she'd keep it.

Better there than to take it to the next level, where he was sure to revert to the protective nature of the species and object to the risks she took. Again the small voice in her head whispered that he was different. That he understood her need to walk the line. That he was in fact a kindred spirit.

But her feelings were too new, too fragile, and she quashed them before they could fully root, determined not to let her heart read more into the night than had honestly been there.

She searched the room for her abandoned clothing, finding her undershirt draped over a lampshade and her panties tangled with the covers at the foot of the bed. Heat crept across her cheeks, and involuntarily she raised her hand to her face, reliving every moment of the night before.

What the hell had she been thinking?

She hadn't, of course, that was the point. She hadn't been thinking at all. With a sigh, she sank down on the bed, her bravado vanishing as quickly as it had come. She wasn't the type to sleep around. And certainly not with a colleague. And yet, here she was—sitting in a hotel room without a stitch of clothing after a night of…well, suffice it to say, great satisfaction.

Sitting alone.

That was the operative word, really, wasn't it? Despite the connection they'd had the night before, he hadn't seen fit to greet the day with her. Instead he'd left her here, on her own, making him no different than any other man in her life.

With a sigh she pulled on her panties. She was back where she started. And if she lied to herself, she could accept the fact that it had been a great ride. But a part of her, a part she tried to keep sequestered, wanted more. Wanted last night to be about something beyond sex. Something spiritual as well as physical. Something romantic.

But those kind of things only happened in movies, and she was an idiot to even give voice to the thought. Little-girl daydreams had no place in real life. Especially hers.

She slipped on her camisole, and walked over to the chair by the window to retrieve the rest of her clothes. Her gun lay on the table, mocking her. Making all her fanciful thoughts seem shallow—ridiculous. There was no such thing as a soul mate, and just because Gabriel Roarke had made her come seven ways to Sunday didn't mean there was more to it than raw passion.

She stepped into her pants, and was just zipping them up when a sound outside the bedroom made her freeze. She reached for her gun, and moved slowly toward the door, her caution probably unnecessary, but as automatic to her as breathing.

The door slowly swung open, and Gabriel's smile faded to astonishment. "You going to shoot the waffles?"

He held a tray and Madison immediately recognized the smell. Lowering the gun, she felt the rush of heat as emotion threatened to swamp her. His hair was wet, and he wore only his jeans, his feet bare.

He hadn't left at all.

Some investigator she was—jumping to conclusions without even checking the facts. "I guess I overreacted a little."

The smile was back, this time with something she thought akin to tenderness. A lump rose in her throat, and she struggled to swallow, feeling all of about ten inches high, despite the fact that he was not even aware of her mistaken logic.

"Occupational hazard." He shrugged, walking over to put the tray on the bedside table. Then in two strides he was beside her, his arms closing around her. "I didn't want to wake you. You seemed so peaceful." He said it with a note of longing in his voice, as if he hadn't slept like that before.

"I was having good dreams." Her smile came of its own volition, her fingers stroking the unshaven stubble on his chin.

"Funny," he said, his breath tickling her cheek, "I had really good dreams last night, too." His hands were stroking her back, sending little shivers of pleasure dancing through her. Whatever her feelings for the man, he certainly knew how to rev her engine.

"I thought you were hungry." She wasn't sure what she'd meant by the comment, but it came out on a provocative note, his eyes darkening in response.

"I am," he said, one hand moving lower, cupping her bottom, the other closing around her waist, pulling her so close their lips were only centimeters away. "Just not for waffles."

She could smell the soap lingering on his skin, and she watched as a droplet of water fell from his hair to cling to his shoulder. Without thought for the consequences, she leaned forward and licked him dry, savoring the taste of his skin on her tongue.

With a groan, he crushed his lips to hers, their shared passion igniting into full flame again. The kiss was as much a contest of wills as anything, each of them trying to find control, and each knowing it was a losing battle.

Whatever it was between them, it couldn't be stopped. And suddenly Madison wasn't at all sure that she wanted to. He walked her backward toward the bed, each of them struggling to remove clothing without breaking contact, the effort making them both laugh.

There was an ease present this morning that hadn't been there the night before. As if somehow they'd crossed a barrier, opening themselves to each other in ways neither would have thought possible.

Madison pressed against him, reveling in the feel of his hard body next to hers, anxious to prove that the night hadn't been a fluke, that together they were better than apart. She fell back against the covers, pulling him with her, their lips still joined in an endless kiss that seemed to take and give and fill her all at once.

She explored his body, memorizing every part of him. Delighting in the daylight and the new sensory experience of watching him respond. He had scars everywhere. Symbols of who he was—how he lived. She kissed each with a sort of reverence, wanting to know everything about him.

He in his turn kissed her from head to toe, sucking and licking and tickling until she was writhing with need, all cognizant thought banished as she concentrated on the rising heat between her legs.

With a swift thrust, he was inside her, and they were

again one. Soaring together, reaching higher and higher, searching for release, craving it, yet cherishing the intensity of the ride. She bucked against him, wanting him deeper, wanting to lock them together, savor the moment, keep it as a treasure forever.

And then the world splintered into a kaleidoscope of color. She heard him call her name, his voice hoarse with his frenzy, his body slamming into hers, the rhythm almost desperate.

And for the first time in her life, Madison let go, surrendering herself completely to the moment and the man.

THE INCESSANT MELODY of a cell phone pulled Gabriel out of his postcoital lethargy. Madison was draped across him, her legs tangled with his, their bodies still linked together despite being totally satiated. He hated to break contact, but whoever the hell was calling didn't seem to want to give up.

He shot a look at the clock, surprised to see that it was almost noon. Not that he regretted a minute of his morning. He smiled at her, pushing the hair from her face, and she muttered something incoherent and turned in his arms, snuggling against him without waking.

God, she was amazing. He felt stirrings below, and quickly put the kibosh on them. First things first. Sliding out from under her, he sat up, and searched the room for the offending phone, only to have *Eine Kleine Nachtmusik* joined by the *William Tell* Overture. He wasn't sure what either ring said about the owner, and quite frankly, with the current cacophony he wasn't up to trying to figure it out. More important to stop it.

He reached Madison's phone first, and answered it with a terse hello, only to immediately wish he'd not picked it up at all. Philip Merrick was on the other end, and from the bated silence he was currently enduring, none too happy to have his daughter's phone answered by a man.

"Where's Madison?" Merrick finally barked into the phone.

Gabe looked over at the bed, only to see her burrowing deeper underneath the covers, a pillow thrown conveniently over her head. He had no idea if she was honestly sleeping or faking it to get out of a conversation with her father, but he wasn't inclined to put it to the test. Let the old man stew.

"She's sleeping."

"Well, wake her up. I want to talk to her." The man's apoplexy carried from tower to tower across Manhattan, probably sending electric meters surging along the way.

"I'll have her call you back, I promise. Right now, I need to answer my phone. So if you'll excuse me…" He didn't give the man the chance to answer, disconnecting and reaching for his jeans and the other phone—still happily playing the theme from the *Lone Ranger*—in the pocket.

"Roarke."

"Where the hell are you?" It seemed everyone was a little testy this morning. Cullen's tone was just this side of irate.

"None of your damn business." He felt a bit like Romeo and Juliet, only no one was on his side. And the Capulets were in bed with the Montagues.

"Is Madison with you?" The voice was more controlled now, as if his anger were being held in check.

"Yes. And except for everyone calling us, we're fine."

"I'm sure you are." Cullen sighed, the action negating some of the sarcasm in his voice. "But in case you've forgotten, there's a killer on the loose, and every moment matters. I was all for Madison having a bit of time to herself, but enough is enough. I want you both in my office in fifteen minutes. We need to regroup, and I need to provide tangible evidence to Philip that you haven't eaten his daughter alive."

Gabe contained a grin, thinking about doing exactly that. "An hour."

"Half an hour," Cullen insisted. "And not a minute longer. I've got a crisis on my hands, and the two of you are supposed to be fixing it—not each other."

"Fine. Half an hour." Gabe hated being dictated to, but Cullen was right; the respite was over. He clicked off the phone, turned toward the bed.

Madison had removed the pillow, and was sitting propped up against it, her hair spilling down over her breasts in a way that made his throat turn dry. "Anything new?"

Gabe shook his head, fighting hard against his hormones, feeling the effect of her nudity on his lower anatomy. "He just wants us in the office pronto."

"I'm not surprised, considering the body count. We should have been in an hour ago." She was reaching for her clothes, avoiding his gaze.

"You needed a break. Besides, until we get the forensics reports back, there really isn't that much we can do." He followed her lead, and began to dress, trying not to think about what her withdrawal might mean. "Cullen is just worried about the accord."

"Considering Jeremy's death, I'd say the concern is legitimate." She pulled her hair back into a ponytail, and then tucked her shirt into her pants. "But I'm still not convinced we're looking at organized terror. The M.O. is all wrong."

"The first half maybe. But not so much now." He frowned, still trying to pull out of his libido-driven haze. "And I think everyone agrees that the murders are tied to the accord somehow."

"It certainly seems that way."

"You don't sound convinced." He buttoned his shirt, his mind finally shifting to business.

"I'm not completely. But I don't really have anything to base it on, just a feeling. I think we'll know a lot more when we find an identity for W. Smith. Did Cullen mention whether Harrison had found anything?"

"No. He was more concerned with making sure we got the lead out."

She nodded. "When did you say we'd be there?"

"Half an hour." He felt like he was talking to a stranger, the resulting kick to his gut almost winding him.

"No good." She shook her head, slipping into her holster. "I need to go home and grab a shower. Why don't you go on ahead, and I'll meet you there. It'll…" She fumbled with her gun, finally sliding it into place. "It'll be better that way." She shot him an automatic smile, and with an angry grimace, he walked over and grabbed her by the shoulders.

"Just because your father disapproves doesn't mean that he's right."

Her lower lip trembled. "I know that."

"Then why the withdrawal?" He searched her face, trying to understand what was going on inside her mind.

"I just thought it would be better if we concentrated on business. Last night…" She trailed off again, looking down at her feet.

He placed a finger under her chin, bringing her head up, forcing her to look at him. "Last night?" he prompted.

"Last night was wonderful. You know that. But I don't want you to think I expect anything more. I…I appreciate what you did for me, but—"

"Don't give me that crap." He cut her off with a wave of his hand. "Last night was a hell of a lot more than me comforting you over Jeremy Bosner's death and you know it. Whatever is happening between us, Madison, it's real. And no one, not your father, not Cullen, not *you,* is going to stop us from seeing where we go from here." His anger peaked and then died, and he forced himself to meet her gaze head-on.

A tremulous smile threatened as she chewed her bottom lip. "I didn't mean to belittle it. It's just so new, and there's so much happening and—"

He cut her off with a hard kiss, and then abruptly pulled away. "We've got work to do. I'll head to Cullen's and you go home for that shower. But make no mistake, Madison, things between us are a long way from over. And I for one intend to make certain you don't forget."

The smile appeared again, and then she was gone, taking the light from the room and leaving Gabe more alone than he'd ever been in his entire life.

Whoever said that love was a bitch was abso-fucking-lutely right.

CHAPTER TWENTY-TWO

"I WANT TO KNOW what the hell has gotten into you?" Philip Merrick stood at the breakfast bar in Madison's apartment, looking like he was about to go three rounds with Mike Tyson.

"Nothing has gotten into me." Well, something had, but she wasn't about to share it with her father. "I just needed some decompression time, and I knew if I came home last night I wouldn't get it." She eyed her father over the top of her coffee cup, waiting for him to offer rebuttal.

"I'm sorry if I came on too strong." His attempt at contrite was just this side of believable.

Madison smiled. "Dad, the day you stop meddling in my life will be the day you're dead, so stop trying to pretend otherwise. And for the record, I'm fine. Honestly. I was a little shaken up last night, and Gabriel offered me a way out for a bit." An understatement that almost had her blushing.

"I'm glad you had the time you needed, but I hate the thought that you didn't come home because of me. I only want what's best for you." His expression was one she recognized, frustration and pride mixed together with a bit of bewilderment. Her father never had been comfortable dealing with a daughter.

"You want what's best for *you*. Or maybe just what you believe is best for me. But neither of those alternatives *is* what's best for me. I'm the only one who can determine that, Dad. And the sooner you get that, the easier it will be for both of us." It was an old argument, and she didn't really expect a breakthrough today. It was just an obvious way to turn the conversation away from Gabriel.

"I try."

He did not, but if he thought he did, then he got credit. She shot him a tolerant smile, thinking of Gabriel growing up all alone. At least she'd always had her parents—to some degree. And God's honest truth, it was better than the alternative.

"I love you, Dad. And I appreciate that you worry about me. But right now, I've got to get over to Dreamscape and my team. There's a murderer on the loose, remember?"

He opened his mouth to protest, but shut it again. Wise man. "Can I give you a lift?"

"That'd be great." It was as close to peace as they were ever likely to come, but he was her family, no matter how dysfunctional. "Just let me grab my gun." Even as the words came out of her mouth she realized it was the wrong thing to say.

"Damn it, Madison, I wish you wouldn't carry that thing around with you." He'd gone from penitent to mulish in something under fifteen seconds. Might be a record.

"It's hard to kill the bad guys without it." She shuddered as the thought brought back vivid memories of Jeremy Bosner taking a bullet. Her gun hadn't done him a bit of good.

"I'm sure you did everything you could, honey." Philip Merrick didn't use endearments, he didn't even do comforting very well, and here he was mind reading to boot.

She forcibly closed her mouth, her eyes on her father.

He shrugged, a smile lighting his usually stark features. "I won't pretend that I like what you do, Madison, but that doesn't mean I'm not perfectly aware of how good you are at your job. If anyone could have saved Jeremy it would have been you. So stop blaming yourself. All right?"

Madison wasn't sure how to take the new and improved version of her father, but she decided face value was usually best—with caution, of course. "Thank you for that."

Her father reached out to hug her, the gesture awkward and touching all at the same time. "I just don't want to see you hurt."

She pulled back, knowing that they'd stopped talking about her profession. Even without words, she knew her father was referring to Gabriel. And she would have shot back something pithy, except she wasn't sure that he wasn't right.

Whether she wanted to admit it or not, Gabriel Roarke certainly had the power to hurt her. Only time would tell if that in fact would turn out to be the case. She supposed she ought to guard her heart or at least pull back, but she'd tried that without much success. There was something about the way he looked at her that turned practical intentions to hard-boiled mush.

He'd said they'd take things as they came. That there was something worth nurturing. But she wasn't as sure. Experience was a hard teacher, and she'd learned from the master. Still, there was always the exception to the rule.

And on that thought, she rinsed her cup, and grabbed her gun.

GABRIEL WAS HAVING a hell of time concentrating on the files in front of him. If he were honest, he'd admit that it was because he couldn't keep his mind off last night, but instead he pretended he was just irritated with her for being late.

"You taking medicine?" Harrison asked without looking up from his computer terminal. The man had eyes in the back of his head. "That's the third time in the last half hour you've checked the clock by the door."

Gabriel didn't bother to answer, just shot another look at the blasted clock.

"I've got a ballistics match," Nigel announced. "Or at least I think I do." He was sitting at a separate computer station, looking at a graph of the bullet's serrations.

"I thought Tracy's forensics people were working on that." Payton, too, was working on tracing forensics data. He had spent the last couple of hours comparing the partial fingerprint they'd found at the abandoned apartment to those listed in AFIS.

"I just thought I'd get a jump on it," Nigel responded. "Beats chasing my tail. Anyway, I think I've got something."

Gabe pushed all thoughts of Madison aside and looked over Nigel's shoulder at the computer screen, Payton and Harrison flanking him on either side.

"Based on striation and composition, it looks to me as if our .223 is a match to one used in a confirmed terrorist attack in Beijing two months ago. Two shots were fired during an informational meeting between the Department of Defense and the Chinese equivalent. No one was hurt, and a local dissident group claimed credit. However, officials never identified the shooter."

"Was anyone from the consortium present?" Gabe asked.

"No." Payton shook his head in response. "I remember the incident you're talking about, Nigel. And at least when I cross-checked it, I found no personnel on either side that are currently involved in negotiations. In fact, I don't remember finding a ballistics report."

"I have a bit more pull than you do these days." Nigel tipped his head back to meet Payton's gaze. "The report is obviously need-to-know information. But considering the ballistics match, I made it clear that we needed to do just that."

Payton frowned, but held his tongue, and Gabe was grateful for his self-restraint. Nigel could be a bit of a prima donna at times, but it didn't change the fact that there was a match and that there was an apparent connection to their situation.

"So we have a tenuous tie between two events," Gabe said, "but nothing to lead us to the killer."

"Well, we do have the name of the group. And unless I'm mistaken, it's one of the two that Payton mentioned earlier as possible organizations that had reason to want the accord to fail."

"So who do they use for black ops?" Gabriel stepped back from the computer, the wheels in his brain cranking. "Payton, can your sources help pinpoint any names? Maybe there's a link between our W. Smith and someone they use in the U.S.?"

Payton nodded, his attention still on Nigel, his expression masked.

"I can check the data in our computers, as well," Harrison added. "By cross-checking the incident with the group itself, I might be able to come up with something I missed before."

"Good. At least it's something positive I can report to Cullen. Have you found a match for the fingerprint, Payton?"

"Nothing local. I'm checking state by state now. And I've got a call into Interpol to see if they have anything. I'll get back to you if something turns up. But to be honest I'm not that hopeful. There's not much here to go on. Certainly not enough for a statistically significant match. But I figure it's still worth a try." Payton shrugged.

"It's a step in the right direction. Anything else come back from Tracy's with regard to Bosner's shooting?"

Harrison picked up a report. "No casings or fingerprints on site. The building was supposed to have been locked, although there's no apparent tampering with the door. So either it was inadvertently left unlocked, or our killer knows his way around locks. Based on the epicenter of the shattered glass, the location of the slug in Bosner's wall, and the entry wound on the man, they're almost one hundred percent certain the shot came from the second floor window you found open." He looked up from the papers. "For someone to make that kind of shot he'd have to be really good. And have the right equipment. You said you heard a hiss?"

"Silencer, but not a big one. Just enough to muffle the report."

"All of which supports our theory that it's a pro," Harrison said, holding out the report.

Gabe took it, wishing that it held something more in the way of answers. Something that would help him nail the killer.

"Cullen's asking for us." The sound of Madison's voice surrounded him like an embrace, and he steeled himself to keep the resulting emotion off of his face.

She was dressed in black, her white button-down perfectly pressed, not a hair out of place. But in his head, he saw her naked, gleaming with sweat, her body locked against his. His blood pressure shot up, his heart pounding in his ears. Through sheer force of will, he banished the thought, managing somehow to keep his smile impersonal.

But their eyes met, and the message sent and received was purely sensual in nature. A promise of things to come.

"Let's go," he said breaking eye contact, trying to compose his jumbled thoughts. "I've just been getting an update of where we are, I'll brief you on the way."

She nodded, smiled at Harrison, which irked him more than he'd like to admit, and turned to go. He followed after her, knowing full well that three pairs of eyes were still locked on them. Eyes that were trained to see even the smallest detail. To find truth in lies, and reality buried beneath subterfuge.

In short, he was toast.

"SO BASICALLY WE'VE GOT nothing." Cullen Pulaski sat at his desk, hands clasped in an effort to remain calm.

Gabriel sat in a chair across the desk, next to Kingston. Madison sat on the windowsill, fidgeting with the blinds' cord.

"We know that the murders are tied together, and we believe there may be a link to an organization in China," Gabriel said. "Harrison and Payton are working to follow up on the lead."

"Where do things stand with the accord?" Madison asked.

"The Chinese are running scared, just as we suspected." Cullen picked up a pencil and twirled it between his fingers. Anything to help him maintain an illusion of calm. "The president got a call this morning."

"It's gone that high?" Gabriel frowned, surprise blending with concern.

"Started there, actually," Kingston said. "This has been the president's game from the beginning. We're merely the lucky players who get to dodge the bullets."

"And bring home the money, if it succeeds." Gabriel's eyebrow lifted, a hint of cynicism coloring his voice.

"There's always a payoff, Gabriel, you know that." Cullen shrugged, wondering again if he'd been wise to bring Gabriel and Madison into this.

"Yes, but is this one worth the price?" Madison's voice was soft, her eyes probing as she watched him.

"That's not a question I can answer." Cullen dodged the question as best he could, struggling to shift the conversation to safer ground. "Besides, it isn't my call. The president is the only one that can put an end to negotiations."

"The president or the Chinese," Kingston reminded.

"Which leaves us playing a bluffing game. We have to convince the Chinese government that everything here is fine, when in fact everything here is far from that."

"But you can't hide it from them, surely?" Madison stood up, rubbing the small of her back, and Cullen noticed the shadows under her eyes. "I mean Jeremy and Candace's murders have been all over the papers. You've managed to quash it a bit, but not entirely."

"Yes, but the connection between the two of them has been nothing more than speculation at this point. And that gives us what we need to create doubt."

"But there isn't any—" Madison started, but he cut her off with the wave of a hand.

"It's enough for now. And unless I hear something different from Washington, it's the way we're going to proceed. The summit is on unless I tell you otherwise, which means that we must work all that much harder to find the culprits and bring them to ground." He snapped the pencil in two, the pieces clattering across his desk.

There was silence for a moment as Gabriel, Madison and even Kingston stared down at the broken pieces of wood.

"A bit overdramatic that." Cullen laughed uncomfortably. "Why don't we write it off as symbolic of the tension we're all feeling. The clock is ticking, and I'm afraid we're at endgame, so to speak. If we don't stop it now, whoever is behind all of this is going to win."

"We're working as hard as we can, Cullen. But I can't make any promises." This from Gabriel, who was still looking at the pencil pieces.

"You'll make it happen, because it must be so." Cullen heard his voice rising, and struggled for control. It would never do to let them know just how panicked he really was.

"I'm not a miracle worker, Cullen, I can't conjure up a

killer just because you want me to." Gabriel stood up, towering over the desk, and just for a moment Cullen actually felt afraid. But just as quickly as it had come the emotion passed, and Cullen reminded himself that he was the one in charge, not the other way around. Gabriel Roarke worked for him.

He stood up, as well, the rising tension in the room palpable. "If I need for you to do so, you'll do just that. The president needs this accord to go through. Much of his economic policy rests on its success. And if he needs us to embellish the truth, then that's exactly how we'll proceed. Am I making myself clear?"

"Perfectly." Madison's voice was like balm. Calm and to the point, she obviously wasn't ruffled by their posturing. "But as far as I can tell, we haven't reached the point where untruths are necessary. All we have to do at the moment is keep as much information as we can away from the press, and continue our full-court press to find answers. Right?"

"For now." Cullen nodded, his gaze still locked with Gabriel's. "But if you don't find those answers soon, we may have to take more drastic action."

"Like lying," Gabriel growled.

Kingston shrugged, like Madison, purposefully ignoring the undercurrents. "Whatever it takes, I'm afraid. This is about a hell of a lot more than the money we have invested. And with Washington pulling the strings, anything is possible."

"But right now it's status quo." Again Madison was the voice of reason.

"Yes," Kingston admitted.

A knock on the door interrupted the moment, and Cullen for one was grateful for the reprieve. He hated pissing matches, and even though he usually won, taking on Gabriel Roarke was not a task he had any particular relish for. "Come in."

The door swung open, and Harrison Blake poked in his head, his expression reflecting his obvious reticence to interrupt. "Sorry to barge in," he said, stepping fully into the room, "but I thought you'd all want to know."

"Know what?" Gabriel swung around to face him, the line of his back still radiating tension.

"I think we may have found W. Smith."

CHAPTER TWENTY-THREE

EVERYONE HAD MOVED to the operations room, and as far as Madison was concerned it couldn't have been too soon. She had no idea what had gone down between Gabriel and her godfather in Iraq, but it was pretty clear from the posturing in Cullen's office that there was a certain amount of animosity still present.

She shook her head, clearing her thoughts. Maybe it was nothing more than the fact that neither Cullen nor Gabriel was the kind of man to take orders easily from another. And the truth of the matter was that she had enough to deal with without trying to understand the dynamics between the two of them.

Point in case: W. Smith.

Harrison had moved to his computer, as usual preferring the anonymity of his kiosk to center stage. Low-profile, old-fashioned and charming, Harrison was the kind of man who opened doors for women, and really listened when they talked. He had that sunny grin and Southern charisma that made him irresistible to the opposite sex. Which was only heightened by the fact that he was totally oblivious to his effect on women. He was too immersed in his own little world.

"So I tried aliases like Payton suggested," Harrison was saying, his voice holding an edge of excitement that meant he'd found something more than just a name, "but I couldn't find anything remotely connected." He paused, looking up at the assembled players, a smile twitching at the corners of his mouth. "And then I ran the *W* as a middle initial."

He clicked on the computer database for effect, and the scanning names flashed by to settle on one.

Ernhardt W. Schmidt.

Madison shot a look at Gabriel, surprised to see a similar look of excitement reflected in his eyes. He was enjoying himself. She fought her own smile. She was surrounded by little boys.

"Ernhardt *Wilhelm* Schmidt." Harrison read the words on the screen, supplying a name for the W. "His sheet is a mile long. Everything from suspected bombing to sniper activity. But the best is that he's a crack shot." He hit another button and a face filled the screen.

Ernhardt Schmidt had blond hair and blue eyes, and the aquiline nose of a German. His features were hard, but it wasn't the face of a killer. Not that they ever were. Killers came in all shapes and sizes and rarely were they recognizable. Most of them had had years to perfect their masks.

Only someone who spent their life observing them could read the signs. The cruel twist of the lips, the hard edges to the smile. The total lack of emotion in the eyes. This was a man who'd ceased feeling anything a long time ago. Or perhaps had never felt at all, something inside him programmed differently from others.

Not a fiend in the sense of a serial killer, just a man without remorse or regret, driven by his own needs, interested in getting paid more than the pleasure of the kill. Although the kill itself would yield some form of release, just not an end in and of itself.

She pulled away from the photograph to meet Gabriel's questioning gaze. She knew that he'd seen her withdraw. Watched as she put herself in another man's place, tried to think with his mind. Some men would have been frightened by it. Or repelled.

But not Gabriel Roarke.

His mouth curled into the smallest hint of a smile, and she would have sworn she read approval in his eyes. Hope fluttered inside her.

Maybe she'd finally found someone who could understand.

"Madison," Cullen interrupted her thoughts, and reluctantly she turned from Gabriel's icy gaze, "have you seen this man before?"

"No." She shook her head. "But I know the type." She proceeded to outline her thoughts for the group.

"So he fits the profile for our killer?" Kingston asked, his brows drawn together in a frown.

"I can't say for certain without more evidence." Madison blew out a long breath. "But if I had to go with my gut alone, I'd say he meets all the necessary criteria. Unfortunately, if he's any good, he'll be hard to trace. I'm surprised we've been able to find out as much as we have."

"I agree." Payton's expression was troubled, his eyes narrowed in thought. "I've said all along that this has been too easy."

"Easy?" Cullen exploded. "Eight people are dead, a crucial economic accord is hanging by a thread, the president is politically vulnerable and we still have nothing concrete to tie us to a killer or a group behind the murders. Just what about all of that, may I ask, is easy?"

Payton shrugged. "I don't pretend to understand the ins and outs of the political maneuverings of governments, Cullen, but I do know how these kind of men work. And they don't leave calling cards. If they do, they wind up dead."

"So what?" Kingston asked, clearly intrigued. "You think the man wants us to find him?"

"I've no idea," Payton said. "I just know it feels off to me."

Madison understood exactly how he felt. "One doesn't last very long in this business without trusting gut instincts, Kingston. Even if they aren't quantifiable." She shot a look at Gabriel, disappointed to find his expression masked.

"Well, I think we're well on the way to finding our man." Cullen's tone was decisive, clearly intent on taking control of the discussion.

"If only it were that easy," Harrison mumbled.

"Do we have any idea where Schmidt is?" Gabriel asked.

Harrison responded with a shake of his head. "He moves a lot. Last known address was in Hamburg. But that was almost a year ago. I've got sources there checking to see if it's still valid."

"I'm betting not," Gabriel said. "If he's our man, he's been here for quite some time. Although he could be going back and forth. Any known aliases for him?"

"The list is pretty long." This from Nigel, who was holding a printout. "We're cross-checking the computers to see if there's anything in any of the other data banks. He's been tagged by your home security forces, so with a little luck that means they're watching him for entry into the States. I've got a call in to London to see what they know."

"How about W. Smith? Does it show up as a known alias?"

Harrison shook his head. "We only found him because of the correlation between the names. Other than that we have nothing to tie him to our murders, really."

"Except that the M.O. for the last few murders fits him to a tee." Gabriel shot a look at Madison for confirmation, and she reveled in the fact that at least for the moment he'd accepted her as part of the team. "Payton, have you talked to Lin Yao?"

"Yes. He'd heard the name. But couldn't confirm that the man had actually worked with either of our suspected groups. He's supposed to see what he can run to ground in Beijing and get back to me as quickly as possible."

"All right." Gabriel was all business now, preferring action to cerebral gymnastics. "I'll check with some folks I know at Langley. Madison, you talk to the FBI, and the rest of you follow up where you can. Cullen, you and Kingston talk with anyone you think needs to know the situation, but other than that keep it as low-profile as possible.

"If this guy is in the city, I don't want to scare him off." Gabriel glanced down at his watch. "Why don't we all meet back here in an hour. We're running out of time. And we need answers ASAP."

MADISON SAT in the office of the FBI's regional director in New York. She'd met the man a couple of times, but had never actually worked with him, and even though she had clearance from a presidential level, she still was uncomfortable coming to him for help, particularly since she could only give him sketchy information at best.

"Ms. Harper." Loren Waxman was short by FBI standards, and perhaps a tad long in the tooth. She figured he was nearing sixty, which was surprising in an organization that prided itself on only hiring the best, the brightest, and the youngest. Still, the man moved with a grace that belied his age, and although his hair was gray, his dark eyes sparkled with intelligence.

"Mr. Waxman." She stood up and offered her hand, pleased when he shook it with vigor. "Thank you for agreeing to see me on such short notice."

Waxman took a seat across from her, laying a manila envelope on the table between them.

"You'll have read the file I've provided."

He nodded, waiting for her to explain further.

"As you know, I've been pulled out of active duty to work on a task force for Cullen Pulaski."

A muffled cough was indication of his disapproval. Not that Madison disagreed. "I know about the task force. And to some extent its purpose. What I'm not clear on is what you think I can do to help you."

"I need access to any information we might have on a mercenary by the name of Ernhardt Schmidt. Most importantly his present location, if we're aware of it. The files I need to check are eyes-only, and I need your permission to access them."

She could have gone above his head, but she wanted to ruffle as few feathers as possible, and following chain of command would go a long way toward keeping things on an even keel.

"You think this Schmidt has something to do with the case you're working on?" Waxman's expression was bland, disinterested even, but she could see the spark of curiosity in his eyes.

"Yes. I have reason to believe he may have been responsible for a series of deaths I've been investigating." And that was as far as she could go by way of explanation. Hopefully, it would be enough.

"You have friends in high places, Ms. Harper." There was a note of disdain in his voice that Madison wished she could erase, but there was nothing she could do about it. She did have friends in high places. Or at least family members who liked to throw their weight around.

She fought off a sigh, smiling instead. "My godfather is well-placed politically, yes. But I've never used it to my gain."

"Nor your father, it would appear." If it was meant as a compliment, the slight edge to his tone took anything positive out of the remark.

"I didn't request this case, Mr. Waxman, but now that I am working on it, I intend to give it my all." She tried but couldn't keep the note of resentment out of her voice.

"Whether you requested the case or not, you've obviously made some powerful allies. I even received a call from the director, and I assured him I'd help in any way I can." He pushed the manila envelope over to her. "Inside you'll find everything you need to access the secured computers. There's also a dossier on Mr. Schmidt. He's a nasty character from the looks of it. I hope you know what you're doing."

"I'm doing my job." Madison took the file, and stood up, more than ready for the meeting to end. "And if that's not enough, I've got good men at my back."

She'd almost said "powerful men," but that would have been a bit much, and besides, Waxman probably would have missed the point anyway.

"WHAT'VE YOU GOT?" Harrison looked up as Madison walked into the operations room. He was sitting at the conference table with computer printouts spread all around him.

"Not as much as I'd have liked." She dropped down into a chair, and slid the FBI file across to him. "I just got back from meeting with Waxman. That's the file he gave us."

"You met with Waxman? I've heard the old buzzard's a real piece of work."

"He wasn't thrilled with the fact that I came with presidential backing, but other than that he wasn't too bad. Although I doubt he'd have given me a plug nickel without the call."

"Not a fan of the young and upcoming agent, eh?" Harrison's smile held sympathy.

"Not exactly." She shrugged out of her coat. "Anyway, the point is that we got what we needed."

"Anything helpful?"

"I scanned the file and it fills in a few blanks here and there. Schmidt definitely works for the highest bidder with absolutely no loyalty to anything but a paycheck. He has been tracked to the U.S., but never tied to any kind of illegal activity here. Although there have been questions."

"Anything that would connect him to the accord?"

"Nothing in the dossier, but it's pretty general. There are also some user IDs in there, stuff that will give you access to the highest-level information the FBI has on the man. I figured you'd be better at ferreting it out than me."

Harrison opened the envelope with a relish he usually reserved for a Big Mac. "This is pretty impressive stuff."

"That's what an alliance with the president will do for you." She smiled, but knew the gesture wasn't reflected in her eyes. Truth was, she was dead tired. Too much was happening too fast, and she hadn't any idea how to sort it all out. Personal vs. business getting all jumbled together in a way she'd never intended.

"You okay?" Harrison was looking at her suspiciously, seeing far more than she wanted him to.

"I'm fine," she chirped brightly, knowing immediately that he didn't buy a word.

"You don't look fine. And if I had to call it, I'd say it had something to do with Gabe."

She started, and fought a blush. "He helped me evade my father."

"And that's all?" Harrison asked.

She wanted to tell him, to ask his advice, but no matter how close they were, there were some things she simply couldn't share. At least not until she understood them herself.

"Isn't that enough?" she asked, dodging his question.

"I was pretty shaken by Jeremy's death. And I wasn't up to battling my dad. Gabriel realized it, and bought me some time. And I can't say that I wasn't grateful."

"I agree you needed time to decompress. Your dad can be a bit overwhelming. But I'm not sure you didn't jump from the frying pan into the fire."

He was absolutely right, of course; she'd swapped one set of problems for another. Granted, the latter had been incredibly pleasurable as far as problems went, but she still had no idea where she and Gabriel could go from here.

All she knew for certain was that he'd muscled his way into her heart, and the idea scared her to death.

NIGEL STOOD OUTSIDE the building, counted to ten, and when he was certain no one was following, walked quickly down the street, ducking into a blind alley about two blocks away. He pulled out his cell phone and dialed a series of numbers, entering two passwords, one vocal and another alphanumerical.

Finally he was connected, the voice at the other end impatient.

"What do you mean they found the man?"

"Just what I'm telling you. They've connected W. Smith to an Ernhardt Wilhelm Schmidt. And they're pretty damn sure he's the one. Gabriel has everyone running down the details as we speak."

"And you?" The man at the other end sounded more annoyed than angry, which surprised Nigel no end.

"I'm supposed to be talking to London."

There was a burst of laughter from the earpiece of the phone. "How convenient. And what will you report back?"

"That Ernhardt is indeed connected to the subversive group in China. But I'll need physical evidence to support the fact."

"Consider it done. And Nigel—" there was a pause, and

then the voice continued, the tone almost menacing "—I want you to find the man and make quite certain he doesn't surface. Am I making myself clear?"

Nigel swallowed, not certain how he was going to accomplish this latest command, but not willing to indicate his concern. "Of course, sir. I'll get right on it."

"See that you do." The line clicked dead, and Nigel gripped the phone in anger, wondering how in hell he'd ever allowed himself to land in such a position. A rock and a hard place if ever there was one, and a misstep in either direction could very well leave him dead.

Which was a position he didn't relish in the slightest.

CULLEN HUNG UP the phone and sat staring at it for what seemed an eternity. Even with the team close to unraveling the whereabouts of Ernhardt Schmidt, he was still battling with the Chinese and the president. Fighting to keep things alive, when in reality they were probably already dead and buried.

He sighed, and buried his head in his hands, wondering exactly how he'd found himself in this position, knowing the answer without even having to think about it. Greed. Pure and simple greed. His desire for more outstripping all common sense.

He'd played the game and now potentially he'd lost it. Only a last-minute Hail Mary could save him now. The grandfather clock in the corner ticked ominously, the great pendulum swinging back and forth as if it were a death knell.

A requiem for all that he was and had been and perhaps would never be again.

Greed.

What a nasty word.

CHAPTER TWENTY-FOUR

"ALL RIGHT, so what have we got?" Gabriel paced in front of the operations room window, his gaze encompassing the group gathered around the conference table.

Harrison fidgeted with a pile of papers, his ever-present laptop open in front of him. Payton sat in the corner, the back of his chair tilted against the wall. Nigel straddled the chair next to Madison, his attention apparently focused on a report he held in his hand.

"The FBI dossier confirms what we already knew," Madison said. "Unfortunately there's not a whole lot else. Waxman did provide passwords for computer access and I turned them over to Harrison." She shot a smile at her friend, ignoring the resulting scowl from Gabriel.

"And what did you find?" Gabriel snapped at Harrison, the sound making the younger man jump.

"Ernhardt has been on a watch list since the early '80s. He's been tracked to the U.S. at least fifteen times, spending most of his time at various places on the East Coast. As expected, he keeps a low profile. Generally uses an alias, and to date has not been attached to any particular scheme. Although he has been linked to several plots against various political personalities—including some speculation that he may even have taken part in U.S.-sanctioned operations abroad. In fact, the bulk of his activity has been in Europe, which effectively takes him out of the purview of the FBI."

"Interpol also has him on a watch list," Payton said. "But has likewise been unable to definitively tie him to anything substantial. He's been hauled in on numerous fishing expeditions, but no pay dirt. He's suspected of involvement in two assassination attempts. A NATO ranking official and a German subversive." He handed a typed report to Gabriel. "The man is definitely a spook. I also talked to various underground contacts and though they'd all heard of him, no one had actually met him."

"By contacts I take it you mean other mercenaries?" The question came from Nigel, his expression inscrutable.

"Black ops people, yes." Payton seemed unruffled by the barb. But then it was his profession, and Madison assumed he was probably used to disapproval—even from friends. "I also followed up with Lin Yao, and he could find nothing concrete to connect Schmidt to Chinese dissidents. However, according to Chinese intelligence, he did make a trip to the western frontier sometime last year."

"They were tracking him?" Gabriel stopped, moving to lean against the windowsill.

"No, the report came from British reconnaissance. But they seemed satisfied with its validity." Payton shot a look at Nigel, who shrugged.

"I don't work the Far East, but if you like I can have the report verified."

"Thanks, Nigel, but it won't be necessary. I trust Payton's sources." Gabriel frowned, obviously trying to put the information together. "I talked with the counterintelligence people at Langley and they report much the same as their counterparts at the FBI. The man has been on a watch list for years, and has been in and out of the country on numerous occasions."

He shifted on the windowsill, his frown still firmly in place. "They haven't been able to verify that he is currently in the country. And when I talked to the European department, they also seemed to be unaware of his current location. He's deemed low threat, so not watched with the fervor of some of his more anti-American counterparts. Nigel, what did London have to say?"

"Very much the same, I'm afraid. That he's a shadow, and low threat, but worth watching. They did also hint at the fact that he might have worked with the U.S. on several black ops missions. Did anyone at Langley mention that?"

"No." Gabriel shook his head with a smile that indicated he wouldn't trust them if they had.

"And I suppose it wouldn't be relevant anyway," Payton said.

"Unless the CIA is trying to upend the accord," Nigel offered.

"I doubt very much it's even on their radar. It may play out as an important economic boon for the United States and/or the president, but I don't think it figures much in the day-to-day operations of the CIA." Gabriel's tone was dry, but there was a barb there. Something between him and Nigel that Madison hadn't seen before.

She glanced at Harrison to see if he'd noticed the exchange, but he was as usual oblivious to everything but the computer screen, the tapping of the keyboard a soft underscore to the conversation going on around him.

"So how do we find out if the man is in the States?" Nigel's question held a note of frustration that Madison understood on more than one account. It seemed every way they turned they hit another dead end.

"If the LUDs from Candace's cell phone are to be believed, then someone called her just after she talked to Smith. If we find that person, maybe we can find out more about who Candace was meeting. And if it turns out that Smith and Schmidt are the same person, then maybe that information will lead us to him."

"Well, no one who was there that night is owning up to the call," Payton said. "Nigel and I talked to all sixty."

"And Cullen claims not have talked to her at all that day."

"No big surprise." Gabriel sighed.

"Well, someone called her," Madison said.

"Unfortunately," Nigel sighed, "the problem is compounded by the fact that there's a phone in the lobby. Which means that there's access without needing to clear security."

"But surely the guard would have noticed someone unknown in the building at that time of night." Madison frowned.

"Possibly," Gabriel admitted. "But there are over six hundred employees here. The guard couldn't possibly know all of them. Still, it's worth checking out."

"I could recanvas the apartment building where W. Smith supposedly resided," Nigel offered.

"Good idea." Gabe nodded. "And Harrison, you recheck the information we had on the man from Virginia. Maybe there's something there we missed. We're going to find the man. It's just a question of when."

Payton's face reflected his skepticism. "Unfortunately we don't have an unlimited amount of time."

"So we work all that much harder."

"I'm afraid time has run out." Cullen stood in the doorway, his face ashen. "There's been another murder."

ANDERSON MCGEE'S HOUSE SAT on the back half of ten acres in Connecticut, the long drive from the road and dense brush an effective camouflage for the old farmhouse. If Gabe hadn't have known it was there, he'd have never found it.

Weathered clapboard and crooked shutters adorned the once-magnificent house, now dilapidated from age and lack of care. McGee had been an invalid of sorts, a semi-recluse, living on family money, and having little to do with the outside world.

More interesting than all of that was the fact that he had no relation with the consortium at all, unless one counted the fact that his family's corporation was a member. But the link between Anderson and the company was slight, his activity limited to the role of major shareholder.

His involvement with the accord was another thing altogether. A self-taught expert in Chinese diplomacy, as a younger man he'd traveled often to the Far East, and built quite a reputation as an historian and a scholar. When he'd returned to the U.S. he'd come to Connecticut to live in relative seclusion.

But when the consortium began negotiations with the Chinese, it was Andy McGee who had fronted the operation, at least on paper. He'd drafted and reviewed almost every single document that had traveled to Beijing. His knowledge of protocol was critical to the success of the endeavor.

And now he was dead.

One shot to the head, while listening to a Bach concerto.

The fact that he'd been found at all was only due to the diligence of the grocery delivery boy, who was determined to leave his boxes with or without the owner answering the door, and managed to shimmy through an open kitchen window.

A cursory check of the house had revealed McGee prone on the recliner, blood staining the plaid upholstery with a garish flare.

Gabe stood to the side, watching as the techs measured and photographed the body, while Madison questioned the still-shaken boy. There was no missing the similarities between Bosner's death and McGee's. Both had been shot through a window with a high-powered semiautomatic rifle of some kind.

Here, as in Bosner's Manhattan apartment, shattered window glass littered the floor, and here, too, a brandy bottle sat open on the table, McGee's spilled glass on the floor beneath his now flaccid hand.

"The kid didn't see anything." Madison appeared at his elbow, the sound of her voice warming him, despite the situation. "According to the techs, McGee had already been dead for at least twenty-four hours. They'll be able to give us a more exact time when Tracy does the autopsy."

"Any employees or family?"

"No family nearby." Madison moved a little closer, and his body responded to her nearness. He sucked in a breath, forcing himself to concentrate on what she was saying. "There's a housekeeper, but she only comes in twice weekly. And the last time she was here, McGee was hale and hearty." She glanced down at her notes. "There's also a groundskeeper. He lives in a cabin just over that hill." She pointed out the broken window toward the driveway. "No one's talked to him yet. According to the housekeeper, he's an odd sort. Likes to keep to himself."

"He'll fit right in, then." Gabriel nodded toward the body.

"I'll grant you he was a bit of an oddball, but that doesn't change the fact that he was murdered in much the same way as Jeremy. And that he had ties to the accord and, to a lesser degree, the consortium."

"And I'll lay dollars to doughnuts that Tracy will find a .223 lodged in his skull," Gabriel finished. "But that still leaves us without a clue as to the whereabouts of the illustrious Herr Schmidt."

"I've got people combing the ground underneath the window, trying to ascertain where exactly the shot was fired from. But unless they turn something up, we're at a standstill, I'm afraid. What we need is a witness. Someone who either saw Schmidt, or something to tie him to the case more directly than our leap from W. Smith to E. Schmidt."

"There's something else you don't know about."

Madison frowned up at him. "What?"

"Something Harrison told me. I didn't share it with the group because I'm not sure exactly what it means." He ran a hand through his hair, trying to order his thoughts. "Harrison did another check on the hacker. Ran the same diagnostics he used to trace the relays that led us to Virginia and W. Smith."

"And—" Madison's frustration was apparent.

"And he may have found something new. Evidence that the hacking occurred from inside the building."

"But he traced the relays." Madison's frown deepened, suspicion darkening her eyes.

"Yes, he did, but he's not completely convinced now that they were genuine. It may be that they were put there on purpose."

"To send us down the wrong track." She crossed her arms, looking up at him as she pieced it all together. "Payton said that he thought it had all been too easy. But if someone is purposefully steering us in the wrong direction, the big question is why?"

"I don't know yet. Harrison wanted to do some more tests. See if he could find anything else. And in the meantime, there didn't seem any point in speculating. My guess is that Schmidt was worried we'd be looking for him, and so sent us on a wild-goose chase instead."

"But why use a name so similar to his own? Surely that's a dangerous game to play?"

"Maybe." Gabe smiled, knowing the gesture lacked any real humor. "But men like Schmidt are an arrogant lot. It's possible that he liked the idea of us eventually finding the truth. Sort of rubbing it in the wound so to speak."

"But it puts him at risk."

Gabe shrugged. "Not really. I mean we still aren't any closer to catching him than when we thought he was W. Smith. Quite frankly, I'd say he's probably laughing his ass off at our expense as we speak."

"Or maybe we're missing the bigger picture." Her brows were drawn together in serious thought now. He could almost see the wheels turning.

"What do you mean?"

"I'm not sure. I want to think on it a bit. Maybe talk to Harrison. But I think Payton's right. There is something else going on here, and I, for one, don't like the idea of being led around by the nose."

"I don't see that we have an alternative."

Madison smiled, their gazes colliding. "There's always an alternative, Gabriel."

"I THINK I'VE GOT HIM." Harrison stood up waving at the computer screen with a flourish.

"Got who?" Madison asked, not bothering to look up from the file she was reading.

They were waiting on Tracy's autopsy for confirmation and a possible ballistics match. Gabriel had gone over there, unable to wait for the phone call, and Madison was wishing she'd gone along. She'd stayed with the intention of reading over the forensics reports for both Bosner and McGee, but she was having problems concentrating.

"Schmidt."

That got her attention. And Payton's, too. He hung up the phone with a decided click, leaving someone sitting on dead air. "What have you got?" He moved so that he stood behind Harrison, looking expectantly at his computer.

"I've been running Schmidt's known aliases against passenger manifests on international flights into New York and D.C."

"And you got a hit." Madison, too, crossed to stand behind her friend, the stirrings of something suspiciously like hope in her gut.

Harrison smiled up at her. "I did. A couple of months ago, a man named Smith Williams entered the country, ostensibly on a business trip. According to the customs declaration he hails from London, working for a company called Houghton Limited. Only problem being that there is no such company. At least not physically. It exists, but only on paper. A slick trick to avoid taxes."

"And the perfect cover for someone who needs a cloak of legitimacy." Madison frowned down at the computer. "And I assume there are no employees."

Harrison nodded. "And the owner has never heard of our guy."

"Was there a destination listed for Mr. Williams?" Payton asked.

"Nope. But there was a hotel."

"Bogus, I assume."

"Actually not." Harrison smiled again. "It's downtown in Battery Park City. And according to their registry a Smith Williams checked in about the same time."

Madison felt excitement rising. "And is he still there?"

"According to the records, yes. But when the manager checked the room it was empty."

"Damn it." The blasphemy was out before she had time to think about it. "I'm sorry. I just feel like we're always one step behind."

"Well, it's not as bad as all that. I ran the name through the NYPD computers just for the heck of it and I got a hit."

"But how is that—"

"It was a traffic ticket." Harrison cut her off. "Issued to one S. Williams for running a red light." He hit a couple of keys on the computer. "And the beauty of the thing is that he had to give an address."

"The hotel, right?" It was obvious from his tone that Payton was starting to get irritated with Harrison's dog and pony show.

"No." He grinned up at them. "An apartment complex on the Upper East Side."

"And you think it's real?"

"I'm waiting for confirmation from the leasing agent right now. It looks like our Mr. Schmidt finally made a mistake."

CHAPTER TWENTY-FIVE

TRACY BRAXTON WAS in the process of cutting into the subcutaneous layers of the chest cavity of a man who'd quite obviously been burned to death. The disfiguration of the body and face lent an air of fantasy to the scene, like some horror movie gone amuck. And in doing so, it removed it somehow from reality.

Tracy looked up briefly as Gabe walked into the room, then resumed cutting. "You're here about the autopsy."

He contained a terse reply, knowing that Tracy had other cases besides theirs. "I'd hoped you'd have something by now."

"I'm sorry. This guy was already waiting in line."

"Burn victim," he said, stating the obvious in an effort to contain his frustration.

"Vagrant." Tracy nodded. "Or at least we think so. It's hard to get a positive ID with what's left of him. He died in an abandoned warehouse. Suspected arson. I need to know when he died, and more importantly how his death relates to the fire."

"And it's important to do it now?" Gabe clenched his fists against his anger.

"I'm afraid so." She actually looked apologetic, and some of Gabe's anger dissipated. "There's a short window here, he's already degrading, and I've got to get inside before it's too late."

"And McGee?"

"Is up next, I promise. But right now I need to concentrate on this guy. All right?"

"I'll wait for you in there."

"Gabe—" Tracy's gaze was tolerant but firm "—I'll call you. There's no telling how long this is going to take, and I'm not going to rush it just because you're impatient. McGee will keep. This guy won't."

"Fine," he said, the word coming out more sharply than he'd intended. But he needn't have worried, Tracy was already back at work on the burn victim, forceps gently separating the ribs.

His cell phone rang, and he turned away from the gruesome scene to answer. "Roarke."

"Gabriel." As always her voice sent heat waves chasing through him. "Harrison thinks he's found Schmidt."

His heart started to pound, all thoughts of Madison pushed away in the rush. "Where?"

"Here in New York. An apartment building on Eighty-sixth." She repeated the address, and he grabbed a pen to write it down. "We're on the way now."

"We?"

"Payton, Harrison and I."

He recognized the sound of traffic in the background, and realized she was in a cab. "I'll meet you there. Have you contacted Nigel?"

"Yes," Madison said, her voice fading as the cell phone cut out. "He's still in the Village canvassing. He wasn't quite finished, so he suggested we go on without him. But he's going to try and meet up with us there."

"I'm on my way." He closed the phone, adrenaline pumping through him. Finally, the game was on.

THE APARTMENT BUILDING WAS a walk-up. Decidedly nicer than the one attributed to W. Smith, but it was still a climb to the seventh-floor apartment supposedly rented to Smith Williams aka Ernhardt Schmidt.

Madison followed Gabriel, in a reenactment of their earlier attempt to nail the man. But this time Payton was along for the ride, leaving Harrison to wait for Nigel and watch the entrance of the building. They all wore headsets, communication being crucial if they were to make certain the *ghost* didn't vanish again.

Static rippled in her ear, followed by Gabriel's voice, barely above a whisper. "One more floor to go. When we get there I want you and Payton to hang back. No sense tipping him off with the sound of our footsteps."

Payton answered affirmatively, and Madison followed suit, although the sneaking suspicion that he was protecting her lingered in her mind, refusing to be dismissed. Still, she wasn't one to flout orders, and there had definitely been a note of authority in Gabriel's voice.

The landing was more opulent than the one in the Village, and as they stepped out Payton moved to the right, securing the hallway in that direction, and Madison followed suit to the left. After signaling all clear, she shifted to the side, allowing Gabriel to pass her.

He moved down the hall, keeping his back to the wall and his eye on the door at the end. 7F. Schmidt's home away from home. Static filled her ears again as Harrison checked in, noting that no one had been in or out of the apartment since they'd entered. After a terse response, Gabriel signaled silence, and inched forward, shifting slightly so that Madison had a full view of the apartment doorway.

The door stood open.

Payton tapped her on the shoulder, and signaled that she should move, taking her position at Gabriel's back. Sliding forward on silent feet, she drew her gun and waited. Payton followed her, taking position on the opposite wall.

The triad complete, Gabriel signaled entrance, and slowly they moved forward, Gabriel disappearing into the open doorway.

The apartment was dark. Blinds closed, dust motes dancing in the light from the door. An abandoned pizza carton sat on a pass-through, a half-eaten piece of pizza on top. There was no sound at all, not the ticking of a clock, or even the caterwauling of the traffic below.

Holding her breath, Madison followed Gabriel as he moved into the living room, Payton turning left into what appeared to be a spare bedroom. He popped back out seconds later with a shake of his head, and they headed through the room toward the bedroom. Unlike the earlier apartment, this one was obviously lived-in. There were other take-out containers, and various newspapers strewn across the floor.

If this was in fact Schmidt's apartment, he wasn't a neat man. Something that didn't quite fit with her mental image of a methodical killer, but it took all kinds.

The bedroom door was open, and something like a squeak caught their attention, all three of them freezing on the spot. Gabriel motioned toward the door, and they fanned out as he burst through, gun barrel leading the way.

He stopped so quickly Madison almost ran into him, and she could feel Payton skidding to a stop behind her.

"Nigel." Gabriel's voice was guttural, his anger evident. "What the hell are you doing here?"

"I thought I was meeting you." The Englishman was standing at the end of the bed, a mixture of alarm and sheepishness coloring his expression. "Instead, I'm afraid I found this."

For the first time Madison looked at the bed, and stifled her intake of breath. There was a man lying there.

A *dead* man.

And unless she was badly mistaken, the man was Ernhardt Schmidt.

"I THOUGHT YOU WERE going to wait for us." Gabe watched his friend through narrowed eyes.

"I was." Nigel held his hands up in defense, his revolver ominously waving with the motion. "But when no one was here, I figured I'd check things out."

"So you just walked in?" Gabe asked, trying valiantly to maintain control.

"It seemed the expedient thing to do." Nigel shrugged. "The guy's door was open."

"I see." At the moment that was the best he could come up with. He turned his back on Nigel, concentrating instead on the body lying across the bed. The man's eyes were closed, the bullet hole in his head the only thing marring the illusion that he was sleeping.

Madison reached over to feel for a pulse, a shake of her head confirming what they already knew.

"Is he still warm?" Payton had moved to the window, testing the sash to ascertain that it was locked.

Madison lightly touched Schmidt's arm, and then nodded again. "I'd say he hasn't been dead long."

Gabe shot another look at Nigel, who was now walking the room, looking for evidence. Harrison's voice broke into his thoughts, the static reminding him that man was still downstairs. In a few terse sentences he reported the situation, leaving Harrison to call it in, and get Tracy's folks over for a look-see.

It seemed they were becoming a magnet for dead people on both sides of the game.

Payton was standing now at the head of the bed, carefully observing the body, using a pillow sham as a glove in an effort to preserve the scene. "Single shot to the head. Looks like small caliber, but I can't say for sure without seeing the bullet."

He shot a meaningful glance at Nigel, and then met Gabe's gaze, their minds moving in tandem. Nigel obviously followed the internal discussion, his face darkening with anger. "I had nothing to do with this, if that's what you're thinking. I just picked a lousy time to arrive, that's all. Besides, if I had shot the bloody bastard, why wouldn't I just tell you?"

"I wasn't thinking that."

"The hell you weren't." Nigel glared at Gabe, then Payton and then Gabe again. "I saw you both. You were thinking that I had opportunity. But you've forgotten I don't have motive. Would you like to see my gun?" He pulled it out of his holster and held it out. "The barrel's clean." He waved the weapon at Gabriel. "Go on. Have a look."

"Ballistics will test the gun, Nigel. It's procedure. I don't need to look at it."

"You'd have thought the same," Payton said to Nigel, "if the positions were reversed."

"No. I wouldn't have," Nigel said, anger still twisting across his face. "Unlike you, I trust my friends."

Payton opened his mouth to respond, then seemed to think better of it, turning back to examine the body instead.

Madison hadn't said anything, and when Gabe looked over at her, he was surprised to see suspicion clouding her eyes. Suspicion, and something else he couldn't quite recognize, but when he opened his mouth to ask her, she shook her head almost invisibly, the gesture meant only for him, her expression clearing by sheer force of will.

"I can't believe it. We finally find him and he's dead?" Harrison appeared at the doorway, cell phone in hand. "What the hell happened?"

"Single shot to the head," Gabe said.

"Execution?" He moved into the room, his eyes on the body.

"Possibly. Definitely close range. And probably while

the poor bastard slept." Contrary to his words, Payton didn't sound particularly concerned about the man.

"I can't say I'm particularly sorry that he's dead." This from Nigel, his words provoking a startled look from Harrison.

"How the hell did you get here?"

"That seems to be the question of the moment." Nigel laughed, the sound far from jovial. "But despite everyone's suspicions, I walked up here just like the rest of you to find Schmidt there already dead."

"Any sign of an intruder?" Gabe asked.

"Nothing that I saw." Nigel shifted slightly, his expression reflective. "I waited outside for maybe fifteen minutes. No one came in or out. When I couldn't stand it any longer—" he shot Gabe an apologetic look "—I thought about going up. Unfortunately the door to the building was locked."

"Not exactly a major obstacle for you," Payton said.

"No. But I didn't think it was the best thing to do in broad daylight in this kind of neighborhood. So I waited for someone to come out, and when they did, used the moment to walk in before the door closed again."

"The stupid generosity of mankind." Again Payton had a hint of sarcasm in his voice.

"Something like that. Anyway, from there, you know the rest. I walked up here, saw the door open, assumed you were already inside, and found Schmidt. You came along a few minutes later. You must have been just behind me."

Gabe nodded, his attention still on Madison, who seemed to be processing the information with added intensity.

"What did the person who let you in look like?" she asked, her brows drawn together in thought.

"An old lady." Nigel smiled. "Hardly the type to execute someone."

"There have been cases…" Madison's smile was brittle, and Gabe wondered exactly where her mind had taken her, but decided now was not the time to press the issue.

"At least Cullen will be happy about all of this," Nigel continued.

"How do you figure that?" It was Gabriel's turn to frown.

"If the killer is dead, then there won't be any more murders, the Chinese will be pacified, Cullen will get his accord and all will be well with the world."

"Hardly," Madison said, the vehemence in her voice making them all turn to look at her. "We've changed killers before, remember? And you know as well as I do that if Schmidt was involved in all of this he was only a hired gun. Whoever was pulling his strings is alive and well. And thanks to someone, Schmidt here is unable to tell us anything that might lead us to the real mastermind. Kind of convenient, don't you think?"

"You think that the person behind all of this killed Schmidt just so that we couldn't talk to him?" Harrison asked.

"It makes sense." Madison nodded. "What I'm not sure about is why he didn't want Schmidt to talk. Was it because he'd give the plan away? Or was it because he knew something we weren't supposed to find out?"

Madison looked directly at Nigel, and as Gabe watched, the man flinched.

"So tell me what you were thinking." It had taken every ounce of restraint Gabe had to keep from questioning her right there in the room, and then it had taken a little maneuvering to manage to be in the cab with her alone.

His only regret was that he'd had to leave Payton to watch over Nigel. Not that he expected Nigel to run, but there was something going on here, and he didn't want to make a tactical error. Enough had gone wrong with this case already.

Madison stared out the window, her profile backlit by the late afternoon sun. "I hate to say it. You're not going to like it at all."

"You think that Nigel shot Schmidt."

"I think it's possible. Look—" she turned to face him, her face reflecting her indecision at sharing with him "—if Harrison is right, and somebody planted the false information, then someone on the inside is probably behind it."

"I'll buy that, but what makes you think it's Nigel?"

"Well, for one thing, the British have been pretty vocal about their disapproval of the accord. They've got their own interests in China to protect. It's bothered me from the beginning that Nigel was part of the team. Not so much because I had reason to distrust him, but because it didn't make sense politically for his government to pull him off of another assignment to come and help preserve an economic alliance they're categorically against."

"Why didn't you say anything?" Gabe asked, studying the curves of her face, trying to see the evidence with her eyes.

"Until recently, you didn't exactly inspire confidences, especially mine." Her smile was wry, but her eyes remained serious. "And I didn't have anything concrete to go on. I still don't really, just a lot of coincidences."

"Like what?"

"Like our disappearing vagrant. You saw that gap on the roof. No one could have jumped that. He had to have gotten out another way."

"The alley."

"It seems the most likely." She shrugged, turning away from him again.

"So you think Nigel lied."

"I think it's possible."

"What about Payton? He had the entrance."

She shook her head. "The only way off the fire escape is through the alley. And I heard someone in the bedroom, remember? He had to have gone out that way."

Gabe didn't like the turn of the conversation, but he had to admit there was a certain amount of logic there. "That's not enough to base your distrust on, surely."

"There's the fact that we found him holding a gun, standing over the body. But we can rely on ballistics to clear that up."

"And that's it?" It was pretty damning, but nowhere close to airtight.

"No." She tucked a strand of hair behind her ear and sighed. "There's more. Nigel has been awfully handy. He's the one who found the supposed connection between the ballistics for Jeremy's murder and the assassination attempts in China. Remember, Payton said he'd looked into the matter, and hadn't been aware a ballistics report existed. I saw his face, Gabriel. He didn't believe Nigel for a moment."

"So why didn't he say anything?"

"I don't know. Maybe like me he didn't have anything concrete."

"Is there anything else?"

The taxi honked at a pedestrian, and they both jumped.

She turned to meet his gaze, her gray eyes clouded with distress. "The alleged intelligence report placing Schmidt in China. Doesn't it seem just a little bit coincidental that it was a *British* intelligence report?"

Gabe sighed. The evidence did seem compelling. "You think that Nigel is behind the murders?"

"No, actually, I don't. Remember I said that I thought it was possible that someone was leading us around as a sort of decoy?"

"Yes. And I thought it might be an attempt by the terrorists to deflect us from their real targets."

"Well, what if they're not related? At least not like we've been thinking. What if it's an attempt to keep us from finding the real culprits? If we fail, so does the accord…" She trailed off, chewing on her bottom lip.

"And Britain wins," Gabe finished for her. It fit. He hated the fact, but he couldn't ignore it.

His stomach twisted as he faced the probability that Nigel Ferris had betrayed him.

CHAPTER TWENTY-SIX

"I CAN'T SAY that this particularly surprises me. I knew the ballistics test was bogus." Payton sat on the sofa in Gabriel's suite, his expressing reflecting disgust more than surprise.

"Why didn't you say anything?" Gabriel asked, his arms crossed in a forbidding manner that had even Madison on edge.

"Because initially it was just a suspicion, and then when Lin Yao confirmed it, I still didn't have tangible proof. I figured it was better to wait it out and see what else surfaced." The line of Payton's scar shone white in the lamplight, the only real sign that he was anything but totally relaxed.

Madison marveled at the fact that these men could have any relationship at all. Their entire lives consisted of lying and protecting interests that more often than not must be at odds with one another. Yet here they sat, talking about another friend, who for all practical purposes appeared to have betrayed them all.

Harrison was keeping an eye on Nigel, pretending to take him out for a night on the town, with the promise that Madison would fill in the details for him later. She wished suddenly that he were here with her. A known quantity in a suddenly unfamiliar world.

"Well, if Madison's hunch is correct, I'd say we have a hell of a lot more than speculation."

"So what do we do with the information?" Madison asked, searching Gabriel's eyes for something of the man she'd spent the night with.

"Hang on to it for the moment. I want full confirmation of the facts before we act. And then I suppose we give Nigel the opportunity to defend himself."

"But won't he lie?" Again Madison was surprised at the degree of acceptance between the three of them. It was almost as if they were playing a game and Nigel had merely been caught out cheating.

"Not to me." Gabriel shook his head, his smile meant to be comforting. "If you're right, he's only been doing his job, and I suspect it hasn't been particularly pleasant for him. He could even be relieved to have it all out in the open."

"What about retribution?"

"Things don't necessarily work that way in espionage, Madison."

"All's fair in love and war?" She was surprised at the note of bitterness in her voice.

Gabe shrugged. "Something like that. Retribution is a funny thing. It tends to keep reciprocating and sometimes the better part of valor is to simply let things slide. The CIA isn't likely to go on record condemning a British operative. Especially when the Agency had a part in his involvement in the first place."

"So they care more about their own reputation than right and wrong?"

"It's a gray area, right and wrong. As I said before it's all perception. What we view as right is wrong for someone else. In this case the accord is a good thing for the president, and a disastrous thing for England's prime minister. And while it would have been better if they hadn't become involved, the price of exacting retribution from them would cost more than the original transgression."

"I suppose you could call it a question of diplomacy," Payton said.

"A man died, for God's sake. And Nigel may very well be responsible."

"It's not as if Schmidt was an exemplary member of society." Payton shrugged.

"Like you'd know anything about that." The words were out before she had time to think about them, and she immediately wished them back.

But Payton smiled. "Things aren't always what they seem, Madison."

Gabe was smiling, too.

Understanding dawned. "You're not really a mercenary, are you?"

Payton's smile widened. "As far as the world is concerned, I am."

"But if I were to access CIA secured files?" She probed, already knowing the answer.

"You'd find Payton listed as a top operative." Gabe's icy gaze met hers, the trust there almost unnerving her. "But of course you can't access those files."

"Nor would she want to," Payton said, his unruffled gaze meeting hers, the only expression one of acceptance, and as easily as that, Madison realized she'd crossed the line from outsider to full membership in their little group, Payton accepting Gabe's trust in her without question.

"But no matter what kind of brotherhood exists between respective espionage agencies, you still can't discount the fact that Nigel purposefully sabotaged our case. Three *innocent* people have died in the time it's taken us to chase after his mythical man."

"Not so mythical, it turns out." Payton tipped his head toward the forensics pictures of Schmidt.

"So you think he meant to frame Schmidt?"

"I don't know for certain. It could be that Harrison

stumbling on the connection between W. Smith and Ern-hardt Schmidt was as much a surprise to Nigel as it was to us. That would certainly explain his beating us to the scene."

"To kill Schmidt."

"Possibly," Payton said. "But if so, someone clearly beat him to the job."

"But you thought he was guilty…" Madison trailed off uncertainly.

"For a moment, yes." A shadow of something crossed Payton's face, but Madison couldn't read it. "But Nigel didn't have a silencer. I checked. So if he'd killed Schmidt, we'd have heard it."

"There are lots of things that can be used as a silencer, Payton." She wasn't certain why she was arguing, maybe because she no longer understood the rules of the game.

"I'm not saying he didn't want to kill the man, Madison. Especially if his talking would have put an end to the game. But I honestly don't believe he actually did it."

"Then who did?" Madison asked, frustration building.

"That's the question of the hour, really. And I'm not sure I have an answer."

"Not the British," Gabriel said, echoing her earlier thoughts. "It's one thing to run interference with the task force, and quite another to kill U.S. businessmen in an attempt to stop negotiations with the Chinese. There's no way the legitimate British government is behind this. I'm guessing the only thing they're guilty of is taking advantage of an already developing situation."

"And Nigel's friendship with the two of you." Madison saw a flash of something in Gabriel's eyes, and her heart twisted. He wasn't as immune to Nigel's betrayal as he'd have her believe.

"So we're back to Chinese dissidents."

"I'm not so sure," Payton said, walking over to the

minibar to pull out a Coke. "They'd certainly be delighted to see the accord fail, but the M.O. is all over the board, and even allowing for personnel changes, I just don't see it as a terrorist act."

"Great, that puts us back at square one." Madison bent her head forward, rubbing her temples.

Gabriel sat down beside her, his strong hands taking over the massage, and she leaned back against him, oblivious to Payton and what he might surmise from their intimacy.

"As soon as we're certain of the facts, we'll confront Nigel. If we're lucky, he'll have information that can help." Gabriel's voice rumbled through his chest, her body absorbing the vibrations.

"It's possible he's tampered with clues," Payton said.

Madison opened her eyes, something popping from the back of her mind to the forefront. "The LUDs. I thought the page Nigel showed us looked funny. Remember it was fuzzy. Especially around the entry that connected Candace to W. Smith."

"So maybe he changed the entries." Payton opened the can and took a sip. "Or at least added the bit about Smith."

"Should be easy enough to verify." Madison pulled away from Gabriel, immediately missing the contact. "All we have to do is request the original."

"Or ask Nigel."

"I'd feel better if we saw the original records." Madison wasn't as ready as Payton to trust their so-called friend.

"We can do both." Gabriel, despite his proximity and the warmth of his hands still resting on her shoulders, sounded more like a commander than a lover. And she sighed, moving to break contact completely.

"Now?" Payton's eyebrows rose in surprise.

"No." Gabriel stood up to walk to the window, shifting

the curtains to peer outside. "It's late. And we've no reason to believe that Nigel will run. I think the best thing is for you and Harrison to trade watch and make sure Nigel doesn't do anything drastic. Madison and I will follow up on some of our hunches, and we'll face Nigel in the morning, hopefully armed with more than speculation. Sound like a plan?"

Except for the fact that Payton was leaving them alone, it sounded reasonable. Madison thought about making an excuse and leaving them to deal with the problem on their own, but she couldn't.

She was part of a team, and nothing, not even her burgeoning feelings for Gabriel should be allowed to stand in the way of accomplishing their objectives. Besides, her relationship with Nigel was unfettered by the past, and that fact alone meant that she was the most objective of the lot.

"Works for me," Payton was saying, already heading for the door. "I'll go and relieve Harrison now. Shall I fill him in?"

Gabriel nodded. "It's best he knows. But let's keep it between the four of us for the moment. I'd rather take this to Cullen when we have all the facts."

Payton nodded and slipped out into the hall, the door shutting ominously behind him.

"So." Madison stood up, turning to face Gabriel. "Where do we start?"

GABE STOOD AT THE WINDOW of his hotel room, stretching. It was late, almost one o'clock, but in the past three hours they'd managed to accumulate quite a bit of evidence, thanks in part to Cullen's long and very powerful reach, and in part to the task force's myriad connections.

Primarily his and Madison's.

Between them they'd obtained solid confirmation that the British had no intel on Schmidt and a purported trip to the Himalayas and that there had been no ballistics report connected with the assassination attempt in China.

Further, Payton's friend, Lin Yao, had reported back to say that there was no known connection between Schmidt and any dissident groups in China. The man was evidently in bed with most everyone else, but not the Asians.

And most damning of all, they'd obtained a separate copy of the LUDs from Candace Patterson's cell phone. There had been no call from W. Smith. The call Candace had received right before she died, the call that had caused her to leave Lexco, had emanated from Dreamscape. Identity unknown, but totally unrelated to Ernhardt Schmidt.

Nigel had been playing them all.

Gabe gripped the windowsill, swallowing his anger. Thoughts of retribution were pointless. Nigel had been following orders. In their world, ultimate loyalty had to mean something. And always, the players must keep that thought in the backs of their minds.

The truth was that no one could ever be completely trusted. Not even a friend. The only person he could really count on was himself. Hell, he'd learned the lesson often enough. Even with the events that bound the three of them together, there would always be a higher loyalty.

Other people who held title to their souls.

He turned then to look at Madison, dozing on the sofa. What kind of life could he possibly offer her? Deception and subterfuge, certainly. But love and trust? He laughed, the taste bitter against the back of his throat. What a load of garbage. How in hell had he thought he would be able to have a relationship with her?

Just because she was in a similar business didn't mean she'd understand him or the game he played. And there was certainly no turning back. He was who he was. He turned to the window again, trying to push it all away, to wall the emotions in.

There was no such thing as happily ever after. If nothing else, Nigel's betrayal proved it once and for all. Everyone was in it for himself. And he was a sentimental fool to entertain any notions to the contrary.

"I wish I could make it go away." Her voice was soft, hesitant, but still it touched him deep inside, easing his pain in a way he wouldn't have thought possible.

He felt her hand on his shoulder and turned to face her, his heart hammering. "I'm not sure anyone can make it go away, Madison. But I appreciate the thought." He started to move, to dismiss the moment of intimacy, but she tightened her hand on his arm and he stopped.

"Don't shut me out, Gabriel. You said yourself we were worth the chance." She tipped back her head, her eyes searching his, her hand tracing the line of his jaw. "We're two of a kind, remember? I know you. As well as I know my own heart. And I know you're hurting. So let me in. Let me help."

"You can't." He hated the bitterness in his voice and wished he were stronger.

"Then just let me hold you." The simple words cut deep, leaving a burning warmth that felt strangely fulfilling, the idea of letting go suddenly more appealing than he could have imagined. No one had ever offered to hold him before. At least not without motive.

He studied her face, seeing nothing but concern and love reflected there. *Love.* The word sent shivers of desire lacing through him. Not physical need, but a soul-deep yearning for something—someone. He'd shut out those kinds of thoughts for so long, and now here she was standing in front of him, offering herself with no strings attached.

It humbled him. It shattered him.

And with a groan he pulled her to him, his lips crushing against hers, his need igniting the flame between them.

He stroked her face, her neck, her shoulders, unable to get enough. He kissed her eyelids, her earlobes, and the soft hollow of her throat. He reveled in the taste of her skin and the smell of her perfume. They belonged together, and nothing could be allowed to come between them.

Least of all his own self-doubt.

As if she could read his thoughts, she pulled back, her eyes searching his, a smile playing at the corners of her lips. "I love you."

He'd meant to say it first, to make a gift of the words, but suddenly all that mattered was that they be said—no matter who went first. And as effortlessly as if he'd been saying it all of his life, he told her he loved her, as well. The words new and familiar all at the same time. A covenant—a bond no one could break.

He pulled her close again, wanting to feel her heart beating next to his. To know that this moment was real. Their kiss this time was gentle, reverent, and he cupped her face in his hands. Then passion burst back into flame and he wanted them skin-to-skin, fumbling in his haste to remove her clothes.

Finally when they were both naked, he swung her into his arms and carried her into the bedroom, laying her down upon the sheets, the moonlight from the window kissing her skin. For a moment, he stood, simply marveling at her beauty, and the fact that she was here, offering herself—her love.

And with his heart in hand, he joined her on the bed, and as he thrust deep inside her, joining his body to hers, the act taking on new significance because it was Madison.

Her hands massaged the muscles of his neck, rising higher then to twine her fingers in his hair, pulling him closer, moving against him, the sweet tension mounting between them unlike anything he'd ever experienced before.

Together they climbed, higher and higher, until they were no longer two separate people, but instead two spirits fused together as one, the sum of the parts greater than anything they had been before.

And somewhere in the darkness, lost in the magic, Gabriel surrendered, the last of his walls tumbling down, his heart demolishing his hard-won defenses, hope filling even the darkest corners of his soul with light.

MADISON SNUGGLED AGAINST Gabriel, aware that morning was near and there was reality to be faced, but just for the moment, she wanted nothing more than the feel of his arms around her, and the solidarity of the two of them against the world.

It was a silly notion. A romantic fallacy. But somehow with him next to her everything seemed possible. Of course the world couldn't be held at bay long, and there were repercussions to everything, but she wasn't going to think about that now.

"You're awake." His voice rumbled through his chest, and she snuggled even closer.

"I was wishing we could keep the world out for just a little bit longer." Reluctantly she sat up, pushing the hair out of her face. "But I guess we can't."

He rolled onto his back, his hand still linked with hers. "Maybe we can't stop the world from coming in, but that doesn't mean we can't be together."

"No." She smiled down at him, her eyes soft. "But it makes it harder. I mean if you were a plumber and I was a teacher, we'd buy a house and a ring and make two-point-five kids. But that's not who we are. We've said it before. You spend months at a time pretending to be someone you're not, and I spend my time trying to second-guess monsters. What kind of life is that?"

His fingers tightened on hers. "Our life. For better or

worse, it's who we are, Madison. And I don't believe that, just because we're outside the norm, we can't find happiness."

She moved so that she was on top of him, his breathing matching the rhythm of hers, their bodies fitting like two halves of a whole. "I want that. But I'm afraid."

His laugh was harsh, his gaze intense. "So am I. But I'm also determined to take the chance. To take a leap of faith. To believe in you—in us. It won't be easy. We're both headstrong, and reckless, and dedicated to our careers. But lots of couples are like that."

"Most of them don't take their lives in their hands on a daily basis. You'll want me safe. And I won't be."

He reached up to stroke her hair, pulling her head down against his shoulder. "I will want you safe. There's no question about it. But I also want you happy. And I know that to do that, you have to follow your heart, even if it leads you into danger. Just as I have to follow mine. Can you really say you would prefer that I take up plumbing?"

She laughed, her heart feeling lighter. Whatever was in store for them, they were at least starting in the right place—with trust and understanding. It was a heady feeling. She lifted her head to kiss him, loving the feel of his morning stubble against her chin, his breath hot against her cheek.

They made love leisurely, learning about each other, giving and taking, hearts and bodies joined, keeping the world at bay for just a little longer.

CHAPTER TWENTY-SEVEN

"HE'S ON HIS WAY?" Madison pulled Gabriel's comb through her hair and gave a last quick look in the mirror. She'd had a shower, and was wearing her sweater as a shirt, abandoning the suit jacket and blouse from yesterday, but she still felt as if she looked the part of lady ravished. And despite their talk, she wasn't certain she was ready to face the world with it written all over her face.

"Yeah. Payton and Harrison are with him." Gabe looked rested and refreshed, the only outward sign of their nocturnal activities the gleam in his eye.

Despite herself she smiled, and catching sight of her face in the mirror, he pulled her back against him, dropping a kiss on the top of her head, the gesture comforting and sensual all at once.

She turned so that she was facing him, searching his face. "You sure you're okay with this?"

His eyes darkened, his thoughts turning to Nigel and his betrayal. "I have to be. There really isn't a choice."

She nodded, reaching up to kiss him. "So let's do it."

They broke apart, and Madison immediately missed the contact, but knew it was time to shift gears, to prove to herself she could be professional, even in the presence of the man she loved—especially in his presence.

A knock at the door signaled that the time had come, and with a last glance at Gabriel, she took a seat on the sofa, ready for the inquisition to begin.

Payton and Harrison looked as if they'd been up all night, and Madison was almost grateful to see that Harrison hadn't had time to change clothes, either. Nigel, on the other hand, looked as dapper as always, his sweater pulling out the blue in his jacket.

"What's with the tag team?" Nigel asked without preamble, his eyes hooded, suspicion coloring his expression. "Frick and Frack here hardly gave me a moment to piss. And unless I'm mistaken I had a bodyguard well into the night, even after I retired to my room."

Harrison shot a look of surprise in Nigel's direction and then sat down in the chair in the corner. "How'd you know we were there?"

"My dear fellow," Nigel said, his accent seeming exaggerated, "it was hard to miss you. I wouldn't advise a career in surveillance."

Harrison's ears turned red, a sure sign Nigel's barb had hit home, but he didn't say anything.

"If you'd played it straight with us, there wouldn't have been the need for a baby-sitter." Payton shrugged, the gesture overly casual, but like Gabriel there were fine lines of tension etched into his face. "Did you kill Ernhardt Schmidt?"

Nigel frowned, his gaze darting first to Payton and then to Gabriel. "Is that what this is all about? You think because I was there before you that I killed Schmidt?"

"Did you?" Gabriel's tone brooked no small talk.

Nigel swallowed visibly. "No."

Gabriel nodded, and leaned back against the windowsill, his arms crossed over his chest. If she hadn't been watching him so closely she'd have said he almost looked calm—but with close examination she could see the muscle ticking in his left cheek, the line of his mouth tight against clenched teeth.

"We know about W. Smith, Nigel," Payton said. "It must have been one hell of a surprise when Harrison produced the real thing."

Nigel eyed Payton coldly for a moment, shot a look at Gabriel, and then shrugged, dropping down to sit beside Madison. "What the hell. I could deny it all, but if I know Gabriel, you'll have proof in triplicate by now."

"Why?" The word cost Gabriel a lot, but only Madison recognized the fact.

Nigel shrugged again. "Because Downing Street wanted it that way."

"You could have just declined my request."

"And let Chinese commerce fall into American hands? My dear boy, that's not bloody likely."

"But people died because of you." The words were out before Madison could stop them.

Nigel turned to her, his expression scornful. "So what are you, fucking Pollyanna? In our world winning costs, dear. A couple of lives is nothing at all, believe me. I'd have thought you were made of sterner stuff."

Anger flared, and then she saw a flicker of regret in his eyes. Nigel was posturing. Making the most of a very bad situation. She refrained from answering. Whatever he said now was purely in defense, and she'd not let him goad her into a response.

"Well, the game's up now." She could have just imagined it, but she thought that she heard an additional edge of anger in Gabriel's voice. "And we need to know what all you've done."

"If I tell you, I'll be handing you victory. And I don't think that's exactly in my best interests, do you?" Nigel had regained at least a semblance of calm.

"Damn it, Nigel, cut your losses. Tell us what you know, and we'll make sure you're safely on British soil before the brass hears about this."

"Cullen Pulaski?" Nigel's laugh was more like a hiss. "I hardly think I need to fear him."

"Don't underestimate the man," Gabriel said, his eyes shooting sparks now. "And don't underestimate me."

Nigel blanched, his face suddenly pale beneath his tan. "Are you threatening me?"

"Let's just say I'm calling in all favors."

"This accord means that much to you?" He frowned as he tried to understand. Then he shot a look at Madison, a small smile playing at his lips. "Or is it her? Has she brought out a streak of decency? Imagine that—after all these years." The smile turned to a sneer. "I'd have never pegged you for a sap, Gabe."

Gabriel's fists clenched, and Madison willed him to see Nigel's words for what they were—bravado and bluster.

"It's about honor among friends, Nigel. That's why we're even having this discussion," Payton said, obviously sensing the impending explosion, and cutting it off before it could begin. "We were under the mistaken notion that we owed you this much. I'm beginning to think we were wrong."

"You hacked into the system and left the trail to Virginia," Harrison said, cutting through the building tension to bring things back to the issue at hand. "What I need to know is what else you did to the system."

"Nothing that you haven't already found," Nigel said. "That was the whole point, and you performed admirably—beyond expectation, actually. Which is more than I can say for Payton." He shot a wry look in the other man's direction. "I hadn't counted on you remembering the attempted assassination. I assumed you had your mind on more mercenary objectives."

"And Lin Yao didn't help matters, did he?" Payton asked, his tone light, belying the anger reflected in his eyes.

"Well at first he played into my hands, actually, but then in your usual thorough manner you managed to throw things off, but I rallied with that bit of intelligence. You'll have to give me credit for that much." They might as well have been discussing the home farm over tea.

"Enough with the recap," Gabriel boomed. "I need to know what else you've done."

"I think you've managed to nail it all, old boy." Again the English accent was put on a bit thick, as if it were a shield; but then again, maybe it was.

"What about Schmidt?" she asked.

"What about him?" Nigel turned his banal gaze on her. "I've already said I didn't kill him."

"Did you see the killer?"

"No. And I would tell you that." His eyes softened ever so slightly. "I was sorry about your friend Jeremy."

Madison bit back a retort. There was no guarantee that they could have stopped his murder even if Nigel had played fair. "How about at the first apartment—the ghost?"

"Me, I'm afraid." Nigel grimaced. "Left a print, too. Although so far, Payton, you've missed calling it."

"You wanted us to think someone was there." Madison was speaking to herself as much as Nigel, but he responded anyway.

"That was the general idea. Look, I was just supposed to keep you distracted. Let things take their own course." His gaze met Madison's. "Even if people had to die. As I said, it's the price of doing business."

"Well, the cost is too high." She knew she sounded priggish, but there had to be a line, didn't there?

"Maybe." For a moment Nigel lost his buoyancy, his face almost gray, the strain obvious. "But it wasn't my choice to make."

"What about the LUDs?"

"That was easy." He waved his hand in dismissal. "You

wanted information fast. So you didn't really question it."
Again he shot a look at Madison. "Except you."

"But I didn't know."

"Yes, you did. I saw it in your face." He smiled. "The
pieces of the puzzle just weren't in place yet."

It was an odd compliment, but she accepted it with a
nod, feeling like she'd fallen down the rabbit hole along
with Alice.

"So where does this leave us?" Harrison asked, clearly
as perplexed by the situation as she was.

"It leaves me on a plane home, I suspect." Nigel
shrugged. "And it leaves the rest of you a tad off your
game. But I've no fear that you'll put it all right in no time.
After all, the pieces are still the same, you just need to re-
assemble them—throwing out the bits I added, of course."

"You'll need to talk to Cullen. Tell him what you've
done." Payton sounded as if he'd rather pull teeth. Which
wasn't a bad analogy, really.

"Not me, mate. I'll exercise my right to a get-out-of-
jail-free card. I'll not deny any of it if pressed, but I won't
talk until I'm safe on British soil, as you so eloquently put
it, Gabe." He stood up, straightening his collar and tie, his
image as dapper Englishman restored.

"You've already packed, I take it?" Gabriel asked, his
face still shrouded with a combination of frustration and
anger.

"In the likely event that I'd need a fast getaway, I never
really unpacked. And with the night's baby-sitters—" he
tilted his head toward Harrison and Payton "—the writing
seemed to be on the proverbial wall. So I guess this is it."
He stuck his hand out. "All's fair and all that?"

Gabe ignored his hand, and refrained from comment.

Nigel's face tightened at the affront. "So it's to be like
that, is it?"

Gabriel's gaze met hers, and she tried for encouraging,

but wasn't sure if she succeeded. There simply wasn't an easy fix for a situation like this. And despite the fact that she abhorred what Nigel had done, she also could see the strain between the three men, and understand their pain.

"Right, then." Nigel dropped his hand. "I'll just be off." And with his head held high, he walked out of the room.

Silence followed, heavy like a blanket or the first fall of snow. And Madison shivered in its wake.

"So he just gets away with it?" Harrison said, his voice not much more than a whisper.

"He'll be reprimanded. I called Langley this morning. They'll have already begun negotiations with the British. There'll at least be an attempt to save face. Nigel will get the brunt of it no doubt." His face was impassive, but the muscle in his cheek was ticking again.

"He was lucky you let it go at that," Payton said.

The two men exchanged glances, then Gabriel turned to face the window. "We need to reconsider the facts and come up with a new theory. And then we'll have to present it all to Cullen."

"I can do that," Madison said, determined to shoulder some of the burden. "He'll listen to me."

"We'll do it together." Gabriel turned around with a sigh, lines of exhaustion creasing his face. "But first let's figure out where the hell we are. There's still a murderer out there, and we've got to find him."

"IF IT ISN'T the Chinese, then who the hell are we looking for? We've already identified at least twenty-five groups that have reason to want the accord to fail." Payton stood up to stretch, his attention still on the white board, and the list of names they'd written.

"Well, we know it wasn't Ernhardt Schmidt, and that could possibly rule out any of the groups he worked for," Madison offered.

She looked as tired as Gabe felt. What he'd like to do was pick her up and carry her away from all of this. To take her to bed and never come out again. But he couldn't allow himself to deviate from the mission. He needed to stay focused.

"Right," Harrison was concurring. "We found a Walther WA2000 in his apartment, along with enough ammo to blow away half of New York."

"But Jeremy's killer used a lighter gun," Payton said. "Maybe an M-16 or a Bushmaster. The cartridge was .223."

"And Schmidt's rifle takes .300 Win Mag," Gabriel finished.

"Isn't the Bushmaster the gun that was used by the Washington sniper?" Madison asked, her nose scrunched up in thought.

"Yeah. I think so, why?" Harrison turned to look at her, recognizing as Gabe did that she'd come to a conclusion.

"Well, it's probably nothing. But consider Schmidt. We're all agreed he's a pro, right?" She waited for everyone to nod, then continued. "And he had a Walther—what was it?"

"WA2000. One of the best sniper rifles made." Gabriel was watching her now with interest.

"Exactly. And expensive no doubt," she said.

"Something along the lines of ten grand, I'd guess, without any modifications." Payton looked to Gabriel for concurrence. He nodded, keeping his attention on Madison.

"So on the one hand we have a professional killer, with a ten-thousand-dollar rifle and on the other we have a murder committed with a six-hundred-dollar rifle that could have been bought at almost any gun store in America."

"So what are you saying?" Harrison frowned, trying to follow her logic.

"Well, it's certainly not Schmidt. Even if we didn't have other evidence, I'd have to go off the gun itself. Professional killers rarely change their choice of weapon. Stock-in-trade and all that. And they certainly don't use garden-variety weapons."

"So you're saying the killer wasn't a pro? But if that's true how did he managed to off Schmidt?"

"That's a bit of a puzzle, but leaving that aside for the moment. I think we can safely say that we're not dealing with a highly trained professional. Which could mean two things. First, the person who hired our killer doesn't have or doesn't want to spend top dollar. And second, he quite possibly doesn't have the expertise or contacts to hire someone of Schmidt's caliber."

"It's easy to hire a hit man, but quite another thing to find a mercenary. Is that what you're getting at?"

"Yes." She nodded, shooting him a smile. "And that tells us something about our killer. He's not organized at an international level. He has enough money to hire some-one but isn't willing to take it to the level of someone like Schmidt. And none of that sounds to me like organized dissidents or terrorists."

"So what is it?" Payton asked, his frustration cresting.

"I don't know. But I think we need to take another look at our victims. Maybe in the wake of Nigel's deception we've been on the wrong track. Maybe there's something else. Something besides the accord that links them together."

"It's worth a shot." Gabriel trusted her instincts. He'd seen them in action on more than one occasion.

He'd like to believe he would have eventually come to the same conclusions she had about Nigel, but the fact remained she got there first, and she was dead-on. And with sudden conviction, he had a gut-level feeling that she was right this time, as well.

"Harrison, let's dig deeper into their lives. Everything you can find about them. They're all public figures, it shouldn't be hard to put together a complete dossier. We're looking for commonalities. Anything in their pasts that might make them the target of this kind of violence. Payton, you help him. And in the meantime, Madison and I will go break the news to Cullen."

CHAPTER TWENTY-EIGHT

"So you just let him walk away?" Cullen's voice was pitched so low, it was almost impossible to hear him, the vein beating at his temple threatening any second to explode. Gabe had to hand it to him, he was reacting better than expected. Or at least managing a modicum of control.

"Yes."

He waited for the explosion, but instead, Cullen sank down into his chair, releasing a long sigh. "But he says he didn't kill this Ernhardt Schmidt."

"And I believe him." Gabe shrugged, not interested in discussing the ins and outs of Nigel's defection.

"But he's your *friend*." Kingston spit the word out as if it were a curse. "Why should we believe you?"

"Because ballistics backs him up," Madison said. She was sitting on the edge of the desk, arms crossed, her gaze encompassing both Kingston and Cullen. "Nigel carries a 9 mm Beretta. He had it out when we found him with Schmidt. But the slugs they got out of Candace Patterson and Ernhardt Schmidt were .38s. No match. He didn't kill Schmidt."

"Well, if he hadn't already been dead, Nigel would have killed him," Kingston stated, stubbornly sticking to the point.

"Probably," Gabe said, fighting against his anger, not willing to divulge anything more. Whatever had happened between the two of them, it stayed there. He shot a glance at Madison, hoping she'd understand.

"It doesn't really matter. Whatever his intentions were, they've been thwarted." The hint of a smile played at her lips and then was gone. As usual they were communicating on a level separate from the others. Like a team. And he couldn't deny that it felt really good.

"Which, unless I'm missing something here, leaves us back at the beginning." Cullen reached for a small ball on his desk and began to squeeze it. "Everything we've gathered in the way of evidence is now shot to hell."

"Something like that." Madison shrugged, working to convey a sense of nonchalance Gabe knew she was far from feeling. "Anyway, it's not all a wash. We've got the correct information now, and we're trying to rethink the issue. It's looking like maybe something beyond the accord is motivating our killer."

"That makes absolutely no sense at all," Kingston said, jumping up from his chair. "Of course it's the accord. Every one of the people murdered held a key role in the negotiations. How could it be anything else?" His face was turning red, his anger apparent for all to see.

"I tend to agree." Cullen's voice was calmer, but no less concerned. "It just doesn't make sense for it to be anything else."

"We haven't dismissed the idea that the deaths are tied to the negotiations," Gabe assured them. "But we have to explore all the options."

"I suppose so," Kingston said, taking his seat again. "I didn't mean to yell. It's just all so frustrating. Like waiting for the other shoe to drop. And I can tell you right now being on the hit list isn't helping matters any."

"I assume you've taken additional precautions?" Gabe asked. If Kingston's outburst was anything to judge by, the man probably had an army of bodyguards 24/7.

"Of course." He waved a hand in dismissal. "Cullen, too. I doubt anyone could get to us, but then I'd have thought the others were safe, too."

"I don't think anyone is really safe, Kingston." This from Madison, who was obviously thinking of Jeremy.

"It wasn't your fault, Madison." Cullen leaned over to pat her hand. "You did what you could."

She nodded her agreement, but Gabe knew she wasn't agreeing at all, merely putting an end to the conversation.

"Have you ruled out Chinese dissidents?" Cullen asked, judiciously changing the subject.

"More or less. We're still making some inquiries, but it isn't looking likely. We've also ruled out the groups Schmidt usually works with. Since he was here, it would seem likely he would have been our man if one of his usual employers was involved."

"And you're sure it wasn't him?" Kingston asked.

"Absolutely," Madison said. "Again it's a matter of ballistics. Ernhardt favored a Walther WA2000. We found it at the apartment. Our killer uses .223 cartridges."

"He could have changed weapons," Kingston offered, but didn't sound convinced. "I mean he's used both a rifle and a handgun."

"True." Gabe shook his head. "But most mercenaries tend to get pretty comfortable with their weapons. Kind of like a violinist and his violin. It's almost a signature. And since being caught isn't the norm, Schmidt wouldn't worry much about it being a tip-off."

"But someone found him and killed him. If he knew he was being hunted, maybe that would warrant the change in M.O.?" Cullen leaned forward, obviously interested.

"Still no go." Gabe leaned back against the bookcase. "The guy was killed in his bed, which means he had no idea anyone was on to him. Otherwise he'd have been watching. Between that and ballistics, I'd say we can rule Ernhardt out."

"So you think the real killer is the one who shot him?" Kingston frowned.

"It seems probable," Madison answered. "If it was our killer though, it would mean he's getting inside information. No one else knew we were even chasing Schmidt."

"Nigel," Cullen spat.

"It's possible," Gabe acquiesced. "But not likely. If Nigel'd been in contact with the actual killer, then he wouldn't have needed to try and kill Schmidt himself."

"I thought you weren't sure?" Cullen's eyes narrowed shrewdly.

"I said probably." He shrugged, pretending he didn't care, knowing Cullen saw right through him.

"The point is, it doesn't make sense to assume that Nigel was the leak." Madison neatly turned the conversation away back where it belonged.

"Then who is?" Kingston's question was for Cullen.

"No one here. I can guarantee that. But we haven't exactly been keeping our operation a secret. Hell, the press has been nosing around here for days. Anyone could have found out with a little effort."

"Maybe." Gabe wasn't really buying into the idea, but until they had more information he wasn't ready to speculate, either.

"What about the killer?" Cullen asked. "Are you still thinking there's more than one?"

Madison nodded. "It fits the pattern. Particularly if we're talking about someone with the desire to cause havoc with the accord."

"And if it proves to be something else altogether?" Kingston shifted in his chair to look at her.

Madison shot a look at Gabe, and he returned a slight nod. At this point it didn't seem worth the effort to try and hold their cards, especially with Cullen and Kingston.

"Then it could be one killer. If this is emotionally motivated, variation in M.O. isn't as unusual. There's a lack of planning. A tendency to act in the moment with materials at hand."

"But all of the murders, with the possible exception of the fire in Robert Barnes's warehouse, seem premeditated." Cullen frowned, trying to follow her train of thought.

"Yes. But there's a lack of sophistication even with the methodology. And that could mean something."

"Well, either way it's going to hurt the accord," Kingston said, stating the obvious.

Cullen nodded his agreement. "The president has been reduced to emergency teleconferences with Beijing. I can tell you he's not pleased with the current situation, and he'll be even less so when he hears about the prime minister's part in all of this."

"He'll deal." Gabe had no time for politics. It seemed inexplicable to think that an economic agreement meant more to Cullen than the deaths of his so-called friends and colleagues. But it was par for the course. Gabe thought his job required selling his soul, but Cullen probably had a direct feed to hell.

Cullen's eyes narrowed, and Gabe wondered for a moment if he could read minds, then snapped out of it. Cullen was just a man, a greed-driven one, but still wholly human.

"I don't need to remind you how important it is that we find whoever is behind this—whatever his motive." Cullen leaned forward, his gaze encompassing them both. "We're against the wire now, and starting from scratch. I pulled the two of you into this because you're supposed to be the best. So prove it. Find me a killer. And find him now."

"LOOKS LIKE YOU TWO ESCAPED more or less in one piece." Payton looked up from the report he was reading. "How did Cullen take the news?"

"Pretty much as expected," Gabe said, dropping down into a chair at the conference table. "Kingston Sinclair was there, too."

"Wonderful," Payton said, "double the fun."

"I don't know about that. But at least we lived to tell the tale." Madison smiled, walking over to the computer terminal where Harrison was working. "You finding anything?"

"Nothing earth-shattering," Harrison said, fingers still clattering away at the keyboard. "Everyone killed falls into the same income bracket. Most of it inherited. And with the exception of Jeremy, they're all around the same age. Late forties and fifties. Without exception, they attended prep schools, followed by Ivy League colleges, but they're all over the map as far as which ones. Most of them have lived in New York at one time or another, but not necessarily at overlapping times, and I don't think Alan Stewart was ever north of the Mason-Dixon line."

"How about commercial enterprises?" Gabriel asked, coming to stand next to Madison, his proximity as always making her hyperaware. "Anything in common?"

"The only ones that encompass them all are the accord and the consortium." He looked up with a shrug. "I told you there was nothing to write home about. A majority were lawyers, but given the number in the sample it falls within the statistical norm for the population, given their education level. And most of them weren't practicing anyway."

"Rich kid's occupation." Payton sat down in a chair at the adjacent terminal.

"What?" Madison asked, confused.

"It's a catchall for rich kids. Something that lives up to Daddy's expectations without any real strain on the offspring. Look at JFK Junior."

"You're saying they do it for legitimacy?" Harrison asked, his curiosity piqued.

"Yeah. It's not that hard to get into law school with the right connections, and once you're out, no matter what you wind up doing, you can always say you're an attorney. Instant gratification."

"Madison's an attorney." Harrison grinned. "And her father's rich. You saying she only did it to please her father?"

Madison's stomach churned, and she stepped back, ready to make a quick exit, hurt that Harrison would set her up for the kill. But Gabriel blocked the way, his hands on her shoulders holding her still.

"Madison doesn't do anything to please her father." The tone of his voice brooked an end to the discussion, but Payton ignored him, his steady gaze locked on Madison's.

"Whatever she does, I'm quite sure she does it for herself. And does it well." He smiled, and Madison was warmed by not only their acceptance, but their jumping to her defense. "But I stand by my generalization." His smile widened. "There are of course always exceptions to the rule."

"I didn't mean it like it came out." Harrison ducked his head, obviously chagrined. "I was just trying to prove Payton wrong."

And suddenly they were all laughing, at ease with one another in a way they hadn't been since Nigel's betrayal.

Gabriel was the first to sober. "So what we've got is a bunch of middle-aged wealthy men—"

"Don't forget Candace," Harrison interrupted.

"And a woman," Gabriel amended, releasing Madison to walk back over to the conference table, "who worked together on the accord, but other than that seem not to overlap consistently in other areas of their lives."

"That's it, more or less," Harrison said, coming over to sit at the table along with Madison and Payton. "Except that Jeremy Bosner was fairly well past middle age."

"But other than that he fits the profile?" Payton asked.

"Yeah, I guess so." Harrison frowned. "Although he didn't inherit his money, either. At least not the bulk of it."

Madison propped her elbows on the table, resting her chin in her hand. "You mentioned that before. Are you saying that most of the victims inherited their wealth?"

He nodded. "That, or they stand to inherit the bulk of their father's estates. The point was I guess that the apple doesn't fall far from the tree. Most of them are either working for their families, or living off family money."

"Which, except for the amount of work involved, is essentially the same thing," Payton said thoughtfully. "You said most. How many exactly?"

Harrison reached over to pull a piece of paper from the printer, then scanned it. "Actually all of them, except for Jeremy Bosner. Candace Patterson is a little outside the norm, I guess when you consider that she didn't know Lex Rymon was her father until recently. But she's still working in the family business."

"So how does it break down? Working in the business vs. living off of trusts or something?" Gabriel asked, doodling on the piece of paper in front of him.

Again Harrison consulted his notes. "Of the nine victims, McGee and Macomb were out-and-out living on their trust funds. Frederick Aston used his when needed. He was an actual practicing attorney—" he shot a snide look at Payton "—when he wasn't running for office. Bingham Smith used his family's money to start his business, as did Alan Stewart. Candace Patterson worked for her father, and Dashal and Barnes each ran their family's companies. Jeremy was the only one that made his own money. Although his parents would definitely qualify as upwardly mobile."

"Are they living?" Madison asked, an idea forming in the back of her mind.

"The parents?" Harrison frowned down at his sheet,

then abandoned it for a second one off the printer. "Looks like Jeremy's have been dead for quite a while. Ten or fifteen years. Stewart's father passed away just recently, looks like about a month ago. Bingham Smith's mother appears to have passed away when he was a child. And Dashal lost his mother to cancer five years ago. Other than that, the rest are living." He looked up from the report. "Why?"

"I'm not sure, really. Just a hunch. And with Jeremy Bosner in the mix it really doesn't fit. But what if this isn't about the victims at all? What if it's something to do with their fathers?"

"Seems a little far-fetched," Payton said. "Unless the fathers are all involved in the accord, as well."

"None of them in a major way," Harrison said. "In fact, most of them not at all."

Madison sighed, unable come up with anything substantial to back up her idea, but unable to completely dismiss it, either, now that it had popped into her head. "I'll grant you the connection through the accord makes a lot more sense. It just seems coincidental that they all come from old money, and with the exception of one, seem to have used it one way or the other to make their way in the world."

"At this point, I'd say anything is worth checking out."

She was certain Gabriel had meant that as support, but it was somewhat lacking in the enthusiasm department.

"I'll look into it," Harrison volunteered. "There's no harm in checking."

"Good. And in the meantime, Madison and I have a meeting with Anderson McGee's parents. Not that I'm expecting anything earth-shattering."

"You never know," Payton piped up with uncharacteristic enthusiasm. "The case has to break sooner or later. Might as well be now."

THE PENTHOUSE APARTMENT rivaled her father's in opulence, the view only slightly less coveted than Philip Merrick's. Martha and Thomas McGee had obviously produced offspring early in life, their relatively unlined faces testament to the fact.

Madison sat on the sofa, teacup in hand, wondering what, if anything, these two septuagenarians could possibly know that would help. Gabriel sat in a wing-back, dwarfing the chair, his teacup balanced on the arm. He looked as if he'd like to run, and she swallowed a smile, not wanting to show pleasure at his discomfort. Still it was perversely enjoyable to see him out of his element for a change.

"I'm not sure there's anything we can do to help." Martha McGee echoed Madison's thoughts, her face a mixture of anxiety and doubt. "We really didn't have much contact with our son."

"But you provided him with a place to live, and money to support him." Gabriel observed, leaning over to put the teacup on the coffee table.

"Yes," Anderson's father agreed. "We've always taken care of him." His smile was strained, his red eyes reflecting his grief. "You probably know by now that Anderson wasn't exactly right in the head."

"He was clinically depressed," Mrs. McGee elaborated.

Her husband reached over to take her hand, the gesture obviously familiar and comfortable. "It was more than depression. He was diagnosed five years ago as a paranoid schizophrenic. But I suspect the condition has existed undiagnosed for years."

"He took medication," his mother offered in an effort to negate what she obviously perceived as an embarrassment.

"He was medicated, but it really didn't do much but keep him sedated."

"But I thought he was working with the accord?" Gabe

asked. "It was my understanding that he wrote or at least edited all correspondence between the delegation and the accord."

Mrs. McGee smiled. "He was an expert at dealing with the Chinese."

"He had his moments," his father qualified. "But you have to understand that there were days when he couldn't have even told you his own name."

"So he wasn't helping?" Madison asked, exchanging a glance with Gabriel, his confusion mirroring her own.

"He thought he was. And the world thought he was. It suited Cullen's purposes, and it helped Anderson to feel needed." Mrs. McGee's smile indicated the high opinion she had of Cullen Pulaski.

Mr. McGee, on the other hand, didn't seem to share her enthusiasm. "He was using the boy. It's as simple as that. Pushing him when there was no need."

"I'm afraid I don't understand," Gabriel said, his dark brows knitting together.

"Cullen needed an expert, but he didn't want someone with the possibility of ulterior motives. Anderson fit the bill."

"But if he was incapacitated—" Madison began, only to have Mr. McGee wave her off.

"He was lucid enough to play the part when necessary. But the effort cost him a great deal."

"It gave him dignity." Mrs. McGee pulled her hand away, squaring her shoulders.

"Dignity." Mr. McGee's laugh was harsh. "How can someone that sick ever have dignity? Cullen Pulaski took advantage of him. It's as simple as that."

"But he did help with the negotiations," Gabriel urged.

"Sometimes, when his head was clear." Mr. McGee shrugged. "But I think Cullen did the bulk of the work himself."

"And didn't claim responsibility? That doesn't sound like Cullen."

"I can't tell you more than that," Mr. McGee said. "I've never been high on Cullen's need-to-know list. All I can say is that my son was in no condition to offer anyone advice about anything."

"He was just trying to help Anderson, Thomas, you know that." Mrs. McGee's eyes were pleading now.

"He was using Andy. I've no idea what kind of game he was playing, but you can bet it had a bottom line. Cullen doesn't do anything unless there's something in it for him. And now thanks to his meddling, my son is dead. As far as I'm concerned, Cullen Pulaski is as responsible for my son's death as the man who killed him."

CHAPTER TWENTY-NINE

"I THINK I MAY HAVE FOUND something interesting." Harrison greeted Gabe and Madison as they walked through the door to the operations room, a glimmer of excitement in his eyes.

After the strange conversation with the McGees, Gabe welcomed anything that could remotely be considered a step forward. Following Madison, he crossed to the conference table where Payton and Harrison had spread out what looked to be half the paper in the free world. Despite an overall chaotic effect, stacks, piles and fans of the stuff indicated there was at least some degree of order.

"We've pulled all the information we could come up with on the nine victims. And then grouped it according to category. Duplicating as necessary." Harrison swung out an arm indicating the paper-laden table.

"It looks like World War III." Madison laughed. "I'm surprised you can find anything at all."

Harrison laughed, too, the easy camaraderie between the two of them sending shards of jealousy piercing through Gabe. He frowned at himself, surprised at the depth of his feelings. They'd both made it absolutely plain that there was nothing going on between the two of them, and even if they hadn't denied it, last night should have made it abundantly clear. Apparently though, his psyche hadn't gotten the memo.

"Actually there's a lot. Most of it we already touched

on. Schools, background, that sort of thing." He moved over to the far side of the table. "This is where we've started grouping data based on the victims' fathers. And interestingly enough, these fellows have a lot more in common than their children."

"What do you mean?" Gabe asked, coming around to stand by Harrison.

"Almost all of them served on the board of directors of a company called Vrycom," Payton said.

"Never heard of it." Gabe pulled out a chair and sat down, frowning up at his friend.

"I have," Madison said. "They were an acquisitions firm, right? In the '80s?"

"Yeah." Harrison shot her a look of surprise. "How did you know that?"

"Because they approached my dad about serving on the board. He turned them down. No idea why, but I remember because a couple of years later they ran into SEC problems."

"Exactly." Payton looked impressed. "There were allegations of collusion. Vrycom existed only on paper. And its sole purpose for existence was for leveraged buyouts. A down-and-dirty way to deal with the competition, if the allegations were true."

"Were formal charges ever brought?" Gabe tried to fit this new information alongside the evidence of nine murders.

"No." Harrison shook his head. "The company disbanded before anything official could happen, and the SEC dropped it. I guess they thought pulling the plug on the organization was enough."

"Any civil actions?" Madison asked, chewing on her lower lip, a sure sign that she'd gone into overdrive thinking.

"We're working on that now." Payton waved at another

pile of papers. "So far we've only come up with one. A company called Bluemax. The suit was apparently dropped before it went to trial."

"Maybe it had something to do with the SEC investigation?" Gabe leaned forward picking up a prospectus on Bluemax.

"I don't think so," Payton said. "The suit predated the SEC's interest by about two years."

Gabriel flipped through the prospectus, noting that Bluemax was a start-up. "So who else served on the board?"

"Now there's the interesting twist," Harrison said. "Eight of nine of the vics' fathers served on the board of Vrycom."

"I'm guessing the exception was Jeremy Bosner." Madison's frown was speculative, as she considered the new evidence.

"You'd be guessing right," Payton said. "There's no indication that his company was involved at all. Although he certainly ran in the same circles. But that's not the most interesting part." He leaned forward, lowering his voice to a whisper, and a shiver ran up Gabe's spine, the prospectus from Bluemax sliding out of his fingers. "There was one other board member. In fact, he served as chairman."

Realization dawned as the puzzle pieces rearranged themselves in a new pattern. "Cullen Pulaski," Gabe muttered.

"You're an apt pupil," Harrison said, obviously pleased. "It's an interesting fit, too, because Cullen is younger than the others by something like ten years. Basically the generation between the victims and their fathers."

"That one I can actually explain," Madison said with a wan smile. "Cullen was a wunderkind. A whiz at mathematics, he was a natural for the computer, and quickly morphed that into taking advantage of the technological revolution. Bill Gates with an industrial slant. He made his first million before he was thirty."

"So he was far more of a player than his age would suggest," Gabe said.

Madison nodded. "Put it this way, the big boys of the day would have fallen all over themselves for a piece of his action."

"Even if it involved collusion," Harrison concluded. "Unfortunately, that's as far as we've been able to take it. We were just beginning to read the SEC documents when you all walked in. So far there's not any kind of link between Vrycom and the Chinese or the consortium, other than a few repeat players."

"Namely Cullen." Madison's forehead was furrowed with worry.

"You've got to admit his name keeps coming up at very inopportune times," Gabe said, his gaze meeting hers.

She chewed her lower lip. "You're talking about the McGees."

"Among other things."

"What about the McGees?" Harrison asked, straddling a chair at the end of the table.

Madison blew out a long breath and ran her hand through her hair, the gesture reflecting just how tired she really was. "According to Anderson McGee's father, any involvement he had in the accord was a ruse."

"Anderson was a diagnosed paranoid schizophrenic, and from what we could tell, most likely not capable of providing the degree of support he is supposed to have been giving the negotiations."

"But he's an expert in Chinese custom, right?" Harrison asked, frowning.

"Was," Gabe said, still watching Madison. "He evidently came home from China a sick man. That's when he moved out to Connecticut. And according to his father, even on his best days there was no chance he was operating at the level necessary to provide support to the negotiations."

"So it was a scam."

"We don't know that." Madison's voice was quiet, but firm. "What we do know is that whatever arrangements were made, Anderson wasn't doing the work he was credited with."

"So who *was* doing it?" Payton put down the paper he'd been reading, curiosity at war with speculation.

"Cullen." The name hung in the air, taking on a life of its own, and Gabe suddenly felt as tired as Madison looked.

"So we've got a lot of odd incidences without seeming connection or motive," Harrison said. "First we have a paper company with SEC problems that took over vulnerable companies in the '80s. And Cullen was chairman of the board. Which would have been just about the time his empire was taking off. Then we have the consortium. Again with Cullen as a major player. And ultimately the chairman of its board."

"And the accord—" Payton took up the story "—apparently with Cullen as one of the two or three who masterminded the original idea."

"But from the get-go there are problems. And people start dying," Gabe added, his mind moving over the facts, trying to put them into some kind of coherent order. "But no one knows it. Or at least recognizes it as murder."

"Except Cullen." This time it was Madison who hammered the nail home. "He knew something was wrong."

"But apparently not before he had the opportunity to tamper with evidence and persuade survivors against autopsy. And enlist a mentally unstable man to handle crucial portions of said negotiations." This from Payton, who had moved to stand by the window, twirling a pen between his fingers. "Eventually however, he begins to see signs of something amiss and calls you in."

"And Madison," Gabe added.

"But why?" Madison asked. "I don't see how any of this fits together. We have no connection between Vrycom and the Chinese negotiations. In fact, it wasn't even in existence when the first idea for an accord was discussed. There could be any number of reasons to explain any of the things we've mentioned here. All of them perfectly innocent. Cullen is a major player across the board. There are probably hundreds of ways he connects with all of the people involved. Six degrees of separation and all that."

"And you don't believe a word of that."

She blew out another breath, her sigh audible. "No. I guess I don't. But I'll be damned if I understand how it all fits together."

Gabe shrugged. "There's only one way to find out for certain."

"I know." She tipped back her head, tears shimmering in her eyes. "We've got to talk to Cullen."

MADISON DIDN'T WANT TO believe anything she was hearing. Didn't want to think about Cullen involved in anything as nefarious as murder. But there were questions here that couldn't be answered easily, and the only way she knew to deal with the matter was to tackle it head-on.

They'd spent the past half hour putting facts together, preparing for what they hoped was a cogent attack. One Cullen would have to answer truthfully. All that remained was to face the man.

Her godfather.

Some part of her refused to accept that there was any possibility of wrongdoing on Cullen's part, but she also knew that at his level of business it was kill or be killed, and that often meant tough tactics. But surely not murder.

The truth was, there was no motive. It made no sense for Cullen to try and ruin the accord. And the SEC violation at Vrycom was just part and parcel of doing business. She wasn't her father's daughter for nothing, and it was a ruthless world out there. Hadn't Nigel just proved that very fact?

"Maybe you should let me handle this." Gabriel's voice was warm and concerned, and Madison suppressed the irritation that flashed through her.

"I'll be fine. If there's a connection somewhere in all of this, we need to find it. And Cullen appears to be the link."

"But you're not willing to go as far as admitting he might be the problem." His eyebrow lifted in question, the gesture, as always, adding a hint of the devil to his expression. Madison might love him, but she sure as hell didn't know him. And the two facts ought to be mutually exclusive.

But of course they weren't.

And a part of her did know him.

Just like she knew Cullen, the little voice in her head whispered. It was almost as if the world had turned topsy-turvy, someone she trusted suddenly suspect, and someone she'd never thought to trust, her lover.

But then, she overanalyzed everything. It was a part of the job that she took home with her all too often. Surely there was a point where faith had to come into play. She trusted her instincts every day when it came to profiling. So why not now?

Why couldn't she trust her instincts where Cullen was concerned? Or Gabriel?

She felt his hands on her shoulders, and looked up to meet the icy intensity of his gaze. She wanted to trust him, to believe they had a future, but suddenly it was all too much. More than she could handle, her fear taking hold and digging into the dark recesses of her mind.

He leaned down to kiss her, his lips warm as they moved against hers, taking possession. Possession. Her heart hammered, and she felt faint. Part of her wanted to pull him closer, to throw propriety to the wind, but she couldn't. Not when the other part of her kept singing the word *possession*.

She didn't want to belong to anyone.

Ever.

She'd been there and done that. Playing the role of little woman wasn't what she was cut out for. Better to be alone.

With a little cry she pushed him away, ignoring the flash of hurt in his eyes, and Payton and Harrison's astonishment. She simply wasn't ready. What had felt right in the dark of the night felt wrong here in the light of day.

She swallowed hard, avoiding his gaze. "You ready?" She pasted on her most winning smile, her emotions still reeling, her thoughts tangled together in a mess of present and past and impossible future.

"Sure." The word was clipped, and he might as well have stabbed her, considering the pain. But even as she had the thought, she knew she'd brought it on herself. It was her fears that were threatening the best thing that had ever happened to her.

Her fears alone.

"Madison?" Payton's voice was hesitant, more timid than she'd have thought possible with him.

She turned to face him, knowing her face was red and that her feelings were transparent across her face. But all she saw reflected in his green eyes was concern. "I just got a call from your father."

Great. All she needed now was another male in her life trying to tell her what to do. "What did he want?"

Payton's glance took in Gabriel standing at her elbow

and the tension radiating between the two of them, and he actually took a step back. Not a bad idea, actually, as she'd always found it better to avoid a battle zone. "He wants to meet you at your apartment."

Gabriel mumbled something and moved away, the lack of physical presence making Madison's heart shrivel. "Did he say why?"

"Yeah," Payton said. "Something to do with Cullen. He said it was really important."

That got her attention. A welcome relief against her surging emotions. Maybe her father had something to tell her that would help clear things up. Exonerate Cullen.

"I'll go with you." Gabriel had returned to her elbow, but his voice was all business now.

"He said alone." Payton looked apologetically at his friend.

"Fine," Gabriel barked. "You go talk to your father, and I'll tackle Cullen. Then we'll all meet back here and see where we stand."

He turned to go, and Madison reached out to stop him, then dropped her hand. What was the use? By the harsh light of day she could see clearly that there was no future for them. Their paths would always take them in different directions.

"Sometimes you have to grab what you want, no matter how ridiculous the notion may seem." Payton's voice was soft, his words meant only for her ears. "He's a proud man, Madison. It took a lot for him to show his feelings here in front of us. If it matters at all, I've never seen him care about someone like this. He's finding his way, too. Don't shut him out, unless you're sure that's what you want."

She nodded, not willing to look at him, certain she'd fall apart if she did. Instead, she hurried through the door, praying that Gabriel would still be in the hallway, that she'd have the chance to make it right.

But it was too late. Gabriel was gone.

CHAPTER THIRTY

GABE SAT in the vestibule of Cullen's office, trying not to dwell on what had just happened. For all practical purposes, Madison had rejected him. Or run scared, the voice in his head insisted loyally.

Either way, she'd disengaged, and done it in a very public kind of way. His heart twisted at the memory, his stomach churning. Women were unpredictable, that was for certain. But he'd thought there was more between them. That they'd decided to at least give a relationship a try.

But then what the hell did he know about relationships? He'd spent his entire life alone. On purpose. And here he was trying to preserve a connection with another human being. Not exactly something he had experience with. Maybe he'd made a mistake. Read more into it than was really there.

He replayed their conversations in his mind, trying to find his error, to understand why he could have thought there was more to it than there obviously was. He sighed, knowing there wasn't an easy answer, wishing there was a way to quell the uneasiness in his heart.

He wanted her. Hell, he loved her. But it took two to tango. Still, she'd said she loved him, too. So what the hell was the withdrawal all about? He wasn't certain. It was all too new. But he did know one thing, he'd be damned if he would let her run away.

She was too important. *They* were too important.

He was halfway out of the chair when the door opened and Cullen beckoned him in. He pushed his thoughts about Madison away; he'd have to deal with it later. Right now he needed to handle business, and judging by the somber expression on Cullen's face, he knew what was coming.

"I'm sorry to have kept you waiting." Cullen gestured toward the chair in front of his desk, choosing the adjacent chair for himself, rather than keeping the desk between them. It was a move calculated to make the conversation more intimate.

Gabe suspected Cullen might soon prefer the barrier of the desk. "We've uncovered some new evidence."

"Something to do with Anderson McGee." It was a statement, not a question. "You found out he wasn't actually taking part in the negotiations."

"According to his father he wasn't capable of reading the paperwork, let alone negotiation." Gabe watched Cullen, looking for something to give away his thoughts, but the man hadn't gotten where he was by wearing his emotions on his sleeve.

"He wasn't." Cullen shook his head and sighed. "But he did have moments of lucidity. And memories. He knew what he'd been. Can you imagine what that must be like? To know that you were once capable of greatness, only to wind up losing it all to a chemical fluke in your brain."

"It still doesn't explain his part in the accord."

"He didn't have one." Cullen sighed, absently twining a loose upholstery thread around his finger. "It was a ruse. Just as you suspected. But not for any sinister reason. We were all in on it. Bing, Jeremy, Kingston and I. It gave Andy purpose. Helped him to get up each day."

Gabriel sat back, waiting, realizing there was more.

"About eighteen months ago, Andy tried to kill himself.

At first his father thought it was an accidental overdose, but it soon became apparent that it had been intentional. Martha and Thomas are old friends." He shrugged as if that explained everything.

"So they came to you for help."

Cullen nodded, still fingering the thread. "Martha actually. She thought that if Andy had a reason to get up in the morning—if he honestly believed his life mattered—he wouldn't try again. She knew we were working on the deal with China. Had Andy been well, he would have indeed been an asset to the team. So we concocted a plan to make him believe he was handling parts of the negotiation. The written work primarily."

"But he couldn't have been contributing anything helpful."

Cullen ran a hand through his hair, the gesture uncharacteristic. "You'd be surprised, actually. The talent and knowledge was still there, but unfortunately it came out a bit on the garbled side. Bing and I fixed it. At times even rewrote it, but let the credit stay with Andy. It seemed harmless at the time. But now, I feel like I dragged him into the quagmire. Caused his death, even."

"You couldn't have known this was going to happen." Gabe studied Cullen, surprised to find that he believed him. It made sense in a convoluted kind of way. And besides, the story could easily be checked. "What about Thomas? Did he go along with the idea?"

"No. He thought I was taking advantage of his son."

"But surely with Martha involved…" Gabe frowned, trying to understand the dynamics between the three of them.

"I didn't tell him she came to me. He thought it was all my idea. It was easier that way."

"For who? Martha?"

"Everyone, really." Cullen shrugged. "Thomas and I

had a falling-out a while back over a business endeavor. We've remained cordial, but he doesn't trust me."

"Vrycom?" The name seemed to hang in the air, and Cullen's eyes widened.

"I'm surprised you've heard of it." Whatever surprise there'd been at the question was gone as quickly as it had come, replaced by a mask of polite indifference.

"Harrison stumbled across it, actually. He was trying to find a connection among the dead."

"But none of them had anything to do with Vrycom."

"Come on, Cullen, you're more on the ball than that. What do you say we cut the games?"

"I'm not sure I'm following." The words were cold. "But if you're referring to the fact that some of their fathers sat on the Vrycom board with me, I'm more than aware of it. But I don't see how it could possibly have anything to do with the murders."

"More than a few, Cullen. Eight of nine." Gabe frowned. "And we're not sure if there's a connection, but you've got to admit it's a hell of a coincidence. What do you know about Bluemax?"

It was Cullen's turn to frown, this time with an obvious effort to remember. "It was a company we wanted to buy out. They had some patents we needed. Small-time business, but they weren't interested in anything Vrycom had to offer. So things got ugly." He shrugged. "That's what Vrycom was for."

"What about the lawsuit?"

"A minor annoyance. They had no chance of winning. It was just a matter of time. As I recall, the case was dismissed, the takeover was accomplished, and we dismantled the company and used the patents. Sounds a bit harsh in the telling, but it was just business. And Bluemax was hardly the biggest fish we took on."

"Until the SEC stepped in." Gabe shifted in his chair,

watching Cullen, listening, hoping for something that might tie into the murders.

"Again, it was standard operating procedure. They didn't really have a case, but it wasn't the kind of publicity any of us wanted, so we abandoned the company. It had quite obviously outgrown its usefulness and so we all went our separate ways."

"Considerably better off, I'd imagine."

"Of course." Cullen looked surprised at the question. "That was the whole point of the endeavor."

"And you can't think of anything that would link your activities there with the murders?"

"None that are stronger than the potential failure of the accord. Besides, as you've already noted, Jeremy's death breaks the pattern."

"There are still a lot of anomalies surrounding your behavior, Cullen. We'd be crazy not to suspect you're guilty of something."

"Does Madison agree?" It was a personal question, and it was Gabe's turn for surprise.

"She doesn't want to." He saw no point in not being honest. "But it's hard to deny the coincidences. There's the fact that you told Alan Stewart's wife not to authorize an autopsy. And the fact that you were pretending that Anderson McGee was doing work that he wasn't. There's also the odd connection between you and the murder victims' fathers. And you're responsible for bringing me into this and you knew damn well I'd bring Nigel. And you can't tell me that you hadn't considered the possibility that it might be a conflict of interest for him."

"Of course I thought of it, but I thought you'd keep him in line."

"Well, you obviously thought wrong." Unwanted bitterness filled his throat.

"In any case—" Cullen dismissed Gabe's discomfort

with the wave of his hand "—there's nothing in what you've listed that hasn't been explained. And more importantly, there's no logical link between them."

"Except the very real possibility that you want the accord to fail."

Cullen tipped back his head and started to laugh. Not with the maniacal laughter of someone caught out, but with the genuine amusement of something found funny. "Oh, my dear boy, you're on the wrong track, believe me."

"I want to," Gabe said, frowning at the sudden turn of emotion.

Cullen dabbed his eyes with his handkerchief, sobering. "If anything, Gabriel, my financial life, no, my very corporate existence, depends upon the accord's success."

"That's easy enough to say," Gabriel prodded, but he was beginning to feel certain they were barking up the wrong tree.

"But it's true." Cullen got up to walk around behind his desk. "And I can prove it." With a sigh, he unlocked a small drawer and removed a file, tossing it onto the desk. "When the dot-com industry went belly-up, I lost a hell of a lot of money. On paper, I still looked good because I had the common sense to use dummy corporations for my transactions, but the financial hit couldn't be ignored. I managed to stay afloat, barely. But I can't do it indefinitely, and even with the economy on the rebound, it's not happening fast enough for me to cover my losses. So I'm in trouble." He pushed the file toward Gabe. "Real trouble."

Gabe picked it up and thumbed through the papers it held, skimming the documents. They were primarily financial in nature. IRS proceedings, notes overdue and foreclosure notices. If these were the real thing, Cullen was on the brink of financial disaster.

"They're genuine," he said, correctly reading Gabe's thoughts. "But no one knows about them. Except the banks of course, and the government. And if the accord fails, I'll be down for the count, and believe me, there are any number of vultures out there who'll be quite happy to pick my bones."

"And if you go down, the president's bankroll is gone." It explained a lot.

"Thanks for the vote of confidence." Cullen gave him a wan smile. "But the president can survive losing me. However, it'd obviously be better if one of his chief contributors stays out of the tabloids."

"Who else knows about this?"

"I told Madison's father. He's been a good friend. And I think Jeremy had an idea what was going on. What Jeremy knew, Kingston was most likely privy to, but other than that, no one."

"You're certain?"

"I can't be certain of anything. But I've certainly tried to keep it all under wraps. If the Chinese got wind of it, it certainly wouldn't help the negotiations." He sighed. "Anyway, the point of telling you was to clear the air. To let you know once and for all that I am not behind any effort to stall the accord. There is nothing on earth that would make me do that. It would be like signing my own death warrant, and believe me, I'm not that kind of man."

There was absolute truth in that, but Gabe also knew that somewhere in all the rhetoric there was a clue to what was happening and why. They just had to find it. "There's still got to be a connection between Vrycom and the current accord. Or at least the fathers and their children. Maybe Jeremy was the link?"

Cullen shook his head, frowning. "I don't see how. I mean, the man had nothing to do with Vrycom. I didn't even know him at that time. If there's a connection it's something really obscure."

"Well, someone is killing your colleagues, Cullen.

We're not imagining that. Candace Patterson received a
call from here the night she died, and someone knew that
we were mistakenly zeroing in on Ernhardt Schmidt. The
only way either of those things could have happened is if
someone on the inside is behind all of this. And if it isn't
you, Cullen, I'm betting it's someone you know."

"IT ISN'T CULLEN," Gabe announced to no one in particular, striding into the operations room.

"You're sure?" Harrison asked, looking up from his
ever-present laptop.

"Positive. The man's in debt up to his ass. If the accord
goes down, he goes with it."

"Any chance he fed you a load of bull?" Payton asked.
"It wouldn't be the first time."

"No." Gabe shook his head. "I've seen proof. He's leveraged to the hilt. If this thing falls apart, there isn't going
to be much left of Dreamscape."

"So he's on the level." Harrison frowned. "Where does
that leave us?"

"I don't know." Gabe dropped down into a chair, running a hand through his hair. "Any word from Madison?"

"She called a little while ago to say that she was stuck
in traffic. She hadn't even made it home yet. So I figure
it'll be a while before she's back here."

He nodded, disappointment washing through him.

"She ran out of here looking for you," Payton said, his
voice pitched low so that it didn't carry over to Harrison's
cubicle. "I take it she didn't find you."

Gabe shook his head. "I must have already been in Cullen's office."

"It'll work out," Payton said, his somber gaze meeting
Gabe's. "You just have to take it slow."

"Not my strong point." Gabe grimaced. He'd always gone
full tilt for the things he wanted. And he wanted Madison.

"Hey, guys, I think maybe I've got something here."

Gabe pulled his thoughts away from Madison, and followed Payton over to the computer terminal. "What did you find?"

"Something more about Bluemax." He pointed to the screen. "According to this, the owner of the company was a man called Edward Clinton. He patented a process for producing semiconductors that dramatically cut the cost per unit. If it had worked it would have revolutionized the industry."

"If it worked?" Payton frowned at the monitor. "You're saying it didn't?"

"He never got to find out. Vrycom leveraged his company, and took everything, including the patents. Clinton was left with nothing but debt. The official press from Vrycom was that the patents were worthless. But considering the fact that at least three of the men sitting on the Vrycom board had significant investment in the old process, I'd say it was a little suspect."

"So you're thinking this Edward Clinton is out for revenge?"

"Not unless we're talking ghosts. The man killed himself about six months after the takeover. Right after his court case was dismissed."

"So it's another dead end." Gabe blew out a frustrated breath as his cell phone began to ring. He nodded for Payton and Harrison to continue, and turned away from them, his mind already jumping to the possibility that it was Madison. "Roarke."

"We need to talk." Nigel's voice sounded tinny on the other end, traffic noise and static making it hard to hear.

"I thought you were on your way to London."

"Not for a couple of hours. I'm outside the building right now. Can you meet me in front?"

"Why don't you come up here?"

"Not a chance. Not everyone is as understanding as you are, and I don't relish the idea of running into Cullen Pulaski."

"I never said I understood, Nigel. It's just the way the game is played."

"Among like minds, perhaps, but Cullen plays differently. Anyway, I need for you to come down here."

His instant reaction was to refuse. There was nothing left to say. But instinct kicked in, and his gut answered for him. "All right. I'll come."

"There's an alley half a block away. I'll be there." Nigel clicked off, and Gabriel closed his phone, his mind churning.

"Who was on the phone?" Harrison's interest was cursory. His attention still focused on forcing the computer to yield answers.

"Nigel."

That got his attention. Payton's, too. "What the hell is he doing? I thought he'd be halfway to England by now."

"Evidently not." Gabe started toward the door. "I'll be back in a bit."

"You're going?" Payton's eyebrows rose in surprise.

"He said it was important." Gabe shrugged. "It beats sitting here banging our heads against the wall." An understatement actually. At the moment he was more inclined to ram his fist through it.

Every step forward seemed to send them back three, and he wasn't used to being on the losing end of the stick.

NIGEL FERRIS STOOD in the shadow of the alleyway, waiting. Sooner or later, Gabe would make an appearance. He owed Gabe and he wasn't leaving until he had the chance to talk to him. A crowd surged through the revolving door of the adjacent building, and Nigel glanced at his watch. 5:30 p.m. Quitting time.

His plane for London was at eight. Not much time. He pulled his coat collar closer around his neck and willed his friend to appear. If he'd read the signals between Gabe and Madison correctly, there was something going on between the two of them. Something significant. And if he was right about things, then they might not have the opportunity to build on what they'd started.

As if he'd heard Nigel's silent plea, Gabe turned into the alley, his shoulders hunched against the chill of the wind. Nigel waited until he was certain Gabe was alone, and then stepped out of the shadows.

"So what's with the cloak-and-dagger routine?" The words weren't much more than a mumble.

"I'm the enemy, remember? I figured it was best to watch my back."

"We've said everything that needs to be said." Gabe stopped in front of him, avoiding his gaze.

"About my part in the operation, yes. But not about Madison."

Gabe's head jerked up. "What the hell does she have to do with you?"

Nigel pulled Gabe deeper into the shadows. "Nothing at all, but unless I misread things she has everything to do with you. And I think we missed something important when we were at the scene of Jeremy's murder. It's been bothering me since then. But by the time I worked it out, I had been banished from the kingdom, so to speak."

"And so you thought you'd come back to share?" There was bitterness mixed with Gabe's anger. Not that Nigel blamed him.

"I thought it was important enough to risk your wrath. Whether you choose to believe it or not, I still consider you my friend. And if Madison is important to you then she's important to me, too."

"So tell me what the hell it is you think you know?"

Nigel waited a moment to be certain he had Gabe's full attention. "It's about the trajectory of the shot."

"The one that killed Jeremy," Gabe prodded.

Nigel nodded. "Something felt off to me at the time, but I couldn't quite place it. Then this morning it came clear. Look, Jeremy was moving from the wing chair to the drinks cart when he was shot."

"Passing in full view of the window."

"Right. But he was shot in the neck. And you know as well as I do that that's a risky shot. Much better to go for the head. And if the man was in plain view, the killer had plenty of time to aim for the head."

"Maybe something jarred his hand." The remark was a throwaway, Gabe's complete attention zeroed in on Nigel now.

"Or maybe he was never aiming at Jeremy at all."

Gabe sucked in a breath, the importance of Nigel's words hitting with brute force. "Madison."

"Exactly. She said she was standing to the side of the window when she thought she saw movement. And then she stepped into clear view."

"And saw the flash." Gabe's brows drew together as he visualized the events of that night.

"And dived to protect Jeremy." Nigel spread his hands in fait accompli. "If she hadn't moved, she'd have been hit. In the head. She's shorter than Jeremy."

"By a head. Oh, my God." Gabe's gaze locked on Nigel's. "That's why there was a second shot. The killer had missed his target. And if I hadn't shown up there'd have no doubt been a third shot."

Nigel nodded. "I thought you should know."

Gabe turned to go, his mind obviously on finding Madison. Nigel stood watching, wishing he could take back the past few days. Turn back the clock and restore their friendship. But then perhaps it had all been a myth anyway.

People in their line of work couldn't afford attachments. Allies maybe. But not friends. And certainly not lovers.

Still, Nigel found himself wishing Gabriel and Madison godspeed.

MADISON GLANCED for the forty-fifth time at her watch, hoping her father hadn't given up on her, wishing that the taxi driver had taken the FDR instead of fighting the traffic on First Avenue. Patience was not one of her father's virtues. A trait she'd obviously inherited.

Finally they rounded the turn onto Seventy-second and with squealing brakes came to a stop in front of her building. She shoved a twenty through the window separating the front and back seats, and without waiting for change slid out of the cab.

She'd spent the ride over replaying every word of her last encounter with Gabriel over and over in her mind. Wishing there was a way to call it back. Knowing that there wasn't. One made one's bed and all that.

The wind off the river slapped her in the face, pulling her thoughts to the case and the possibility that her father had information. Something to do with Cullen. Her heart rate ratcheted up a notch as she considered the possibility that the news might not be good. After all, he'd chosen to meet her away from Dreamscape.

She quickened her pace as she walked under the canopy fronting her building, grateful when Harry, the doorman, gave the revolving door its usual spin. Gabriel was probably talking to Cullen now. She felt a moment's guilt for not being there to act as buffer, and then shook her head. The two of them were perfectly capable of dealing with each other. They'd done it before. They certainly didn't need her. She was far better off finding out what it was her father knew.

A handsome older man at the front desk waved, and she struggled for the name. Ed, maybe. He was new. She'd only met him a day or so ago.

"Ms. Harper," he greeted her, smiling.

She nodded distractedly, still working on her courage. "Is my father up there?" she asked, hoping for a positive answer. He hadn't answered the phone when she'd tried to call.

"Yes, ma'am. He arrived about an hour ago, and has been calling down periodically ever since." The concierge shifted on his stool, looking a bit conspiratorial. "I told him traffic had been hell."

"Thanks, Ed." She smiled, relieved that her father was still there. "I was afraid he'd given up on me."

The older man returned the smile, and patted her hand. "Fathers never give up on their daughters."

She grimaced, heading for the elevator. Clearly Ed didn't know *her* father.

The doors chimed open and she stepped in, pressing her floor's button, her thoughts turning again to Gabriel. She'd almost called him twice, her hand on the cell phone keys before she'd managed to stop herself. Despite what commercials said, a cell phone wasn't the proper vehicle for an apology.

That was better done in person. On bended knee if necessary. She swallowed back a sigh. She'd made her bed, and now it was up to her to rumple it up again. She laughed at herself in the elevator's mirror. Gabriel had her so flustered she was screwing up metaphors.

Better to concentrate on the task at hand.

She'd deal with Gabriel afterward. If he loved her, he'd have to understand. She'd make him understand. Whatever it took. She'd waited a long time to find him, and she wasn't about to let her own paranoia screw things up between them.

The door dinged open, and she scrounged through her purse to find her keys, walking around the corner and down the hallway to her front door. She stood for five minutes rummaging through her junk and was just about to give up and knock, when her hands closed around the reticent key.

She slipped it into the lock, turned the key and opened the door, calling out as she came inside. "I'm home, Dad."

She threw her purse on the table, and slid out of her coat, placing her gun beside her purse. Hanging the coat on a hook, she called out again, then rounded the corner into the living room, stopping in surprise.

"What are *you* doing here?"

CHAPTER THIRTY-ONE

"WHERE'S GABRIEL?" Cullen stood in the doorway of the operations room watching Harrison and Payton. The former was ensconced at his computer as usual, the latter sitting at the conference room table, feet propped up, a fat file in his hands.

"Not here." Payton didn't even bother to look up, and quelling a surge of irritation, Cullen walked into the room.

"Any idea where he might be?"

The two men exchanged glances, and then Harrison spoke. "He went out for a walk. Should be back any minute. Is there something we can do for you?"

Closing ranks. He recognized the signs. Harrison had been absorbed into Gabriel's world. He noted the fact with no emotion. After all, it was to be expected, and despite the fact that it meant he would no doubt be shut out, it was to his advantage in the long run. "I suppose he told you all that I'm no longer a suspect."

"He mentioned it." This from Payton, who was watching him now from beneath hooded eyes. "Sorry to hear about your financial problems."

It was a dig. The perfect passive-aggressive attack. "I'll survive."

Payton shrugged.

"So where are we?" He purposely walked past Payton over to Harrison. "Anything new?"

Harrison blew out a breath, and swiveled to face him.

"We're still looking at Vrycom. Did you know that the owner of Bluemax killed himself shortly after Vrycom took over his company?"

"I heard something about it, of course, but I don't know the details. It really didn't have that much to do with me."

"You don't feel responsible?" Payton had walked over to stand by the window.

"For what, the man killing himself?" Cullen frowned. "Why should I? I didn't hold the gun. Hell, I didn't even give him a motive. We paid him more than market value for his company."

"You'd have had to pay him ten times that to get rid of his debt. He'd sunk everything into the company. By the time he paid off his creditors there wasn't anything left," Harrison said, his expression impassive.

"It's not my fault the man had no backbone. I'm in debt up to my ass, too, and you don't see me holding a gun against my temple." The minute the words were out he realized how cold he sounded, and wondered when he'd stopped seeing his associates as people, and begun to see them instead as markers on the way to success.

"The game isn't over yet." Payton shifted so that the sunlight hit him square in the face, highlighting his scar, and Cullen knew in that instant that Payton blamed him for everything that had happened in Iraq. It had been his vanity, his overriding sense of one-upmanship that had driven him to prove that he could in fact get his man out when everyone else was saying it was impossible.

He'd been right of course, but the cost had been too high.

Especially for Payton.

"I'm sorry." The words were inadequate, but he meant them for what they were worth.

"Some things aren't to be forgiven." Payton held his gaze for a moment, and then dismissed him as easily as if he were a beggar on the street.

Cullen had made a fortune out of knowing when to cut and run, so with a shrug he turned to Harrison. "So besides the fact that the Bluemax's CEO killed himself, what else have you found?"

"Nothing concrete. I've been trying to find out more about the man, but so far I haven't turned up much. He wasn't much of a player before Bluemax, and quite frankly I'm not sure people took him all that seriously even with the company. His one big claim to fame seems to have been his company's encounter with you."

"Not me per se. I was only part of the process. My primary role was to identify companies that either had technology we needed, or were standing in the way of something we were trying to accomplish. Then it was up to someone else to get the dirt on them, so to speak."

"Keeping your hands clean?" Payton's comment was an observation, nothing more. Whatever animosity he carried was safely masked again.

"No. It just wasn't my forte."

"So what do you remember about Bluemax?" Harrison asked.

"Not that much really, it was a long time ago. They had some patents we wanted, and we offered to buy them out, patents and all. But Bluemax turned us down, so we organized a forced buyout. As I said, we needed what they had and if we couldn't get it the old-fashioned way—"

"You took it by force," Payton finished for him, not attempting to hide his disgust.

"It was just business." Cullen shrugged. "Vrycom existed for the sole purpose of furthering the technological revolution. Our job was to make sure new advances were kept within the circle of people most likely to be able to do something with them. It was a cooperative of a sort. We worked together for a common good."

"Yours." It was a statement, not a question, and Cullen chose to ignore it.

"There was financial gain certainly, but on both sides of the coin. A lot of the companies we bought out welcomed our involvement. And even the ones who didn't made money. I can't help it if it wasn't enough. If you're going to survive in this business you have to develop a thick skin. If I told you all the times I overextended only to come back from the brink it would surprise you. It's the nature of the beast. You learn to cope."

Payton opened his mouth to argue, but Harrison held up a hand to stop him. "I think we'd best all agree to disagree on this point. Besides, Cullen's culpability isn't the issue here. Finding the killer is. And to be honest, what happened with Bluemax may be totally spurious. Even if we assume that there is a connection between the CEO's death and the murdered victims, there's still a problem with pattern. Jeremy Bosner had nothing whatsoever to do with the Vrycom."

"I might be able to explain that." Gabriel walked into the conference room, his face flushed with anger. "According to Nigel, Jeremy may not have been the intended victim."

"What the hell were you doing talking to Nigel Ferris? I thought he'd tucked tail to run back to the prime minister." Cullen fought against a rush of anger. Ferris deserved to be hung by his thumbs and if Cullen had his way he'd see that it happened, international diplomacy be damned.

"He should be at the airport now. But before he left, he had some information to share."

"About Jeremy Bosner," Harrison prompted.

"No, about Madison."

Cullen's gaze collided with Gabriel's and his blood ran cold. "What about her?"

"Nigel studied the trajectory of the bullets at Jeremy's

brownstone. He believes that the shot was meant for Madison, not Jeremy."

"But why would someone be gunning for her?" Cullen asked, his heart constricting. "She has nothing to do with Vrycom or the accord."

"Yes, but *you* do."

"I'm sorry, I'm not following." Cullen frowned, his hands closing around the edges of the table, trying to find something solid to hang on to.

"Then let me spell it out for you. With the exception of Jeremy, all the victims are the children of members of the Vrycom board." Gabriel was standing over him, towering actually, and Cullen felt a moment of real fear.

"And Cullen doesn't have any children." Harrison, too, was standing, his eyes narrowed in understanding.

Gabriel nodded. "But he has a goddaughter."

"Oh, my God." Cullen felt the blood drain from his face, his hands still clenching convulsively at the conference table. "Where is Madison now?"

"She's with her father," Gabriel said.

"That's impossible." Cullen stood up, leaning against the table for support.

"What do you mean?" Gabriel shifted so that they were standing eye-to-eye.

"I mean that Philip is in Brussels. He was called away this morning. So unless Madison has left the country, she can't possibly be with her father."

"KINGSTON, WHAT ARE YOU doing here?" Madison asked, her mind already sorting through possible explanations. "I was expecting my father."

"I know." He walked over to her, taking her hands. "I'm sorry for the intrusion, but it was easier to wait up here." He gave her hands a squeeze. "Your father asked me to let you know that he'd been called away. Brussels,

I think. He said you'd be here waiting, so I figured I'd just swing by. But when I got here you hadn't arrived yet, so when the concierge mistook me for your father and gave me the key, I'm afraid I didn't bother to correct him." His smile was somewhere between impish and apologetic, the expression making him look younger.

"You could have called." She squeezed his hands and let go, walking over to the refrigerator for a bottle of water.

"I was in the neighborhood." He shrugged. "Besides, I thought maybe you'd give me an update on what's been happening with the investigation."

She nodded, pulling out a bottle of Evian. "You want something?"

Kingston shook his head. "I'm fine. Had a latte on my way over."

She opened the bottle and the two of them walked over to settle on the sofa. "Did Dad say why he wanted to see me? He told Payton it was urgent."

"He didn't say anything. But I think he was a bit distracted. Something to do with a drop in the European bond market."

Par for the course. Philip Merrick had chosen his business over his daughter almost since the minute she was born. "No big deal."

"It is, obviously." Kingston reached for her hand again. "I'm sorry."

She pulled her hand back, and slid back to the corner of the couch, suddenly feeling inexplicably uncomfortable. She'd known Kingston forever, but he'd never been up here with her alone. She shook her head at her own foolishness; she was jumping at shadows again.

He obviously felt the tension, too, because he walked over to the bookcase, making a play of examining the titles there. "So why don't you give me an update?"

"We're trying a new tack." She didn't want to share Gabriel's suspicions about Cullen. Despite evidence to the contrary, she didn't really put that much stock in the idea. Cullen was ruthless when it came to business, but he'd never be party to killing someone. "Have you heard of Vrycom?"

Kingston's shoulders tightened, and she could see the tension radiating down his arms. "I'm not familiar with the name."

He was lying, but she wasn't certain why. "It existed during the '80s. A paper tiger meant to take out rivals. Companies with technology the cartel needed or wanted to bury. A company called Bluemax was one of the victims."

Kingston swung around to face her. "I thought you were working on the angle that it was something to do with the accord."

"We were. But there's evidence that an association with Vrycom could be the real motivation. Cullen served as the chairman, and eight of nine victims' fathers also sat on the board."

"Eight of nine? That leaves an anomaly, surely."

"Yes. Jeremy." She smiled, with what she hoped was confidence. "But we're working on that angle, as well."

"I see." He reached out to pick up a photograph of her and Cullen taken the previous Christmas. "You and Cullen are close."

Madison nodded, wondering why the abrupt change of subject. "He's been there when I needed him."

"More than your own father sometimes."

"Dad does the best he can. But he's consumed by his work. Nothing will ever change that. And I guess Cullen has sort of filled in the gaps. Tag-team fathers or something like that." She kept her voice light, but she could see from Kingston's expression that he was aware of how much her father's absences had hurt.

"I had a son, you know," Kingston said, staring down at the photograph.

Another non sequitur, but Madison contained her frown of impatience. "You've never mentioned a son." Which, considering how long they'd known each other, seemed more than just odd.

Kingston's smile was sad. "He died."

Again Madison had the feeling that there was more going on here than the surface conversation, and gently she probed for details. "Was he a baby?"

"No. He was a grown man. Or at least he thought he was." There was deep sadness there, and maybe just a hint of guilt.

"What was his name?" She walked over to him, placing a hand on his arm, the gesture meant for comfort.

He looked at her, almost as if he were surprised to find someone else in the room. "Edward. Edward Clinton." He sighed. "His mother got custody when we divorced. I never really had the chance to know him."

"I'm so sorry, Kingston."

"Are you?" he asked, his expression changing again, darkening somehow. "Yes, I guess you would be. You always were a sympathetic child."

She stepped back, not certain why, but letting instinct take control. "How did he die, Kingston?"

He lifted his eyes from the photograph in his hands, his gaze meeting hers, and she recognized anger glittering there. "He killed himself."

"Oh, God. I'm so sorry."

"No, Madison." He shook his head, carefully placing the photograph back on the bookshelf. "It's me who should be sorry. I always liked you."

She frowned, trying to understand what one thing had to do with the other. "Are you all right, Kingston?"

He didn't look well at all, one hand clutching the bookshelf, the other stuffed in his pocket. Her gaze automatically followed the line of his arm, locking in place on the familiar bulge in the immaculate Armani blazer.

A gun.

Before her body could react to the emphatic signal from her brain, he pulled out his hand, the silencer-clad .38 sending the message full stop. "I'm not all right at all, Madison. But in a few moments, I will be."

CHAPTER THIRTY-TWO

GABRIEL TOOK THE CORNER on two wheels, then ground to a halt behind a long line of waiting cars. He cursed under his breath, wishing he had a siren or something to clear the way, knowing that even that wouldn't necessarily be enough to break up a traffic jam in the city.

He wasn't certain what he'd find at Madison's, but the fact that her father was in Europe combined with Nigel's information about her possibly being a target had sent him running after her. Or more precisely slugging along in Cullen's Maserati in rush-hour traffic. He banged a hand on the steering wheel, almost rear-ending a taxi.

He'd tried her cell phone and her home phone, and she wasn't answering. He'd even talked to the personnel in her building, but to no avail. Payton was working to try and get someone up there, but in the meantime, even if it turned out to be a wild-goose chase, he couldn't sit still and take the risk that something could be wrong.

Except that sitting is exactly what he was doing—along with apparently half of New York City. With another curse, this one not mumbled, he dodged another taxi and pulled into the far lane and up to the curb, blatantly ignoring the posted no-parking sign. He'd never been one for rules anyway. And right now his gut was screaming that Madison was in trouble.

Nothing else really mattered.

Slamming the car into Park, he leaped from it, barely

stopping to turn off the engine. Patting his jeans pocket to be certain he had the set of keys Cullen had given him, he set out toward Seventy-second on a run.

His cell phone rang as Gabriel rounded the corner onto First, and after five insistent rounds of the *Lone Ranger,* he slid to a stop, fumbling in his pocket for the damn phone.

"Roarke." He knew he was yelling, but his irritation was fueled by fear.

"It's Harrison." To his credit Madison's friend sounded as worried as Gabe did. Maybe more so.

Gabe sucked in a breath, and fought for control of his voice. "Did you find her?"

"No." Harrison sounded apologetic, and he rushed to finish before Gabe could hang up. "Look, I don't know how this will impact things, but I thought you should go up there armed with all the facts."

"What did you find out?" Gabe started to walk again, his pace just short of a run, still intent on reaching Madison.

"I found the link we were looking for. The CEO of Bluemax was Kingston Sinclair's son. I don't know if that makes Kingston our killer or not, but I thought you ought to know."

"I thought you said the man's name was something else."

"It was. Apparently he used his mother's name. There's not a lot there. Father and son were estranged for years, but rumor has it that Kingston helped with the funding for Bluemax. That's how I tracked it down initially—" Harrison stopped suddenly as someone grabbed the phone.

"Gabriel?" Payton's voice was just this side of alarmed. "You need to hurry. I sent the NYPD to Kingston's and he's not there, but they found the sniper rifle. And at least on surface examination it fits the ballistics for Jeremy's murder. I don't know where he is, but if he's at Madison's she could be in trouble. We're on the way. But you're closer."

Gabriel started to run again, still clutching the phone, not bothering to hang up. Three blocks to go—he just prayed there was still time. He'd only just found her, and he'd be damned if he was going to lose her now.

"I TRIED TO DO THIS BEFORE, you know. Twice in fact." His eyes were slightly unfocused, the sheen of sweat on his brow indicating he wasn't as calm as he'd have her believe.

"What do you mean?" She asked, playing for time, trying to figure out how to get to the foyer and her gun.

"The first time was in the operations room. Do you remember? I closed the blinds. I intended to do it then, but that computer boy interrupted." He frowned, and took a step toward her, and she forced herself to hold her ground. "But I heard you say you were going to Jeremy's. So I followed you there, and waited in the apartment across the way. It should have gone down easy, but you moved faster than I'd expected. And then Gabriel Roarke showed up." He spat the name out as if it tasted bitter. "You're a lucky girl. But I'm afraid your luck has finally run out."

"Your son was the CEO of Bluemax. That's why you killed the others. An eye for an eye." It was all starting to make perfect sense—in an insane kind of way. But then that was the type of mind Madison was used to dealing with.

"Right answer, wrong quotation. *The gods visit the sins of the fathers upon the children.* Euripides. They took my son, so I took theirs."

"But why me? My father had nothing to do with Vrycom." As soon as the words left her mouth, she knew the answer. "Cullen. This is about Cullen, isn't it?"

Kingston shrugged. "He has no children, but he loves you like a daughter. The loss will be as great."

"But it won't bring back your son."

His eyes hardened, clarity returning with a vengeance. "No, it won't. But I can at least assuage my anger and exact a bit of revenge."

"Like you did with the others." She was staring down the barrel of a gun, and still she wanted a confession. If the situation hadn't been so dire, she'd have laughed.

"I killed them all. And I wouldn't have been discovered if it hadn't been for Cullen's meddling. That's when I decided to bring you in. Make things a little more personal. I was the one who convinced Cullen that you should be a part of his famous Last Chance team. And I was the one who kept them running in circles."

"With a little inside help. Did you know about Nigel?"

His smile was slow. "Nice bit, that. At first I didn't know who it was. But then when I realized where his loyalties lay, it made sense. And quite honestly I couldn't have recruited a better partner. Poor bastard had no idea how much he was helping me."

"You killed Schmidt."

"Yes. I had to. If you'd found him alive he'd have screamed his innocence, and with a little digging you'd have been able to verify the fact. It wasn't part of the plan, but I couldn't afford to take the chance."

"But in killing him you risked discovery."

"Believe me, my dear, no one on your little team is going to connect the dots. It's too obscure."

"Gabriel will figure it all out. He's close to the truth now. He'll catch you in the end."

"Doesn't matter to me. All I ever wanted was to avenge my son. And with your death, I'll have completed the task."

He leveled the gun, and she heard the click as he sent a bullet to the chamber, the sound indicating that she had mere seconds to move. The obvious thing was to dive for cover, but then she'd still have the disadvantage of his being armed and her not. Her weapon was still lying in the foyer, the fifteen feet or so she'd have to travel to retrieve it a death trap.

Better to immobilize the threat. And it was now or never.

Without waiting to analyze further, she dived for Kingston, feeling a bullet rip through her shoulder before she even heard the hissed report. As she crashed into him, she swung her arm upward trying to dislodge the gun.

They fell to the ground, each struggling for control, and Madison grabbed his right wrist, slamming it hard on the floor. The gun, finally freed, spun off to the left, and slid under the open drapes. Not much help, but at least it leveled the playing field.

Kingston was surprisingly fit for a man his age, his maneuvering a sign that he'd studied martial arts somewhere along the way. Wrapping his arm around her neck, he managed to lever them both to their feet, her body locked against his.

Swinging backward with her left leg, she hooked it around his knee, simultaneously swinging her elbow back into his diaphragm. The quick release of breath signaled that she'd hurt him, and she took full advantage of the moment, twisting free, scrambling toward the window and the gun.

But Kingston was faster, grabbing her hair and yanking her back to her feet, his fist making contact with her chin. Her vision swam for a moment, but she managed to turn and get in a blow of her own, the contact sending her adrenaline rushing.

Locked together, they did a macabre dance around the living room, each of them trying to maneuver toward the gun lying beneath the drapes. She tried again to bring him to his knees, but he twisted his hands in her hair, yanking back her head with enough force to make her dizzy.

Ignoring the pain in her head and shoulder, she kicked out again, making contact with his knee. The pop was audible, and he screamed in pain, falling backward, his hold on her tightening as he continued to fall.

Their combined weight shattered the window and Kingston slid through the broken glass, pulling her with him. For a moment she felt weightless, and then as she grabbed for a handhold on the windowsill, Kingston's body pulled taut as his fall was broken by his grasp on her calves.

The pain in her shoulder was searing, and her left hand slipped, causing her to list to the right. Kingston's grip loosened slightly with the surprise of the movement, and she took advantage of the fact, regaining her grasp on the window and kicking her legs against his hold.

One hand released her, and closing her eyes in concentration she slammed her right leg against the side of the building, taking his hand with her. He yelped in pain but held firm, his other hand trying to find purchase. Again she swung her legs, this time both of them, the impact against the building sending shards of hot pain searing through her body.

But the result was worth it. Kingston screamed again and then released her, the relief of the reduced weight on her arms making her feel suddenly stronger. Holding herself as still as possible, she looked down in time to see him shatter the atrium window below, his body impaling itself on the point of the statuary adorning the fountain.

Kingston Sinclair was dead.

And unless she found a way to get herself back over the sill, she was going to follow suit. Her shoulder was strained beyond the point of endurance, and she could feel the muscle beginning to shake, the fingers of her left hand starting to go numb.

She tried to pull herself upward, but her left arm simply wasn't following her brain's command. She could see people moving in the gym below, but by the time they reached her it would be too late.

There were no balconies on this side of the building. Nothing protruding that might serve as a ledge to break her fall. The windows on either side of her were closed tightly and probably too far away to reach even if they were open.

The cold wind whistled around the building, and she felt her hand start to give way. She was out of options, and the only thing she could think about was the fact that she wouldn't see Gabriel again. Wouldn't be able to make things right, to make certain he understood how very much she loved him.

Her left hand slipped farther, the bulk of her weight now pulling against her right hand. She swallowed her fear, knowing that it was an enemy, and that if she was going to use these last few moments productively she had to keep a clear head.

Fear helped her hang on longer than she'd have thought possible, but she could feel the blood dripping down her arm, and knew that her left arm was soon going to be completely useless, and that her right arm simply wasn't capable of supporting her entire body as she hung from the sill.

People were screaming below her now, pointing upward, watching with the horrified fascination that comes from realizing the inevitable and knowing there is nothing one could do about it.

She gave one last attempt at getting her left hand to perform, the fingers responding to the effort by releasing the sill altogether.

She wanted to continue fighting, but she simply didn't have the strength....

Something grabbed her free hand, her heart registering

the reality before her brain, and she shot a look upward, expecting angels but finding Gabriel instead.

He grasped both of her wrists, the determination on his face beyond anything she'd ever seen. "Hang on," he mouthed and began to inch her upward. Her brain finally clued in to the situation, and using her feet she helped him "walk" her up the wall, until she was halfway in the window, and with a final jerk he pulled her over the sill and onto the floor.

Their hearts beat in tandem as Madison enjoyed the simple act of breathing, not even the pain in her arms and shoulder dimming the pleasure of the process.

"You all right?" Gabriel had rolled over to cradle her in his arms, his hands stroking and exploring, trying to assess the damage.

She nodded, smiling up at him, content for the moment just to be in his arms. "I thought you'd never get here."

His smile was crooked and endearing, the love in his eyes humbling and exciting all at the same time. "I thought you didn't want my help."

"I guess I changed my mind." She leaned up to kiss him, savoring the feel of his lips against hers, knowing that no matter the obstacles they belonged together.

Now and for always.

EPILOGUE

"HERE'S TO MY GODDAUGHTER." Cullen Pulaski refilled Madison's glass with champagne, and she smiled up at him lovingly. He'd certainly made sure she had the very best. A private hospital room with a view of New York that rivaled the best apartments.

Harrison and Payton stood on one side of the bed, while her father and Cullen stood at the end. Gabriel sat on the opposite side, holding her as close as her cast would allow. The surgery on her arm had been a success, and with physical therapy and some TLC she'd soon be good as new.

"Here's to Last Chance, Inc." Madison held her glass high. "We might have been slow out of the gate, but you have to admit it was a hell of a finish."

"A bit too close for me," Gabriel said, pulling her closer, his breath teasing her hair.

Harrison raised his glass, echoing both sentiments. His gaze met Madison's, the relief there almost palpable. "I'm just glad you're here for the celebration."

"Me, too." Her whispered response brought a cluck of concern from her father. He'd flown back from Belgium as soon as he'd heard, and wouldn't have left her side for a minute if Gabriel hadn't insisted they be allowed at least a few minutes alone now and then.

"Well, it's all in the past now," Cullen said. "The summit is on, the negotiations occurring even as we speak. If things continue going so well, I fully expect a signed agreement by the end of the week."

"So a winning situation all the way around." As usual there was a mocking edge to Payton's voice, but his smile was genuine.

"I still don't understand how Kingston was able to manage the variations in M.O.," Harrison said, reaching for the champagne to refill his glass.

"That one's actually pretty easy," Payton said. "Turns out Kingston did two tours in 'Nam. One as a sharpshooter, and the other in medevac. So his skills covered the gamut. And especially in the beginning, he had the element of surprise. The victims trusted him."

"Well, it's over now," Madison's father said, with a wave of his glass. "That's all that really matters."

"Yeah, time to get back to our real jobs," Harrison concurred. "I don't know about you guys, but I've got a pile of work waiting for me."

"Not us," Gabriel said, shooting her a wicked smile. "We're set for a little R & R. Right after I get her to the justice of the peace. I'm thinking Hawaii, or maybe a deserted island in the Pacific somewhere."

"As long as there aren't any cell phones," Madison agreed, laughing, her heart soaring at the thought of spending the rest of her life with Gabriel.

"I'm still miffed I won't be here for the wedding," Payton frowned playfully.

"It's not our fault you got called off to the wilds of South America," Gabriel said, his expression turning serious. South America was all Payton had been willing to divulge of his next assignment, and they really weren't even certain he was telling that much truth, but Madison knew she had to be content with not knowing. Payton would always have secrets, but he would also always have a place in her heart.

"I don't know that any of you should be making those kinds of plans just yet."

Almost in unison the four of them frowned at Cullen, suspicion raising its ugly head.

Cullen took in their expressions, and answered with a benign smile. "It's not my fault you all did such a bang-up job. And it isn't my fault that the president called this morning to say that there's been a bit of a problem at the border. Something to do with a Mexican cartel. DEA's been on it for years with no success."

"Don't tell me," Gabriel said dryly, his gaze meeting Madison's. "It's a 'last chance' situation, and no one else is equipped to handle it like we are."

Cullen's smile broadened, his eyes twinkling with the success of a battle won. "Exactly."

Turn the page for a look at Dee Davis's next exciting
LAST CHANCE, INC. *adventure...*
ENIGMA

coming in Summer 2005
from HQN Books

PROLOGUE

San Antonio, Texas

THERE WAS SOMETHING off in the air. A smell, or a sound. Something that didn't feel right. And he wasn't the type of man to let that pass by—long years of practice, or maybe just gut instinct kicking in. He'd planned everything to the last letter. Position, fuse, blast ratio, timer. Everything had been perfect.

But not now.

Nolan Ryan nodded in agreement from the dashboard, the bobble-headed baseball player a reminder of everything at stake. Better to be sure.

J.T. turned his car around and headed back to the hotel. The Prager was situated in the heart of downtown San Antonio, right across from the Alamo. Twenty-three years younger than the Texas monument, the hotel was nevertheless a landmark, an elegant memoir to times gone by.

Currently, it was undergoing renovation. Which made it perfect for his purposes. An empty shell. The original design was flawless, and in destroying such beauty he'd be creating his own art.

But there was more to it than that. It was a tribute. A moment he could manipulate. Her mourning would be his pleasure—the circle completed. Yin and Yang. They would be whole. Or at least a step closer.

He stopped a half block away, his eyes trained on the building, trying to figure out what was bugging him. Traffic surged past him, pedestrians waiting for a light to change, totally unaware of what was about to happen.

He took a step forward, thinking that maybe he'd recheck everything, but a glance at his watch confirmed that there wasn't time. He shifted again, searching the area.

Another step closer and he had his answer—a large black sedan parked illegally across the street. Federal plates. Someone was in the building. As if to emphasize the thought, another car pulled up behind the first, this one white with state plates. A large man wearing a suit and a Stetson stepped out of the Lincoln. He stopped for a moment, his gaze taking in the other car. Then, with a sigh, he crossed the street and entered the hotel.

J.T. forced himself to think, to try and consider his options. All the while the man's face teased his memory. He recognized him, but had no idea from where. Not that it changed things. He glanced again at his watch. There simply wasn't enough time. Nothing he could do would change anything.

It was a regretful development. Certainly not part of the plan, and if anything he hated deviation. But the end result would be the same. And that's all that really mattered. Besides, he firmly believed that everything happened for a reason. And he smiled at the thought that perhaps destiny had stepped in with a helpful hand.

His step was almost light as he turned and headed back up the street, sliding into his car, key in hand. Less than a minute later, he was turning off of Dolorosa onto the feeder for I-10, Nolan's head dancing with joy in the silent vibration of the distant blast.

CHAPTER ONE

Waleska, Georgia

ONE MORE JILTED LOVER pissed off at being dumped. At least that's the way it seemed to be playing out. Unfortunately, the jiltee knew his way around bombs, and the jilter was a preschool teacher.

Which meant a hell of a problem. And to make matters worse, Frank Ingram, the rejected suitor, had swallowed a bullet less than an hour ago. A neighbour had found the body and the note. That was about the only break they'd caught so far.

The device, located in a second-floor classroom of the First Baptist Preschool, was attached to a motion detector. Too much vibration and it was all over. Which of course meant there could be no evacuation. And very little access to the bomb.

The only reason the thing hadn't already detonated was that the classroom where it had been placed wasn't currently being used. A small quantity of mold had been found beneath an air-conditioning unit, and until the sample could be tested, the children had been removed from the room.

Which left Samantha Waters with two scenarios. Either the bomber hadn't been aware of the mold, or he wasn't really interested in killing anyone. Considering the alleged lethal nature of the device, and the fact that the room was

normally occupied by the woman he'd wanted dead, Sam
was opting for the former. And thanking her lucky stars. If
not for the mold, she'd be picking through the body parts
of toddlers instead of trying to figure out how to evacuate
them.

The thought sent a bolt of anger coursing through her.
She'd seen the aftermath of a day care blown to hell. It still
haunted her dreams. And she'd be damned before she'd let
the same thing happen again.

There were three other classrooms in use on the second
floor, one across from the room with the bomb and two
down the hall. The staircase was at the opposite end of the
building, which meant there was no way to use it.

The intended victim and her class had been working in
a different room today, a twist of fate that probably saved
her life, since the Cherokee County Fire Department had
successfully evacuated everyone on that level. So Maggie
Carmichael and the three-year-olds of Waleska were safe
for the moment. But that left the rest of the children. And
Sam didn't like their odds.

Normally she wouldn't have been involved with a local
situation, but she'd been returning from another case when
she'd heard the radio dispatch. And quite frankly, she
wasn't a sit-on-the-sidelines kind of girl.

"We've evacuated everyone we can, and deployed the
robot." The county bomb tech slid to a halt beside Sam,
the gleam of sweat across his forehead a reflection of the
slight tremor in his voice. Not that Sam blamed the man.
He couldn't be more than about twenty, the fine stubble
of his beard indication that he probably hadn't been shav-
ing all that long.

Most men volunteered for the bomb squad out of some
sort of misguided testosterone-cowboy need to physically
stand down the enemy. Unfortunately, the rush was the
kind that induced incontinence, and more often than not

the bad guys won the day, the carnage in places like the World Trade Center and the Murrah building silent testimony to the fact.

"There's a problem, though," the kid was saying, and Sam forced her attention back to the scene at hand. "In order to get the robot up there, it'll have to climb the stairs, and what with the age of the building and all, there's a good chance the clatter will set that sucker off before Max has a chance to make it halfway."

Max was a TR2000 robot. The ten-wheeled apparatus weighed less than forty-five pounds and was designed to operate in tight spots. Unfortunately, it wasn't known for its athletic grace. She sighed, eyeing the school building. It was an unusually warm spring day and all the windows were open—including the ones leading into the room with the bomb.

She lowered her binoculars, a rush of adrenaline ratcheting up her heart rate. Maybe there was a chance. "I think I've got an idea." She smiled at the young tech, and moved past him toward the cluster of emergency personnel standing in the parking lot of the building.

"Captain McBane," she called, waving at the fire chief, the ranking officer at the scene and therefore technically in charge. He turned with a frown, his expression clearly stating what he thought of women on the job, especially tiny little women who soaking wet weighed less than the bomb.

She'd heard it all before, and didn't really give a damn, except that it sometimes made getting her way a bit more difficult. She forced a smile and approached the little group. "I think I know a way we can get at the bomb."

Two other firemen, both pushing fifty, turned to face her, shooting sideways glances at their captain, waiting to follow his lead.

"Well, now," he drawled, stopping just short of adding *little lady.* "I'm open to hearing anything you've got."

He probably wasn't, but at the moment Sam didn't care. "What I want you to do is move the fire engine closer to the building."

"Sure thing, and then we can all stand back and enjoy the show. There'll be body parts spread over three counties," McBane said.

One of the firemen contained a snicker, and the other spat, refusing to look her in the eye.

She bit back her frustration. "The playground's covered with recycled rubber, it's meant to absorb a fall. In fact it'll absorb most anything. Even the movement of the truck. And it's practically under the damn window. If you approach it slowly from the south—" she pointed at the open field that flanked the playground "—the bomb won't detonate."

McBane's posture was still combative, but there was a flicker of respect in his eyes.

"If we load Max onto the extension arm," she continued, pressing the advantage, "I think we can lift it close enough for me to maneuver the robot into position for an X-ray. Once we have that, I can use the disrupter to shoot out the motion detector and our bomb won't be able to spray anything anywhere."

Silence followed as the three men digested the information. She waited, knowing already they'd have to capitulate. If they didn't follow the advice of an ATF EEO and things went south, there'd be hell to pay. And if she fucked things up, then they had an out. It was a win-win situation, but that didn't mean it had to sit easy.

"I guess it's worth a try." McBane's words were accompanied by a sigh meant to insult, but Sam was already halfway across the parking lot, motioning for the young tech to follow.

"What's your name?" she asked the kid.

"Jason Briggs."

"Well, Jason, you've been drafted to help me. Got a bomb suit?"

He nodded, his eyes widening as the meaning of her words sank in. "We're going in there?"

She laughed and shook her head, stopping at the back of her open Chevy Suburban. Her suit was state of the art. A Med-Eng EOD-7B, it weighed in at around sixty pounds—over half her body weight. "We're sending Max up there." She pointed at the fire truck, already moving into place. "But it never hurts to cover your ass, you know?"

Jason nodded, his expression solemn. "You been doing this long?"

A fair question, considering he was about to trust her with his life. She stepped into the pants, adjusting the grounder straps. "Almost sixteen years. Started out in a department a lot like yours."

"How long you been with the ATF?" He reached down for the ballistic inserts, automatically tucking them into place for her.

"Couple of years." Her voice was muffled as he helped her with the helmet.

"You're EEO?"

She nodded, standing patiently while he tested her air lines. An Explosives Enforcement Officer was a coveted job. There weren't many and you had to earn the position. Sam had been selected young, but then she'd had more experience than most.

"Wow."

The word stood on its own, and with a thumbs-up, she headed over to the fire truck, indicating that he should follow as soon as he was suited up. The fire truck was in place now, Max precariously balanced on the extension arm of the vehicle.

She slid into place beside a similarly clad fireman and checked Max's operating panel. The signal was clear, the digital picture showing them the side of the school building. "Let's do it."

The fireman nodded, and headed for the cab of the truck, ready to hoist the arm. Jason arrived and with a last pat for Max, Sam signaled the lift. The arm rose slowly, inching over as it went upward, the robot finally swinging into place near the open window.

It took a moment for her to acclimate herself to the video, but once she had her bearings she realized the camera lens was showing her the room's door, and across the way she could see the other classroom. And the children inside. They were huddled near the far wall, eyes wide, motion held to a minimum—as much as anyone could keep a four-year-old still.

Sam sent a silent curse down to Frank Ingram and lowered the camera to search the room. Fortunately, Frank was into hiding things in plain sight, and she found the bomb almost immediately. As improvised explosive devices went, this one was pretty straightforward—two pipes with end caps, covered in construction paper and duct-taped together. There was also a battery, various wires, a wristwatch and a blinking green light.

The motion detector.

"Whatcha got?" Jason had arrived, suitably decked out in his bomb suit.

"Pipe bomb." She gestured to the screen. "Question now is how sensitive the trigger is."

"Hell of a question." The fireman was back.

She ignored him in favor of the little screen, her mind running through alternatives, each of them carrying significant risk. There was no way to remove the device. And no way to evacuate the kids. Which left her with one shot.

Disrupt the bomb. Sever the motion detector and the device would be rendered safe. It was a gamble. But at the moment it was the only one she had. "I'm going to shoot it with the disrupter." She reached down for Max's controls, adjusting the PAN-disrupter, a machine capable of firing a variety of projectiles at variable speeds, the idea being to hit the bomb with enough speed and force to knock out the motion detector without triggering an explosion.

The primary question still being how sensitive the sucker was.

A cry filtered through the open window, and Sam shifted the camera, eyes back on the monitor. A small child dashed to the door of the room across the way, obviously intent on making an escape. Sam held her breath, eyes glued to the screen. The preschooler began to step into the hallway, but before he could make the move, his teacher appeared, snagging him by the shirt, and jerking him back into the classroom.

Sam counted to ten and then sucked in a breath. At least she had an answer. Reaching down for the controls, she adjusted the speed of the water cartridge.

"You sure as hell better know what you're doing." The fireman was standing too close, and Sam glowered up at him. The man shrugged and backed away, leaving her to the machinery. Slowly she began to raise the disrupter, trying to line it up with the bomb.

A grating noise, followed by a pop, sent her heart racing.

"Something's wrong with Max." Jason's whisper held a note of fear—a healthy emotion for someone in their line of work. "The arm's not extending."

Sam swallowed a curse, and made some adjustments on the controls.

Nothing.

"I'm going to have to do it manually." Sam stood up, meeting the eyes of the older fireman. His expression held no trace of mockery now. He simply nodded, accepting that it was their only alternative, then stepped forward to pull Sam's visor into place.

"I'll lower the basket." He started toward the truck, but Sam reached out to grab his shoulder, motioning for him to move slowly.

He nodded, and headed for the cab. In a matter of minutes, the extension arm was brought back to the bed of the truck, and Sam clambered aboard, freeing the disrupter from the robot. She heard the truck's arm shift into gear as she began her ascent, but her attention was focused solely on the window, the disrupter armed and ready.

Once she was in place, she visualized the shot, and then using the laser sight, centered on the motion detector's blinking light.

One Mississippi… She sucked in a breath and steadied herself.

Two Mississippi… She positioned the laser.

Three Mississippi… She shot.

Seconds turned to hours as she waited for success or failure. And then she noticed the quiet. Absolute complete silence.

The bomb was disarmed, the motion detector halfway across the room.

Cheers erupted below and Sam felt her knees begin to shake, the pressure finding physical release at last. Leaning over the edge of the basket she gave a thumbs-up, and watched as the firemen headed into the building, first to evacuate the children and then to dispose of the remains of the bomb.

Her job was done.

She sank down and pushed back the visor, grateful when she felt the basket sway as it was retracted. In just a few minutes she was down and with Jason's help removing her suit.

"That was really something," he said, his face red with excitement. "*Really* something."

She smiled and searched for something meaningful to say, but was saved from the exercise by the ring of her cell. Reaching into the Suburban, she grabbed the phone and flipped it open.

"Waters."

"Hey, Sam." Raymond Seaver's voice held a hint of laughter and rebuke. "I thought you were on your way back to Atlanta."

"Sort of got sidetracked." She frowned into the phone.

"So I hear."

News traveled fast, but there was no way Seaver had called just to talk about her latest escapade. Her boss was too focused for that. "What's up?"

"Got a call from a guy named Cullen Pulaski." There was a pause as Seaver waited for the information to sink in.

"The industrialist?" Sam shivered in anticipation. Something big was coming down.

"Yeah. There's been a bombing in San Antonio. Senator Ruckland and two of his colleagues were killed." Again he paused for impact.

"So?" She urged, trying to contain her impatience.

"So," Seaver drawled, "there's some kind of task force. Last Chance something-or-other. Best of the best sort of thing. And Pulaski wants you."